FANGED

ANGEL WITH ATTITUDE

more . . .

"Divinely funny . . . A subtly provocative paranormal romance that shines a new light on angels and demons and witches, oh my!"   —*Heartstrings Reviews*

"Fun and fast-moving . . . Valerie is a wonderful character. Kick off your shoes on a cold winter's night and relax with this. You'll be glad you did."   —*Mythprint*

"You have to read this book! It is quirky, funny, and sweet. If you love original and hilarious, you have to pick up *Angel with Attitude*."   —**FallenAngelReviews.com**

BITTEN & SMITTEN

"A terrific vampiric chick-lit tale filled with biting humor."
—*Midwest Book Review*

"4 Stars! Fun and clever . . . this novel is bound to appeal to those who like their romance a little offbeat and definitely humorous."
—*Romantic Times BOOK Reviews Magazine*

"A study of contrasts: frothy chick-lit wrapped around a grittier reality and a flip side featuring a modern heroine paired with a Brontean hero. Let us welcome this fresh voice to the genre."   —*Booklist*

Stakes
&
Stilettos

ALSO BY MICHELLE ROWEN

The Immortality Bites Series
Bitten & Smitten
Fanged & Fabulous
Lady & the Vamp

Angel with Attitude

Stakes & Stilettos

Michelle Rowen

FOREVER

NEW YORK   BOSTON

Cover photography by Herman Estevez
Book design by L&G McRee

Forever
Hachette Book Group
237 Park Avenue
New York, NY 10017
Visit our Web site at www.HachetteBookGroup.com

Forever is an imprint of Grand Central Publishing. The Forever name and logo is a trademark of Hachette Book Group, Inc.

Printed in the United States of America

First Printing: April 2009

10 9 8 7 6 5 4 3 2 1

Acknowledgments

Huge thanks to . . .

. . . my wonderful editor, Karen Kosztolnyik, without whom this book would have very unwisely ended a chapter early. Definitely a good call!

. . . my fab agent, Jim McCarthy, who keeps doing what he does so very, very well, and I thank my lucky stars every day to have him in my corner.

. . . Bonnie Staring and Laurie Rauch for beta-reading my vamps and making sure they had enough fang to go the distance.

. . . Michèle Ann Young, who gave the "Interludes" in this book a once-over to make sure I wasn't just making things up when it comes to historical detail. I have a tendency to do that. Research is cool but it hurts my little brain.

. . . my fantastic parents, who have taken on the mantle as Official Unpaid Rowen Publicists. I find my bookmarks in bookstores near and wide, much like Zorro's mark, and I know they've been there spreading the word.

Stakes
&
Stilettos

Prologue

Ten weeks ago

She wasn't wearing any shoes. That was his first impression.

His second impression was that the attractive brunette was completely insane. She had to be if she was approaching *him*.

He watched warily as she struggled through the narrow opening in the barrier and stared out at the sight before her. She was now perched alongside him on a support beam of a tall bridge high above a very dark, cold river.

Her eyes, wide with fear, finally landed fully on him.

"Hey!" she called out. The swift wind blew the bottom part of her thin, silky dress up above her knees to show off her long legs. Her leather coat, more fashionable than adequate as protection against the cool early winter chill, gaped open in the front.

Don't come any closer, he thought. She was going to

get herself killed climbing out past the safety barrier of the bridge. Dying was *his* goal that night, but he'd rather not see anyone else suffer the same fate.

"Go away," he said simply.

She didn't go away. Instead her gaze moved around erratically. "Holy crap. This is high up, isn't it?"

A marvelous observation. He eyed her as she shuffled closer to him. *Insane. Most definitely insane.*

"Help me!"

He frowned. "Help yourself. Can't you see that I'm trying to kill myself here?"

Quelling any thoughts of empathy, he gazed down at the dark waters of the Don River hundreds of feet below them. Quite honestly, there could not be a worse time for him to have been interrupted. She was putting herself in extreme danger.

"Help me first and then kill yourself," the woman suggested.

Who was she? What was she doing there? Did she know who he was? Had she been sent to stop him from ending his already overlong life?

No. The young woman who'd chosen to climb out onto the bridge in bare feet at the very end of a particularly cold November hadn't sought him out. He could see it in her eyes. He could taste her fear. This was merely a coincidence.

A very inconvenient coincidence indeed.

The woman bore unmistakable fang marks on her neck. She'd recently been bitten by a vampire.

There was fresh blood on her throat.

He ignored the dark hunger that swelled within him and the ache of his lengthening fangs. He hadn't drunk blood in a hundred years. No need at his age, but the want was still there. Every day. Every hour.

Long shadows appeared behind her as three men approached. His breathing hitched. Were they after him? Had he been followed to the bridge?

Tonight was to be the end of his long life. The end of a so-called master vampire. Thierry de Bennicoeur, dead after nearly seven hundred years. Had they followed him to witness his fate?

No, the men's gazes locked onto the woman instead. A tall blond man—a human—smiled as his eyes flicked to Thierry and then back to her.

"A friend of yours?" he asked.

"Yes," the woman said quickly, her troubled gaze moving to Thierry again. "A *good* friend. And he's going to kick your ass if you don't leave me alone."

Thierry raised an eyebrow. *Kick his ass?*

The blond man snorted. "That I'd like to see."

"Vampire hunter," Thierry said out loud. He had confronted so many hunters in his time that it was obvious to him what the fair-haired man was, and the wooden stake the hunter held tightly in his grasp was only one clue.

"Who wants to know?" The man's gaze slid from the woman's bare feet to her long, lean legs. It was the gaze of a predator, and not one who wished only death for his victim.

Hunters enjoyed playing with their prey—especially helpless and attractive female fledglings—before killing them.

"Who I am is none of your concern." Thierry forced his voice to remain impartial. "You are invading my personal space. Kindly take your business elsewhere."

And leave the woman in peace or I will kill you.

"We've just come to claim this little piece of vampire ass," the hunter said, "and we'll be on our way, so you can get back to whatever it was you were doing."

The young woman drew closer with shaky steps and grabbed the hem of his coat.

"Don't let them hurt me," she implored. "Please."

He could feel the warmth from her body.

Walk away, Thierry told himself sternly. *Leave them. Leave her. You don't know this woman. Where is her sire? This should be his responsibility.*

Now on his hands and knees in an attempt to crawl through the crudely cut opening of the bridge's fenced barrier, the hunter grabbed her ankle. To Thierry's surprise, the woman kicked the hunter directly in his eye.

Good aim. One of the best self-defense targets on the human body—groin or eyes. The hunter screamed and clutched at his face.

The woman scrambled away and almost lost her footing. Thierry reached out and steadied her, pulling her against him.

She looked up at him with surprise. "Thank you. I thought you weren't going to help me."

"Reflex," Thierry said. And it had been. For the most part.

There were two other hunters who began to climb through the barrier. They both had sharp weapons. While Thierry didn't really care about his own fate that night, he had now made a stand when it came to the woman's. Her safety, at least for the next few minutes, was his only priority.

Unfortunately, there was only one choice of escape.

He looked down. "I suppose we'll have to jump."

The woman's grip tightened at his waist. "Wasn't that your original plan? And wasn't your original plan to kill yourself?"

He thought of the stake tucked into the back of his pants with which he had truly planned to kill himself before allowing his remains to be swept away by the river below.

It would have to wait for another time.

"With my luck the fall tonight won't kill me," he said with a sigh. "But you just might."

He tightened his arms protectively around her and without waiting for another protest, he jumped off the bridge. Her scream rang loud in his ears.

He couldn't remember the last time he'd had a beautiful woman cling to him so fiercely. For the briefest of moments it made him feel alive and wanted—very dangerous feelings for someone like him to have.

However, when they landed, the freezing-cold water managed to douse those feelings and reality quickly set in.

He'd have to get rid of her as soon as possible. There was no other choice. Having a woman like this in his life—so young and fresh and filled with vitality—could only prove to be a deeply dangerous mistake.

For both of them.

Chapter 1

My name is Sarah Dearly. Fledgling vampire and part-time bartender, at your service. Welcome to my highly dysfunctional life.

Two and a half months ago I was bitten and turned into a vampire by my blind date from hell, chased across the city by vampire hunters, and managed to meet the handsome master vampire of my dreams right before we had to jump off a bridge together to escape getting killed. And that was all the *very first night*.

Since then things have been steadily . . . oh, *insane* would be a good word. But I've managed. Ten weeks as a vampire had changed a whole lot of things in my life, but I was still me. Still Sarah. Still not anyone to be afraid of in a dark alley. Ten weeks without my biting any necks or magically turning into a bat. "Evil" is definitely not my middle name.

I'd been damn lucky, all things considered. Although I do think changing into a bat would be a nice gift-with-purchase for this whole unfortunate vampire deal.

"Sarah, are you ready to meet the man who'll change your life forever?"

I glanced up from the dirty martini I was shaking and looked across the top of the bar at the grinning redhead. Her name was Heather, a former waitress at Haven, and her enthusiasm was almost contagious. *Almost.*

"Change my life forever, huh?" I said. "Is that a promise or a threat?"

"Definitely a promise. New directions, new opportunities. A chance at a fantastic future."

"If I even get the job."

"You know me. Of course you'll get it!"

Okay, I had to admit it. I was a little excited. Especially since Heather had asked me personally to interview with her new boyfriend that very night. We were meeting at a café just down the street from the club. We weren't meeting at Haven because it was vamps-only. It was a rule. Heather's boyfriend was human, but obviously pro-vampire since he was with her, so it was all good.

I liked Heather a lot. She was fun and funny and never gave me a hard time when I worked the bar and she waited tables. She'd quit two weeks ago after she met the man of her dreams, who had started a brand-new merchandising Web site called Vamp International that was set to launch next month. The job I would be interviewing for dealt with the fashion end of things and it sounded, from Heather's description, too good to be true.

Plus, it paid big bucks.

I pulled my tip money out of a small juice glass next to the till. A small juice glass was all I needed. Nobody tipped the bartender here. Or very rarely. I'd noticed that on the average, vampires were extremely lousy tippers.

Haven was my boyfriend's nightclub, which catered to the fanged citizens of Toronto, open from 9:00 P.M. until nearly dawn.

Less than a week from now Haven would be transferring over to the new owners. Thierry had recently made the decision to sell the club, and apparently the new boss wanted to bring in his own servers. A bummer, but not an unexpected one. Luckily, it would still be a vampire club—one of only two in Toronto at the moment—so it was nice to know there would still be somewhere to hang out, but I couldn't count on getting a semiregular paycheck anymore.

Therefore, this job opportunity had seriously come at exactly the right time for me. I was broke.

I felt a warm hand at the small of my back, and I turned away from Heather to see Thierry now standing next to me. I hadn't even seen him approach. Master vampires—they were a sneaky lot.

Thierry was, in a word, gorgeous. At first glance, or even second, you'd never guess he was pushing seven hundred years old. He looked more like he was in his midthirties, and super hot with the whole tall, dark, and fangsome thing going on.

A lot of people were either scared or turned off by his sometimes cold and aloof manner, but I preferred to think of that as part of his charm. I knew underneath that icy exterior was a man as wonderful on the inside as he was on the outside. But I was fine with it being my little secret.

"Is everything all right over here?" he asked.

I nodded. "I'm about to take off for my interview."

"Hi, Thierry," Heather said, smiling widely at him even

though I knew she was one of those who didn't like him very much. "Why don't I wait over here for you, Sarah?" She moved far enough away to give us some privacy.

Thierry moved his gaze to mine. His eyes were a medium gray color, but somehow managed to look metallic, like silver. It was a bit spooky until you got used to it.

"You don't need to get another job," he said.

"Oh, but I do. I definitely need a nice, normal job to help pay the bills." I fished into the juice glass and pulled out the penny that was stuck to the very bottom, and then knelt to tuck the money into the front pocket of my purse. "I wanted to buy a new dress for the reunion, but since I can't afford it, I'm going to ask Amy if she has something I can borrow."

My ten-year high-school reunion was in two days. Despite my life being in constant peril in the ten weeks since I'd been turned into a vampire, things had cooled off enough that I felt I didn't want to miss it. It was to be my last gasp as a normal person before I finally, grudgingly, accepted my new life as a vampire. And yes, *life* as a vampire. Vampires being the walking dead was just another unfortunate rumor, like me being a weapon of mass destruction.

The rumor currently going around was that I was the "Slayer of Slayers." Sheesh. You kill one vampire hunter in self-defense—an act that had now grown in legend to twelve hunters and counting that I'd taken down with my well-manicured but lethal hands—and a girl gets a reputation.

I hated to admit it, but I think that's one of the reasons Heather's boyfriend, Josh, had agreed to meet me for an interview at this crazy hour of the night. He was impressed by my rep. Hey, if it helped to get me a cool new job, I would milk it for all it was worth.

Thierry frowned at me. "Of course you should have something new to wear. Why didn't you say anything to me earlier?" He slid his hand into the front pocket of his black suit jacket, pulled out a money clip, and proceeded to peel off a few bills. "How much do you need? Will a thousand be sufficient?"

"Uh . . . yeah, that should just about do it." My mouth began to water at the sight of the money, but after a moment I forced myself to hold back the drool. "Wait, no. No, Thierry, please. I don't want to take any more of your money."

"What do you mean?"

Ninety percent of my body reached out to that roll of money, but 10 percent was holding me back. That 10 percent was surprisingly strong. "Look, I feel like I've sponged off you for over two months. Now I have this opportunity to interview with Heather's boyfriend so I can make my own money. You shouldn't have to be there with a handout whenever I get sick of what I'm wearing."

"I don't mind," he said.

"Well, I do. I need to find my own way when it comes to this sort of thing."

God, I was being so mature. It was a little sickening. For my entire life I thought having a rich boyfriend would be the perfect solution to all of my problems, and don't get me wrong, it was fantastic. But it also made me feel . . . dirty. And not in a good way. It made me feel that by taking his money I was less of a person. Less of a vampire. *Whatever.*

Ten weeks ago I'd been fired from my full-time, lousy-paying, but regular job as a personal assistant. My funds had dwindled away to practically nothing. I was down to bartending tips and Thierry's generosity. A real job was way overdue.

A small smile curled up the side of his mouth. "Are you saying that you don't want me for my money?"

I smiled back at him. "Oh, I want you. But the money thing is something I need to work out for myself."

He reclipped the money and slid it back into his pocket. "If you insist."

I felt a quick pang of regret but stifled it. It was the right decision. I wasn't a kept woman. And it's not as though we were married and half of Thierry's bucks immediately became mine.

No, the position of "Thierry's wife" had already been filled by a gorgeous seven-hundred-year-old French vampire named Veronique.

She wasn't in the country at the moment.

Not that she minded our relationship. In fact, strangely enough, she encouraged it. They'd been married "in name only" now for over a century. Apparently divorcing somebody you'd been hitched to for six hundred years wasn't something you could do by simply hiring a lawyer and signing some paperwork.

Didn't bother me.

Much.

Okay, it bothered me a lot, but I tried not to dwell.

"Stay close to Heather," Thierry said. "And promise to return here as soon as this interview is over."

"I promise."

It sounded bossy, but he was just being careful. When my reputation first became known I'd had a couple of bodyguards assigned to guard my body. I now had just one. A big brute of a guy appropriately named Butch. He was also a vampire, which definitely helped. My last bodyguards had been human. One of them had also tried to kill me, but that was another story.

However, Butch had recently requested a few personal days for unknown reasons, which I would assume were personal. This meant that I was currently bodyguard-free, so it was vital that I be with somebody trustworthy at all times.

Frankly, it felt as if I was constantly being babysat, but if it kept me breathing I would tolerate it for as long as I had to. The reputation would fade away and the hunters would move on to something more interesting sooner or later. I hoped it would be sooner.

Lately things had cooled off considerably on the hunter front. I'd been informed there was some kind of vampire-hunter convention going on down in Las Vegas right now that the hunters were flocking to like wooden-stake-carrying birds flying south for the winter.

Remind me to stay away from Vegas at the moment. Only a crazy vamp with a serious death wish would show his or her face down there with all of those hunters lurking about.

"Then I wish you the very best of luck with your interview." Thierry leaned over and brushed his lips against mine. Our relationship had definitely improved lately. Sure, he tended toward the strong silent type, and he did have a bit of a . . . *dark side.* To put it extremely mildly.

But kissing me in public was a definite sign that things were better than ever.

After another kiss and a whisper in my ear to be

careful, he left the main club area to return to his office to deal with last-minute paperwork regarding the ownership transfer. Exciting stuff. Yawn.

"Ready?" Heather asked.

I nodded. "As ready as I'll ever be."

The new bartender had already signed in, so Heather and I left the club and headed the short distance to the café, a little place called the French Connection. It specialized in overpriced cappuccinos and pastries. Since my vampire stomach couldn't handle solid food now that I was on a purely liquid diet, I ordered a coffee. Black.

Heather's boyfriend, Josh, sat at a small table in the corner. He was cute, somewhere in his twenties, and had dark shaggy hair and liquid brown eyes. I liked him immediately.

He got up and embraced Heather, kissing her hard on the lips, and then shook my hand very firmly.

"Sarah, it's such a pleasure to finally get the chance to meet you." He settled back down into his chair. The café was empty except for the three of us, and the cashier behind the counter was busy organizing the display of scones and muffins and croissants into perfect high-caloried lines.

"You, too," I said. "Heather's been raving about how great you are. And thanks for giving me the opportunity to talk to you."

"No, I should be thanking you for agreeing to consider my offer." He reached into his pocket and pulled out a small stack of bills. "Consider this a small sign of my appreciation. It's a four-hundred-dollar advance on your first paycheck."

I blinked. Wow, this was getting off to a fantastic start.

"Maybe we should skip the interview and I can start right away," I joked.

He smiled and glanced at Heather, who squeezed his hand. "I do have some questions. Important ones."

Would it be rude if I shoved the cash into my pocket right away? Probably. "Shoot. My life is an open book."

"How long ago, precisely, were you sired as a vampire?"

I frowned. "That's kind of a strange question for a job interview, isn't it?"

He shook his head and laughed. "Yeah, I guess it is, sort of."

Heather laughed, too, and reached across the table to pat my hand reassuringly. "Josh is just trying to get to know you. Besides, the company does cater to vampire clientele."

"Oh." I relaxed a bit. "Well, okay. It was exactly ten weeks ago yesterday."

"Ten weeks." He nodded. "And you've adjusted well?"

"As well as can be expected, I guess."

"I think you've done very well."

"I try." I took a sip of my coffee, cringing a bit at how bitter it tasted. I reached over to grab a few packets of sugar, tore them open, and stirred them into the dark depths.

"And since you were sired, do you notice having any special abilities now?"

I thought about that. "Well . . . I'd say that my senses have increased a bit, but nothing too crazy. Like my hearing's improved. And I can smell really well. Seeing in the dark is a little clearer. Do you mean things like that?"

He nodded. "That's helpful. And do you have any prophetic dreams?"

"Prophetic dreams?"

"Dreams that seem to foretell the future."

"Uh . . ." I frowned again. "Actually I did have a dream a few weeks ago that sort of told me that trouble was coming. And a few more that have been rather vivid. Would those count?"

He nodded. "Any other uncanny psychic abilities?"

"I won twenty bucks on the lottery last week."

"Increased strength?"

"Maybe a little, but I'm not signing up to be a professional wrestler yet." My frown deepened. "Listen, these questions are making me a little uncomfortable. What does this have to do with the job?"

"I'm human," Josh said, "and I'm hiring vampires. I need to know these things. It's important."

I glanced at Heather, but she looked completely fixated on Josh and not in the least bit frazzled by his vampire-related interview. I brushed away my sense of weirdness about the situation and took a sip of my now too-sweet coffee. "Okay, if you say so."

"So . . ." Josh continued. "There's a rumor that you've drunk the blood of not one, but two master vampires. Is that true?"

I grimaced. Another rumor. Just what I needed.

Well, there was Thierry, of course. He'd saved me when my original sire was slain by vampire hunters before I'd had the proper fledgling nutrition to keep me breathing. I got to ingest some of his supercharged vampire blood—apparently the older the vamp the more potent his blood was. Since master vampires rarely, if ever, shared blood or sired fledglings, this caused my vampire side-effects—namely losing my reflection and developing my fangs—to happen months if not years before they normally would have. Becoming a full vampire apparently took time.

And I guess Nicolai was a master vampire, too. Or *was*, anyhow, until he'd ended up on the wrong side of a wooden stake. As one of the elder vampires in the Ring—the international vampire council—he'd stopped by Toronto three weeks ago to investigate my Slayer of Slayers reputation. Unfortunately there was some major bad blood—no pun intended—between him and Thierry. When he found out Thierry and I were involved, the insane vamp tried to kill me to seek his revenge. Before I'd learned about his ulterior motives, I'd had some of his blood by way of his wrist stuck in my mouth when I was near death. A girl can't be too choosy in situations like that.

"Sure, two master vamps," I said after a few moments of silence. "I guess I'm popular. Why do you want to know?"

Josh studied me without saying anything. From my dark brown shoulder-length hair, currently tucked behind my ears, to my eyes, nose, mouth. Then along my neck to my white camisole tank top, and, if you ask me, lingered a little too long for comfort on the boob area. My black winter coat hung behind me on the chair.

"I think I have all the information I need," he said.

"So do I have the job?" I asked, still forcing myself to ignore the weird feeling.

He glanced at Heather. "What do you think?"

"I think it'll work out perfectly." She smiled and kissed him. "Just like we planned."

I swallowed. The strange feeling of dread that had taken up space in my gut from the very first interview question began to spread through the rest of my body. "Can we talk about Vamp International now? Do I have the job?"

Heather stroked Josh's face before kissing him on his lips, then turned her attention to me, her smile as bright and shiny as it had been all evening. "Okay, Sarah, I don't want you to be mad, but there actually isn't any Vamp International."

I felt a rush of disappointment. "Then what exactly is this interview for?"

She pushed the wad of money in the center of the table closer to me. "It's four hundred dollars now, and another four hundred once it's done."

I eyed her suspiciously. "Once what's done?"

"You need to sire my boyfriend," she said simply.

"I need to *what*?" My heart began to pound hard enough for me to hear in my ears. "What the hell are you talking about? I thought I was here to interview for a full-time job."

Her smile faded slightly around the edges. "Well, I knew you probably wouldn't immediately jump at a siring opportunity. I wanted you to meet Josh and see how awesome he is and how happy I am with him. And we *are* paying you for your services."

"For my *services*?" I repeated. "This is completely ridiculous."

"Please." Josh leaned forward. "I love Heather. I

want to be a vampire so we can be together forever. Heather told me that you were a romantic. That you'd understand."

"Oh, I understand perfectly," I said, feeling the seething annoyance building up inside me. "You want to be a vampire? Then why don't you just get *her* to sire you?"

He shook his head. "She's the last in a long line. The strength in her blood is way too diluted. If she sired me I'd be too weak. But because of your connection to two master vampires your blood would make me strong, even as a fledgling. You *have* to sire me."

"Forget it." I shook my head. No way. That would require biting him—possibly on the neck. Something I've never done before nor did I plan on starting tonight. *Gross.* I'd have to drain his blood while keeping my fangs in long enough to transmit the vampire virus that had changed me from a normal, everyday twenty-eight-year-old into a friendly neighborhood bloodsucker.

Hell, no.

Now, I *did* require blood to live. I was a vampire, after all. But that was why there were vampire bars. Vampires went to these places to get their blood—blood that was available in kegs delivered by companies that got the red stuff from paid donors. It was a business. The rarer the blood type, the more the blood cost. It worked very well and nobody I knew had a problem with it, especially since it meant that we didn't have to get our blood from the original source. That would be wrong on too many levels to count. No humans were harmed to meet the requirements of my daily nutrition. Amen.

Although, even drinking blood from a keg, knowing I wasn't hurting anybody, had been a hard thing to accept. However, if I didn't want to die in agony—which I *didn't*—some aspects of being a vampire couldn't be avoided.

"I'm out of here." I stood up from the table and grabbed my coat, ignoring the money completely, and I left the café to emerge into the chilly night without looking back.

Honestly. Some people. What had they been thinking? And lying to me about a fantastic new job? So not cool.

Pay me to sire her boyfriend. Did they think I was a vampire prostitute or something? I wasn't biting anyone for money. I didn't care how broke I was.

Dammit. I was disappointed. Obviously a job that sounded too good to be true was just that. And to think that I'd trusted Heather—even thought of her as a friend. Talk about adding insult to injury.

I heard two sets of footsteps behind me but I ignored them.

"Sarah, wait!" Heather called after me.

I ducked into the little snow-covered park across the street from Haven. Through the park, up the street, down an alley, and I'd be back in the club.

"Please, just listen to us." There was a pleading in Heather's voice now.

I stopped and turned around to face them. "Look, I understand that you two are in love. That's super. Really. But I don't like being lied to and I don't want to bite anyone. Like, ever. So let's just forget this ever happened, okay?"

"We'll pay two thousand dollars," Josh said with a glance at Heather. She nodded.

Two grand? That was a lot of money and would cur-

rently solve a great many problems. "That's very generous, but no. I can't do it. Listen, don't become a vampire.
It's not really that great. Be a human. Stay a human. Less
stress, trust me on that."

Disappointment filled Josh's expression. "That's not
an option."

"I'm sure somebody will help you if it's what you really want."

"No, it has to be you," Josh said, and he began to
shiver from the cold night, since he only wore a sweater,
and he wrapped his arms tightly across his chest. "You're
currently the only vampire alive who has the blood of two
masters coursing through her veins."

"I'm the only one?" I said with surprise. "Seriously?"

He nodded. "There was another fledgling who had
the blood of *three* master vamps, but he was recently set
on fire by hunters and pulled apart by dogs. Apparently
he saw it coming in one of those prophetic dreams." He
shrugged. "I've researched it. It has to be a fledgling and
it has to be the blood of more than one master vampire.
That's you. You're so lucky. Masters almost never let
fledglings drink from them."

My stomach lurched. "I'm going back to Haven."

"You need to bite me. Please, bite me, Sarah."

"Bite him, Sarah," Heather echoed. "Don't worry, I
won't be jealous."

The cold wind picked up and I could hear it whistle
through the dry branches overhead, shifting the loose snow
so that it fell lightly to the ground close by. I sighed with
frustration. "How many different ways can I say no?"

Heather's eyes narrowed. "You bitch. How can you be
so selfish?"

I glared at her. "Selfish? Because I don't want to bite your boyfriend? How is that selfish?"

Then I felt a hand at my waist and the unmistakable feeling of a sharp wooden stake at my throat. Josh was now behind me.

"We tried to do this the easy way." The friendliness and pleading were now gone from his voice. "Ask you nicely. Pay you, even. But I'm not taking no for an answer."

Immediate panic gripped me as tightly as Josh had. "The easy way? By lying about a job?"

"God, get over it, would you? *This* is the job. You're going to sire me or I'm going to kill you."

Any move I made would send the stake directly into my jugular so I tried not to budge, even though my entire body felt like a live wire. Perhaps a different tactic would be a good idea.

"The Slayer of Slayers doesn't take kindly to threats, asshole," I growled, trying to sound as tough as I could through the fear as sharp as the stake at my throat.

He snorted at that. "We know it's just a rumor that you killed all of those hunters. However, everything else about you isn't a rumor. You've drunk the blood of two master vampires. That makes you very special. But you don't have to bite me. The virus is in your blood as well as your fangs. Doesn't matter if you're alive or dead. All I need is enough of your blood." He dragged the tip of the stake along my neck and I felt a stinging pain and a warm trickle of blood slide down my throat. "See? Not so tough after all."

"Let me go right now." My gaze whipped over to where Heather stood, hoping she would see that her darling boyfriend was actually a violent sociopath, but she just looked at him with love and devotion.

"Kill her," she prompted. "We can save the money we were going to pay her for our honeymoon."

I breathed out, trying not to shake with the fear I felt, and tried to think as calmly as I could. This wasn't the first time I'd been in a life-or-death situation. However, I wasn't quite the victim I'd been ten weeks ago when I was made into a vampire by my blind date.

"Josh," I said shakily. "Listen, we can talk this out."

The stake eased off a bit from my throat. "Can we?"

"Not really." I stomped on his instep and twisted away from him. Then I curled my hand into a fist and socked him as hard as I could in his jaw. Not too much vampire strength, but since he was only human it was enough to knock him back a few feet. Enough for me to get away.

That is, if I didn't suddenly have his vampire girlfriend behind me, pinning my arms down at my sides.

"Let go of me, Heather," I snarled at her. "Right now."

"Not a chance."

"I thought we were friends. Why would you do something like this to a friend?"

"Because I love Josh. But I guess somebody involved with a cold, emotionless jerk like Thierry wouldn't understand what true love feels like, would you?"

"This isn't love," I managed.

"We're going to be together forever."

"You've only known him for a few weeks, haven't you?"

"It doesn't matter. I know it's forever." Her fingernails dug painfully into my arms. "Do it, Josh. Do it now."

"Let go of me!" I yelled and struggled so hard against

her that I almost broke free. She had a fight on her hands to keep me in place. I wrenched to the side, twisting my body to possibly bite her on the nose, but then I felt something very bad slam into my chest.

I gasped.

It was something sharp.

Something extremely painful.

Heather finally released me. "Sorry, Sarah. I wish you'd given us another choice."

My eyes widened as I looked down at the wooden stake protruding from my chest. I touched the end of it with shaking hands, blinking hard.

"Wh-what . . . ?" My mouth was dry. I fell to my knees on the cold, hard ground and stared up at Heather, who'd gone to stand next to Josh. They both looked down at me coldly.

Oh, my God. I'd been staked. They'd staked me.

I couldn't breathe. The pain in my chest was like a living thing that was burrowing into my body. The night that surrounded me began to fill my vision with a growing darkness.

I thought she was my friend. I trusted her.

Too good to be true.

I gasped for breath and fell to my side, my head landing on a patch of thick white snow.

I couldn't see anything. I was blacking out. I was going to die.

Then suddenly there was a whir of movement in my now dark and cloudy peripheral vision. I heard both Josh and Heather yelling.

And then there was only silence.

I felt hands on me, pulling me up to a standing position. Gloved hands prodded at my chest, pushing the camisole to the side. I wanted to protest being groped by whoever it was, but I couldn't find the words at the moment. The world began to fade.

A sharp smack resounded on the side of my face. "Stay with me, Sarah."

Unfamiliar deep voice. Male.

"Who . . . wh-what—?"

"They won't hurt you again. The stake . . . it's not in your heart. Almost, but not quite. You're a very lucky woman. I'd heard that about you—that you're damned lucky. You'll be all right. I promise."

I forced myself to focus my vision enough to see the vague outline of a man close to me, his face mostly covered by a black winter scarf. I couldn't see his features other than a glimpse of his eyes. He wore dark clothes—a long black coat. His hands were encased in black leather gloves. He was tall and strong and he lifted me up into his arms.

"Th . . . the . . . st-stake . . . ?" It wasn't more than a whisper. It hurt to talk.

"I'll let someone who knows how to remove it properly do the honors. I don't want to hurt you. I can't stay, though. I'll get you back to your friends."

I blinked and that hurt, too. "Wh who are you?"

"They call me the Red Devil."

Frowning also caused pain. "The R-Red Devil?"

What the hell kind of a name was that?

"Shh . . . save your strength. You're going to need it."

The Red Devil—or whatever his real name was—pressed me protectively against his chest and swiftly began walking out of the park. I sensed that we were headed back to Haven, at least I hoped so, but I couldn't be sure since after another moment I passed out from the pain and shock.

It was official.

Being staked sucked.

Chapter 2

She's dead! Sarah's dead!" It was George's voice. He was a vampire waiter at Haven and one of my very best friends. "No, wait . . . she's not dead! She's still breathing!"

"We need to go to my office," Thierry said tightly. "*Now*, damn it. Hurry up."

The fact that I could hear voices was a good sign. It meant that I was conscious. Or sort of conscious. I currently couldn't see anything, although that was probably because my eyes were closed and they wanted to stay that way. I groaned.

"She's waking up! Sarah! *Don't go toward the light!*"

"Wh-where did h-he go?" I managed.

"Who? Sarah, please don't try to talk. There was no one outside. Only you. You knocked on the door or we never would have known you were there."

I didn't knock. I couldn't have. I'd been much too unconscious to knock. The Red Devil . . . he brought me back here and he must have left before the door to Haven opened.

"George," Thierry said. "Please help me bring her to the office."

There was a scuffle. I heard more voices murmuring as we passed through the main area of the club. I was being carried in someone's strong arms. I forced my eyes open a crack to see that it was Thierry. He held me tight against his chest, and his expression was tense as he focused on the direction he was quickly moving in.

"Thierry . . ." I moaned against his black shirt.

His jaw clenched and he glanced down at me. "Shh, Sarah. Conserve your strength."

He kicked open his office door and entered the room to place me as gently as possible down on his black leather sofa. It still hurt like hell.

"Close the door," he told George.

I opened my eyes wider. George stood by the door wringing his hands. He was a vampire who was over eighty years old but looked like a twenty-something Chippendale dancer with shoulder-length sandy-colored hair, a tall, ripped bod, and a tendency to wear leather pants and tight shirts. He closed the door and came over to my side.

"Sweetie," he said with an audible shake to his voice. "You're going to be okay."

"Really?" My mouth was very dry.

"It might not feel like it right now, but it'll be fine."

I coughed. "Thanks for the vote of c-confidence." I looked down at my chest. The stake was still sticking straight out of it. My breathing was ragged. "That is s-so going to leave a mark."

"Who did this?" Thierry asked.

I swallowed and cringed at the pain that caused. "Heather's b-boyfriend. He . . . he wanted me to sire him." I gasped for air. "There was no job. She let him stake me when I told him n-no . . ."

His silver eyes narrowed. "I will kill him for this."

"One thing at a time," George suggested.

"Yes." Thierry's jaw clenched and his expression was grim. His eyes reflected a brewing storm inside. "Sarah, please be brave for me. I need to remove this stake, and since it's so close to your heart, I will need you to be very still."

"Do you want me to leave?" George asked.

"No," Thierry said quickly. "I need you to stay. The blood . . . there will be too much blood. You need to keep Sarah safe."

Anyone else might wonder what he meant by that. Was George a trained nurse? No. Was Thierry squeamish when it came to blood and worried he might pass out and George would have to finish the job?

Nope.

I glanced at the bright red blood already soaking through my nice new white lace camisole. White, of course, because that's always the way, isn't it? Then I looked up at Thierry. His eyes had already turned from their normal silver shade to the black of a hungry vampire, and when he spoke his words were slurred due to his lenghtening fangs.

Thierry had a bit of an addiction to blood. When he got a taste of it he went a little crazy—to say the least. It had happened only once before, by mistake, and he'd nearly drained me dry. Vampires at his age don't need to drink blood at all, and when they do, it only makes them want more. And more. Thierry normally drank cranberry juice now and I'd prefer to keep it that way.

At the moment, his concern for me was mixed with a healthy dose of . . . *primal hunger.*

Terrific.

If I hadn't been dealing with the big piece of wood sticking out of my chest I'd have been a little more concerned for my neck.

"It's fine," he said, although it sounded as if he was speaking to himself instead of me. His black gaze tracked from my wound to my eyes. His forehead was deeply creased. "I won't lose control."

George came to my side and held my hand. He stroked back the hair that had fallen across my forehead.

"Just hold on, Sarah," he said. "Think happy thoughts. Really, it's no big deal."

George had been staked before, and I'd been there to witness his reaction to having the stake removed. Therefore I knew it *was* a big deal and he was a big fat liar.

"Just g-get it out of me," I said through clenched teeth.

Thierry's hands were shaking slightly as he gripped the end of the stake.

"Be brave, my love." And then he pulled the stake from my chest.

I screamed. I tended to do that when my insides felt as though they were being torn from my body and set on fire. The stake clattered to the ground, and Thierry pressed his palms against the wound to stop the bleeding.

"Knife," he growled at George.

George disengaged his probably broken hand from my crushing grip and hurried to Thierry's desk to grab the knife he kept in the top drawer. He brought it over and handed it to Thierry.

"Compress the wound," Thierry said, and George, who was very good at following orders in tense situations, did as requested.

Then Thierry drew the knife across his left forearm to draw his own blood and held it against my mouth.

Master vampire blood. Filled with power and strength—like a well-aged liquor that made a regular vamp's blood seem as potent as Kool-Aid. This was the reason Josh wanted me to sire him. Because the strength of Thierry's blood, of Nicolai's, was inside me.

No. It didn't make any sense. I didn't feel any different. He'd been wrong. He'd made a horrible mistake and then that bastard had staked me.

Hell, maybe I should have said yes. Instead of dealing with a stake wound I'd have two grand in my pocket.

I shut off my racing thoughts and drank.

Blood. Yeah, it was disgusting—at least in theory. As a human I thought that the very idea of drinking blood was completely and utterly nasty, not to mention unhygienic. In reality it was not so black or white or right or wrong.

I was all about the shades of gray now. And Thierry, even in a horrific situation like this, tasted really, really good to me. I knew doing this would help me to heal faster and even help to lessen the pain. My eyes locked onto his and he stared down at me, his eyes still fully black and filled with something that looked a whole lot like lust. With his free hand he stroked the hair off my face.

"Sarah . . ." he said softly. "That should be enough."

"Okay," I managed, finally and reluctantly letting go of Thierry's arm.

"I need a drink!" George exhaled shakily. "And it's

not just because I've been clutching your breasts for five minutes."

"Don't get any ideas, Georgie." I laughed a little at that and it hurt. "Ow."

"Don't worry," he said. "You're still not my gender preference."

Thierry stood up from the side of the sofa and rolled down his shirt sleeve but not before I'd caught a glimpse of the knife wound that had already begun to heal. "Sarah, George will help to clean you up. I have an extra shirt you can wear on a hanger behind the door."

"Me?" George pointed at his chest. "You want me to clean—"

Thierry turned his still-black gaze away from me and walked quickly out of the room.

George looked down at me. "Feel like a sponge bath, you sexy little thing?"

After George cleaned and patched me up, I fell asleep and had one of those prophetic dreams. At least I think it was one now that I was paying more attention to that sort of thing.

The man with the black scarf wrapped around his face walked toward me. Other than the scarf obliterating his features, he wore a very nice black tuxedo. The background flickered as though changing channels on the television from day, to night, to the inside of a gray factory, to a wall of flames.

"Red Devil?" I said out loud. "What does that even mean? Do you have another name? Should I just call you Red, maybe?"

"Yes, Red as blood." He held a gloved hand up to the

side of my face. "We're so close now, Sarah. Soon you'll know your true destiny. It is to help me."

I blinked. "Well, I am currently looking for a new job. How much does this helping you thing pay?"

"Every moment you exist, Sarah, you are helping me."

"With what?"

"I can't tell you yet." He shook his head. "What do you want more than anything else in the world? Right now, right at this very moment?"

I thought about it, hard. I looked down at my chest, at the bandage that was there to cover the stake wound. "I want to be normal."

"You can't be normal anymore. You're a vampire."

"I know that. But I can be as normal as possible. I want my friends to be safe. I want to be happy."

"With Thierry."

"Yes."

"That can never happen."

I frowned at him. "Tell me who you are. I'm not really in the mood for riddles or games. It's been a rough night."

"This isn't a game." He attempted to put his arms around me in an odd, stifling hug, but he was pulled back before he touched me. Thierry stood behind him.

"Sarah," Thierry said. "Is he trying to make you do something you don't want to do? You can tell me."

I opened my mouth but found I couldn't reply to him.

Thierry took a step closer to me, but the Red Devil grabbed him, turned him around, and then sank a wooden stake into his chest. I let out a horrified scream.

Thierry met my gaze. "Why did you help him, Sarah?"

I shook my head. "I . . . I didn't mean to. I love you, Thierry!"

He whispered something that I couldn't hear and then he disintegrated before my eyes.

"No!" I cried.

My dreams about Thierry—prophetic or not—always seemed to end with him getting staked. But it hadn't happened in real life. It wouldn't happen. I wouldn't let it.

It was just a dream.

I would be normal. I would be happy.

I would.

"Ow," was my first word upon waking up. There was a cool cloth pressed to my forehead. George blinked down at me.

"Morning, sunshine," he said to me, and then, "She's awake."

"Good." Thierry was back in the room, his eyes now returned to their normal silvery shade of gray. His arms were crossed and he frowned deeply. "How are you feeling, Sarah?"

"Like I should be checking my spleen for splinters."

"Can you sit up?"

"I don't know."

His right hand was on my shoulder, the other on my back, and he supported me as I slowly brought myself up to a sitting position. It hurt, but not as much as I would have thought it would. He sat beside me so I could lean against him.

"Yes, sitting I can apparently manage," I said.

Thierry reached over to undo the top buttons on his spare black shirt, which I now wore, and he peeled the bandage away from my chest. My bra and camisole were ruined and had been thrown into the garbage.

"You're already starting to heal." His warm fingers stroked softly over my bare left breast.

I sucked in a quick breath. My chest ached from my wound, but it didn't stop the rest of my body from tightening with desire at his touch. "Good to know."

He didn't remove his hand. We stared into each other's eyes.

George cleared his throat. "Uh . . . should I leave the two of you alone?"

"In a moment." Thierry moved his hand away so he could replace the bandage. "Sarah, I went outside to see if I could find Heather and her boyfriend."

"Did you find them?"

"Yes." He stood up from the sofa. "A man, who I am assuming is the boyfriend, was left dead in the park next to the remains of what I'm sure is Heather. They were both killed. However, I did retrieve your coat."

My eyes widened. "Was it . . . did you—?"

He shook his head. "No, I didn't kill them, although I definitely wanted to."

I frowned. "It must have been the Red Devil."

"Pardon me?"

I took a breath. "Right after I was staked a man appeared. He wore a scarf over his face so I couldn't see what he looked like. He called himself the Red Devil and he carried me back here and then I guess he left. If it wasn't for him, I'd be dead. He *saved* me."

"You were outside the door when the bouncer found you. Someone knocked. I assumed it was you just before you lost consciousness."

I shook my head. "It must have been him. Have you ever heard of him before?"

Thierry eyed George without expression. George, on the other hand, looked beside himself with excitement.

"The Red Devil?" he asked. "He's back? This is so wonderful! I thought he was gone forever."

"The Red Devil is an urban legend," Thierry said.

"No, he isn't." George turned to me. "Sarah, you just met one of the coolest vampires in history. He's a hero. He saves our kind from harm, like the Lone Ranger or Zorro. He swings in, kicks butt, then leaves, and no one knows who he is. At least he used to. He hasn't been seen or heard from in a hundred years. But now he's back. You are so lucky! Was he hot?"

"Scarf on face," I reminded him. I shifted position on the sofa and the leather squeaked. "He was tall, though. And are you serious? He's some kind of a vampire superhero?"

"Urban legend," Thierry corrected. "That some have taken to heart and perhaps are trying to emulate. The Red Devil doesn't actually exist. He never has. But whoever this impostor is, I do owe him my thanks for saving your life."

I frowned. "He killed Josh . . . and Heather."

"Yes, he did."

My masked hero was now a murderer. Vigilante justice. Maybe under that scarf he looked like Charles Bronson, only with fangs.

They'd tried to kill me. I suppose it was an eye for an eye, but still, it was disturbing, to say the least. I'd considered Heather a friend—her betrayal still stung. And now she was a puddle of goo. I guess she was older than I thought she was, since only really old vamps disintegrate when killed. Younger vamps and fledglings stayed in one solid but dead piece.

I took in a shaky breath.

"George," Thierry said. "Please let my patrons know that Sarah will be fine and there's no need to panic. And I'd prefer that you don't tell anyone about this . . . this *Red Devil* nonsense."

"Sure thing." George nodded, and with a quick wink at me he left the room and closed the door behind him.

"I don't understand how this could have happened," Thierry said.

"I know. Sometimes it feels like everybody wants to kill me." I replayed the horrific scene over and over in my mind until I had to force myself to push it away.

"That's not what I meant." He touched my face and looked at me so intensely it felt as though he was trying to memorize my features. "Heather was a terrible waitress, but I never would have thought her capable of something like this. I trusted her."

"That makes two of us." I leaned into his touch and put my head against his shoulder. "She was in love with Josh. I guess love makes people do crazy things."

The pain still throbbed in my chest, but it was becoming increasingly manageable. At some point tonight—or this morning, since by a quick glance at the wall clock it was going on 3:00 A.M.—I might even be able to stand up. It was a goal.

"It does, indeed," he murmured. "I don't want to lose you, Sarah. Please, promise me that you'll be very careful from now on."

"Cross my stake-riddled heart." I smiled up at him, but felt tears welling inside.

"Good." He leaned toward me and kissed me, trailing his fingers along my cheek, my jawline, and then tangling into my already tangled hair. The kiss deepened and a little moan escaped my throat as his tongue slid against mine.

I thought about my dream, about seeing Thierry staked and killed.

It was just a dream. Nothing more than that. This Red Devil was some vampire playing dress-up and trying to save vamps who'd gotten themselves into tight situations. Like me. Since I was all for getting saved when the situation called for it, more power to him.

Thierry moved his face down and peeled the shirt away from my chest so he could gently kiss the bandage over my already healing wound. I bit my bottom lip and slid my fingers into his dark, nearly black hair. His mouth made things tighten and curl inside me, and the ache I was currently feeling wasn't just in my chest anymore.

He smiled up at me. "Don't worry. I know you're weak and injured. I promise not to molest you any further."

I parted the shirt farther and returned the smile. "I may be injured, but I'm not that weak. If you're really careful, a little molesting would be perfectly fine with me."

"Is that so?" He moved back up to kiss me again, a little harder this time.

The phone on Thierry's desk rang. He sighed softly against my lips, and then took a moment to rebutton my shirt before moving to pick up the receiver.

"Yes," he said, and I watched his expression darken. His eyes flicked to me. "She's unavailable at the moment, Quinn. Whatever you need to tell her you can tell me. I promise to relate it directly."

My heart jumped a little at hearing the name. Quinn was a good friend of mine. A vampire hunter who had been turned into a vampire. Up until three weeks ago he'd also complicated my relationship with Thierry—Quinn was hot, available, and interested in me—but I'd made my choice. I cared for Quinn very deeply, but I wasn't in love with him. I loved Thierry. And Quinn had accepted that by going off on a road trip through the United States. With a werewolf.

Poor guy. I'm sure he'll find somebody eventually. Some nice girl who won't give him any problems.

"You're certain?" Thierry said into the receiver. "Yes, I understand. I'll tell her." There was a long pause and then, "As I already said, she's unavailable."

After another moment or two, he hung up the phone.

"I could have spoken with him, you know," I said. "There's nothing wrong with my voice."

"I know." His expression gave nothing away.

Okay, fine. "What did he want to tell me?"

"It seems that Quinn is currently in Las Vegas."

"Vegas?" I repeated. "Isn't that where the hunter convention is going on right now?"

"It is."

"Is he crazy or something? Is he okay?"

He folded his arms across his chest and leaned against his desk. "He sounds fine. He wanted to pass along word that Gideon Chase is dead."

The sound of that name was like a big glass of cold water thrown in my face.

"Gideon? He's dead?"

Gideon Chase was the leader of the vampire hunters, a billionaire who enjoyed his sport a little too much and funded others so they could enjoy it as well. Ever since I'd developed my little reputation as the Slayer of Slayers, I'd been told that he'd set his sights on me and wanted to personally hunt me down. Kind of a notch in his hunter utility belt.

I'd tried not to think about it. After all, dwelling on something like that might cause one to experience a great many sleepless nights while one imagined oneself at the mercy of somebody without any mercy. Yeah. Sleepless nights. Tell me about it. The bags under my eyes lately weren't from partying hard. Gideon wouldn't have missed getting my heart if I'd been at the receiving end of one of his stakes, that's for damn sure.

"This is a good thing, Sarah," Thierry said.

I took a deep breath and let it out shakily. "Of course it is."

"It means that you're safe and the hunters won't know which way to turn until they nominate a new leader."

I frowned. "And the price that Gideon put on your head? Does it mean that you're safe, too?"

Gideon liked master vampires—killing them, that is. They were more of a challenge, and he'd offered a lot of money—millions, in fact—to anyone who brought Thierry to him alive. I hadn't heard one solitary thing about Gideon Chase that made me think he was worthy of anyone's grief. He was dead. He was gone, and I, for one, would sleep a lot sounder from now on.

He smiled thinly. "I will never be safe. That is why I'm constantly vigilant about my surroundings, as you should be as well. I think what happened tonight with Heather was a good reminder of how quickly things can go wrong if we're not careful. When we return to your hometown for your reunion, I'd prefer you stay by my side at all times."

I raised my eyebrows and shifted positions on the sofa to try to ignore the throbbing pain in my chest. "You really think we should still go? After what happened tonight?"

"We don't have to go if you don't want to."

Attending my high-school reunion suddenly seemed like the most important thing in my life. A small reminder of when I was normal and happy. When people accepted me and life was simple. When I didn't ingest blood as my main food source or have to dodge wooden stakes on a daily basis.

"I definitely want to go," I said firmly.

"Then we'll go."

I gingerly touched my bandage and frowned. "Listen, Thierry, can I ask you something?"

"Of course. Anything."

"Josh . . . he said that I had the blood of two master vampires in my veins . . . you and Nicolai. He said that made me special and I could make him a stronger vampire if I sired him. Is that true?"

"He had heard rumors, not facts. His greed led him to want to believe. It also led him to attempted murder, and now he's dead because of it."

My frown deepened. "It's just . . . I don't feel too bad right now. Sure, I feel like crap, but not as bad as I would have thought I'd feel with an injury like this. I thought maybe the blood had something to do with it."

"Yes, my blood does help to improve your healing abilities, but that doesn't mean he was right in his other assumptions."

"So I'm not special."

"You're very special. To me." He leaned forward and kissed me again. "Now, please rest here, Sarah. I will be back shortly."

"Where are you going?"

He moved toward the door. "To investigate this Red Devil nonsense."

"You really think it's nonsense? That he's not the real deal?"

He paused and turned back to me. "I'm certain he's not the real deal."

Okay. Well, that made one of us.

Chapter 3

I bet he looks like Brad Pitt," my best friend Amy said two days after my date with the wooden stake. "Somebody with presence and serious sex appeal."

I was at her house, lying on her king-sized bed, propped up by a multitude of colorful pillows. Amy had been turned into a vampire about five days after I had, but we'd been friends for a long time before that. I'd made the mistake of introducing her to a vampire named Barry and the two had hit it off so much that she'd been sired on their first date and they'd gotten married about two weeks later.

George sat next to me, cross-legged, as Amy went through her closet trying to find the perfect dress for me to borrow from her vast and sparkly collection.

I used to have a vast and sparkling collection of my own, but thanks to vampire hunters and a well-placed explosive in my apartment a few weeks ago, I was currently homeless—living with George until further notice—and slowly but surely trying to replenish my wardrobe and belongings. I was still twitching a little from watching all of my worldly possessions go up in smoke. Luckily, I hadn't gone with them.

But that was in the past. The current subject between George, Amy, and myself was, of course, the Red Devil.

"I'm sure he's very sexy," I said. "But, just remember, he did kill two people."

"Two *evil* people," George added. "I always had a feeling Heather was up to no good. I'm positive she was dipping into my tips." He eyed Amy's latest selection, a little green number. "That one's perfect for you, Sarah."

I'd designated him as my chauffeur for the day as well as my makeshift bodyguard, at least until Thierry picked me up. We were headed straight to Abottsville and the reunion after I borrowed what I needed from Amy.

"Too low-cut," I said. "I've got a healing stake wound to deal with that I'd rather my entire hometown not get a look at."

Amy frowned and combed her fingers through her short, bright-pink hair. Yes, pink. She'd recently had a minor nervous breakdown when she believed that her husband was cheating on her and had taken it out on her previously blond locks. "I don't think I have anything that isn't low-cut."

"That could be a problem."

I peeled the bandage away under my V-neck T-shirt and peeked at the evidence that I'd come ridiculously close to acquiring fluffy wings and a halo.

George eyed my chest. "A little foundation and some pressed powder and no one would ever know."

It looked much better underneath, but was far from being healed completely. What currently remained of the wound was a raw, red mark about the size of a shot-glass opening—like an evil bruise. All in all, I was fairly surprised at how quickly I was mending. But, as Thierry had said, it probably had a lot to do with the master vampire blood I'd had. I wouldn't be siring any supervamps any time soon, but if I could heal up nice and quick it would be worth it.

I looked at the wound very rarely. Even though I was trying to keep up a good front, I was still deeply shaken by what had happened. Being around my friends and going through Amy's closet seemed like a good way to keep my mind off nearly dying.

I had barely gotten any sleep last night or what was left of the night in question. I'd stayed at Thierry's townhome both nights, even though I was officially still living at George's place. Thierry was being very careful not to hurt me, therefore I hadn't gotten much more from him than a few memorable kisses, so that wasn't the reason for my lack of sleep. Unfortunately. No, it was reliving the staking over and over, and throw in my meet-and-greet with the Red Devil and you've got a recipe for insomnia.

Amy held up an electric-blue micromini with a beaded fringe. I made the gag sign. She pouted and put it away. "You know, it's okay if you're attracted to this guy. He does sound super hot."

"Who? The Red Devil? You think I'm attracted to him?"

She and George shared a look. "Well, of course," she said. "He did rescue you. And you said he was really sexy."

"Did I really say that?" I frowned. "Look, even if he *was* Brad Pitt, it wouldn't actually matter. I'm with Thierry."

She rolled her eyes at that proclamation. She had as much of a problem with me being with that, in her words, "boring, stoic jerk" as I had with Barry, the man she'd chosen to marry—a short little creep of a vampire who'd hated my guts from the first moment we'd met.

"You know what they say," George said, taking it upon himself to fluff up the pillows behind me so I'd be comfortable. "There's nothing wrong with looking at the menu as long as you eat at home."

"I'm not looking at any menus," I said firmly. "I don't eat anymore. I just drink. Besides, the menu was wearing a scarf so I couldn't even see what kind of a restaurant it was."

George cringed away from me. "Jeez. It's just a saying, Little Miss Cranky Pants."

I sighed. "I know. Sorry. I'm feeling edgy."

"What about this one?" Amy pulled out a black dress with a bit of glitter on the top and held it up.

"Not bad." I turned to George again. "Listen, tell me more about this Red Devil guy. Who is he? What has he done? Where did he come from?"

He scratched his chin. "Well, I don't know much actually. Other than the fact that he's a hero. Back in the old days when hunters tried to take out a bunch of vamps, the Red Devil would swing in and save them all."

I thought about that. "How come I've never heard of him before?"

"There's a lot of things you've probably never heard of. You've been a vamp for barely any time at all. And besides, until last night I thought he was long gone. Haven't heard any rumors about him for years, and he's never even been active in my lifetime. He did most of the big stuff in the old days stretching all the way back to the Crusades. The guy's got to be over a thousand years old." He shifted position on the bed. "But still hot."

I thought about my scarfed hero. "I just can't figure it out. Why would he be here? Why would he save me?"

George shrugged. "Maybe you should stop overanalyzing it and just consider yourself lucky."

"Yeah, maybe." My stake wound itched so I rubbed it lightly. "I never even got the chance to thank him."

"Maybe you'll see him again some day," Amy said. "That would be so romantic."

I looked at her sharply. "You've seriously got to lay off the Nora Roberts, Amy. I'm not interested in him. I would like to thank him for saving my life, but I may never get the chance. Besides, Thierry thinks he's just some guy dressing up like the Red Devil. Trying to be something he's not."

"Oh, brother." Amy sighed. "Who cares what he thinks? You have a gorgeous vampire superhero who risked his life to save you. *You*, Sarah. And you're worried about what that reclusive jerk thinks?"

"I know you don't believe this, Amy, but I'm in love with Thierry. *Love*, love. Like cupids and hearts and sexy lingerie love."

She made a face. "But he's no Red Devil."

"You don't even know the Red Devil."

"I know he's strong and courageous and incredibly amazing."

George nodded. "Definitely."

"Thierry's none of those things," Amy said firmly. "You just won't accept that."

I glared at her. "Sure, he's a little reserved and sometimes he doesn't talk much."

"Does he ever even go outside?" Amy asked, and I knew she was trying to exaggerate because she was finding this debate funny.

I grinned. "He goes outside at least twice a week. Fresh air is important to a master vampire."

"But only when it's safe," Amy said. "After all, we must be vigilant about the dangers that lurk around us at all times." She did a surprisingly good impression of him and I couldn't help but laugh.

"An ounce of prevention is worth a pound of wooden stakes," George added.

"Look, he is who he is," I said. "You should give him half a chance."

"But you wish Thierry could be a little more like the Red Devil." Amy raised a thin, perfectly plucked eyebrow.

I shrugged. "Maybe I do. A little. The Red Devil was rather . . . *forceful*. I'd be willing to bet that he'd charge right into a dangerous situation instead of staying inside where it's safe."

Amy and George didn't reply to that. The cheery smiles had fallen away from both of their expressions.

After a moment, George cleared his throat. "Hey, Thierry. I guess Amy left the front door unlocked, huh?"

I glanced at the doorway. Thierry leaned against it. There was a small smile on his lips.

Terrific. And how much was I willing to bet that out of that entire conversation, he'd only heard the very last thing I'd said. I was such an asshole.

"I hope it's okay that I let myself in, Amy," he said.

She was frozen over by the closet with a sparkly red dress held up in front of her as if for protection against the forces of evil. "Sure. Uh-huh."

"That one." I pointed at the dress. "It's perfect. Can I borrow it?"

She nodded stiffly and flung the hanger in the general direction of my lap.

"Are you ready to go?" Thierry asked me. "Your overnight bag is in my trunk. We can be in Abottsville in three hours."

I nodded and began to get up from the bed, but since I was still nursing the healing wound it took some effort. He came over to my side and assisted me to my feet.

"Bye, Thierry." Amy stayed over by the closet. She was looking at her chosen object of disdain, Thierry. But as I focused on her expression I realized that there wasn't much disdain to be seen in her wide eyes.

She looked like a teenager at a rock concert.

I frowned.

And then I had the sudden and profound realization that, despite all of her harsh and nasty words, my pink-haired best friend had a crush on my boyfriend.

Her gaze flicked to mine and I think she saw it in my eyes—that I knew her dirty little secret. She looked away and actually started to whistle innocently.

Great. Just what I needed.

Thierry helped me out to his black Audi without saying another word. He pulled out of the driveway in front of Barry and Amy's apartment complex.

"About what I said in there," I began.

"What did you say?"

I didn't even remember, actually. But I knew it had something to do with me wishing that he was more courageous, like the Red Devil. I didn't mean that. I'd been joking around. I knew Thierry was courageous. I'd seen it with my own eyes. I felt horrible that he might have overheard me say something I didn't even believe.

"Nothing." I shook my head and forced a smile. "You know I love you, right?"

He smiled as he eased the car onto the highway. "I know. You love me despite my many flaws. But just so you know, this Red Devil person is not perfect either."

Shit. He *had* heard.

"I never said he was."

"In fact, I think he may be dangerous, whoever he truly is under that disguise. If he approaches you again I want you to tell me immediately."

I nodded. "Okay. But let's forget all about him just for today."

He turned to me and met my eyes briefly before focusing on the road again. "Agreed."

And even though I wondered who he was, what he wanted, and where he came from, I forced myself to forget all about the Red Devil.

Or, at least, I tried damned hard to.

Interlude

Thierry, I'd like you to meet Marcellus."

He came to Veronique's side and raised his eyes to meet those of the man he'd heard about for two hundred years. The man his wife had never stopped caring for, even though he had left her to fend for herself during the darkest days of the Black Death plague.

It was very difficult to be married to someone who was hopelessly in love with another.

Difficult, but not impossible.

Thierry nodded at the vampire and forced a semblance of a smile to appear on his face. His collar felt stiff at his throat, as if he was being choked by it. Veronique constantly accused him of being unfriendly to others they met in their travels through Europe, of being a miserable man filled with a festering darkness.

He had to admit, the woman was an excellent judge of character—except when it came to Marcellus, that is.

Marcellus was a handsome man. Tall and imposing, with fair hair and skin, but with a charming smile—the ease of which Thierry admired—and an obvious taste for fashion. His clothing was perfectly tailored and expensive enough that the cost of it could have fed Thierry's entire family for years.

His family. They'd all died during the plague. Four sisters, two brothers, and his mother. Gone. His father had died years earlier, and as the eldest by five years, Thierry had taken on a parental role with his siblings. Yet, only he had survived.

Survived, he thought with bitterness. Yes. After two hundred years of life, survival was all that mattered anymore.

Veronique, he had to admit, was a beautiful woman. Hair as dark as night that she wore in the latest styles. She dressed in the latest fashions. Her wrists and neck and ears dripped with jewels—all of which Veronique had acquired for herself. Thierry didn't know how she had paid for such luxuries, but there was always money to spend. He had long since stopped questioning their resources.

Marcellus had invited them to a performance of the *commedia dell'arte* and then to dine in the vaulted cellar of a tavern near the river.

The tavern was filled with vampires—something that stunned Thierry. He'd never seen so many of his kind in one place before. He'd been a vampire for two centuries but he was still amazed that such a thing existed. Veronique had sired him into this life after the point he'd wanted to continue living. He had already made his peace before he'd been saved from the death and disease of the plague years.

Now he was to live forever. Much like the beings that surrounded him. They laughed and drank and danced and listened to the music in the tavern as if they were normal.

But they weren't normal. They were creatures who looked human but needed blood to survive. He ran his tongue along the sharp tips of his fangs. Veronique indulged her thirst frequently but he did not. He didn't care for the feeling of intoxication when he drank blood—the feeling of being out of control. He valued his control above all things.

"Don't be silly," Veronique always told him. "You should relish this second chance at life I've given you."

"I do," he assured her.

He wondered if she regretted siring him. Or marrying him. He did care for the dark-haired beauty in his own way. After all, despite her self-involved actions and behavior, Veronique was not evil. She did what she could with the life she'd been given. As did he. She made for a fine companion and had taught him many things about being a vampire.

But he didn't love her.

He had loved his family, but they had been destroyed by the plague. One of his sisters had still been healthy when the villagers had taken her late one night and burned her body among the dead to prevent the spread of the disease. There had been nothing he could have done to prevent it. That was the night Thierry ran as far away from his village as he could, only to end up in the same situation as his sister.

Veronique had saved him. She'd been hungry and he'd apparently looked appetizing enough for her to pull his half-dead body from the pile of burning corpses.

The plague had long since left Europe, leaving behind a path of death and destruction. Thierry was still alive. Still breathing. His heart still beat, but now he had to drink the blood of others to keep it that way.

It was a monstrous life.

The only thing he had was Veronique. Yes, the woman who was now seated upon her sire and old lover's lap with his tongue down her throat. Thierry watched them from the shadows. Veronique hadn't even noticed his departure from the table.

She would be unfaithful to him. Thierry was surprised that the thought didn't bother him as much as it should have.

He watched as a man approached Marcellus to touch his shoulder and then whispered something in his ear. Marcellus nodded and disengaged from Veronique's embrace long enough to stand up, smiling as he left the table to venture outside. Thierry followed, keeping to the shadows, watching as Marcellus's easy smile faded to a tense but determined expression.

"And the man who told you this?" he asked the man next to him sharply after he'd taken the stairs to street level.

"A solid source. It is good, reliable information. They are almost upon us."

Marcellus's expression shadowed. "I only wish I had more time. There are arrangements to be made." His serious gaze then moved to where Thierry stood silently. "You there. Perhaps you can be of help to me tonight."

"I didn't mean to overhear anything," Thierry said, feeling exposed and ashamed to be caught lurking in the shadows.

Marcellus's lips curled. "Of course you did. And I can't say that I blame you. After all, I have been preoccupying Veronique all evening."

"Are you apologizing for that?"

"No." His gaze was steady and unflinching and Thierry felt uncomfortable for a moment.

"What do you want from me, then?"

"Leave us," he told the other vampire, who bowed and with a glance at Thierry left them in privacy.

Marcellus pulled a chain out from under his collar. There was a key on the end of it. "If I ask you to do something for me, will you do it?"

"It depends what it is you ask."

The smile returned as he slipped the chain over his head and glanced down at the gold key. "This is the key to my home near the city wall." He told Thierry the precise address. "I want you to take this key and let yourself into the house. Destroy the papers you will find there."

"Why?"

"Because tonight I shall die, and if those papers get into the wrong hands, many others shall die as well."

"I don't understand."

"No." He shook his head. "I don't suppose you do. I am a very good judge of people. I know those I can trust by looking into their eyes. Do you know what I see when I look into yours?"

Thierry didn't reply.

"I see a man who has suffered, and even though that which has caused your suffering has left, you still hold on to that pain. However, I sense that you are honest and honorable. I don't know how you came to marry Veronique, nor does it matter anymore."

"You left her."

"Only because I had to. For her own safety. You see, I am a hunted man. There are those who wish to do me great harm, and they have finally found me. I cannot escape. They will end my life tonight and I must embrace it. My death must be on public record so my secrets shall die with me."

"The papers."

"Yes, the papers must also be destroyed. There is no other choice."

"Why can't you simply leave?"

He walked off to the side and gazed out at the dark, empty street outside the tavern. "Have you ever heard of the *Diable Rouge* . . . the Red Devil, Thierry?"

"Yes." The Red Devil was a vampire rumored to save other vampires from the threat of hunters. His identity was not known, but his deeds were legendary.

Marcellus turned to him. "The Red Devil dies tonight. The hunters believe that they know his true identity and they want to end him."

Thierry frowned deeply. "I don't understand."

Marcellus smiled. "It is best that Veronique never learn the truth. I want her to believe that I left her years back for selfish reasons. She must never know how deeply I loved her, how much I still love her and have missed her for all of these many years. I felt great jealousy when I first met you, Thierry, for you have what I cannot: *Veronique.*"

"*You* are the Red Devil?"

"It is a silly name, but yes. I am. Until tonight."

Thierry shook his head. "Then it's too important for you to continue. You must escape."

He smiled, but it was a sad smile. "Do you know what it feels like to be betrayed by those you consider your friends? All is lost. The papers have names, locations, details that in the wrong hands would do too much damage . . . If the Red Devil is gone, then that information must follow."

"How can you accept something like this? So easily? After all that you've done to help others?"

"I am almost five hundred years old and am weary with life. To be a vampire is to live forever, but it is finally time for me to rest. Seeing Veronique again has given me a last happiness."

The other man stepped back outside. "Marcellus, they approach."

Marcellus nodded to him and then handed Thierry the key. "Take this."

Thierry took it and looked down at it with a frown. "But, Marcellus . . . you cannot—"

"I must."

"What about Veronique? She is still downstairs."

"I will ensure her safety if it is the last thing I do. I swear it." Marcellus smiled, and Thierry could see the strain of such a long life in his expression. "Now go . . . hide yourself. They must not find that key." He paused and grasped Thierry's shoulder. "Take care of Veronique for me. Farewell, *mon ami*."

Thierry watched his wife's sire and ex-lover descend the stairs to the secret tavern and knew there was nothing he could do or say to stop what was to come.

His mind buzzed with the information he'd received.

The Red Devil. Marcellus was the Red Devil and he was about to die. Thierry's throat felt thick at the thought.

Then he clenched the key in his fist and turned away from the tavern to disappear into the shadows.

That night, Thierry traveled to Marcellus's home near the city wall. He found the papers. Lists of the names of vampires pretending to be human. Lists of names of humans who now hunted vampirekind. Lists of the names of informants, both vampire and human, and how much money these informants expected to be paid for their information. There was a bank of weapons hidden in the home. And money. A great deal of gold and other coinage spilled forth at his touch.

He also found Marcellus's detailed journals of the *Diable Rouge*. What he had done. Where. When. Why. Thierry sat in Marcellus's home and read the many journals twice through, amazed at what he discovered. The Red Devil's identity was a closely guarded secret and had been for nearly five hundred years. Through Thierry's investigation, he could not find one living person who knew what Marcellus had done during the dark hours of night. Even Marcellus's assistant the other night, the man who warned of the approaching hunters, might not have known the whole truth.

The truth was that Marcellus was saving his kind from slaughter at the hands of the hunters.

The thought that it was now over, that the Red Devil was dead, disturbed Thierry greatly. Even though his past relationship with Veronique soured him in Thierry's eyes,

Marcellus had done such good with his long life, had saved so many people, that it couldn't be over.

There was a letter tucked into the journal at the last entry made. It had not yet been opened. It was from an informant and told of a planned massacre later that week.

A closely knit clan of vampires with loose ties to French royalty had been targeted to be an example to others. Three men and four women. And now that the Red Devil was dead, there was no one to save them from certain death.

Thierry's knuckles were white from clutching the journal so tightly. He had watched his family die and had been able to do nothing to prevent it. The Black Death had not been selective. It had eaten through the surrounding lands with an insatiable hunger, destroying those left behind with grief, despair, and poverty. But a disease couldn't be stopped.

However, a few hunters with sharp weapons *could* be stopped.

Thierry thought of his sister, the one who had not died from the plague, but instead at the hands of crazed villagers who, so afraid of death, killed anything they saw as a potential threat. He'd been too late to save her. It was his fault she was dead. The guilt ate at him even after so many years.

There was a wooden box, ornately carved with the symbol of a sun, on a side table near him. He opened it expecting to see more jewels or money, but it contained only two things, which he removed: a miniature painting of Veronique and a red mask. He gazed down at the portrait of his wife, at her perfect beauty, flawless complexion, and haughty expression. There was no denying that she was the most beautiful woman he had ever seen.

He placed the painting back into the box and closed the lid. He held the mask up to his face. It felt right against his skin.

The decision was made in that instant. He would continue Marcellus's secret work. He would take on the Red Devil's persona. In the memory of his family, he would help those who couldn't help themselves.

He took the mask, some weapons, the journal, and as much gold as he could carry. And he left the small house the following day to return to his wife in Paris.

Her expression was beautiful but annoyed when he found her.

"Where have you been?" she asked.

He had already decided to tell her nothing. It would be safer that way for her. Marcellus had wanted his secret to die with him. It would.

"I had to leave. I'm sorry if you were worried."

She laughed lightly. "Worried? No, Thierry, I wasn't worried. I was disappointed."

He eyed her warily. "Why?"

"After you disappeared the other night there was a raid of hunters. I barely escaped with my life. Marcellus . . ." She brought a handkerchief to her mouth. "Marcellus was murdered. I watched him die."

He frowned deeply and felt a surge of anger at that. Marcellus had told him that Veronique's safety was assured. "You shouldn't have stayed. You should have left and hidden yourself at the first sign of danger."

"As you did?" Her eyes flashed. "No, I would not

leave him in such a way. Marcellus was brave. He fought
against those who meant to kill me. You ran away like a
scared child. So yes, I am disappointed that I am married
to such a coward. In fact, I'm surprised that you returned
at all. I thought perhaps you would be too ashamed to
face me again."

He fought to keep his expression emotionless. "And
yet, here I am."

She sniffed and dabbed the handkerchief to her eyes.
"I miss him, Thierry. I don't know if he knew how deeply
I loved him."

"Had he lived, would you have left me for him?" he
asked.

She looked at him with surprise, concentration creas-
ing her forehead. "I guess we shall never know the answer to that question." She sighed. "Now, please get my
bags. Let us leave this horrible place once and for all. I
wish to go somewhere else. Anywhere else."

"No, not yet. There's some business I must attend to
later this week."

Her eyebrows rose. "Some business? You?"

"Yes."

"Very well. Perhaps you have returned from your hiding place with more motivation than you've had in the
past. It will be a good thing if you have found some goal
to achieve other than looking sullen."

The woman was in mourning for her lover. He would
forgive her sharp tongue. Forgive, but not forget.

Her beauty was as incredible as it always had been,
but it dimmed slightly for him around the edges from that
day forward.

It didn't matter. Her grief would fade. Their relationship

would become comfortable again. She would always think of him as a coward who had run away from a fight. He had to admit that it was an excellent cover.

Thierry kept the truth in a tight ball deep in his chest. It warmed him on many cold nights to follow.

Chapter 4

Attending my high-school reunion tonight, I'd decided, was going to prove one very important thing to me.

I was normal.

No matter what had happened to me—becoming a vampire, killing a hunter in self-defense, being incorrectly labeled the Slayer of Slayers, having my apartment blown up, getting staked and nearly killed—none of that mattered. I was still perfectly normal.

It was a goal.

So, what had seemed like a vaguely okay idea a couple of weeks ago—going to the reunion—now was a vital necessity to help me feel as if my life hadn't gone completely out of control. Even though it had.

Being staked had aged me. Significantly. I felt older and more wary and paranoid than ever before, at least until we reached the border of Abottsville, which, the sign reminded visitors in hand-painted letters, was still "the home of the largest pumpkin in Ontario." Just seeing that sign helped me to relax a bit.

Just a bit.

"You're very quiet," Thierry said.

Wow, if he was commenting on how little I was speaking, considering how little *he* usually spoke, then I was definitely not acting normally.

"Sorry," I said. "Just having an internal monologue about life and death."

"Are you still all right with us coming here?"

"Yes. Absolutely." I pushed all other thoughts away.

"If you'd rather we turn around and go back to Toronto—"

I shook my head. "No, it's fine. I'm glad to be here. Plus, I really want to see my mom and dad. I can't wait to introduce them to my wonderful new boyfriend."

"And since he couldn't make it, what will they think of me?"

I eyed him. "Was that a joke?"

"An attempt."

One thing Thierry didn't really possess was a funny bone. I'd searched. I'd found nothing. But it was sweet of him to try.

We were to check into the motel and then go for a superquick visit with my parents, who didn't know their only child was a vampire, and I'd prefer it stayed that way. What they didn't know wouldn't hurt them. Or me.

Then tonight we'd go to the reunion dance. There had actually been a couple of days of reunion-related activities, but too much of a good thing is not good at all. It was the dance, a little schmoozing, and then it was over, and ideally I'd get rid of this vampire-related funk I was going through and feel better about life, liberty, and the pursuit of vampiric happiness.

Mom had offered to let us stay with them in my old bedroom—even though she'd made it clear that she didn't approve of us sharing the same room out of wedlock (her words)—but I decided that a motel room would be the best option for all involved.

The motel was the only one in town, the Abottsville Motor Inn with an adjoining restaurant called the Breakfast Nook. It was just as classy as it sounded.

The room itself was what the management considered a "luxury suite" and did boast a king-sized bed underneath an oh-so-elegant ceiling mirror. I normally would have found that terribly amusing, especially with the irony that vamps didn't have reflections, but instead it just seemed embarrassing.

Once the supreme tackiness had settled in, I hung the dress I'd borrowed from Amy in the closet, threw my overnight bag in the corner, and checked the bedsheets for any potential cockroach infestations. Then I had a quick shower and freshened up my makeup using my shard compact mirror, which Thierry had bought me as an early Valentine's Day gift. Vampires didn't normally have reflections, but a *shard* wasn't a regular mirror. It was very special and very expensive and I could see myself just fine and dandy in it. I had a bigger one on the wall at George's house, but it wasn't exactly portable.

Thierry waited for me as I finished up. I'd decided for casual comfort by wearing dark blue jeans and a fuzzy white sweater under my winter coat.

Then we headed across town. It only took five minutes before I could see my parents' house looming large on the horizon at the end of a cul-de-sac. I frowned. The driveway was full of cars. This was supposed to be a short visit with just my mom and dad. Who else had they invited?

Thierry pulled the Audi alongside the curb and gave me a look. "What is going on, Sarah?"

I got out of the car and felt the cold winter breeze on my face. A few flakes of snow were falling. "No idea. But I promise it won't take long. We go in. I introduce you. They will be suitably impressed by your charm and good looks. I down a glass of wine and we are out of there in ten minutes."

He raised an eyebrow as he looked skeptically at all the cars. "Ten minutes?"

"Fifteen at the very most. We don't have that much time before we have to be at the reunion, anyhow." I eyed the front lawn and the collection of winter decorations that included a family of reindeer that lit up at night and a big inflatable snowman. "And no mention of my staking. I don't think my mother would take too well to knowing that I almost died. Especially after what happened to my apartment."

Since my parents didn't know about the vampire thing, I'd blamed the explosion on a gas leak and that I was staying with a friend until I found somewhere more permanent. My parents had freaked out, of course, and insisted I move back home with them until I could piece my life back together.

I was still piecing. But I wasn't planning on moving back into my old bedroom, still decorated with Madonna and Bon Jovi posters. Not going to happen.

Thierry hadn't asked me to move in with him yet. Despite everything going rather well between us lately, it did make me feel a little uneasy about the future.

No dwelling. Dwelling would be bad.

"Why would I tell her you were staked when she doesn't know that you are a vampire?" he asked as we walked toward the front door, decorated with a big-ass wreath.

"Semantics," I said. I reached for the doorbell, but Thierry stopped me with a hand on my arm.

"Sarah, I know you are weary of my mentioning this, but every time we leave Toronto and go outside of our comfort zones we are putting ourselves in grave danger. Even here."

"I know." More than ever, I knew that. My chest still hurt like a stake-shaped elephant had sat on it. It hurt a little to breathe. Even vampires enjoyed breathing regularly, so it was a bit annoying. But I was there, I was going to make the most of it, and everything would be just fine. Or else.

I reached for the doorbell, but the door swung open before I got to it.

"Sweetie!" My mother's arms were open and she gave me a big, warm hug. "I'm so glad to see you!"

"You, too, Mom." I smiled. She smelled like freshly baked chocolate chip cookies. "So who's here?"

She looked vaguely guilty. "Well, honey, you visit so rarely that I thought I should make the most of this opportunity. A few of your aunts, uncles, cousins. I tried not to make a big to-do out of it."

A family reunion. In ten minutes?

"Great," I said with as much enthusiasm as I could muster.

Thierry stood next to me silently. I disengaged from my mother and glanced at him.

"Mom, I'd like you to meet Thierry."

Her gaze traveled politely up his six-foot-tall frame to a face that would make any woman—no matter her age—feel a bit weak in the knees. He had that effect. As evidenced by Amy's newfound crush, that his cool and stoic temperament might rub some people the wrong way didn't mean he was hard on the eyes.

"A pleasure," he said.

"What is your last name, Thierry?" she asked.

"It is . . . *de Bennicoeur*."

"Goodness, that's quite a mouthful isn't it? What is that, French? Italian?"

"It's French."

"French Canadian? Are you from Quebec?"

"No."

She blinked and smoothed her dark hair in place on the side of her head. I recognized it as a nervous habit. "You don't have an accent."

"I came to North America a very long time ago."

"But you speak French?"

"Yes, I speak several languages."

"Yes, well." She shuffled back a few steps. "Please, leave your shoes right there"—she nodded at a large pile of muddy and snowy footwear—"and come in and join the rest of us. Care for a glass of wine?"

"Yum," I said halfheartedly. Why had that greeting felt like the most awkward thing I'd ever witnessed? And mostly on Thierry's part.

He didn't feel comfortable here. It was obvious.

"We can leave," I whispered to him as we moved along the short hallway to the family room.

He shook his head and squeezed my hand in his. "It's fine. It's an honor to meet your family, Sarah."

He was *so* earning the brownie points today.

In the family room we were both given a nice large glass of Baby Duck sparkling wine—a Dearly family favorite—and Thierry was introduced to every relative of mine who lived within a hundred-mile radius. Three uncles, five aunts, seven cousins . . . including my cousin Missy, who made a beeline toward me at first sight.

"Sarah!" She gave me a huge, smothering hug. "Oh, my God, it is so great to see you."

"You, too." I gave her a closemouthed smile. "How's married life treating you?"

"Fantastic . . . or should I say *fang*tastic? Could not be better."

I glanced over in the corner to see her new husband, Richard, in a heated discussion with my uncle Charlie. I assumed it had something to do with fishing, since that was Uncle Charlie's favorite subject. Richard wearily raised a glass in my direction and flashed a quick smile at me that revealed his small fangs.

My very human cousin Missy had married a vampire. He was also an accountant. I'd been at their wedding—one of the bridesmaids, in fact—when I realized that Richard and I had more in common than simply knowing Missy. That's when I realized also that vampires, while keeping their existences secret, were more prevalent in everyday society than I'd ever imagined. That was also when Missy discovered my little secret—and she'd been more okay with the discovery that I was a vampire than I was.

I shuddered slightly at the memory of that fateful wedding. Bad, bad dress.

"Who's the hunk?" Missy asked, nodding at Thierry.

I told her. As briefly as I could. She seemed suitably impressed that I'd landed a master vampire. I didn't share with her the fact he had already been previously landed by another woman.

"Listen," she said. "I wanted to tell you and I'm hoping it doesn't mean anything whatsoever, but it's about the reunion."

"What about it?"

"I consulted a psychic about the decorations."

Missy, although a few years older than me and not attending the reunion tonight, was on the reunion organizing committee. It was a yearly thing and it kept her busy.

"You consulted a *psychic* about the reunion decorations?" I repeated it to make sure I'd heard her right.

"It's hard to make a gymnasium look like a fairy-tale castle. A little help goes a long way."

"I'm sure that it does." I took a sip of my wine. "And what did she have to say?"

"She said that a beautiful varnish wouldn't change the darkness that lurks inside." She swallowed hard. "I have no idea what she meant by that. Her eyes went all white and weird and then she snapped back to normal and didn't even remember what she said at all."

"White eyeballs? That *is* weird."

She chewed her bottom lip. "Do me a favor and be careful tonight. Madame Chiquita is apparently extremely accurate."

"I promise to be on the lookout for any dark, lurking varnish." Great. White-eyeballed psychics were giving unpleasant predictions about the reunion. Or maybe Missy was just paranoid.

That made two of us.

"Missy!" Richard called. "Uncle Charlie wants to plan a fishing trip with me. Can you come over here, please?"

She grinned at me. "Duty calls."

I turned away, wondering how much money Missy had been charged by her reunion psychic, and realized my father was standing directly behind me.

"Hey, Dad." I smiled without showing my fangs and gave him a hug. "Great to see you."

My chest gave out a weak twinge of pain and I had a quick and unexpected flashback of the stake being in my chest.

Just relax, I told myself. *Act normal. You're normal. Everything is fine.*

My father eyed Thierry, who, across the room, seemed to be having an awkward conversation following a rather tight hug from my aunt Mildred.

"Who is this fellow, anyhow?" he asked. "You've never mentioned him before. What happened to George? I thought you two were engaged."

Long story. A case of mistaken identity at Missy's wedding. Hilarity ensued. Ancient history.

I cleared my throat. "I'm with Thierry now. I'm sure you'll love him."

"He doesn't seem your type."

"Oh, he is my type. Trust me."

"Where's he from?"

"Toronto mostly."

"What does he do for a living?"

"Uh . . . he owns a nightclub."

He gave me a look that informed me he didn't consider that a worthy or respectable occupation. Until five years ago when he retired, my father was on the Abottsville police force. He was well known for his excellent interrogation skills.

"How old is he?"

I swallowed. "He's thirty-six. Just turned."

"Eight years older than you? That is a significant age difference, Sarah."

Right. If only he knew the truth. "It doesn't make a difference to me."

"He's wearing a very expensive suit. He has money?"

"Sure." I gulped another mouthful of wine.

"Have you gotten another full-time job yet?"

"Um, no, not yet."

"So are you saying that this new rich boyfriend of yours is supporting you?"

"More wine, please!" I hollered. My mother came by and topped off my glass.

My father's expression softened a bit and he put his hand on my shoulder. "I'm sorry if it seems that I'm being judgmental, but I only care about what's best for my little girl." His eyes narrowed and he took another look at the suspect in question. "I get a strange vibe from him. Like there's something off. But you say you're happy with him?"

"Ecstatically so."

He looked at me sternly. "What is the rule about sarcasm in this house?"

"Only on Saturdays?"

"Sarah—"

"Look, Dad, what do you want me to say? I'm in love with Thierry. I wanted you and Mom to meet him. He's really great."

He nodded and watched my mother tentatively approach Thierry and a couple of aunts to see if they wanted some cheese and crackers. The aunts went for it. Thierry declined.

"Are you planning on getting engaged?" he asked.

I choked a little on my latest sip of sparkling wine. "Not in the immediate future."

He frowned. "Why not? Doesn't he want to commit?"

"Look, can we lay off the twenty questions already and talk about something else?"

My mother approached with the tray of cheese and crackers. "Talk about what?"

"Sarah and Thierry have no plans of committing to each other," my father commented. "Perhaps he's not the marrying kind."

My mother looked distraught. "But, Sarah, why waste your time with someone who doesn't want to marry you? You're still young, but time is a fleeting thing. You know what they say about the cow and the milk, don't you?"

"Mom—"

"You're not giving away free milk, are you, honey?"

I sighed heavily. "What is marriage? I mean, seriously. It's just a piece of paper. Or, possibly, a chiseled ancient tablet of some kind or however they did it back in the fourteenth century. It doesn't mean anything. I like things just the way they are."

"But you always dreamed of a perfect wedding," my mother persisted. "With a white dress and a long veil and doves released at the end of the ceremony!"

"Dreams can change," I said. And I meant it, too.

"I think I know what's going on here." My father's arms were crossed. "He's a married man, isn't he?"

My eyes widened. Damn, he was a good cop.

Mom gasped and held a hand up to her mouth. "No! He's married? To another woman? Sarah, what on earth are you thinking?"

Instead of throwing up on the pale green wall-to-wall carpeting, which was my first inclination, I glanced over to where Thierry was surrounded by the aunt entourage. They'd popped a tape into the VCR and were taking the liberty of showing him my secret shame, aka the only commercial I'd done when I'd been an aspiring actress. I hadn't even known it was still in existence.

"Feel fresh as the morning dew," the twenty-year-old me (with much longer hair) said with a big, bright, and shiny smile. "With Daisy Fresh personal deodorant maxi-pads, you'll never worry about not being as fabulous as you can possibly be!"

Obviously things could not get any worse than they already were.

I turned back and fixed my parents with a steady look. "Hey, guess what? I'm a vampire."

They frowned.

"What did you say, dear?" my mother asked.

"I'm a vampire. It happened a couple of months ago.

So, I won't be aging anymore. I'm immortal. I've come home to go to my reunion so I have a chance to feel happy and normal again. Still waiting. I just thought you'd like to know."

"You're a *vampire*," my father repeated.

I rubbed my stake wound absently. "That's right."

He shook his head. "And you think that this is some sort of excuse for taking part in a shameful, adulterous relationship?"

My mother sniffed and drew a Kleenex out of her shirt sleeve. "My little girl. My poor little girl!"

I blinked. "Didn't you hear the part about me being a vampire?"

"Yes, and we're ignoring that. Obviously you are racked with guilt over these life choices and it's making you delusional." My father sighed heavily. "I really think you should move back here for a while. Get your head straight."

"Sarah." I felt Thierry's arm come around my waist. "How is everything over here?"

My father fixed Thierry with an icy glare. "Just so you know, I do not approve of the kind of life you're subjecting our daughter to."

Thierry's expression didn't change. "I'm sorry?"

"You should be sorry. Sarah deserves better. She deserves a bright future with a man who adores her, not someone who wants to use and discard her like a dollarstore hanky."

"I assure you that is not my intention and apologize if I've somehow given that impression in the short time I've been here. I only want the best for Sarah."

My father's face was as cold as I'd ever seen it. I'd seen him look at criminals with more kindness in his eyes. "I'm going upstairs to watch the Golf Channel." He moved past us but touched my arm. "Remember what I said, Sarah. Your room is always open for you."

He left.

My aunts were replaying my maxipad commercial for the fifth time and commenting on how pretty I'd looked and how unfortunate it was that I chose not to pursue a career in acting. They beckoned for me to come and join them.

I looked at my mom.

She cleared her throat. "Would anyone care for some more wine?"

My ten-minute estimate was very optimistic, since it took two more hours until we were out of there, and the reunion was to start in a little over an hour. I had barely any time to get ready. The sun had already set by the time we walked down the ice-and-snow-covered driveway. Thierry was silent as he steered the car away from the curb and got back on the main street of Abottsville.

"I'm sorry about that," I said. "Really."

"Did I say something I shouldn't have?" he asked. "If so, then I do apologize."

I shook my head. "I'm not even sure what happened, myself. They just freaked out."

"About what?"

I pressed back into the leather seat. I so didn't want to talk about this. "I told them I was a vampire."

He took his attention briefly off the road to glance at me with surprise. "Why would you do that?"

"Because I wanted them to know."

"And that's how they reacted to this news? They hold me responsible for this change?"

I chewed my bottom lip. "Not exactly. Somehow they figured out that you're married and then they completely disregarded the whole vampire thing. Being a vampire isn't as bad as dating a married man to them, I guess."

His jaw was tight. "I don't blame them."

I raised my eyebrows at that. "You don't?"

"No."

"I'll explain to them why it's different for us. That Veronique is out of the picture. Etcetera, etcetera. They'll understand."

Then again, I didn't really understand, so how could I hope that my parents would?

He shook his head. "It still isn't right."

I shrugged and glanced at the clock—it was already after six. "Look, don't worry about it. I know that things aren't going to change—that it's impossible—but it doesn't change my feelings for you."

His attention was steady on the road ahead. "It's not impossible."

I frowned. "What did you say?"

He pulled the car off to the side of the road just past downtown Abottsville, next to a very large hot-dog-shaped building that in the summer sold—believe it or not—hot dogs, and shifted into park. He turned to look at me with those silvery eyes of his. "I said, it's not impossible."

"I don't know what you mean."

His throat worked as he swallowed. "Veronique has been a part of my life for so many years I can't remember ever not knowing her."

I cringed inwardly at that. "Of course. You've known her since practically the Stone Age. Plus, she's completely gorgeous and perfect and well-dressed. *And* she speaks French."

"That's not what I meant." He frowned deeply. "It was different years ago. Most marriages were arranged or were entered into for the sake of convenience. One never had to worry about falling out of love with someone and wanting to get a divorce, since love rarely played a part in such agreements."

"One out of two marriages end in divorce these days," I said, feeling strange and uncomfortable sitting here in the car and talking about marriage. Besides, we were now running really late for the reunion.

My stake wound itched.

"A disheartening statistic," he said.

I forced a smile. "Listen, Thierry, you don't have to get all analytical on me. I understand your situation." *Not really.* "I know that, even if you wanted to, divorcing Veronique is impossible."

"That's not entirely true." He leaned back in his seat. "I have contacted several people in the Catholic Church—vampires—who are looking into the possibility of arranging an annulment between Veronique and myself."

My heartbeat sped up. "An *annulment*?"

"Yes."

Stunned didn't even begin to cover what I was feeling at the moment. I forced my gaping mouth closed. "After six hundred years of marriage? Is that even possible?"

He nodded. "My marriage to Veronique has long since been over. I would be surprised if she would take issue with this decision. We're very different people who want very different things. She desires a life of beauty and excitement in Europe surrounded by young, handsome men."

I swallowed hard. "And what do you want?"

His gaze was steady with my own. "You," he said simply.

My mouth opened a little but no sound came out. There was silence in the car for several moments.

The corners of his mouth curled. "Have I rendered you speechless? I didn't even know that was possible."

A breath hitched in my chest. "Thierry—"

"I can see it in your eyes when I speak with Veronique, or when she is in town, that her role in my life disturbs you greatly." He reached forward to stroke the dark hair off my forehead and tuck it behind my left ear. "It's been over between Veronique and me for many, many years, but it hasn't been official. I'm striving to make it so."

He pulled back a little from me and slid his hand into his inside jacket pocket. "I can't make any true commitments to you at this time, at least none that your parents would approve of, but I can make you a promise."

I looked down. There was a ring sitting on the palm of his hand. A woman's ring that was studded with diamonds all the way around the circumference.

An eternity band.

My gaze snapped back to his.

"I want you to have this, Sarah," he said softly. "For you to wear it knowing that it's from someone who loves you very much." He slipped it onto the ring finger on my right hand and then brought my hand to his lips. "Is that acceptable to you?"

"Yes, that's very acceptable." I looked from my new ring that seemed to sparkle even in the growing darkness, to Thierry, but his face was blurred because I was now crying like a baby.

He leaned forward to kiss me and I wrapped my arms around his shoulders to draw him closer to me.

If I was dreaming, I never wanted to wake up.

Chapter 5

Back in the motel room I started to get dressed for the reunion, but I couldn't help gazing down at the ring Thierry had given me. Talk about a distraction. It was gorgeous. I felt happier than I'd felt in recent memory while looking at it, and it wasn't just because of the pretty bling. It was because it *meant* something.

Thierry had bought it for me. *Me.*

Would he really get an annulment from Veronique?

The future was so bright that if I could find the dough, I might even buy a new pair of sunglasses.

Thierry'd had his cell phone pressed to his ear since we'd returned to the room ten minutes ago. "It's official. Gideon Chase is dead. All active hunters are en route to his funeral in Nevada as we speak."

And the good news kept coming. It seemed strange to celebrate the death of somebody, but in this case, I'd make an exception.

"Where's the champagne?" I studied his noncelebratory expression. "Why don't you look happier? Isn't this a good thing?"

He shook his head. "It doesn't feel right to me."

"You think there are still hunters lurking around?"

"It's not that. It's simply difficult for me to believe that he is truly gone forever."

I smoothed out the sparkly red dress I'd borrowed from Amy on the top of the bed. "You're not going to miss him, are you?"

He shook his head. "Definitely not. The man relished death and destruction too much for me to mourn his passing. He had too much power at too young an age."

Billions of dollars, male-model good looks, and the dude had spent his life hunting vampires. What a waste. "May he rest in pieces. One less wooden stake for me to worry about."

He gave me a grim look. "I had a personal acquaintance with a member of the Chase family two hundred years ago. He nearly killed Veronique and me. He pledged to wipe out all elder vampires from the face of the planet. He didn't bother with fledglings, since they weren't much of a challenge to him."

"He hurt you?"

He paused before answering. "I heal remarkably well."

My jaw felt tight. "I'm glad they're dead."

"There will always be someone to take the place of a true monster. Especially a rich one."

I nodded. "That's why it's a good thing that somebody's decided to revive the whole Red Devil thing."

Being staked had left more than an itchy healing feeling in my chest. It had left me with a ton of empathy for all the poor vamps who hadn't been lucky enough to be rescued.

"While I do owe him my deep gratitude for saving

you," Thierry said, "I fear that he is simply a misguided vampire who is in well over his head."

"You think that's all he is? Misguided? Because the Red Devil never truly existed, right? That's what you said the other night."

He walked over to the little curtained window that looked out onto the parking lot. "There was a time when there was a true Red Devil. A very long time ago."

I frowned. "Hold on. First you said it was an urban legend and now you're saying he really existed? Which is it?"

He turned to look at me. "The *Diable Rouge* came forth when hunters began to grow and organize their numbers. Vampires were helpless against them."

"And?"

"And he endeavored to save those who needed his assistance from the clutches of hunters who viewed us as monsters needing to be slaughtered. He saved as many as he could, whenever he could. It became an obsession for him. But that was a long time ago, when such a man as the Red Devil was needed. To have someone acting as the Red Devil now would be merely a drop in the bucket of righting wrongs."

The hunters still looked at us that way. That's why most of them sharpened their stakes. Because they really believed we were evil, bloodsucking things that needed to die. It was so Hollywood. "I guess we see differently on this. I figure a drop in the bucket is better than no drops at all." I shook my head at him. "Have you always been this way?"

"What way?"

"Mr. Pessimistic. You've got to remember, along with

that bleak worldview, there is a whole lot of hope to go along with it. Otherwise, why even bother getting up in the morning? The world is a pretty good place, actually. You've just got to look for the good in it instead of the bad."

"Eternal optimism. I wish for you to always possess it." He moved toward the bed and leaned over to kiss me on my lips, but it felt like a sad kiss instead of a passionate one. I captured his mouth before he had the chance to pull away, and deepened the kiss, pulling on his shirt to draw him closer to me. He didn't resist.

"You know what?" I breathed against his mouth. "How about we forget about the happily departed Gideon Chase and the Red Devil? I haven't had a chance to say thank you for my new ring."

He gazed down at me. "You've just said it."

"That's not exactly what I meant." I swung my legs around so I was kneeling on the bed next to where he stood and I let my hands move over his shoulders and down his back, pulling his suit jacket off as I went. I kissed him again and slid my tongue against his, tasting him deeply. "Wouldn't want this snazzy room to go to waste, you know."

"Snazzy is not the word I'd use to describe it." He inhaled sharply as my hands slid to lower places on his body. They had a tendency to do that.

I smiled up at him. "Just because the artwork is nailed to the wall and I wouldn't want a CSI team in here with their black light doesn't mean this can't be a romantic getaway, you know."

"Agreed." He leaned over and crushed his mouth to mine and, with a hand at the small of my back, lowered me to the bed. His weight pressed firmly down on top of me and the bed let out a mournful creaking sound. After a moment he broke off the kiss and gazed down at me with a small smile. "But later."

With effort, mostly because I was wrapped very firmly around him, he managed to pull away from me.

"Later?" I glanced up at the ceiling mirror that lacked my reflection. "Why later?"

He raised a dark eyebrow. "Your reunion starts in less than forty-five minutes."

"I'm okay if we're fashionably late. Really."

With an amused look and another soft brush of his lips against mine that made me groan with frustration, he stood up from the bed and walked into the bathroom. I heard the shower being turned on just as there was a knock at the door. I sat up and swung off the bed. Being careful not to make a sound, I crept toward the little window and glanced outside. My eyebrows went up and I unlocked the door so I could swing it open.

"What the hell are you doing here?" I asked.

George leaned against the doorframe. "I just love this town. Where is that monster-sized pumpkin? I totally brought my camera this time."

I frowned at him. "What's wrong? Why are you here?"

"I needed to talk to you."

"To me? Not to Thierry?"

"No, just you." He was grinning so I could see his fangs. "Guess who I met?"

"I have absolutely no idea."

"Let me give you a hint. First name Red, last name Devil?"

"Are you serious?"

He nodded. "He is awesome, Sarah. So amazing. Everything I'd ever heard about him is totally true. He was waiting for me by my car outside Amy's and he scared the bejeezus out of me, especially with the whole scarf-over-his-face thing. But then he asked me personally to come here and keep an eye on you. He wants to make sure you're okay. Isn't that fabulous?"

Fabulous, sure. Also extremely strange and suspicious. "Why you?"

"Obviously because he knows I'm the right person for the job."

"The job of spying on me?"

He laughed at that. "Very funny. No, of course not. Of course he wants you to be safe, which is cool, but obviously he's interviewing me to be his trusty sidekick. Since I need a new job anyhow, the timing couldn't be more perfect." He pulled a compact digital camera out of his back pocket and held it up to his face. "Say cheese."

"Cheese." I blinked as the flash went off.

He eyed the display screen of the shot he had just taken. "You forgot to smile."

"I didn't forget." I chewed my bottom lip as I studied George, as enthusiastic as I'd ever seen him. "How did the Red Devil know where I'd be staying?"

"He didn't have to. Thierry gave me the address in case of emergency. The Red Devil didn't have to say anything. And now here I am." The flash popped again. "Okay, that was even worse this time."

I glanced past George at the dark and silent parking lot, and then grabbed his shirt and dragged him into the room, closing and locking the door behind me.

"Are you crazy?" I sputtered.

"What?"

I tried to breathe normally. "Whoever this guy is could have just used you to find out where I am right now. He may have followed you here."

He shook his head. "No way. He wouldn't do something like that."

I listened to the shower still going in the bathroom. Damn, that man loved his hot water.

I smoothed out George's shirt under his winter jacket from where I'd wrinkled it. "I know he saved my ass, and for that I'm very grateful. But I don't know anything else about him. What if he's one of the bad guys?"

"Bad guys don't save people." He put a hand on my shoulder. "Look, Sarah. Relax. I know the other day with the stake was really traumatic for you, but don't let it make you even more paranoid than you already are. If the Red Devil was one of the bad guys he would have let you die, not brought you back to the club."

Paranoid. Yeah, that sounded about right. "You really think so?"

"The Red Devil is not a bad guy."

I let out a long and shaky breath and willed my heart to stop beating so fast. "Maybe you're right." A great sense of relief flooded over me and I gave George a hug. Then I eyed him now that I was able to focus again and noticed he was dressed to the nines in an expensive red silk shirt and black leather pants. "Why are you all dressed up? Got big plans tonight?"

He shrugged. "Well, since I was in town I was hoping I might be able to come to the reunion, too."

"To help keep an eye on me for the Red Devil?"

"Well that, of course, but, I would assume, there's free

fruit punch of some kind? Possibly some finger sand-wiches? A good old small-town hootenanny?"

"You can come, but if you tell Thierry why you're really here he's going to blow a gasket, and even though I'm not entirely sure what a gasket is, that would not be a good thing."

"Then I won't say a word." His gaze moved to my hand. "New ring?"

I rubbed it. "It's from Thierry."

His eyes widened. "Is it an engagement ring? Did he pop the question?"

"Of course not," I said bluntly. "He's already married, remember?"

He sighed. "You are absolutely no fun today. Did somebody take her depressing pill this morning?"

"Do I really sound that bad?"

He nodded. "Don't worry, we'll have fun tonight. There's dancing, right?"

"Allegedly."

He shook his head sadly. "You're even starting to sound like Thierry now. He's starting to rub off on you. I think that's the problem."

I pointed at the door. "Begone with you. I will see you at the high school in an hour."

He went. I shut the door after him.

I tried not to think about the Red Devil potentially fol-lowing George all the way to my hometown to find out where I was. The thought was decidedly creepy. Who was this guy? What were his ulterior motives?

Was I starting to sound like Thierry? All careful and cautious? Maybe that's the way you became after being less than an inch away from getting killed. Careful and cautious.

And tonight I would have a very careful and cautious evening with some mild dancing with old friends. Possibly some of that fruit punch.

With any luck, the sparkly red dress I'd borrowed from Amy would be the most exciting thing to happen to me tonight in my single-minded quest to feel normal and be happy.

Fingers crossed.

Chapter 6

The reunion dance was being held in the gymnasium of the Abottsville District High School, and I had to admit that Missy and her crew had done a wonderful job of making it look like something out of a fairy tale. Sparkling lights flickered across the dance floor. The walls were adorned with murals that looked like castle walls.

The last time I'd been here had been for my graduation ceremony. I'd whipped that little tasseled hat off and thrown it into the air so quickly that by the time it hit the ground I'd already moved to Toronto to start university and find my way in the big city.

It was just after eight o'clock by the time we got there. The dance was to go until midnight. Four hours of walking down memory lane seemed like more than enough, especially now that I felt on edge about the Red Devil's motives. I tried to relax and feel normal, but it was difficult. The red dress I'd borrowed from Amy was even shorter than I'd anticipated, and the low-cut neckline barely covered the fading but really itchy stake wound on my chest. I'd positioned my nametag over the general area, so that helped a bit.

"Why is George here?" Thierry asked.

I glanced over at the dance floor. George waved at me.

"Oh, didn't I mention that to you? He wanted to come and I said he could. I think he's lonely."

Thierry had been in such a good mood, by his standards, that I didn't want to put a damper on the evening by telling him about the Red Devil's continued interest in my well-being.

Maybe it was early, but there weren't as many people in attendance as I'd expected. In fact, at first glance I didn't even see anyone I remembered.

"Sarah?" I heard from over my shoulder. "Oh, my God. Sarah Dearly! I don't believe this!"

I turned, relieved to see somebody I definitely recognized. I smiled at the pretty woman with dark red hair and a cute black shift dress on her trim figure. "Claire!" I hugged her. "Wow, it's so great to see you."

She smiled so widely it could be classified as beaming. I didn't. I'd trained myself to smile without showing off the fangs. Kind of a subdued Mona Lisa deal.

"I was wondering if you'd make it to the reunion," she said. "Can you believe it's been ten years already?"

"I really can't." I scanned the floor. "So where is everybody?"

She shrugged. "I did see a few people. I guess most decided they didn't want to show off their balding heads and big beer guts. And that's probably just the women."

I laughed at that. "Maybe you're right."

"So what have you been up to? How's the acting thing going? I know you had a big plan to do movies. Have you been in anything lately?"

"Plans change." I glanced over at Thierry, who was giving me and Claire a little room to speak relatively privately. "You know, after I left Abottsville I realized that acting wasn't really my thing. Way too superficial."

Not to mention, ridiculously hard to break into without sleeping with directors and/or producers. Even for the maxipad commercial I'd had to agree to go out with the casting agent. I strongly disagreed when he suggested a three-way with his "understanding" girlfriend and I never worked in showbiz again. Strange how things work out.

Claire nodded. "So what are you doing now?"

As glamorous as a short-lived career of being a personal assistant and now a part-time bartender sounded, I decided to vague it up. "You know, I do a little bit of this, a little bit of that. How about you? I know you wanted to go into . . . what was it? Corporate law?"

"Actually, I work at McDonald's," she said. "In Niagara Falls. Come by some time and I'll sneak you a free Big Mac." She turned to the side and waved her hand. "Reggie, come over here and meet my friend Sarah." She waited a moment. "Reggie! Now!"

A nice-looking dark-haired man came to her side. He had a receding hairline and a suit that looked as though it didn't fit him too well, since he kept tugging at the collar. "I'm here, I'm here."

I extended my hand. "I'm Sarah."

"Nice to meet you." His gaze immediately went directly to my super-short red skirt, before snapping guiltily back to Claire.

But she wasn't looking at him. Instead she squinted at Thierry's nametag. "Thheeerie?" She sounded it out. "That's an unusual name."

I slid an arm around his waist. "Actually the 'h' is silent. It's French."

"Oh." She nodded. "Teeeerie."

"It's pronounced *Tyair-ee*." Thierry took her hand in his. "A pleasure."

She grinned. "So are you two married?"

I moved my arm from his waist to hook around his and found that he was more tense than he appeared. "Nope."

She presented her left hand for me to inspect a tiny diamond ring. "I'm engaged. Reggie popped the question at Christmas."

Reggie nodded. "I did. I've never been happier."

If you asked me, he sounded more scared than enthusiastic. Then again, I'd known Claire in high school. I knew she kept a tight leash on her boyfriends.

"Congrats," I told them. "Hey, want to hear something strange? My cousin's on the decorating committee and a psychic gave her an eerie prediction about tonight."

The smile faded from Claire's face. "What kind of a prediction?"

"Something about darkness lurking around. It sounded a bit scary, and with the week I've been having it would have fit right in. So far, so good, though. Nothing seems to be lurking, dark or otherwise."

Claire closed her eyes and held her hands up to her sides for a moment.

"What are you doing?" I asked.

"Just give her a moment," Reggie suggested, sipping from a small glass of punch. "She's sensing the aura of potential evil in the room."

Claire's eyes snapped back open and her smile returned. "Nope, everything feels fine to me."

O-kay.

We chatted for a while longer before the crowd slowly began to swell, although still not as many as I would have expected. Maybe it had something to do with its being held in February. Due to construction on the school scheduled for the summer, the reunion had been moved up this year as opposed to canceling it altogether. That was probably why the attendance was spotty. Abottsville was well known for getting dumped on with snow at any given winter moment, and the threat of that might keep some people away.

Claire and Reggie finally moved away to schmooze with others with a promise to return later. Standing at Thierry's side, I waited for the huge wave of nostalgia to wash over me and make this into a fantastic night that would help me to feel better about my life. An hour later I was still waiting.

George took a break from the dance floor to come over toward us. He wore a nametag that said "Jim-Bob" on it.

"Everyone remembers me," he said. "Apparently I was popular."

"You were."

I remembered Jim-Bob. And he *had* been a popular guy. Strangely enough, George was nothing like him, since Jim-Bob was short and fat and a major womanizer—

also, definitely *not* a vampire. I could have sworn I'd read in the paper last week that the real Jim-Bob had been indicted on four counts of Internet fraud. I guess that's why his nametag was available tonight.

"I'm going to make a trip to the ladies' room," I told Thierry. "Too much fruit punch."

He nodded and leaned over to brush his lips against mine. "I'll be waiting."

I could tell by how quiet he was that he wasn't having a very good time. I decided not to torment him for much longer.

Five people recognized me on my way out of the gym, but I didn't recognize them until I looked at their nametags. It was amazing how much people could change in ten years.

In the ladies' room, I picked the stall closest to the door so I wouldn't have to walk past the mirrors on the wall. Not having a reflection sometimes brought up questions I didn't want to answer if I could help it. Questions like, "Why don't you have a reflection?" That was the most common one. It came just before whoever asked it freaked the hell out.

When I exited the stall I noticed a blond woman leaning against the wall opposite it. I figured she'd been waiting to use it, despite the multiple other options in the room, but she didn't make a move to go in.

"Sarah," she said. "Great to see you again."

Didn't recognize her. Damn. I glanced at her nametag and realized she wasn't wearing one. "Hey there . . . *you*. How's it going?"

She wore a tight-fitting blue dress that encased her

Playboy Bunny–esque body. Definitely fake boobs. Her hair was so light blond it looked like Barbie doll hair. She was beautiful, but in an unnatural sort of way.

"I'm fantastic," she said, and then paused. "You don't remember me, do you?"

"Of course I do," I lied, feeling bad about not remembering somebody who obviously knew me. "Silly. How could I forget you?"

She smiled. "What's my name, then?"

I tried to laugh at that but it came out pinched. "Why, don't you remember it?"

The smile didn't quite reach her heavily made up eyes. "Of course I do. But, nobody else seems to. Actually, it's okay. I looked way different back in high school. Ten years can really change a person."

"Except for me," I said. "Except for a couple of things in my life, I feel like I haven't changed a bit."

"And that's a good thing?"

"Depends what you want out of life. I kind of like having ties to who I was back in the day. Keeps me grounded."

And happy. And vaguely normal.

She nodded. "I'm Stacy. Stacy McGraw. Remember me now?"

I nodded. But I didn't. Not even slightly. "Of course. Nice catching up, Stacy. I'm going to head back to the dance now."

She blinked slowly. "Don't you want to wash your hands first?"

I hesitated, glancing at the bank of mirrors above the sinks. "Of course I do. But I have this thing about public washrooms. Dirty Sinkaphobia, I think it's called. My boyfriend has a little bottle of hand sanitizer on him. He's a total germ phobic."

"Your boyfriend, Thierry," she said.

"That's the one."

"He's very handsome."

"Thank you. I totally agree."

"What is he, six or seven hundred years old?" Her gaze was steady with mine.

My throat felt tight. "He just turned thirty-six. He's an Aquarius."

Her cool smile widened. "Of course he is."

I frowned at her. "You know, I'm going to have to come clean here. I don't actually remember you at all from high school. Are you sure we were in the same year?"

She nodded. "Just picture me a hundred pounds heavier. Glasses. Brown hair."

Dammit. I still couldn't remember her. Not for the life of me. What she'd said about Thierry had made me very wary. What was her deal?

Actually, forget it. I didn't really want to know.

"I'm going back to the reunion." I moved toward the door.

She stepped in front of me. "Not quite yet, Sarah."

"What do you want?"

"Just to talk."

"About what?"

She took another step closer to me. "I know you're a vampire."

My mouth felt dry. "Vampires don't exist."

Her dark red lips curled up. "Does that line work for

you often? Or do most people not even clue in to what you really are? Well, I guess I'm a little different than them."

I could smell her perfume. She'd really loaded on the Obsession by Calvin Klein. "What do you want, Stacy?"

Her smile held. "I told you. I just want to talk."

My eyes narrowed. "Then talk. And, not to sound rude, but let's make it quick."

"Why? In a hurry to get somewhere?"

"It won't be long before somebody wants to come in here, you know. They might break up this friendly little convo."

"Oh, it will be a while. Trust me, Sarah. Right now and until I decide, nobody in the building will need to use the washroom. It's just the two of us."

I frowned. "What are you talking about?"

"Just a little magic. A little isolation spell was all it took."

"Magic?"

She nodded. "Same magic I wish I'd had back in high school when I was a loser. When I was picked on."

Screw this. I went ahead and washed my hands. Stacy didn't even flinch when my reflection didn't show up in the mirrors. "Everyone was a loser in high school," I said. "Everyone was picked on at one time or another. I know I was."

She leaned leisurely against the green-tiled wall, glancing at the empty mirror and then at me. "Is that what you remember?"

I thought about it. Yeah, high school had its good points, but there were plenty of bad points, too. That's how high school was for everyone. That's why it was a good thing it only lasted four years.

"I remember trying out for the cheerleading squad," Stacy went on. "But I was laughed out of the room. There was nothing wrong with my performance, I was just too fat."

I'd been on the cheerleading squad and remembered vividly two heavier girls were on it with me. So she was wrong. It would have had very little to do with her weight and everything to do with her performance, attitude, and personality—and if today was any indication, I think I saw why she had failed to make the squad.

"I'm sorry you had a bad experience," I said.

"A bad experience?" Something sparked in her eyes. "*A bad experience?* Oh, it was way more than that, Sarah."

I didn't know why I felt so nervous. The girl was shorter and skinnier than me, if you didn't count the huge knockers. By how tight that dress was I could tell she wasn't carrying any concealed weapons. So what if she knew I was a vampire? As if anyone would believe her if she decided to literally share with the class.

"I think you need to get out of my way now," I said evenly. "I've had enough."

She eyed me with mild amusement but said nothing. I took that to mean the conversation was over. I walked past her to the door and grabbed the handle. It was locked. I looked over my shoulder at her.

"Unlock it." I was surprised to hear the underlying menace in my voice. I was not in a good mood anymore.

She spread her hands. "And what are you going to do

if I don't? Bite me like the evil, nasty vampire that you are?"

"I'm not evil or nasty."

"But you are a vampire."

I hissed out a breath. "I don't bite people. I've never bitten anyone. Even though I'm a vampire I am perfectly in control of myself at all times. I'm not a bad person."

"You sound very sure of that."

"I am."

Her expression darkened. "Sarah Dearly isn't a bad vampire. Well, isn't that special for you. I guess things could have gone much worse than they did, huh?"

"I guess they could have."

"I came to the reunion tonight for a very specific reason."

"Oh? And what's that?"

"To get revenge," she said simply.

I rolled my eyes. I couldn't help it. "Well, you go, girl. You've got the hot body now, you go get the revenge on everybody who made fun of you. Go taunt them like they taunted you, just let me the hell out of here."

"I don't think taunting will quite cover it."

I crossed my arms and tapped my foot. "If you don't let me out of here I'm going to start screaming my head off. And trust me, I'm a very loud screamer."

She turned to the mirror and reapplied her lipstick. "Now, let me think. So many options. How am I going to get my revenge on you, Sarah? What can I do to you that would really make a difference? It's got to be something perfect."

I frowned. "For what? What did I ever do to you?"

She spun around to face me. "I can't believe you really don't remember."

"I don't."

"You're the one who booted me from the cheerleading auditions."

I actually couldn't believe I'd ever been a cheerleader. It seemed so distant from my current life. Not much rah-rah-sis-boom-bah for me lately. Well, maybe just the "boom" part.

"Do you know how many people tried out back then? There were only so many spots."

Her eyes narrowed to tiny, angry slits. "You also went to the prom with the guy I was madly in love with. You ruined my life, Sarah."

"Your life? That was ten long years ago. Besides, I didn't do any of those things on purpose. If it's any consolation to you, that jerk stuck me with the limo bill."

"Don't you dare say anything bad about Jonathan." She walked a slow circle around me. "Now, what shall I do to you? I had a few things planned but I'm rethinking it now. Maybe I should do something to your boyfriend."

I glared at her and my hands curled into fists at my sides. "Touch him and you'll be very sorry."

Her eyebrows rose. "Such menace. I thought you said you were a nice vampire. All noncvil. In fact, I think you might be right. I don't think you have a truly evil bone in your body."

"I don't. But I have a funny desire to protect the people I care about."

She cocked her head to the side and smiled. "Have you ever heard of nightwalkers, Sarah?"

I frowned. "No."

"I guess I'm much more well-read than you are. No big surprise there." Her smile widened. "Ask your boyfriend what they are. I'm sure he'll fill you in. You know, I'm happy that things have worked out so well for you. You've obviously changed over the years. Maybe you're not as cruel as you were in the past. If you want to apologize to me, then I might consider accepting it."

"Apologize to you? I don't think I have anything to apologize for." I sighed. "Look, Stacy, you need to chill out. Do you hear me? Now why don't we leave this washroom and go have some punch and—"

"Shut up," she snapped.

Suddenly I was unable to speak.

"Do you know what I've been doing for ten years?" she asked. "I didn't leave high school with dreams of being an actress like you. I forgot about college or university and instead studied magic. I learned how to create glamours to make myself look thin and beautiful. But every time I managed a successful spell, the darkness inside me grew and grew."

"Mmmmhff," I managed. I felt as if there was a gag in my mouth, but it was just magic. Magic? That was impossible, wasn't it? But I could feel the magic crawling down my arms to my feet, and it kept me frozen in place.

Her eyes flashed and she smiled. "I'm really good now. I can do almost everything I want to. Practice does make perfect." She tilted her head to the side as she eyed my borrowed dress before her gaze flicked back to my face. "I used to envy you in school. Beautiful, popular, people liked you. No one even knew I existed. Everything's always been so easy for you, even becoming a vampire."

"Rrlllkkk," I growled. Translation: *You are one crazy bitch.*

Stacy opened her purse and pulled out a small glass vial, then she took the top off it and sprinkled the contents into the palm of her right hand. "You really should have apologized when I gave you the chance."

There was a knock at the door. "Sarah?" It was Claire's voice. "Hey, are you in there?"

Stacy smiled at me. "Looks like I'm not the only witch in town. I guess I'd better make this quick."

My eyes widened. What the hell? What was she going to do?

She began to speak strange words that sounded a lot like Latin. But she wasn't reading from a book. It looked as if she was reading from the air as her eyes bled to a darker color. Not black like a hungry vampire's, but a dark red. Her lips curved into a smile as she spoke the words I didn't understand. I struggled to move but I couldn't budge.

After another minute, with Claire knocking on the door, Stacy stopped talking. She took a step toward me, and with a smirk, blew the powder into my face. "That should do it."

I closed my eyes and coughed.

When I opened my eyes, Claire was entering the washroom. She ignored Stacy, who winked at me and brushed past her to leave. It was another few seconds before I could speak or move.

"Why did you lock the door?" Claire asked with a frown. "And why do you have glitter all over your face?"

I felt like I was in shock. I touched my face and my fingers came away with a silvery substance.

I swallowed. I had honestly thought she was going to kill me. My heart was pounding so hard I could feel it in the backs of my eyeballs.

"Do I look okay?" I asked Claire shakily.

"Yeah, except for all the glitter you look fine."

"That chick who just left, Stacy McGraw. She tried to freak me out. And she did a pretty damn good job of it."

"Well, she's gone now."

"Thank God."

"She's a witch?"

I blinked at her, still trying to shake the unpleasant experience I'd just had. "You guessed it." I rubbed at the glitter some more.

"No, that won't do. Come over here." Claire led me to the sink. I eyed the mirror skeptically, since it only showed her, not me. Claire patted my back. "Don't worry. I know what you are. It's no big deal."

I looked at her with surprise. "It isn't?"

She shook her head. "I've known tons of vampires over the years. The crew chief at Micky Dee's is one. She's a bitch, but it doesn't have anything to do with her being a vamp." She started to brush the glitter off my face.

"Stacy said you were a witch, too."

She nodded. "It's a hobby, mostly. But if you need a demon summoned or your boyfriend turned into a small furry creature, then I'm your gal." She frowned. "Although I didn't know you could use cheap drugstore glitter like this. I've been buying this shadow salt stuff, which is extremely expensive. What did she do to you?"

"I have no idea. She said some stuff in Latin and then blew the glitter on me."

"Do you feel okay?"

I thought about it for a moment. "Other than being shaken, I feel perfectly normal."

"Obviously whatever she was attempting to do to you didn't work. I think you got off really lucky."

"I think you might be right."

A few minutes later, after I'd freshened up my makeup by looking in my shard compact, I headed back out to the reunion dance feeling weary. I searched the crowd for Thierry and found him standing in the corner clutching a small glass of punch. I hugged him tightly, which must have tipped him off to the fact that something was wrong I gave him the short version of what had happened.

"I think she was all talk," I said. "Because I feel fine."

His silver eyes were filled with concern. "She knew you were a vampire?"

I nodded and let out a shaky sigh. "It was freaky. But it doesn't matter. It's over. I think she ran away, since I don't see her in here." I glanced around at the reunion. It was officially a bust. In fact, it looked like most of the people had already called it an early night. "It's time to go."

"I think that's a wise decision."

George came over. "You're not leaving, are you? But we're having so much fun."

So much for keeping an eye on me for the Red Devil. He'd been too busy dancing. "Maybe *you* are."

"Come on, one dance. I promised that we'd have fun tonight." He eyed Thierry. "You don't mind, do you?"

Thierry raised an eyebrow. "One dance."

"You can join us if you like."

Thierry declined and George pulled me onto the dance floor along with five or six other couples. They were playing the high-school dance song to end all high-school dance songs: "Stairway to Heaven." The one that starts off slow and it seems like a good idea to dance to it, but by the end . . . all six minutes later when the hard-rock riffs come into play and you're dancing with somebody who is nasty and smells funny, you rethink your entire existence.

It was one of my favorites.

George spun me around in a slow circle. "See? We're having big fun."

"Yeah, I guess." I told him about what had happened.

"Sweetie, you are a magnet for trouble. It's just in your nature. What are we going to do with you?"

I sighed. "I have absolutely no idea whatsoever."

He grinned down at me. "So you were a total bitch in high school? I never would have guessed that."

It was getting really warm in that gym. "I didn't think I was. According to Stacy, though, I was a judgmental, man-stealing beeyotch. But I remember always feeling like the one who was picked on. I'm starting to think that high school is traumatic for everyone."

I fanned my face. What, did they turn up the heat in the last few minutes?

"I was homeschooled. The Depression was way depressing. I think that's why I love a good party these days."

"Yeah, probably." I rested my head against his shoulder. "Stacy was obviously crazy and obsessed. She even knew I was a vampire. She seemed surprised that I'd never bitten anyone before when I explained that I was definitely not evil in any way. Actually, it was more like she was amused by that."

"She sounds like a total cow."

I pushed away from him a bit. "Is it seriously hot in here or is it just me?"

He leaned back and looked at me with a frown. "Sarah, what is up with your eyes?"

I frowned. "What do you mean? Is there something wrong with my eyes?"

"Yeah. They're completely black."

My frown deepened. "That is really strange."

And then I sank my fangs into George's neck.

Chapter 7

George screamed and tried to pull away from me but I held on tight. I was so freaking thirsty and I'd never had any idea how unbelievably delicious he was.

"Sarah, what the hell are you doing?" he managed.

I ignored him. Honestly, the guy talked too much for his own good.

I faintly heard the voices of other couples around us on the dance floor.

"What is Sarah doing to Jim-Bob? I thought she was here with somebody."

"Poor Jim-Bob! The woman is obviously a tramp."

"She's giving Jim-Bob a dance floor hickey! That is so hot!"

After a moment, I felt strong hands clamp down on my upper arms and I was wrenched away from George's neck. He stared at me with wide eyes, with his hand now pressed against the side of his throat.

"Sarah," Thierry said sharply into my left ear. "We must leave."

Without another word, he forcibly dragged me off the

dance floor, pulling me through the gymnasium and then out to the bright hallway. After another moment I felt the cold night air as we left the high school to go outside to the parking lot. I glanced back over my shoulder at the interior of the high school I'd spent four years at. I was still thirsty. What was going on? Why wasn't I back inside?

"Sarah," Thierry said, gently shaking me. "Sarah! Snap out of it!"

Slowly, as I breathed the fresh air, my head began to clear. My heart drummed in my chest, making me aware again of my still-tender stake wound, as I reflected on the last five minutes of my life.

"Oh, my God." My eyes widened and I looked up at Thierry's concerned expression. I touched my hand to my lips. "I have no idea why I did that."

The doors creaked open and Claire and Reggie joined us. Behind them was George.

"I'm so sorry!" I managed. "George, I don't know what happened in there. I didn't mean to hurt you!"

"It's fine," Thierry said.

"It's *fine*?" George held a hand up to his neck. "She bit me! In public! I am traumatized!"

Claire approached, with a frown, and studied me. "I take it you don't normally bite a lot of necks?"

"I've never bitten anyone before. Ever. I have a total no-bite policy." My bottom lip wobbled. I felt ill. "It's never even occurred to me before, but it's like I couldn't control it. I didn't even plan to do it until it just happened."

"This witch in the washroom," Thierry said. "She did something to you. Perhaps it was a spell to make you attack a human and create a scene to ruin the reunion. You didn't. There is no harm done."

"No harm done?" George protested. "Hello? Vampire with a neck wound over here!"

Thierry stroked a tear away from my cheek and then pulled me against him. "It is fine, Sarah. It's over."

I buried my face in his black shirt, breathed in the light scent of his cologne, and slowly began to feel normal again. That had been so incredibly strange. Nothing like that had ever happened to me before.

Although, I suppose that wasn't exactly true. The day after I was sired, when I still thought that nothing was wrong, my boss at the time had cut her finger during a meeting with me. I'd temporarily lost my mind and attacked her finger to suck the blood off it. She fired me thinking I was a finger-sucking freak. My fledgling vampire tendencies had kicked in and I couldn't control them. A very unfortunate situation.

But that had been the only time anything remotely like this had ever happened. At least, until tonight.

Talk about a wake-up call.

"She wanted revenge," I said. "Stacy did. And I guess that's what she was saying in Latin. For me to bite somebody. I'm so embarrassed."

"Nobody noticed anything strange," Reggie said. "There were other people making out on the dance floor, and they figured you and Jim-Bob were just doing the same."

"Jim-Bob is not happy!" George exclaimed.

I pulled away from Thierry to tentatively approach George. "Is it bad?"

He pulled his hand away from his neck and I cringed when I saw the raw-looking, dark-red bite marks. "Bad enough, but it'll heal."

"I'm sorry. Seriously. I never would have done that if I wasn't all screwed up by the glitter spell."

He nodded. "I thought you looked sparklier than normal."

"So you forgive me?"

"Of course I do. Just warn me if you're going to go for the jugular again, okay?"

The thought made me feel sick to my stomach. "I didn't exactly plan to do that. Other than feeling a bit overheated, there was no warning at all."

"That's not very comforting."

"I think we should leave," Thierry said.

I nodded. "I think that's a good idea. Can't go back in there. They think I've just compromised Jim-Bob's integrity."

"So you're feeling okay?" Claire asked.

I concentrated. Other than my elevated heart rate and an overall feeling of weirdness, I felt fine. "Yeah, I'm okay."

She pulled pen and paper out of her purse and scribbled something on the paper. "If you need me, you can reach me here."

I squinted at the name and number. "What is this, a motel?"

"My basement apartment was recently condemned due to a minor demonic outbreak, so I've been staying with Reggie there. Call me if there's anything I can do to help you. Hell, call me if you want to hang out sometime. Niagara Falls isn't that far away."

"Thanks, Claire." I gave her a quick hug.

Reggie nodded at me. "Great meeting you, Sarah. And just for the record, you can bite my neck any time."

"Reggie," Claire said sharply.

He blinked. "Uh . . . I didn't mean anything by it."

She smiled tightly. "We're going back inside now."

"We can leave for Toronto right now," Thierry said. "There's no reason to stay, and it's still early."

I shook my head. "No, let's go back to the motel and get a good night's sleep. Everything will be better tomorrow."

"Glad you think so," George said. "I'm leaving. I'll see you back in Toronto."

And we all went our separate ways. I guess biting George's neck canceled out what the Red Devil had asked him to do—look out for me. Can't say that I blamed George much. If somebody had bitten me I wouldn't be hanging around for a potential second course.

I'd hoped that attending my high-school reunion would be a good way to remind me that, even though I was a vampire, I could still be normal.

Okay, so it hadn't exactly worked out as I'd envisioned it.

However, three glasses of punch and one bitten neck later, the ratio was still in my favor. Barely. But I was very glad I wouldn't have to come in contact with Stacy McGraw again. She was a witch with some serious issues to sort out. Preferably far away from me.

I guess it could have turned out a lot worse than it did.

After we returned to the motel room and locked the door behind us, Thierry turned to face me. He had this thing he did with his expression. I would assume it was because after six-plus centuries of practice, he was able to give the ultimate poker face. No expression, no emotion, just a flat, bland look on his painfully handsome face.

However, he wasn't giving me that look at the moment. His dark eyebrows were drawn closely together, his mouth was set in a thin line, and his jaw was tight.

"I'm fine," I told him. "Seriously."

"You would tell me if you were feeling any different?"

"Trust me, I'm now paying very close attention to how I'm feeling."

He studied me for a long moment and then nodded. "I have come into contact in my life with those who practice dark magic, and it doesn't always end as pleasantly as this has."

I threw my purse down on the table next to the television. My stomach churned unpleasantly from what had happened earlier. "I think George might disagree with you on that."

"George will be fine."

"You've known witches before?"

"A few. I also remember a particular fortune-teller I once met. At the time I thought she was a fraud, but I have come to realize she had admirable skill. Another witch I knew of specialized in creating curses for profit."

I slipped off my shoes and flicked them toward the door. "Do you think Stacy was trying to curse me?"

He was silent for a moment. "That was my first assumption. But since you've easily recovered from what happened, I believe it was simply a temporary spell. She is obviously not a powerful witch."

I shook my head. "I can't believe there's so much for me to still learn. Magic, witches, werewolves. Claire said she can summon demons. Was she serious about that?

Why didn't I know any of this when I was human? I just sailed through my life thinking anything remotely like this was fiction."

He crossed his arms. "How would you have reacted if you had learned that it wasn't fiction? That it is, in fact, reality?"

I thought about that. "I don't think I would have believed it."

"Most humans, when shown something out of the ordinary, a flash of fangs, for example, will not make the connection. They see what they want to see and assume that it was a human who had sharper-than-normal incisors. To believe anything else would require them to reassess their entire place in the universe."

"That's pretty deep."

"You've seen for yourself that vampires are not much different from humans."

I nodded. "Other than the fangs, lack of reflection, and immortality thing, we *are* human."

"And the desire for blood," he added.

I felt myself pale a bit. Right. The blood. "I think I'm going to get ready for bed. I'm tired."

He drew closer to me and put his hand against the side of my face. "You don't have to feel as if you've done something wrong. Vampires, especially fledglings, require blood. It's in your very nature to seek it out."

"Not when it involves chomping on one of my best friends."

His jaw tightened. "Better him than an unwilling human."

Vampires took blood where they could get it. I got mine exclusively at Haven, from the delivered kegs, but

I could also put in a special order with the delivery companies if I wanted to keep some on hand in the fridge at home. So far, that hadn't been necessary, since I could do "takeout" from the club when I needed to.

I'd learned that a human's blood was the first choice. A fellow vampire's blood was a good second choice. Then there was animal blood, and the last resort, synthetic, which apparently had all of the nutrients but none of the zing.

I thought of it in terms of the human blood's being the main course, and the vampire blood's being dessert. Only some vamps, like Thierry himself, had more of a sweet tooth than others.

It was so bizarre.

Bottom line, I'd gotten off easy tonight. I should be thanking my lucky stars.

Thank you, lucky stars.

I glanced down at the beautiful ring on my right hand and then looked up into Thierry's eyes. A promise, he'd said. He hadn't exactly clarified what that promise was. A promise he'd help me? A promise he'd be around and wouldn't get any more stupid suicidal "I'm going to jump off a bridge" ideas into his vampire brain? A promise that after he had his marriage to Veronique annulled, we might have a real future together ahead of us?

All of the above. Pretty please.

He raised an eyebrow. "What is that for?"

"What is what for?"

"The smile."

I felt the expression widen on my face. "I'm just reminding myself how lucky I am."

"Lucky?"

"To have somebody who is willing to put up with the crazier moments in my life."

He held out his hand. "Come. Let us get the rest of that glitter off you."

I placed my hand in his and he led me to the bathroom. He moistened a facecloth and worked at gently removing the remainder of the powder Stacy had blown at me. He stroked the hair off my face and ran the warm cloth over my forehead, my cheeks, my neck, and even down between my breasts.

"Wow, she got it everywhere, didn't she?" I breathed. This was starting to feel better than a general cleanup should.

"She did." He pulled the thin red strap of the dress off one shoulder and slid the cloth over my exposed skin there before moving to the other side. That strap fell away as well.

He moistened the facecloth again under the tap water and pressed it against the faint mark of my stake wound. His silver eyes flicked to mine.

"How does this feel?" he asked.

"Really, really good."

His lips twitched into a half smile. "No, I meant your wound. Does it still cause you pain?"

I looked down at the mark. My borrowed red dress had pulled away enough that I was barely covered. The pink mark from the wooden stake was now pale and shiny in the bathroom light.

"I barely notice it anymore." I was such a liar.

He moved the cloth away and stroked his thumb against the mark. "Your healing abilities have greatly increased."

"Another plus to being a vampire."

"Yes. But my blood has allowed you to heal much more quickly than I even thought possible. In this case, I think it's a very good thing."

My dress slipped another inch. His fingers then grazed against my left breast. I think it was intentional. The heat of his touch felt as if it was branding me. His gaze locked with mine again. "I almost lost you that night," he said.

"I'm hard to lose."

"I don't like feeling so powerless to help you. I don't know who this Red Devil really is, but he has my eternal gratitude for saving you."

I could barely concentrate on what he was saying. I was sort of focused on what his right hand was up to. "He . . . he should get a medal or something."

"Or something."

I licked my lips and tried to focus, but his fingers were circling my entire breast now and I wasn't thinking straight. "Have you ever been staked?"

He nodded. "Several times. None of my wounds have come as close to being fatal as this one did, though. Too close." The dress slid down to my waist as he leaned forward to kiss my chest over the wound. Over my heart. I leaned my weight against the bathroom counter, feeling a little light-headed and warmer by the second.

"Your heart," he said, "is beating very fast for a vampire."

Your average vampire's heart beats approximately forty times a minute. Slower than a human's. When I was human my regular heart rate was about seventy beats a minute.

However, thinking about little facts like this wasn't

helping my heart rate go down from its current one-fifty. I was like a half-dressed hummingbird.

He moved as if to release his hold on me, but I grabbed his hand and pressed it against my chest again. He looked down at the connection, and then into my eyes.

"I never did get that chance to thank you for my beautiful new ring," I said, and then reached around to the back of the dress and unzipped it. With a small shrug it slipped past my waist to pool on the floor at my feet.

Thierry's gaze slid down the front of me. "Sarah . . ."

I brought his hand to my mouth and kissed it.

Then I moved my hands up into his dark hair and pressed my now dress-free body against him. Without my stilettos our seven-inch height difference was evident, but I could manage. I pulled his face closer to mine and brushed my lips against his.

"I love you," I told him. "Even in this lousy little motel room."

With a flick of my hands over his broad shoulders, I removed his expensive black jacket, which joined my dress on the white-tiled floor. It was Hugo Boss. He had ten of them exactly the same in the closet at his townhome. I'd counted. Then I pulled the black shirt out from his pants, unbuttoning it from the bottom to the top, and it joined the clothes party on the floor.

Thierry's pale chest had a light sprinkling of dark hair on it. He was toned, but he didn't have a bodybuilder physique, which was fine with me because I wasn't into the big and bulky. His muscles were lean and hard and felt good under my touch. In the center of his chest were some faint scars left over from when he'd been human. He'd been left for dead when Veronique had found him and sired him. This was what was left from his own near-death experience at the hands of the people who'd nearly killed him. I kissed his chest, running my mouth over the scars.

Then I led him to the bed, and I sat down on it and slowly undid his belt. Black, of course, like the rest of his wardrobe. I slipped my hands under the waistband and slid his pants over his hips, and he leaned over and our lips met in a kiss that made my mind go blank to all other worries or stresses. When Thierry kissed me there was only him, the taste of him, and the need for more and more.

After a moment he broke off the kiss, but kept his mouth close to mine so I could feel his warm breath on my lips. "It's been a difficult evening. If you wish to wait until we get back to Toronto, I would understand."

I grinned at him. "And let this fabulous room go to waste?"

I scooted back a bit to make room for him and felt the bed dip as he kneeled on it in front of me.

"An excellent point." He lowered himself on top of me and I felt his hot mouth slide over my collarbone, then down to my breasts. My hands tangled in his hair. He trailed his hands lower over my abdomen to the top of my panties, which he quickly and efficiently disposed of. They were red to match the dress, because matching underwear to outerwear is very important to me, for some strange reason.

I loved it when he touched me like this. His hands and mouth could do things to me that they should teach men in school. I arched off the bed and stifled a gasp at his intimate touch. After a moment he returned to my mouth and kissed me so deeply I thought I would pass out.

"Thierry—" I kissed him back just as hard and wrapped myself around him to pull his body even closer.

I will tell you a secret about Thierry de Bennicoeur. Being a master vampire automatically made him cool with his emotions and actions. It was difficult to get used to, since I was accustomed to dealing with such things as blind dates who wanted to get into my pants an hour into the first date.

Thierry wasn't like that. He was respectful. He was cool and reserved. He was—

I moaned as he slowly entered me.

—he was a freaking sex god.

Some relationships got boring after a while. The physical relationship gets tired and dull. But every time with Thierry—and admittedly it was not a daily, or sometimes even weekly occurrence—but every damn time was better than the time before.

Like tonight.

The man drove me over the edge.

Literally, in this case, because at that moment we fell completely off the bed. That had definitely not happened before. Thank you, small-town motel rooms.

"Sarah—" His voice was hoarse against my lips. "I love you."

"I love you, too."

I suddenly felt warm. Really warm. And not just because my world was being rocked. I wouldn't have noticed the sensation at all if I hadn't already been in tune to it from feeling the same way on the dance floor. I nuzzled Thierry's neck and licked the side of his throat. It made him groan.

"The witch . . ." I murmured.

"What about her?"

"She said something about . . . about hurting you because I'd gone to the prom with the guy she had the hots for."

His hands slid from my breasts down to grasp the backs of my thighs to bring me even closer to him. "And?"

I sank my fangs into the side of his neck.

"Sarah . . . stop . . ." But his tone wasn't terribly persuasive. In fact, it sounded more like an encouragement to continue.

Besides, I couldn't stop. I don't think I could have even if I'd been thinking clearly. All I could think about was the smell of him (*good*), the feel of him making love to me (*very good*), and the taste of him on my lips (*very, very good*).

After a couple of minutes, though, he clamped his hands on my upper arms and with effort managed to pull away from me.

The room was dark but I could see him clearly. My eyesight was one of the things that had improved since becoming a vampire, but this was even better than normal. Definite night vision. All the color was gone but it was a crisp black and white as if the moon shone directly above the room.

Frowning, Thierry brushed his fingers against the wound on the side of his neck. I watched as the fang marks grew smaller and smaller until they disappeared completely. I could heal well, but not like this. Thierry healed like a champ.

I was certain he was going to be angry with me and say cross things, but he simply stared down at me.

"Are you well?" he asked after a moment.

Was I well? What a strange question. I was well. I was damn well. I don't think I'd ever been so well in my entire life, as a matter of fact.

"Do I look well to you?" I asked, and my voice sounded very odd. It had this strange, sultry thing going on.

His gaze lowered to take me in and, in the position I was currently in, there was a lot to take. I was certain he was able to see me as well as I could see him. His eyes flicked back to my face. "You do. But that was not normal behavior for you, Sarah. I'm worried what this means."

"What it means . . ." I sat up and slithered closer to him so that our lips were only an inch apart. "Is that you make me lose my mind. Your touch, your kiss, your body, it's all I can think about."

His gaze darkened. "Is that so?"

"Yes. And I know you feel the same way about me. That's why you want the annulment." I heard the words leave my mouth. It was strange. It was as if I was watching from a long way away. As if this was a movie of some much more confident person with my face. "You want me. You can barely contain yourself when you're around me. You want to do very bad things to me."

His breath hitched as I pulled him closer and flattened my breasts against his hard chest.

"I don't know what you mean," he said.

I raised an eyebrow. My mouth was so close to his I might as well have been kissing him. "Oh, I think you do. Don't you remember? A night not that long ago? The taste of my blood drove you insane with need."

His brows drew together. "That was a horrific mistake."

"Was it?"

"I nearly killed you that night."

I smiled and traced his face with my hands and brushed my mouth over his in a brief kiss. "But you didn't. I'm fine. I'm here, with you. Do you think I would have stayed with a man who I thought would kill me?"

"Sarah," he breathed. "You're not yourself right now."

"Of course I am." I kissed him and slid my tongue into his mouth searching for his until I found it. For all his protests, he didn't stop me and instead kissed me back. Very hard. I smiled against his lips.

I reached around and moved my dark hair away from my neck. "Bite me, Thierry. Sink your fangs into me and drink as much as you like. I want you to taste me."

I heard a low growl and it made my body ache with desire. He brushed his mouth against my throat. "Don't make me do this, Sarah."

"I'm not making you do anything. You want to."

"Yes, I want to. But—"

I pressed my throat against his mouth. "Lose control, Thierry. Lose that control you hold so closely to you. It's the only thing with the power to keep us apart."

His heart beat as rapidly as mine had earlier in the bathroom. "What did she do to you?"

That was a very good question. Even as I wrapped myself around Thierry's body like a slutty anaconda, begging for him to bite my neck, I was asking myself the very same thing.

The last time he'd bit me it had almost killed me. The moment he'd tasted blood he'd lost his control, his center, that I knew he worked so hard to maintain. I was trying to make him do something he didn't want to do, even though a part of him inside was screaming for him to do it. I knew it. I could feel it. I could taste it.

He grabbed my wrists and pushed me down onto my back on the questionably clean motel carpeting and crushed his face against my neck.

Most of me was ecstatic that I was having this effect on him, breaking down all those annoying barriers of his. But a very small piece of me was screaming inside to stop him before it was too late.

The larger part of me told the other part to shut the hell up and stop being a total party pooper.

He pulled away a little and I could see that his silver eyes had changed to black. He searched my face, perhaps for some sign that I wanted him to stop. When he saw no red flags, he lowered his face again and his teeth grazed my throat just over my pulse.

His fangs began to penetrate my skin, a small but exquisite pain, but then he stopped as if frozen in place. He pushed back and stared down at me and began shaking his head slowly. There was a look on his face that I didn't think I'd ever seen before. I'd seen blankness. I'd seen anger. I'd seen concern and I'd seen passion.

But I'd never seen panic.

"No," he managed. "I can't do this."

I tried to draw him back to me but he moved away from my touch.

"I won't hurt you again." His voice was barely a whisper. His eyes were pools of darkness. "There's something wrong and we'll figure it out, but I won't hurt you again."

Before I could say anything, he got to his feet and headed directly to the bathroom, slamming the door shut behind him.

I heard the lock click.

My disappointment slowly faded to disbelief.

What the hell? I looked around the room. *What the hell just happened here?*

But I couldn't claim that I'd blacked out. I remembered everything.

Holy crap. I'd gone all black widow spider on him. I'd bitten him and tried to get him to bite me back.

I'd become a total biteaholic.

I crawled up onto the bed and pulled the covers over me. A sudden wave of extreme sleepiness washed over me and I only had one more thought before I fell deeply asleep.

Maybe going to my high-school reunion to feel normal again hadn't been such a wise choice after all.

Live and learn.

Chapter 8

I pried my eyes open and looked at the digital clock next to the bed. It was ten o'clock. Almost twelve hours of sleep and I couldn't remember a single dream, prophetic or otherwise.

A very good start.

The memory of what happened last night flooded over me. I groaned from disbelief and embarrassment and pressed my face down into the pillow. I honestly couldn't believe I'd suddenly turned into a neck-biting nympho. But that was last night. It was over now. I felt much more centered. A good night's sleep will do that.

"You're awake," a deep voice said.

I grimaced.

I peeked over the starchy white sheets at a fully dressed Thierry sitting on a chair next to the television stand. The curtains were drawn, so it was still dark in the room.

"Good morning," I croaked.

"How are you feeling?" he asked.

"Better."

"That's very good to hear. We'll have to keep a very

close eye on any unusual behavior, Sarah. And we must find the witch you spoke with last night. I've already made several calls to find out her location."

I cleared my throat. "I don't want to see her again. She might turn me into a toad next time."

He didn't smile at that. His cell phone rang and he pulled it out of his jacket pocket. "We must leave shortly. I'll give you some privacy to dress."

He opened the door and went outside the motel room to take the call.

I lay there for another minute and stared up at the ceiling mirror that reflected only a messy bed with an indentation where I lay. Then I forced myself to get up, have a quick shower, pull my hair back into a short ponytail, get dressed, and shove my used clothes into my overnight bag. Then I sat on the side of the bed and tried not to think of much of anything, but that didn't work out too well.

I was fine. I felt fine. Nothing was wrong. The sooner we got out of there and got back to life as usual, the better. I could put this unfortunate little trip out of my mind forever.

Two necks bitten. That would be it. Finito. The end.

Stacy must be some strange witch. What kind of a stupid spell was that, anyhow?

Being turned into a toad would have been so much worse.

My inner pep talk was working, and when Thierry re-entered the room I was ready to go. I was even smiling a little.

He raised an eyebrow. "I'm glad to see that you are looking well."

"I am. Look, I know what happened last night was really strange. I'm sorry. I promise it won't happen again."

He studied me for a moment. "I don't blame you. You weren't yourself."

No, that was very true. If I'd been myself I would have been all awkward and apologetic instead of sultry and seductive. *So* not me. There was a small part of me that wished I could be more confident like that all the time, but if it came with an uncontrollable thirst for blood, then I'd have to pass.

Maybe I'd look at this situation as a good opportunity to be thankful for what I already had. I was always looking for a way out, a way to be what I used to be, aka normal and human. I had never really appreciated that being a vampire fledgling wasn't all that bad. Except for the hunters, of course.

Thierry took my overnight bag from me and held open the door. I slid my sunglasses on and, with a smile as optimistic as I could manage, walked outside—

—into the *blazing hot core of hell.*

I screamed and held my hands up to shield my face. The glare from the sun wasn't just a glare, it was a burning agony that seemed to be trying to fry my brain. My vision went white and spotty and I felt a searing pain on my hands. I'd never felt anything so hot in my entire life.

Thierry grabbed the back of my shirt and pulled me back inside the room and shut the door. The pain eased immediately. I was actually panting when I looked at him. I didn't like the expression on his face.

My hands looked as if I'd been at the beach all day

covered in vegetable oil. Bright pink. Smoke rose off the surface of my skin in wispy curls.

"Your eyes are black," Thierry said.

"Oh, my God." I scrambled to pick up my sunglasses from where they'd fallen on the floor and I put them back on. I stilled myself and concentrated. Did I feel like biting him? No. But my eyes were black?

I almost got my ass completely fried by the sun. By *sunlight*.

But sunlight didn't bother me. Not much, anyhow. Sure, I was a little more sensitive to it and it made me feel like taking a nap after being out in it for too long. But this? This wasn't right. To say the very least.

If I'd been out there any longer I had no doubt that it would have killed me.

"Wh . . . what's a nightwalker?" I asked him.

"Pardon me?"

"Stacy . . . she mentioned something in passing last night. I didn't even pay any attention to it. But she asked me if I knew what a nightwalker was. She said I should ask you."

He hesitated. "A nightwalker is a type of vampire that existed a long time ago. One that has more of the common, mythic traits associated with vampirism. It is due to this rare form of vampire that we have so many misconceptions about what we truly are. But nightwalkers no longer exist." His expression was unreadable. "What else did she say?"

I thought back to the strange conversation I'd had with her after she told me she knew I was a vampire. I'd assured her that I was nice and normal and not a monster.

And she wanted revenge.

Oh, shit.

"She cursed me, didn't she?" I said. "Maybe to be one of these nightwalker things?"

"I believe she cursed you, but since we don't know that you have any more symptoms, we can't jump to any conclusions. It does seem as though she is drawing on common vampiric myths in whatever she's done to you, though."

"And now I can't go outside." After the blazing heat of the outdoors—and being that it was actually minus-ten Celcius in February, that wasn't a good sign at all—what else was wrong with me? "Am I going to be stuck here until the sun goes down?"

I glanced around the room, which now felt like a badly decorated prison cell.

"We must go back to the city."

"You go." My voice was shaky. "I'll stay here."

"No, I won't leave you here like this. We'll return to Toronto and then we'll locate the witch and have her break the curse. It's as simple as that." He sounded so calm and confident that I wanted to believe him.

He stood with his back against the door. He didn't attempt to come any closer to me. I couldn't say that I blamed him much after what had happened last night. Or maybe he was afraid that I'd go supernova and spontaneously combust.

I take it back. This was definitely worse than being turned into a toad.

I sat on the edge of the unmade bed. "But how can I drive back to Toronto with you? Your car is covered in windows. I'll be like a microwavable bag of popcorn in there."

He took in a deep breath and let it out slowly. "It's simple. We will put you in the trunk."

My eyes widened. "Are you serious?"

"No. I was attempting humor again to help lessen the gravity of this situation."

I blinked at him. "Don't quit your day job."

He approached and stroked the side of my face gently. "Don't worry, Sarah. There's a simple answer to this. We'll find the witch. I'm confident that I'll be able to convince her to help."

I felt the weight of those words. Yeah, Thierry had a way of making things happen when he wanted to. Master vampires could be very convincing.

"So that's the plan?" I asked. "Find Stacy? What if you can't find her?"

"I *will* find her. When we return to the city our first stop will be Barry's. He's lived through a curse before. He may be of assistance to us in this matter."

Thierry made another call on his cell phone, and I called my parents from the motel phone to say good-bye. They were vaguely apologetic for their reaction to Thierry yesterday, feeling that they might have overreacted, but they just wanted me to "be happy." I assured them I was happy, and I said it with as much conviction as I could muster. It seemed to work. Luckily, they didn't ask for us to stop by on our way out of town, which was good because I didn't want to have to tell them that they'd be answering the door to a great big ball of fire.

Half an hour later, Thierry's solution to our trip back

to the city arrived. A rented cube van. So, wrapped very tightly in the tacky paisley comforter from the bed, I ran to the back of the van and threw myself inside. The door slammed shut and I was plunged into darkness. I felt the vehicle start moving and I counted down the minutes until we got back to Toronto.

The front door was open and waiting for me at Amy and Barry's place. I could see it from the back of the van.

"As quickly as possible," Thierry said tightly.

With blanket in place I headed with him directly for the door. Amy was there, and she beckoned to me with a wave of her arm. She looked concerned. Possibly because of the ugly stolen comforter I had wrapped around me like a large paisley cocoon. The inside of their house looked so dark, so cool and inviting, that I couldn't wait to get inside. Even under the protection of the comforter, I could feel the sun reaching for me with its fiery fingers of death.

When I reached the doorway I didn't slow down. Which was rather unfortunate because at the threshold it felt as if I'd just walked directly into a plate-glass window. I slammed into the barrier and fell backward. Thierry caught me before I hit the ground.

"What the hell?" I said out loud, feeling bruised and shaken, not to mention charbroiled.

Barry appeared next to his wife. He was a full foot shorter than her and Amy wasn't exactly an Amazon. He wore a small blue business suit and had his arms crossed and he studied me for a moment.

I was getting warmer in my cocoon by the second.

"Yes, it does appear to be some sort of curse," he said.

And then he smiled at me. Smiled! At me!

That little rat bastard. From almost the moment we met he'd rubbed me the wrong way. They always talk about love at first sight. They never mention seething dislike at first sight. I'd tried to like him. Really, I had. And the fact that my best friend had fallen head-over-four-inch-heels for the creep, been sired into a life of fangs and immortality, and married him within weeks of meeting him didn't exactly help the situation.

He seethingly disliked me, too. Something to do with my corrupting Thierry and making life more difficult for everyone involved.

Whatever.

I forced myself not to panic. "I can't come inside. What am I supposed to do now?"

Amy was wringing her hands. "I'll go get the fire extinguisher. Just in case!"

"No, that won't be necessary." Barry sighed. "I invite you into my home, Sarah Dearly."

I glanced at Thierry. His expression was tight and he nodded.

I tried walking through the open door again, braced for any resistance, but there was none. Thierry closed the door behind me.

I let the comforter drop to the floor of Amy and Barry's foyer. Amy hugged me and stroked the slightly sweaty hair off my forehead.

"Poor Sarah!" she exclaimed. "We're going to find that witch and we're going to break this stupid curse."

"That would be a good thing," I said. "It's a little inconvenient."

"Luckily, the sun sets before six o'clock these days."

I summoned a weak smile. "Hooray."

"Why are you still wearing those sunglasses?" she asked.

"Oh, just because." I released her and pulled the shades away to show her my black eyeballs.

Her eyes went wide. "Yikes." Then her gaze moved down to my hand. "You have a new ring! Ooo! Did Thierry give it to you?"

I nodded. "An early Valentine's Day gift."

"It's beautiful!"

"Sarah must now be invited into a home before she can enter," Thierry said aloud as if he were talking to himself. "She has uncontrollable thirst for blood and sunlight burns her."

He shared a glance with Barry.

Barry studied me for a moment with a smile still curling up the corners of his mouth. "A very interesting curse indeed."

I eyed him. "Thierry says you were cursed, too."

"I was."

"What was the curse?"

"That's a little personal."

I sat down heavily on a wooden bench they had in their front hallway. Beside it was a shoe rack that held Amy's top twenty pairs of heels. One, I noticed, was a nice pair borrowed from me a year ago that I'd totally forgotten about.

"Barry was cursed to be unable to speak for a hundred years," Thierry said.

I snorted at that. "Why did you have to break a helpful curse like that?"

Barry scowled at me. "It wasn't funny."

"Neither is this."

"The curse was broken by getting the witch to remove the spell. It is as simple as that," Thierry explained. "Barry, I've made some headway. I know she lives in the city, but her phone number is unlisted."

"I will help you with whatever you require, Master."

I rolled my eyes. It just creeped me out that he called Thierry "Master." He also got a little peeved when everyone else didn't follow suit. I guess I could understand a little. Three hundred years ago Thierry had rescued Barry from being on display as an abused and exploited miniature vampire in a traveling fair. Hearing about that had softened me toward the guy, but not as much as I would have thought.

"Butch called earlier to say that he will be back on the job today," Thierry said. "I told him to come directly here."

Well, that was a relief. As much as I didn't like having a bodyguard around, it did lessen the stress. A bit.

"I'm not sure if you've heard," Barry said. "But Gideon Chase is dead."

Thierry nodded. "I did hear that."

Barry went into the kitchen and returned with a piece of paper. "I printed this off the Internet this morning."

I looked at the paper. It was Gideon's obituary on the VHA (Vampire Hunters of America) Web site. Alongside it was a striking picture of Gideon wearing a tuxedo and smiling for the camera. He'd been a very handsome man with chiseled cheekbones, a strong jaw, hair almost as dark as Thierry's, and piercing green eyes that seemed to stare out at me even through the poor quality of the printout.

My eyes narrowed at the picture. *Better luck next lifetime, creep.*

Amy peered over my shoulder. "Holy cow, he was hot. Too bad he was evil."

"Any hunters in town with affiliations with Gideon are currently at his funeral," Thierry said. "It's quiet right now in the city. It will help not worrying about that so much as we search for the witch."

"You will totally find her," Amy said brightly. "I'm sure of it."

She'd turned her attention away from her husband and the picture of hot-but-dead Gideon to stare up at Thierry. I personally witnessed a small but disconcerting amount of eyelash fluttering.

Thierry cleared his throat. "Your confidence is appreciated."

She beamed.

Right. Her crush on my boyfriend was going to have to be addressed very soon.

"What can I do to help?" I asked.

"The best thing for you to do would be to stay here with your friend until we return."

In other words, I'd get in the way. No big surprise there. I decided not to argue. It had been a hard enough day already.

"Okay, I'll stay here if you can do something for me," I said. "Can you swing by George's and pick up my high-school yearbooks? I had my parents send them a week ago so I could freshen my memory of who's who before the reunion. Maybe if I go through them again I can re-member Stacy better."

He nodded. "I'll get them for you."

"Is it okay if we go shopping later?" Amy asked. "I need a few things."

Thierry appeared to mull that over. He looked at me. "If you're feeling well enough when Butch arrives, and if it's after sunset, then you may leave this house. I've informed Butch of the situation, and he will be on the lookout for any unusual signs."

My babysitter. If it meant I could go out, then I was all for it. I hate being stuck inside for too long. Unless I'm stuck inside a mall.

I chewed my bottom lip. "I'm not planning on biting anyone else. I'm feeling totally normal now."

"Still." Thierry's jaw was set and he came closer to me. He ran a warm hand down my arm. "Please be careful."

I nodded. "I will."

I went up on my tiptoes and pulled his face down for a kiss. Our lips met and held before the kiss grew more passionate. Even with Amy and Barry witnessing this, I couldn't seem to stop. I didn't want to stop. I tightened my hold on him. His hands were firm on my lower back.

Then he tensed against my lips.

I frowned. "What's wrong?"

"I don't think we should be too close until we work this problem out." He looked down at me and his eyes were as black as I sensed mine still were. "There seems to be something about this curse that affects me as well."

I didn't let go of him. He didn't release me either. It

seemed odd to see black eyes, completely without any whites, in someone's face, but it suited him in a very strange way. It looked right. It gave him an extreme edge of danger that I found myself uncontrollably attracted to.

I knew my thoughts were growing cloudy. I noticed this from what seemed like miles away. I wanted to kiss him again. Even his warning didn't lessen that growing need.

"Okay, what exactly is going on?" Amy asked uneasily.

"I can't seem to control this." Thierry ran his fingers along the side of my neck and made a low, throaty growl.

"Then don't," I said.

He pulled me roughly against him and crushed his lips against mine. He began eating at my mouth in a kiss that made it feel as if he was trying to devour me. I wrapped my arms tightly around him and kissed him back just as deeply.

"Separate them," Barry said. "Quickly."

I was wrenched away from Thierry. Barry gripped my arms and I mindlessly began to fight against him. I turned and snarled, and with a push I sent him sailing across the room, where he slammed against the wall. Two framed Monet prints crashed to the floor, the glass shattering on impact.

Suddenly, as quickly as the fog had come over me, it cleared away as if I'd just had a glass of cold water thrown in my face. I brought a hand to my mouth, which felt swollen from the kiss.

"I'm so, so sorry," I said to Barry. "I will totally pay to have those reframed."

Barry brushed himself off and scowled at me. Amy held on to Thierry's arm. He obviously hadn't thrown her across the room as I'd done with her husband.

"Add increased strength to the list," he said to Thierry. "I think it's clear what we're dealing with here."

"The nightwalker thing, right?" I asked as my stomach sank.

Thierry's expression was pained as he looked at me. I watched his eyes slowly return to their normal color. "We'll take care of this. And we must leave now."

Barry nodded, then he approached Amy and kissed her on the cheek. He warned her to be careful.

Thierry stayed where he was by the door. His brow was furrowed. "I will see you soon, Sarah." Then he followed Barry out of the house, careful not to let too much sunlight in past the open door.

Amy slowly turned to look at me. "That's one hell of a curse."

I breathed out a long sigh. "Please remind me not to go to any more high-school reunions, okay?"

"Uh, Sarah? You're not planning to attack me, are you?"

I swallowed hard. "Absolutely not."

Her eyes narrowed and she peeled back the curtain to the side of the door. I had to jump out of the way of the beam of light. "What a jerk."

"Who?"

"Thierry. Honestly, I can barely stand to be in the same room as that guy. I think I finally understand how

you feel about Barry, because I feel the same way about
him."

I sat down on the bench again. I felt tired and I'd
only been awake for five hours. "Actually, there's a
difference."

"Oh? What's that?"

I looked directly at her. "I don't make googly eyes at
your husband."

Her eyes widened. "What on earth are you talking
about? I hate Thierry."

"Yeah, about as much as ·you hate strawberry
cheesecake."

"I love strawberry cheesecake!"

I crossed my arms. "Exactly."

"Sarah, you have it all wrong."

I almost laughed at how mortified she looked. "It
doesn't matter. Seriously. Your little crush on my boyfriend is the least of my worries at the moment."

Her expression faded to one of guilt. "I don't know
what's wrong with me."

"That makes two of us."

She shook her head. "Seriously, I don't like Thierry. I
would never act on it. But there's something about him.
He's just so . . . I don't know." She sighed. "You know?"

I just looked at her. "Right. That's perfectly clear."

"Are you feeling better? Your eyes are back to normal
again."

"Much." I thought about it for a moment. "Maybe
Thierry's right about the curse affecting him as well.
When he's not around I can think a lot clearer."

"The man can seriously kiss," she said dreamily.

I looked at her sharply.

She cleared her throat. "So, we're waiting for Butch and the sunset. That's a few hours away still. Want to watch a DVD?"

"Okay, but nothing weird, violent, or potentially dangerous to me in my current fragile state."

"How about *From Dusk Till Dawn*?"

"Perfect."

Chapter 9

I decided not to share with Amy the fact that I'd almost made Thierry bite me last night. After the near-death experience of the last time he bit me, she probably wouldn't think that was a good thing. I mean, *I* didn't think it was a good thing.

We watched the DVD. I'd had it confused with another movie with a similar title—a romantic comedy. This wasn't. After a character had his throat torn out by the bloodthirsty vampire vixen, I asked her to turn it off and put in something kinder and gentler. We settled on *Winnie the Pooh and the Blustery Day*.

Way fewer bloodthirsty vampires.

Waiting there for my bodyguard to show up, I realized that I hated feeling helpless like this. It was a feeling I'd perfected, but it didn't mean I liked it. I wanted to be out helping Thierry instead of waiting here like a two-fanged sloth.

"The sun has officially set," Amy announced.

This was very good news. I looked out the front window to the street and saw Butch nearing the house. I opened the door to let him in.

Butch weighed close to three hundred pounds. As with a linebacker for a football team, the extra bulk was for brute force rather than running long distances. His head was shaved bald and he had a pale brown goatee. Under his winter jacket, he always wore a black T-shirt with some arbitrary phrase printed on it. Today it read: "You use the Force. I'll use my fists." He came highly recommended as a vampire bodyguard.

Plus, he was a fan of reality TV. It all helped.

I had considered not leaving Amy's house after what happened with Thierry, but it had been almost four hours without incident, the sun was down, and a quick check in my shard confirmed my eyes had returned to normal. Butch gave the thumbs-up for our field trip.

I waited to feel the fog come over me again, but there was nothing. My mind was clear.

"What are we going out for?" I asked.

"Lingerie," she said. "It's Barry's birthday next week."

"And he likes to wear lingerie? I had no idea. What's his favorite color?"

"It's not for him, silly. It's for me."

"Just make sure you don't wear your 'Thierry Is a Hot Tamale' T-shirt. He might not understand that."

She glanced at Butch and her cheeks reddened. "I thought we were going to drop that?"

"Oh, we are. It's dropped." Her crush on Thierry had quickly gone from annoying to amusing. The fact that she was completely embarrassed about the whole situation only made it funnier.

"You're married, Amy," Butch brilliantly observed. "You shouldn't be looking at other men."

"Thanks for your opinion," Amy said dryly, pulling on her winter coat. "Not that I asked for it."

He shrugged his massive shoulders. "I think when you're married you shouldn't look at anyone else. It's wrong."

Amy eyed me. "Sarah's dating a married man. What do you think about that?"

"That's way different," I said quickly. "Can we go now? Pretty please?"

The promise of an annulment was just that at the moment. A promise. I wasn't going to share that news with anyone else until it actually *was* news. Then I would shout it from the rooftops.

But that was the future. I was currently dealing with the present.

The present that included shopping for my friend's lingerie while my married boyfriend searched for the witch who'd put a nasty curse on my ass.

A romantic fairy tale if ever I'd heard one.

With every step I took through the Toronto Eaton Centre, my favorite shopping mall in the very heart of the downtown core, I asked myself:

Am I feeling okay?

Do I want to bite anyone?

The answers continued to be: Yes, I'm feeling okay; and no, I don't want to bite anyone. I felt perfectly normal. It was obvious that this situation was a temporary one. I could deal with it short-term, no problem, especially with Thierry on the case of finding Stacy.

So I allowed myself to relax a bit. Just a bit.

I hadn't been to the mall for a couple of weeks. Mostly due to my acute problem of being broke. What fun was window-shopping if there wasn't the potential of buying something? And sure, I could probably go shopping every day if I wanted to take Thierry's readily available money. Part of me did. Part of me wanted to completely replenish the wardrobe I'd lost when my apartment blew up. But the other part of me wanted to do the right thing and wait. Earn the money on my own—although I still wasn't quite sure how I would do that—and buy myself everything I needed.

The harder road, sure, but it did give me a sense of pride.

But you know what they say about pride.

After being at the mall for an hour already Amy hadn't bought a thing, which was unusual for her. We browsed through a store that specialized in lingerie. It was a virtual sea of silk and lace.

"What do you think of this?" Amy held a bright pink merry widow with dangling garter straps up in front of her. The color matched her current hair color perfectly.

I scrunched my nose. "A little too trampy for my tastes."

She smiled. "Just what I was looking for! Thanks!"

I glanced over at Butch, who stared at the store mannequin dressed in a lavender corset, crotchless panties, and a black feather boa draped over one shoulder. He seemed mesmerized.

I left Amy to continue her trampy shopping spree and wandered the store. It smelled nice in there—a jasmine fragrance filled the air that emanated from a bath and beauty section. A "mood-enhancing" candle flickered on display.

Over in the bathrobe section I stopped in front of a gorgeous dark blue chenille one. I checked the tag. Over two hundred dollars. Ouch. I sighed and ran my hands over the super-soft material.

A salesgirl approached. "Can I help you with anything?"

I stopped molesting the bathrobe of my dreams and shook my head. "Just browsing."

She nodded at the robe. "That's on sale. No tax this week."

"Maybe let me know when you have a 90 percent off sale."

She grinned. "I know. It is expensive, but quality costs money."

I considered my Visa card. Not a chance. I could already hear it practically screaming from inside my purse. It didn't want to come out any time soon or it might charge me with abuse.

"Try it on," the salesgirl prompted, taking it off the hanger and holding it up.

"Oh, you're good." I slipped it on and pulled it around me in a big chenille hug. I felt automatically relaxed. Two hundred bucks for stress relief. No tax.

"Looks great on you!" She must have been on commission.

"I really want it," I said.

She blinked. "Then it's yours."

I frowned at her. "What?"

She blinked again. "If you want it, then it's yours. I will wrap it up for you."

"Hold on. I really can't afford it."

She shook her head. "It's yours. For free."

"Uh . . ."

But before I could say anything else, she pulled the robe off me and took it up to the cash register, wrapped it in tissue paper, and put it in a large bag with some bath beads thrown in to give it a nice scent. She pushed it across the counter to me.

I studied her. What was the catch? "Are you sure this is free?"

The smile seemed frozen on her face and her eyes were a bit glazed over. "Yes. Free. Enjoy your new bathrobe. Good-bye."

She turned and walked away.

Amy joined me at the cash register. "I didn't see anything I liked. Ready to go?"

I nodded.

Maybe it was a promotion. Maybe I was the thousandth customer in the store that day. Weird.

With a last glance at the salesgirl, now helping another customer, I accompanied Amy out of the store. I expected the girl to snatch the bag away from me, but she didn't. Butch finally tore his eyes off the scantily clad mannequin and joined us.

"That was so strange." I took a last look back at the store. "I just got this for free."

Amy peeked into my bag. "Wow, really?"

"Yeah."

"That is so cool. Who says you're not having a lucky day?"

Actually, I did. Major. And a free bathrobe didn't exactly balance the scales.

I shrugged inwardly. But it was a nice start.

"Hey, look, George is here, too." Amy pointed over at the food court as we passed it.

And yes, there was George, drinking a milk shake and reading a magazine. He had a Band-Aid on his neck. Actually, two Band-Aids. One to cover each fang mark I'd made last night. I guess he hadn't healed yet.

I cringed at the memory.

He lowered his copy of *Vanity Fair* as we approached. "Oh, look who it is. Bitey McBitealot."

I sat down across from him. "How's the neck?"

"Tender." He eyed me. "How's your stake wound?"

I automatically brought a hand up to my chest. I'd actually forgotten about it for a few minutes, but just the mention brought back the memory in Technicolor. "Almost healed."

His eyes flicked to Butch. "Who's he?"

"Haven't you met Butch before? He's my new bodyguard."

"Hi there." Butch awkwardly waved his hand in George's direction.

"Charmed." George sipped from his milk shake. "Is it strange having a bodyguard? Somebody following you wherever you go like you're some sort of celebrity?"

I thought about it. "I'm a fan of anything that keeps me breathing."

"Maybe he can make sure you don't bite anyone else."

I held back any witty reply to that because he was absolutely correct. And he did have the right to still be mad at me, which obviously he was. I wouldn't have been too thrilled if somebody had chomped on me without permission. I still hadn't forgiven the blind date that started my new fangtastic lifestyle off in the first place. And he was dead.

My attention moved over to a nearby table—a mom, a dad, and two little girls. A normal, happy little family. I sighed. They probably had a white picket fence in their front yard and everything. They were eating burgers and fries, and had soft drinks in front of them.

My mouth felt dry. "God, I am so thirsty right now."

Butch grabbed my shoulders. "NO!"

"Not thirsty that way. I mean . . ." I made brief eye contact with a woman carrying a tray from the taco place as she passed our table. "I really want a Diet Coke right now."

The woman paused at the table and handed me her drink with a glazed look in her eyes. "Here you go." And then she continued walking.

I looked at the drink in my hand before taking a sip. It was a Diet Coke with lots of ice. I frowned deeply. "Okay, now that's *definitely* weird."

George's eyes slowly and steadily widened. "Um . . . what just happened?"

I shrugged. "Same thing happened in the lingerie store. I said I wanted the robe in there and the girl wrapped it up for me and gave it to me for free."

There was silence at the table for a moment and I took another sip of my free beverage.

Amy suddenly gasped. "Oh, my God, Sarah."

"What?"

"Maybe you have the thrall!"

"The what?"

"The *thrall*," she repeated. "It's when a vampire can

control other people with the power of their brains and make them do things!"

I frowned. "It's really called the thrall?"

She waved a hand. "I heard that term somewhere."

I considered what I'd learned about vampires since becoming one and also took into consideration what I knew from movies and television.

Mind control was definitely on the list.

I chewed my bottom lip. "No, that's got to be impossible."

"What is going on?" George asked.

Amy took the liberty of filling him in on everything she knew about my curse.

Thus far, my symptoms included:

The desire to bite necks. *Gross.*

Potential death by sunlight. *Horrible.*

Inability to enter somebody's home without an invite. *Inconvenient.*

Extra strength. *Kind of cool.*

Potential mind control. *Uh . . . wicked!*

Perhaps an experiment was in order. I made eye contact with George. "Give me your magazine."

He held it against his chest. "Go get your own."

Hmm. Maybe it only worked on the nonvampire members of society.

I stood up, looked around, and walked out of the food court and into the nearest store. It sold electronics and literally buzzed with customers and merchandise. I quickly browsed the shelves and picked up an MP3 player.

"Excuse me," I said to the first employee I saw.

"Yes? Can I help you?"

I held up the device and made eye contact with the guy, a teenager with bad skin and an awkward smile. "I want this. Can I have it?"

His eyes glazed over and the smile fell away. "Of course you can."

"For free?"

He nodded. "Yes. I will put it into a bag for you." He took it from me, removed the security features that would make the alarm go off as I left the store, placed it in a bag, and thrust it in my direction. "Please enjoy the rest of your evening."

Sweet.

But then I frowned and looked down at the small bag. What was I doing? This wasn't right. I was *stealing*.

When I turned I saw that George stood behind me. He smiled very widely at me. "I needed an MP3 player. This is so awesome!"

I shook my head. "I can't do this."

"What? Of course you can. We are going on a major shopping spree. Did I mention that I totally forgive you for biting me?"

I took a deep breath and let it out slowly. Then I walked through the store so I could hand the bag back to the employee.

He frowned. "What?"

"I can't take this."

"But you wanted it."

I met his very eager but glazed eyes. "I'd rather see you do five jumping jacks right now."

He did them.

With a sinking feeling in the pit of my stomach, I turned around and left the store quickly.

Butch was waiting outside with his huge arms crossed in front of him. He raised an eyebrow.

I visited a few more stores and it was the same. Anyone I made eye contact with would hand over anything, possibly including their firstborn child, if I asked for it.

It felt very wrong.

On the other hand, it also felt very right.

It was a split decision. Right in the midst of my curse trauma was this lovely little gift. Sure, I was currently broke, but if I could get anything I wanted for free, that solved that problem, didn't it?

"I need this curse gone." I pulled my cell phone out of my purse and looked at the screen. What was Thierry doing? Had he found Stacy yet? Should I call him?

No. I needed to let him do his thing. I knew I had a tendency to get in the way. I was trying to break myself of that habit. I didn't want him to think I was more trouble than I already was, especially since he was being so understanding and supportive about this bizarre situation. I slipped the phone back into my purse and shifted my lingerie store bag to my other hand.

Now that I thought about it, I *could* use a new purse. Possibly Burberry.

No. Not good.

"We need to leave now," I said, and looked at Butch and George. "Where's Amy?"

George nodded at a jewelry store up ahead. Amy's bright pink head was lowered as she inspected the diamond engagement rings that put her modest ring from Barry to shame.

I approached and tapped her on the shoulder. She turned to me. "Hey, can you get me a free ring?"

"No, I can't."

She pouted. "Why not? I thought you were my best friend."

I cleared my throat and glanced at the girl across the counter. A smile appeared on her face. "Anything I can help you with?"

"Could you give us some privacy?" I asked.

Immediate eye glaze. "Sure thing." She turned and quickly walked to the back room of the store, closing the door behind her.

I sighed and looked down at the display of engagement rings. They were so beautiful. I glanced at my promise ring. Still gorgeous; but in a different way than a big fat three carat princess-cut diamond solitaire.

Amy nodded at my new finger bling. "So that's just a Valentine's Day gift? It doesn't mean anything else?"

I curled my hand into a fist. "It means that he has very good taste in jewelry."

She blinked. "Did he pop the question?"

"Being that he's already married, I think any question popping is a little out of the question."

She looked disappointed. "I forgot about that."

"That makes one of us."

She sighed and moved away from the glass case of engagement rings over to a display of necklaces and started looking through them.

Quick check: Was I feeling okay?

Yes.

Did I feel like biting anyone?

No.

Phew.

My cell phone rang. I pulled it out and looked at the screen to see that it was Thierry.

I answered it. "Thierry, hi."

"Where are you?" he asked.

"At the mall. Did you find witch-face?"

"Not yet. But we will." There was a strain to his voice. "I think we should meet at Haven in an hour. Can you be there?"

I tried to keep the disappointment out of my voice that his search had turned up nothing. I'd had high hopes. "Yeah, we'll be there."

"Have there been any incidents?" he asked.

Define incident, I thought. "No. I'm doing okay."

"I think it would be a good idea if we have you drink at the club to help alleviate any blood cravings for the next day or so."

"Is that an educated guess or do you know that for sure?"

"It is, unfortunately, only a guess." He was quiet for a moment. "I will find her, Sarah. I promise you."

The sincere tone of his words warmed my heart and I felt a lump in my throat. "I know you will."

I glanced over at the store opening to the mall and my eyes bugged out to see that the witch-in-question, Stacy McGraw, currently stood directly in front of the store. Our eyes met. She smiled and waved at me.

"Thierry . . . she's here," I whispered into the phone. "Stacy's here. I'm looking right at her."

"She's there? Don't let her out of your sight. You need to—"

Stacy flicked her hand at me and the phone flew out of my grip and crashed against the floor, where it exploded in a tiny puff of smoke and flame.

She grinned. "I did a location spell to find out where you are. How's it going?"

My eyes narrowed. "How do you think?"

"Ready to apologize to me yet?"

I put my hands on my hips. "Fine. I'm sorry, okay? Is that good enough for you?"

Stacy shook her head. "Wow. Not even slightly. You didn't mean it. I want an apology that you *mean*."

I took a step in her direction just as Amy called my name, and I glanced over at her.

"Sarah, what do you think of this?" She held up a necklace that had a big early-Madonna-like bejeweled cross on it.

I immediately added to my growing list of curse side-effects:

Extreme aversion to crosses. *EXCRUCIATING*.

The cross turned a blinding white color like a tiny death-sun and sent out waves of agony directly toward my eyeballs.

"Put that thing away!" I yelled at her, falling to my knees and covering my eyes.

The light disappeared and Amy rushed to my side. "Oh, my God. Sarah, I'm sorry! I didn't even think about it."

"It's okay," I said weakly. "Just don't do it again. Please."

I looked up at the entrance to the store but Stacy was gone. I staggered to my feet and ran outside looking in all directions.

That bitch. She'd completely disappeared.

I glanced off to the side to see George and Butch

discussing something obviously more important than keeping an eye out for the witch who'd ruined my life. They looked at me.

"What?" they said in unison.

Panic clutched at my chest. I wanted this curse gone. I hated it. I hated everything about it. It was completely ruining my life.

I swallowed past the tears that wanted to fall and went back into the store, got the clerk to come out of the back, and Amy and I walked out five minutes later with two lovely matching diamond pendant necklaces.

Sure it was stealing, but at the moment I didn't really give a rat's ass.

I also kept the bathrobe. So sue me.

Chapter 10

We arrived at Haven at a little after nine o'clock, so it was open for business. A scattering of customers sat at the tables, sipping on their drinks in the upscale club and listening to a mixture of jazz and contemporary tunes. Two waiters—both of whom I knew had already landed jobs elsewhere in readiness for the club's transferring ownership—strolled the floor. Since it was Friday it wouldn't take long before the club was completely filled, as vampires of all professions came in to chill out after a long week at their day jobs.

I currently didn't have a day job, but I sure as hell needed to chill out.

Thierry wasn't sitting in his usual booth; instead he stood at the door scanning the entrance for our arrival. He came directly toward me as we entered the club and seemed about to hug or kiss me, but he didn't. In fact, he took a step back from me.

I swallowed hard. He was afraid to touch me in case we went all vampire-Sid-and-Nancy on everyone. It figured that the moment Thierry was okay with public displays of affection, they were off the menu.

"I was worried," he said, his face tight. "When the phone went dead—"

I held up a hand. "Stacy took off. I don't know where she went."

His jaw tightened. "At least we know she's definitely in the city."

"At least." I felt a tap on my back and turned to see Amy with her arms out.

"Somebody need a hug?" she asked.

I nodded and hugged her. It was better than nothing.

She patted my back. "Just don't bite me."

I pulled back. "Why do you have to say something like that?"

"Better safe than sorry."

George and Butch moved off to the side of the bar and ordered drinks before the bartender moved over to me.

"Hey, Sarah!" he said happily. His name was Ron and he was a big fan of the Slayer of Slayers. He thought I was some kind of hero. I hadn't tried to change his mind yet.

"Order something to drink," Thierry suggested. "Have you had any blood lately?"

I bit my bottom lip and glanced at his neck. "Not since last night."

His expression darkened and he clasped his hands behind his back. "I am finding it difficult not to touch you. Especially after last night."

I blinked. "Seriously?"

He nodded gravely. "It is troubling."

I let that disturbing, yet also slightly exciting, knowledge settle over me, and then I told him about my reaction to the cross jewelry as well as my mind-control abilities. I left off the part about the unpaid-for merchandise.

"Stacy wants me to apologize to her." I turned toward the bar and leaned heavily against it. "I'm getting the feeling that she won't be receptive to helping us out until I do that. But I don't know how to get in touch with her."

"We now know she's definitely in Toronto. It's only a matter of time before we find her or she attempts to contact you again."

I felt his hand at the small of my back then, and I looked up at him. Nothing happened other than the nice warm imprint of his touch. I smiled and slid my right hand up the center of his black shirt to his chest. "See? We're touching and there's no vampire apocalypse. Everything's going to be okay."

"Perhaps I've simply been overthinking the situation." He took my hand in his and kissed it. "I picked up your school yearbooks. They're on the desk in my office."

"Thank you."

"Now, if you'll excuse me for a moment I must speak with Butch."

He left me at the bar and Ron set up three shots of B-Positive in front of me and I took a moment to toss them each back. It was my favorite blood type. I continued to hold on to my theory that it would make me "Be Positive." Ten weeks with fangs and I was still waiting for the positive energy to kick in.

I guess Ron recently had a shipment from the "Blood Delivery Guys," the appropriately named blood delivery company. I saw several self-refrigerating silver kegs were piled up behind the bar neatly labeled with the corresponding blood type.

Ron leaned over the bar. "So have you heard?"

"Heard what?"

"About the Red Devil? He's back!"

The image of my scarf-wearing hero flickered in my mind. "Who told you that?"

"George."

I glanced over at the culprit, who wasn't supposed to say anything about the Red Devil's potential reappearance.

"It's so exciting," Ron continued. "Finally after a century I can start to feel a little bit safe again."

"Has it really been a hundred years since he's been around?" I asked.

He nodded and poured me another shot. "Everyone thought he was dead."

I thought about that. It was a long time to disappear. "So why do you think he disappeared? And why did he choose now to return?"

He leaned closer. "I have a theory."

"Do tell."

He ran a cloth along the top of the bar. "I think that after centuries of being an incredible champion to vampirekind, he became disillusioned with the fight. I think he felt that no matter what he did, it didn't change anything. Hunters would always exist and vampires would continue to be slain, so he quit and has tried to live a quiet, secretive life ever since, feeling that anything he did might only add to the problem instead of being part of the solution. And now, after all these years of self-reflection, he is willing to step back into the ring and do what he can even if it is an ultimately futile battle."

I frowned. "Do you really believe that?"

He shrugged. "Who cares? He's back! He's going to protect us vampires from hunters. And how cool is it that he's chosen Toronto out of all the cities on the entire planet to make his reappearance? Maybe the Red Devil is Canadian!"

"Yeah, that's pretty cool." My frown deepend. If he'd been gone for a hundred years, why did he choose to reappear now? Why here of all places? And why did he save me in particular? Not that I was complaining, but still, it didn't make a whole hell of a lot of sense.

"You two should join forces," Ron suggested. "The Slayer of Slayers and the Red Devil. You could be an amazing team!"

"From what I've heard, the Red Devil works alone."

He nodded solemnly. "He is a loner. Doesn't want outside help. But he might make an exception for you."

"I wouldn't bet on it. Besides, I don't have a shiny cape and mask at the moment."

I surveyed the club. Thierry was talking with Butch and George. Every now and then George's focus would shift over to me. Obviously they were talking about me. Big surprise. Amy was now with Barry, and they also glanced over at me every now and then.

Yeah. Disaster of the week right here. Present and accounted for.

God, I hated just waiting for something to happen. It made me feel so helpless over this whole situation. What if it got worse? What if I hadn't found out all of the curse's side-effects yet?

I hoped, since I had reacted that badly to a cheesy rhinestone cross, no one had any holy water on them tonight. I glanced nervously through the rest of the club.

Holy water *bad.*

I racked my brain for other vampire myths and came up with another one.

The ability to turn into a bat.

I arched an eyebrow. That might be interesting.

Then I downed another shot of B-Positive, closed my eyes, and concentrated. After a moment I opened my eyes and looked down at my hands, but they were still hands, not small leathery wings.

Cross one myth off the list. No shape-shifting abilities.

Then I froze in place as I remembered the most prevalent myth of all about vampires that I used to believe, aside from the whole drinking blood thing.

Vampires were evil.

But I *wasn't* evil. I didn't *feel* evil. I breathed out a long sigh. Along with the bat thing, being evil was obviously a myth that I'd sidestepped.

Thank God.

Then again, Stacy thought I was evil, didn't she? That's the whole reason she'd cursed me in the first place. For revenge.

I walked through the bar and headed toward Thierry's office. I closed the door behind me so the noise and music from the club were muffled.

Sitting behind Thierry's desk, I looked at the four yearbooks he'd placed there.

I remembered high school as being four years of dull, with the occasional school dance, then more dull followed by one year at university before I decided that school and I were breaking up for good. Sure, there was the whole cheerleader thing, but it was no big deal. Obviously I wasn't even that good at it. After leaving university and bombing at the acting thing, I had tried out to be a cheerleader for the Toronto Raptors, but those girls were professional pom-pom shakers. I was small-town. In every way. Hadn't even made the callbacks.

I flipped open my senior yearbook and smiled at the inscriptions from my old friends, most of whom, except for Claire, hadn't bothered to show up for the reunion at all. A good number of the pictures of teachers had mustaches and devil horns drawn on with blue pen. That may have been my doing. I will admit nothing.

There was a picture of the homecoming committee. I wasn't on it. The drama club. I was there in the back row making rabbit ears behind a friend. A glimpse of my leg in an action shot at a basketball game when I fell off the top of the cheerleader pyramid. I still had a small scar from accidentally kneeing another girl in her brace-filled mouth.

There was the picture of the squad itself. Six of us with three alternates all smiling and looking happily at the camera. I shook my head. Now that I thought about it, I'd had a lot of fun with those girls. Being on the squad automatically made us more popular than we might have been without it. And the guys on the teams, both football and basketball, were more likely to go out with us than anyone else. I had a fairly steady boyfriend from the basketball team during my senior year. He was the one who'd popped the question just before senior prom. I believe my exact response had been, "Get married? Are you kidding me?"

Unfortunately, he hadn't been kidding.

And that had been the end of our relationship, which was probably for the best since I hadn't been in love with him in the slightest. That's when I went with Stacy's alleged true love, Jonathan, to the prom.

I flipped forward to the football team's photo. There was the love interest in question. Still as cute as I remembered him, but my memories of him were less than favorable being that he'd decided he'd rather tear my expensive prom dress off in the back of the limo than actually show up at the prom itself.

I recall kneeing him very hard in the groin.

I'd been stuck with the limo bill. And he'd gone to the hospital.

Ah, the memories.

I frowned as I looked at the cute boys in their football uniforms. There was another figure behind them. I squinted at the fuzzy black-and-white photo. I wasn't positive but it might have been Stacy lurking in the shadows.

Creepy.

I flipped forward to my grade and trailed my finger down the page. There I was. Sarah Dearly. Forever immortalized in the yearbook as the girl most likely to close her eyes during a photo.

I flipped forward a few pages to get to the M's. There was Stacy staring out at me with the same icy glare she'd given me in the washroom at the reunion.

Her eyes were the only thing I recognized. The rest of her was completely different. The vengeful woman I'd met in the bathroom had been a petite, yet busty blonde with killer legs. Well dressed in expensive clothes and designer heels. Perfectly applied, though too-heavy makeup. Expensive perfume.

The girl who looked up at me from the small black-and-white photo wasn't the same person at all. She had dark, greasy hair pinned back with barrettes, a sullen face full of pimples, and a couple of extra chins. And she wasn't smiling.

The absolute worst thing about her photo? The fact that as I looked at the teenage Stacy McGraw, the memories started coming back to me. Things I'd forgotten for ten long years.

I chewed on my bottom lip. Yeah, I'd known her. Not well, of course, but I remembered her. She'd been in a couple of my classes. She'd been a loner, and I couldn't even recall that she had any friends.

I let out a shaky breath. *Oh, no.*

The day that I'd broken up with my boyfriend had actually been a lot more traumatic than I'd prefer to remember. He hadn't taken my rejection very well, and it had been a big agonizing hallway scene that had put me in a very foul mood.

That day had also been cheerleader tryouts. We were going to put together a squad for the summer. Just because it was summer vacation didn't mean that there wouldn't be some more games. Abottsville was fairly boring, after all. No multiplex cinemas. No mall. But we had a lot of sports fields: soccer, baseball, football.

Stacy had been one of the girls who'd tried out. I'd been tired, angry, annoyed by life in general. And I'd told her in no uncertain terms not to waste our time. I didn't remember exactly what I'd said, but it hadn't been kind and it had revolved around her appearance. Her weight. Her face. I'd spewed some nastiness at her because I'd been feeling nasty.

I felt it with a clarity I'd rarely felt before—

I'd shown her the dark side of Sarah Dearly.

After that, I must have snapped out of my foul mood and moved on with my day and forgotten all about it.

Obviously Stacy McGraw hadn't forgotten about it. Ever. And if she'd been festering about the hurtful things I had said, add on the fact that I'd been asked to the prom by her secret crush, and it's no wonder that she hated my guts.

And now she was a witch with a very big grudge.

I closed the yearbook and leaned back in the high-backed leather chair, feeling sick to my stomach.

There was a knock at the door and it slowly opened. Thierry entered the room, his gaze steady on me.

"I wondered where you'd gone to," he said.

I held up my yearbook. "Just in here walking down memory lane."

"And how did that go?"

"It's a rocky road."

I told him about my discoveries. My throat was tight as I admitted to being a bitch to Stacy in high school. I expected him to look at me with disgust or shame, but his expression didn't change.

"So obviously I deserve to be cursed," I said.

"That's nonsense, Sarah. You may have spoken poorly during this one moment in your life, but that doesn't mean you're a bad person."

"Sure it does."

He sat on the edge of the desk near me. "No, it doesn't. What happened in the past is just that, the past. You are a different person now. You're older and wiser and see the error of your ways."

I raised an eyebrow at that. "Isn't it funny how you can give me that advice, and yet when it comes to your own past you can't take it?"

"That is different."

I shrugged. "Maybe, maybe not. I know I'm not the same person I used to be. But I've always thought that in high school I was the nice girl. That people liked me. That I had a lot of friends. Sure, I didn't like school very much and I wanted to get the hell out of my hometown at my earliest convenience, but I'd always thought of myself as one of the good guys. But maybe I wasn't so nice after all. If I was a mean girl to Stacy, who else wasn't I nice to? What else might I be conveniently forgetting?"

"You *are* one of the good guys. There is no doubt in my mind that you are good, Sarah."

"If you say so."

He gave me a very rare smile. "I do. I've met many people over my existence, be they human or vampire. Out of everyone I've ever met, I would have to say that you are one of the most genuine and special of them all."

"You really mean that?"

He nodded and reached down to take my hand in his. "Most assuredly."

His hand felt warm against mine. "Should you really be touching me?"

He didn't let go. "I am not feeling the darkness at the

moment, only the light." He paused. "Besides, Butch is waiting just outside the door. I've asked him to intervene if anything . . . unusual occurs."

I grinned at him. "That sounds vaguely voyeuristic, but I'm okay with it."

He drew me closer, the chair rolling smoothly against the floor, and leaned over to kiss me chastely on the lips. He threaded his fingers through my hair. "I know we haven't found her yet, and I am very sorry for that, but it won't be long."

"When we do find her, or if she finds me first, I know what I'm going to do."

"Oh? And what's that?"

"I'm going to apologize to her. Now I know I have something to apologize for, I'm going to beg her forgiveness and hopefully that will convince her to break this stupid curse."

"That's a very mature decision."

"I'm very mature." I kissed him then pulled back a bit. "Hey, listen, Ron has an interesting theory about the Red Devil's reappearance. You should ask him about it."

"As I've said before, it's not the Red Devil. The man you met the other evening was an impostor." He said it with such certainty.

I shook my head. "You don't think it's even possible that he's the real deal? Maybe he is. Stranger things have happened."

His jaw tightened. "If he attempts to make contact with you again, Sarah, please let me know. I am wary of his true intentions."

I crossed my jeans-clad legs and tried to feel comfortable but I only felt tension emanating off Thierry in waves at any mention of the Red Devil. "Wary? But he saved my life."

Thierry stood up from the desk and crossed his arms. "He happened to be in the same area as you when you were in danger, and he acted on that. Whether it was truly to save you or perhaps to wedge his way into your life we don't know."

"Why would he want to do that?"

He shook his head, his expression tense. I don't know what it was about this guy that got Thierry all wound up, but it wasn't a good thing. Not at all.

"Okay, forget it," I said. "I promise you'll be the first person I tell if he sends a smoke signal my way."

His frown remained. "And you mustn't let his charms work on you."

"Charms?"

He raised an eyebrow. "They do say that the Red Devil is a charming man."

"And you think my head would be turned so easily?"

He shrugged slightly. "I don't know."

"Obviously you didn't get the memo that stated I'm only interested in one ancient vampire with issues, and it's you."

"Issues?" he repeated.

"So many you should offer yearly subscriptions."

His mouth quirked. "I see. Well, I could say for your young years you also are the bearer of many issues."

"Tell me something I don't know. But even with our issues we're still together. Even though everybody and their pet rabbit thinks we're doomed."

He raised a dark eyebrow. "Who thinks we're doomed?"

"Everybody. And their pet rabbit."

"And how do you feel?"

I smiled up at him. "I'm starting to feel warm and fuzzy again."

"Is that so?"

I nodded. "Now if I promise not to bite you, can I get a proper kiss?"

He hesitated and glanced at the door, then back at me. His expression was serious, but the longer he gazed into my eyes the more he seemed to relax. "Your idea of proper and mine may be two different things."

"I don't think it's that far apart."

"I'm glad that the events of the day haven't made you more fearful. I would have thought that perhaps you wouldn't want to be near me for a while."

"Then you thought very wrong." I stood up and wrapped my arms around his waist. "I hate coming to the conclusion that I was mean to Stacy, but I guess it's a relief. She wants an apology and I'm going to give her one because she deserves it. Everything will be fine then."

"Then I share your confidence." He leaned over and brushed his lips against mine. I sighed. "You promise you won't bite?" he breathed into my ear.

"Cross my heart."

I guess that was enough to convince him, as our lips met again and held and I kissed him deeply. I waited, feeling a little tense, before I relaxed against him and opened my mouth to the kiss.

I felt a bit of pain as my enthusiastic tongue met the edge of his sharp fang, but I ignored it. Fangs can get in the way of making out, though normally it was my fangs that got in the way. This time it was Thierry's.

With the small taste of my blood, his grip on me grew tighter and the kiss more urgent. I thought for a moment about Butch being right outside the door and maybe this wasn't quite the perfect moment or location for taking things any further, but the thoughts quickly left my mind as I lost myself in the kiss and I wanted more of him. My mind grew cloudy and my skin warmed at his touch. Thierry broke off the kiss and held my face between his hands.

"Do you know how deeply I care for you?" he said, his eyes black and his voice raspy.

"Show me," I said, leaning back on the desk. "Right here. Right now." Again with the sultry voice and rising lust as I looked at the black-eyed Thierry.

Red flag!

Alert! Alert!

Danger!

He pushed me back onto the desk and pressed his weight on top of me, his mouth on me, licking a hot line along the pulse at the side of my throat. I ran my hands down his back under his jacket just as I felt his sharp fangs pierce my skin.

Unlike the last time he'd bitten me, which had been painful and scary, this felt very, very good. I knew on some level that my mind wasn't working the way it should. That this actually *wasn't* good. But . . . but it felt so . . . overpowering. Better than sex. Better than chocolate, even, and that's saying something. True, I couldn't eat it anymore and didn't even get cravings for it, but my memories of chocolate were . . . well, not as good as this.

I vaguely wondered why he hadn't been able to stop himself this time, unlike last night, when I'd begged him to bite me and he'd managed to put the brakes on just in time.

But last night he hadn't tasted my blood first. This time he had, if only a couple of drops—his fangs had been sharper than normal or this never would have happened. He was still hungry from last night. Hungry for me.

He began tearing at my clothes as he drank from me. But no . . . no, I realized through my current fog that he wasn't frantically attempting to remove my clothes and make love to me on his desk, he was trying to hold on to me while Butch was wrenching him off my body.

Thierry was strong, but Butch had leverage. I felt my blouse rip and a few buttons popped right off, and then Thierry was on his feet halfway across the room, his eyes black, the back of his hand held up against his mouth.

"I didn't want to interrupt." Butch sounded embarrassed. "But I think it's a good thing I did."

I touched my neck where I'd been bitten and blinked up at them.

I watched Thierry slowly come to the realization of what he'd just done. Pain and grief filled his expression.

"Sarah," he managed. "No, not again. I'm sorry. Dammit . . . I . . ."

"Forget it." I stood up from the desk and, still in my mental fog, walked toward him, threw my arms around him and kissed him hard on his mouth. I could taste my own blood on his lips.

Butch grabbed my blouse, succeeding in tearing it even more. I spun around to face him.

"Your eyes—" He looked worried. "Sarah, just calm

down. We're going to find help. There's something seriously wrong with you."

"You really think so?" I heard myself say. Then I grabbed him by his black T-shirt and threw him across the room. His head hit the wall hard and he slid down to the ground unconscious.

Chapter 11

As soon as I saw that I'd effortlessly knocked out a three-hundred-pound bodyguard, I snapped out of my monster-madness daze.

Thierry immediately went over to Butch to make sure I hadn't killed him. Luckily, he was just knocked out. I was shaking. I could tell by Thierry's expression as he looked up at me that he could see my distress and wanted to comfort me in some way, but we'd finally learned our lesson the hard way. No more physical contact until we'd figured this mess out.

He was about to say something and I held up my hand.

"Don't apologize again," I said shakily. "I'm the one who should."

"Sarah—"

"Please . . . just take Butch out of here. I need to be alone. In fact, I think it's safer for everyone involved if I stay in here until further notice."

He pulled Butch up to his feet. "I will get him some water. He'll be fine."

I nodded and moved safely behind the desk. Thierry

glanced at me again over his shoulder as he left the office.

"It will all be all right," he said.

"I still believe it," I told him as firmly as I could.

And I did. I believed that everything would be okay. What choice did I have?

He left. His eyes had already returned to normal. I had a funny feeling that mine hadn't, and a quick look in my shard pulled out of my purse confirmed it. Black as midnight and scary as hell. I still felt fuzzy around the edges. I touched the fresh fang marks on my throat and flinched.

I blinked and felt tears splash to my cheeks. This was so wrong. Everything about this was wrong. Damn curse. Damn that Stacy. And damn me for making her hate me enough to want to make my life a living hell.

I tried to find the positive in the situation, but the glass remained half empty.

A few minutes later no one had come to check on me—not that I blamed them—and the private phone line in Thierry's office began to ring. For lack of anything better to do, I reached over to pick it up.

"Haven," I said blandly.

"This is Veronique, who is this?"

I sat up straighter in the chair. "Veronique . . . it's . . . it's Sarah."

"Ah, Sarah, very good. I need to speak to my husband. It's rather urgent and he's not answering his cell phone."

Veronique had left Toronto a few weeks ago to head back to her home in France. She'd called a few times since and never seemed to recognize my voice. I tried not to take it too personally.

"He's occupied at the moment. Can I get him to call you back?"

She sighed and it sounded annoyed. "Occupied. Did he ask you to say that? Is he attempting to avoid me, for some strange reason?"

"Not that I'm aware of. Listen, I'll tell him that you called and he'll get back to you as soon as he can, okay?"

"No, it is not okay."

"What's the problem?"

"The problem . . ." She breathed out the words in her barely noticeable French accent. "Is that I have received paperwork from my husband that disturbs me greatly."

"What kind of paperwork?"

There was a long silence. "He has initiated an annulment of our marriage that he wishes for me to sign."

My mouth went dry. "Oh?" I tried to sound surprised. "An annulment, you say? How very odd and unexpected."

"I don't know what could have prompted this action. A Vatican vampire delivered the papers by hand only moments ago. He'd flown from Rome for this express purpose."

Vatican vampire?

"Well," I began cautiously. "Maybe Thierry wants you to have your freedom. I mean, you two don't live together, you don't spend any time together, for how long now? More than a hundred years?"

"What does that have to do with anything?"

"I'm just thinking that maybe this is something that has been in the works for a while."

There was a pause, and then, "Do you know what he states as the reason our marriage should be annulled?"

I twisted a finger into my hair and tried to will myself to relax. "No idea."

"That I had no intention of staying true to my vows of fidelity when we married."

I waited. "And?"

"And what?"

"Are you trying to tell me that you've been faithful to him for six hundred years?"

She cleared her throat. "That is a little personal, my dear. He also goes on to say that he has reason to believe I was already married when we were wed."

My eyebrows went up at that. "Were you?"

She cleared her throat again. "You know, it was a very long time ago. Certain details are, of course, a tad obscured by time."

"Why are you getting so bent out of shape about this? Your marriage is in name only, isn't it? That's assuming you weren't already married to . . . what was the dude's name you were head-over-fangs for back in the day . . . Marcellus?"

She sniffed. "Yes, my true love, Marcellus. I still think of him every day."

"Were you married to him before you met Thierry?"

"It doesn't matter anymore."

"Sure it does." I felt a hot line of anger beginning to snake through me. This woman, while beautiful and intimidating and ancient, was annoying as all hell. And considering who she was and how completely she screwed up my love life by her very existence, I actually didn't dislike her. Annoyance. That was all. But annoyance wasn't hate.

"I loved Marcellus with every fiber of my being. He was my soulmate."

I cleared my throat. "And what about Thierry?"

"Pardonnez-moi?"

"What was Thierry to you? I mean, you did get hitched, after all, whether or not it was actually 100 percent legit."

"Things were different then, my dear."

"Were you in love with him?" My voice rose a level in volume.

"I don't believe that I remember you being like this before," she said. "You are normally so calm, collected, and polite. Barely noticeable, really. Is there trouble?"

I leaned back in the leather chair and sighed. "You could say that."

"Is there anything I can do to be of assistance?"

"Yes, actually, there is."

"What, my dear?" she asked. "You are one of my truest friends and I would certainly do anything in my power to make your life happier."

"Sign the papers."

"Pardon me?"

My grip on the phone increased. "I said, sign the papers. The annulment papers? In front of you? Sign them. You don't love Thierry and he doesn't love you. You don't even mind that he and I are together, which, let's face it, is not normal loving-wife behavior. Your marriage is a sham and I get the feeling it's been pretty much over ever since the plague-infested honeymoon. There really isn't any problem here. Keep the last name if that's what you want. Just sign the papers and set him free."

There was silence for a moment. "Free to be with you, you mean."

"That's right."

"So you did know about this little matter after all."

"I may have heard about it."

"Was it your idea?"

"No."

"I don't believe you."

I sighed heavily. "Believe what you want, Veronique. I'm sorry that the idea he wants a clean break after all this time hurt you, and I'm sorry if I'm sounding a bit bitchy, but I've just recently been cursed to act like a walking vampire cliché who can't go out during the day in case I get burnt to a crisp, so I guess my mood could be a little better."

"A curse?" Her tone turned curious. "Tell me more."

And I did.

"It sounds as if you are behaving like a nightwalker," she said after I finished telling her about my side-effects.

I felt cold at that. "Yeah, I know. Thierry hasn't completely confirmed that's what I am now, but I'm thinking he's just trying to protect me. Do you think that's what this sounds like?"

"I don't know for certain." Her words were clipped. "All I can say is to be careful, my dear. Be very careful until the curse is broken."

"Can you tell me more about these nightwalkers?"

"I do not wish to discuss more unpleasantries. I must go now."

"Wait . . . are you going to sign the papers?" I asked.

"No, I don't think that I will."

My knuckles were white on the phone. "Why not?"

"I will need to give it some thought."

"What thought? You don't love him. You don't want to be with him."

"Marriage has very little to do with love, my dear. I have tolerated your relationship with my husband only because I felt that it was a minor distraction that had no future. But this is the first time I have been presented with such nonsense as the end of our marriage because of some silly, inconsequential girl. Now, please have my *husband*"—she enunciated the word—"call me at his earliest convenience."

She hung up.

I glared at the phone after slamming it back in the receiver. If she had been here I would probably have bitten her. Hard. And that wasn't exactly an empty threat anymore.

Why did everything have to be so complicated? Couldn't I have what I wanted in life? Just once? Just one time without any gauntlets to run through first?

No, I didn't think so.

So now what? I stared at the phone that I'd decided was the cause of all my problems. Stupid phone. What now?

The phone rang again.

Damn evil phone!

I picked it up and held it to my ear. "What?"

"Is that any way to answer the telephone?"

I frowned. "Who is this?"

"You *still* don't recognize me?"

My eyes narrowed. "Stacy. Good to hear from you. How's it going?"

"You won't even give me the courtesy of sounding surprised that I managed to find out where you are and get the phone number? You think this shit is easy?"

"Save it. I'm not in the mood."

She tsked her tongue. "You can catch more flies with honey than vinegar. Let's get right to it. I want for us to meet. And I insist that you don't bring your boyfriend or your large hulking bodyguard along or I may get very angry with you."

Not that Butch probably would come twenty feet near me at the moment.

I let out a long breath and rubbed my temples with one hand. "Look, Stacy, I've been thinking a lot about high school. And what you've done to me is horrible, but I'm starting to understand it."

"You're ready to apologize to me? An actual, sincere apology this time?"

"Yeah. Definitely. I'm s—"

"No," she cut me off. "Not over the phone. I want you to apologize to my face."

My jaw tightened. "Is that really necessary?"

"Why, are you afraid of me?"

You should be the one who's afraid, I thought darkly, and I knew right then that I wasn't afraid of this messed-up bitch in the slightest. Annoyed and pissed off, yeah. But not afraid.

"Of course I'm afraid," I said instead. "I'd be stupid if I wasn't. You've obviously got a lot of power at your fingertips. I'll never watch reruns of *Bewitched* with the lights off again."

"I promise not to use my magic against you tonight," she said.

"And I'd believe you because?"

"Because you have no other choice, do you? Tell me, is your boyfriend still alive?"

"Yes," I hissed. "Of course he is."

"Hmm, I would have thought that the two of you would have torn each other's throats out by now. Your restraint, or his, is quite admirable. Especially given his past."

"What the hell do you know about him?"

She laughed softly. "Only that he is a man of many secrets. I'd love to tell you one of his best-kept secrets, Sarah. After your humble apology, and perhaps some groveling."

Before I opened my mouth to tell her to go to hell, she continued. "The park across from your little vampire bar. Ten minutes."

She hung up.

I didn't like that she knew where I was. She seemed to know a lot of my business and it made me extremely uncomfortable.

Ten minutes. Okay. I stood up and clutched the side of the desk. I actually wasn't scared, which was a new sensation for me. I think Veronique's phone call had infused me with some seething unpleasantness that was giving me the equivalent of what used to be liquid courage. No liquor. Wouldn't work on me anymore. Seething unpleasantness was now my drink of choice.

I felt no fear. My paranoia had decided to take the night off. Maybe it was the curse making me feel over-confident, but I was ready to kick some skinny-witch butt.

I'd go meet her. I'd apologize. She'd break the curse. Everybody would be happy and dance and sing. It made sense. After all, she wasn't a serial killer, she was a witch with a grudge. She had something I wanted and I had something she wanted. Magic words on both sides—an apology and a few Latin phrases tossed out and all of this nastiness would be over. I might even stay up to watch the sun rise as part of my curse-free celebration along with all the dancing and singing.

I couldn't go out the main doors because Thierry would be there and he'd have a ton of questions. I knew he wouldn't want me to go and meet her, but this was my window of opportunity. Besides, anyone who messed with me tonight was in for a rude awakening. I'd just thrown a three-hundred-pound bodyguard across the room. A bleached-blond, big-boobed witch would be no problem.

I swung the door to Thierry's office open.

I heard an "Ow" and I smelled smoke.

Behind the door was George, rubbing his nose with one hand and holding a cigarette in the other.

I eyed the burning tobacco. "I thought you quit."

He shrugged. "It's been a stressful day."

"What are you doing here?"

"Keeping an eye on you, even though I haven't seen the Red Devil since yesterday. I'm guarding the door."

"Thierry will kick your ass if he sees you smoking in here."

He dropped the cigarette and ground it into the hard-wood floor. "Gone."

"So am I." I walked past him headed for the back door. My coat was out front, but since the weather didn't bother me much anymore I didn't really need it. This wasn't going to take long.

He grabbed my shoulder. "Hold on there, you vicious little vixen. Where do you think you're going?" His eyes widened when I told him. "And you're just leaving? Just like that? Without even telling Thierry?" His gaze flicked to my neck and then down at my half-torn blouse and my black bra underneath. "Look at you, all *Rocky Horror Picture Ho.*"

"I'm getting this curse broken, and this is how I have to do it. You can come if you want. It won't take long."

I heard footsteps. Somebody was coming along the hallway, possibly to use the bathroom or possibly to check up on me. I grabbed George's arm and pulled him along with me to the back door, opened it, and let it swing shut behind us.

"You didn't even wait for my answer," he said, rubbing his arm. "Damn, you're getting a bit pushy, aren't you?"

Everything that had happened began to rush over me in a flood of emotion and my bottom lip wobbled. "I'm sorry. Really, George, I'm sorry for everything."

"Hey, don't cry. It's going to be okay."

"That's what everyone keeps telling me. But . . . but it's not. Not if I don't meet with Stacy and apologize to her. And even then . . ." I swallowed hard. "I don't know. Just as things are going really great with Thierry this had to happen and now if he touches me we want to bite each other and stupid Veronique won't agree to the annulment. Nothing ever seems to go right for me."

He put his arm around me and gave me a side hug. "Nothing ever goes right for you? Well, you met me, didn't you? Obviously after that windfall, fate had to give you a few hard knocks."

That made me smile a little. "Of course. What was I thinking? That must be it."

"And how bad can life be? You're gorgeous. You know amazing people, me at the top of the list, of course. Your fangs are definitely the cutest I've ever seen, and since

I now know them practically in the biblical sense I feel that I can say that in all honesty. And even though he's extremely moody, you have a boyfriend who is beyond crazy for you."

I blinked. "You really think so?"

"Crazy. Beyond. You obviously have a talent for making people crazy, Sarah. It's a gift. Don't deny it."

I laughed. "Great."

He nodded. "Now let's go. Another moment of being all snark-free and complimentary like this and I might toss my cookies. It's so unnatural."

And so we went.

A park at night. A witch with a grudge. A desperate, bloodthirsty, cursed vampire and her trusty sarcastic, nicotine-addicted sidekick.

No problemo.

Interlude

Thierry knew it was a trap, but he went anyhow. He had no choice.

He watched from the shadows.

A nightwalker had managed to lure Veronique to an abandoned house in London's East End with romantic promises. Even Thierry was surprised, despite his wife's weakness for handsome men who showed her the slightest attention, that she had been so naïve as to be led there near the docks—an exceedingly poor and disgusting neighborhood.

It was true that the nightwalker in question didn't show any outward signs of what he was. Despite his never going out during the day, he seemed quite normal indeed. A handsome, well-dressed man of means at first glance.

A nightwalker who had murdered scores of women—all of whom were vampires. He was a tool of the hunters who were trying out nightwalkers as secret weapons.

Only Thierry knew this. He also knew that the hunters had recently decided it was a very bad idea.

Nightwalkers couldn't be controlled. To trust one would be a deadly mistake.

Thierry also knew that the rookery where Veronique was being held was being watched by three hunters. They were to wait until the nightwalker had killed Veronique—a vampiress they considered highly dangerous—and then they would slay the nightwalker himself.

He and Veronique hadn't spoken in months. She'd left him to go to London and play among the rich and fanged citizens, having a string of affairs with men a fraction her age.

Thierry kept waiting to feel jealousy or anger at his wife's decisions, but he felt nothing at all. This disturbed him. He should mind that his wife was unfaithful, shouldn't he? But he didn't seem to care.

Sometimes, late at night, he would stare up at the ceiling and worry that he had no heart. That there was nothing in him that was human anymore. Perhaps the human part of him had died in the plague, now nearing five hundred years ago. It was a long time. It had felt like a long time.

He shook his head. It was no time for dark thoughts. They smacked of weakness.

He slid the mask of the Red Devil in place over his face and slipped into the building.

The nightwalker had already bitten Veronique. The marks on her neck had healed remarkably well, but were still visible. He'd watched from the shadows outside as the monster had swept her hair off her throat and bent to taste her. To begin with, she had welcomed his bite, but it had been obvious that her lust had quickly turned to fear. When she pushed at him he had struck her so hard it had knocked her unconscious. He had tied her up and left her in the room alone. When the nightwalker returned, he would finish her.

She moved when Thierry began to loosen her bindings, and she turned her beautiful face to him, her eyes widening.

"You are . . . you are the Red Devil," she whispered.

"Yes."

"And you've come to rescue me?"

The mask felt warm. He hated wearing it for too long. "Yes."

When the ropes were loose he helped her to her feet. She threw her arms around him and hugged him tightly.

"How can I ever thank you?"

He pulled away and looked down at her. "There's no need for that."

She stared at him. The mask covered most of his face, but his mouth and eyes were visible. He waited to see if she would recognize him. He almost wanted her to find out his secret, but there was no flicker of recognition. The woman he had known for almost five centuries gave no hint that she knew who he truly was.

Then again, she thought her husband a coward who would hide from danger. It would never occur to her that he was capable of knowing, let alone *being*, the Red Devil himself.

No one knew. Not one soul.

"Come with me." He took her hand and led her to the open window.

There was a crash. The nightwalker had returned,

his eyes black as pitch, his lips curled back from his fangs. Without a word of warning, he attacked, and Thierry fought back, keeping Veronique behind him for protection.

And then, suddenly, the hunters burst into the room and there was chaos. The nightwalker turned on them and attacked. Thierry was able to jump out of the window with Veronique, and they ran for three blocks through the dirty and crowded London streets.

"Go," Thierry said. "You're safe."

Veronique threw her arms around him and pressed her half-dressed body tightly against his. "You are as remarkable a man as I have heard."

He didn't quite know how to answer that. He didn't feel so remarkable.

She drew his mouth to hers and kissed him, before leaning back and touching her fingers to her lips.

She must recognize me now, he thought.

She smiled wickedly. "A kiss from the devil himself. It is something I could get very used to."

"You must leave."

"I want to know who you are beneath the mask." She slid her elegant hand down his chest. "And I will show you how grateful I am for your rescue."

He leaned closer. "You don't know who I am?"

She looked confused. "No. Please tell me. I want you. I want to be with you. We should be lovers."

He ignored that and pulled her along with him until they were clear of the worst of the seedy neighborhood.

"Good night, Veronique," he said, and turned away from her.

"No, wait! Please! How do you know my name?"

But he was gone and he didn't look back. After he slipped behind the next building he removed his red mask.

"Sir?" an old gnarled woman croaked at him. "A fortune for you? A glimpse at the future?"

"I am not interested in fortunes."

He attempted to brush past her but she grasped his hand in her dry one.

"Ah." A smile fanned dozens of wrinkles out from her faded eyes. "A vampire."

"How . . . ?" He frowned. "How did you know that?"

"Shh. I will tell you your fortune for free." She stared down into his palm. He watched her cautiously. "I see a very long life, but since you are a vampire I suppose that is to be expected." Her finger traced a line on his skin. "Much danger."

He eyed her warily.

"Ah, and I see romance. A deep and abiding love that shall change your life forever."

He laughed out loud at that. He'd given the old woman the benefit of the doubt after she'd guessed him a vampire, but now she was simply wasting his time. "I have never been in love. And I never will be."

"No," she agreed. "Not now. Not for a very long time. But there will be someone, someday, who shall enter your life and wipe away the cobwebs that have grown over your soul. She shall be the light to your darkness. Despite your many differences, she shall be the one for you and you will fight for her."

"I don't fight for love. It isn't worth it."

She smiled at him and patted his hand. "You will fight. She shall find you when you least expect it, she will see who you truly are behind all the masks you hide behind, and she will change everything for you."

He raised an eyebrow, slightly bemused with the old witch. He reached into his coat pocket and drew out a few coins that he pressed into her hand. "I don't believe in fairy tales, old woman, but thank you for your amusing fortune."

He started to walk away, to disappear into the crowd, into the night.

"You don't have to believe," she called after him. "Perhaps the fairy tales shall believe in you."

Rubbish, he thought. Then he promptly put her words out of his mind, despite the ache in his chest that made him wish he could believe.

Chapter 12

The small snow-covered park across the street from the alleyway Haven was located in seemed at first glance to be deserted. But then I saw her. Standing in dead center, with her arms crossed and a less-than-friendly expression on her face. Her bleached-blond hair contrasted with her blood-red winter coat.

She was all alone. I scanned the immediate area. As far as I could see it was only the three of us.

"Sarah," she said sternly. "I thought I said no bodyguards."

"He's not a bodyguard." I shrugged. "George is just here for moral support."

Her smile widened. "I didn't think he looked all that tough."

"Hey," George protested. "You said she was mean and nasty. You didn't say anything about her being rude."

Stacy walked toward us. "Beautiful night, isn't it?"

"Divine. Let's cut the small talk, though."

She studied me for a moment. "You're ready to apologize?"

"Yes."

She smiled. "Then make it a good one."

I took a deep breath and swallowed my ill feelings. Okay. She deserved this. She did.

"Upon reflection of certain days at high school," I began, "I do remember why you might not like me so much."

"Not *like* you?" she said. "That's a bit of an understatement, isn't it?"

I forced a smile and glanced over at George. He'd lit up another cigarette. "Right. Well, I know that I treated you with disrespect. Everyone can't be flowers and sunshine every day of their lives. There are things like PMS and/or fights with boyfriends, etcetera, that might contribute to someone acting uncharacteristically unpleasant."

"Oh, that was uncharacteristic?"

"It was ten years ago."

"So?"

A wind picked up and blew some of the snow that had gathered on the tree branches at me. It felt cold and wet against my face and I wiped it away. "You unfortunately saw a bad side of me for a couple of minutes one day. I had lots of friends. They would all vouch that I was a really nice person. But I know I was mean to you, and then I went out with what's-his-name to the prom—"

"Jonathan," she snapped. "His name was Jonathan."

"Right, *Jonathan*. High school is bad enough without any extra trauma. I know that. I am so, so sorry if I hurt your feelings."

She snorted.

I raised my eyebrows. "What?"

"That was your apology?"

"It was."

She slapped me, leaving behind a painful sting on the left side of my face. I looked at her, too stunned to be angry.

George took a step closer. "Slap Sarah again, you bitch, and I'm going to blow smoke in your face."

She waved a hand in George's direction and he froze in place and his eyes shut. His cigarette fell to the ground.

I blinked. "What did you do?"

Stacy glared at me. "Your moral support was getting in the way. Don't worry, he'll be fine, but this is a conversation between the two of us, Sarah, and I want it to stay that way."

I curled my hands into fists at my sides, willing myself to stay calm. My left cheek burned from the slap. "I apologized to you. What do you want from me now? I haven't done anything wrong."

She shook her head and took a moment to brush the blowing snow off her red coat. "Isn't it funny how everyone has a completely different view of themselves? How everyone is the hero of their own story and other people are the villains?"

"I'm not a villain."

"You're a vampire."

"Vampires are not villains." *God, how many times did I have to explain this to people?* "We're just like humans only we have a few more issues to deal with. It's the choices we make that make us good or bad. I'd think that somebody who calls herself a witch would understand that. I'm not seeing any green skin, warts, and broomsticks around."

"No, no broomsticks," she said evenly. "But I did bring one of these along."

She pulled a long, sharp wooden stake from the inside of her coat.

My mouth went dry and my heart began to pound hard against my rib cage. Just the sight of the stake was enough to give me an immediate anxiety attack. The last time I'd seen one had been when it was yanked out of my chest.

"It's funny how just the memory of a major trauma can bring it back as if it only just happened," Stacy said, and her smile was back. It made me think that somehow she knew about what had happened to me. My attention didn't leave the piece of sharpened wood for a moment. "Memories are triggered by many things. A smell, a taste. Our senses are amazing for total recall. It's as if we're right back when the bad thing happened. We can live it again and again and again." She moved the stake back and forth between her hands.

"Just put that away," I said shakily.

"Why? Do I seem threatening? I'm just holding it. I'm not trying to do anything with it, am I?"

I had dealt with my stake issues. I had. It was an unpleasant memory, as she'd just said, but I'd gotten over it. Only . . . only I hadn't. Maybe I wasn't dealing with what had happened to me as well as I thought I had. The stake itself wasn't doing me any harm. But I knew what it felt like to be staked. To come as close to being dead as I'd ever come before.

Being staked had been the most terrifying experience of my life.

"I said I was sorry," I said. "What more do you want from me?"

"That's a very good question. Well, I suppose we can start by you telling me what it's like to be one of the bad guys."

"I'm not one of the bad guys!"

Her cold smile widened. "There is so much you don't know, Sarah, and your boyfriend hasn't even begun to fill you in on the subject. But I guess he's too busy trying to drink your tasty blood, isn't he? I suppose it's only a matter of time before he finally goes completely off the wagon and tears out your throat before you can do the same to him. I've heard he has a bit of a problem keeping his fangs to himself when he's around certain women."

My eyes narrowed and I got my breath back when she invoked Thierry's name.

"Don't you dare mention him. I don't know how you know what you do, but my life and his are none of your damn business."

"I mentioned nightwalkers to you before. Have you learned anything about them?"

My attention was still focused on that stake. "Mostly that they no longer exist."

"Nightwalkers couldn't stand sunlight, they thirsted for blood from humans with warm flesh and beating hearts. They were repelled by crosses and holy water. And yes, they were wiped out." The light on the lamppost above us flickered. "As a matter of fact, Thierry is the one who worked side by side with the hunters to get rid of them all, or most of them. From what I've learned, he was the head of some vampire faction."

It felt colder in the park all of a sudden. Thierry

was the vampire who created the Ring—the vampire council—originally, but he'd walked away from his leadership role a hundred years ago. "I don't believe anything you say."

"He felt that these nightwalkers were dangerous to vampire and human alike, so being the brave and noble man he was, he secretly met with the leaders of the hunters to give them information that would help to off all those nasty vamps. Maybe he was right to do that. Maybe it was for the best. But if you ask me, it kind of smacks of genocide, don't you think? Part of his bargain was for them to leave the other vamps alone, but hunters aren't exactly good at keeping bargains, are they?"

I crossed my arms. Even though the temperature didn't majorly affect me anymore, I suddenly felt chilled right through to the bone. "If what you're telling me about these nightwalkers is true, then it would be like getting rid of a bunch of cockroaches. No big loss to the world. I don't think Thierry did the wrong thing at all."

She shook her head. "I figured that you would try to defend his actions. God, you trust so easily, don't you? Considering the well-known fact that he can't control his own monster when he's around you, it's a bit like him throwing stones from his glass coffin with what he did to the nightwalkers, don't you think?"

I glared at her. "You cursed me to be a nightwalker."

She nodded. "And I'm so thrilled with how well it turned out. I'm surprised Thierry can even come near you, let alone want to bite you. He devoted years to wiping things like you off the planet."

"I held up my end of the bargain. You've had your fun. Break the curse." I heard the desperation in my voice and

I didn't like it at all. I wiped away more cold, stinging snow from my face.

She frowned. "Who said anything about a bargain?"

I breathed out a long, steady breath. The thrall. Of course. I'd use the thrall on her to get her to do what I wanted.

I narrowed my eyes. "Remove the curse right now, Stacy."

"No."

I blinked. "Remove it."

"I don't think so. Oh, and if you're trying to use mind control on me, it won't work. I put the curse on you. You can't use any part of the curse to affect me. Them's the rules."

Dammit.

I blinked back tears of frustration. "Look, I know you had a lousy few years at high school, but so did a lot of people. Life hasn't exactly been a daily party for me either, you know. But we get by, we try to forget, and we move on."

"Is that what you're saying I should do? Move on?"

"Yes, that's exactly what I'm saying."

"And maybe we can be friends? Put the past behind us?" It sounded like she was mocking me.

"The fact that you've devoted all these years to hating my guts makes me think that a strong friendship probably isn't in our future."

She laughed, and it sounded cold. "Do you think you're the only one on my shit list, Sarah?"

"What?" I quickly glanced over my shoulder to see that George was still standing in place, now covered from head to toe in a fine layer of snow.

"I have a list of names of people who have done me

wrong, and you're way down at the bottom. I've finally come around to you, but it did give me time to do some research. The timing of the reunion was a coincidence. And the fact that you were already a vampire only made it more interesting."

"There's a *list*?"

"Some of the others didn't apologize at all. Jonathan . . . he didn't understand why I was so pissed at him right up until he took his last breath." She shook her head. "He was clueless. Totally clueless. In hindsight I think it's probably a good idea that we never hooked up."

I stifled a gasp at that. "You killed him?"

She looked appalled. "No, of course not. I'm not a murderer."

I let out a deep breath. "Well, that's good."

"I'm not a murderer because I don't have to be. I curse people and I'm very good at it. However, the curses usually end in death for the people on my list. Oh, well."

"What did you do to him?" I asked tightly.

Her eyes narrowed. "He liked to cheat on his wife. I watched him. Just like he took you to the prom when he should have taken me. He should have been faithful to *me*. I cursed him that every time he did something wrong he'd be caught. And one day when he was with his mistress, her husband came home with a gun." She shrugged. "He definitely got a lot of bang for his buck, if you know what I'm saying."

"How . . . how many have there been?"

She glanced up at the overcast night sky. "You're lucky number seven. And the only one still breathing, although as a nightwalker I'm not entirely sure you need to breathe anymore."

"Please break the curse." I hated how weak my voice sounded, but I felt it now. Weak and tired and I wanted this to be over. "I can't live like this."

"That's kind of the point." She cocked her head to the side and studied me. "You're being sincere now, I can tell. Maybe I will cut you some slack. After all, you were only a bitch to me a couple of times."

"So you'll break it?"

"I haven't decided yet. But I'll tell you this much. If I don't, it will be permanent after three days have passed. It's only been one day. You have two left, if you can make it that long. And a word to the wise, the symptoms get worse the longer you have it." She grinned, and her amusement at my distress made me furious all of a sudden.

I took a step toward her and bared my fangs at her.

She held up the stake. "Oh, and if you're thinking of hurting me, just remember that if I die, the curse is permanent and you can sell all of your designer sunglasses on eBay since you won't be needing them anymore. So no funny business. Maybe I'll be in touch tomorrow. Or maybe not. I'll have to see how I feel. Or if you and your boyfriend live that long."

"Don't you dare hurt Thierry."

"Me hurt him? I wouldn't dream of it. I was thinking that you might kill him. Or maybe a hunter might finally plunge a stake into that dusty old chest of his."

My jaw clenched. "I guess you don't have all the information going around, because there are no hunters in Toronto right now. They're all at Gideon Chase's funeral."

"Some of them are, sure." Two shadowy figures approached her from the other side of the park. As they got to her she handed one of them her stake. "But not all of them. Good night, Sarah."

She turned and walked out of the park without another glance over her shoulder.

I heard George gasp from behind me as he was released from his freeze spell.

"Did I miss anything?" he asked, then looked at the approaching hunters and shrieked.

The hunters were all dressed in black—big scary-looking guys wearing leather dusters. They looked like your average, everyday, deadly hunter types.

"Hi there," one of them said. "You're the vampire, right?"

"Sarah," George managed, clutching at my arm. "We need to run. Need I remind you . . . no bodyguard? Hello?"

My emotions had been riding a roller-coaster all night. Highs and lows and everything in between. And now, after everything else that had happened, to be faced with two freaking hunters?

"Now, just hold still, vampire, and we'll make this a quick one." They both took a step closer.

I looked at them. "I bet you say that to all the girls."

There was a definite tone to my words and it wasn't fear. I was too pissed off to be afraid of these meatheads. These stupid, brainless *human* hunters. I felt the fog begin to move over me and the last thing I was thinking was to be afraid. They were the ones who should be afraid.

"Drop the stake," I said.

The one on the right did as I commanded. He frowned. "What the hell?"

I made eye contact with the other one. "You, too."

The stake hit the ground.

The *thrall*. The thrall was good. It was one thing I might like to keep.

I felt a strange warmth and confidence swelling inside me as I walked toward the men.

"Sarah, what the hell are you doing?" George breathed from behind me.

I looked over my shoulder. "Go back to the club, George. I'll be okay."

"I'm not leaving you."

"That's sweet, but I'm going to have to insist." When he didn't make a move, I raised my voice. "*Now*. Please leave."

"I'll go get Thierry." With a last fearful look, he turned and ran out of the park.

I looked at the hunters again, and I put a hand on each of their chests to feel how quickly their hearts were beating.

"Her eyes," one said shakily.

"Are they black?" I asked. "Yeah, they do that lately. Luckily, since I don't have a reflection, it's not really bothering me too much. Now, if I may ask the question again, what am I going to do with you two bad boys?"

They eyed each other. "Well, you could let us go."

"Or you could kill them," another voice said over my shoulder.

I raised an eyebrow but didn't turn around. "Long time no see."

The Red Devil came to my side. "I've been watching."

"Enjoying the show?"

"Actually, yes. I had heard that you were the Slayer

of Slayers, but to see it with my own eyes is something I never expected."

One of the hunters whimpered. "The Slayer of Slayers? You?"

The other hunter whimpered. "We should have gone to Vegas!"

The Red Devil turned his scarf-covered face to the men. "Why are you in town? I was under the impression that all hunters were south for your leader's funeral."

"Not all of us are," one said. "A lot of us are glad he's dead."

"He was really bossy," the other added.

"Shut up," I said. And they shut up.

I could so get used to this if I had to.

Just the thought made me grimace. I didn't want to have to get used to this.

"Kill them," the Red Devil said. "They would have killed you without any conscience. The least you can do is return the favor."

I frowned at that. Kill them? I knew I was acting all nightwalker at the moment, but I had no intention of killing anybody. Not even a hunter.

"I don't think so," I said.

"No?" Red said. "But you're the Slayer of Slayers. You slay slayers. Isn't that right?"

I clenched my fists tightly and looked at the hunters. "The two of you, listen to me. I want you to turn around and leave this park. And don't look back or I'm going to do very bad things to you. And I don't mean that as a come-on."

They both nodded and had that glazed look that I

noticed was a trademark of my new thralltastic mind-control ability.

But they didn't move.

I frowned. "Turn and leave. Right now."

One of them finally did. With a glazed expression, he turned and ran out of the park without waiting for his friend. But the friend continued to stand there. His face was tense and strained as if he were lifting some heavy weights.

"He's attempting to resist," Red said. "Some humans are resistant to vampire control. The weaker the mind the easier it is."

"So this one doesn't have a weak mind?" I said, and turned to look at Red. "I find that hard to believe."

"Watch out."

The hunter had taken the opportunity to grab the stake off the ground and arc it in my direction, directly toward my almost completely healed chest wound.

I caught his arm but still felt the tip graze my skin.

"I'm going to kill you," he growled.

I glanced at Red.

He cocked his head to the side. "I think I'll simply observe from a safe distance."

"Great."

Although I had extra strength now, which was definitely helpful to hold him off a bit, the guy was a trained hunter. He twisted away from me and tried to come at me from a different direction.

"You're dead, Slayer of Slayers!" he bellowed.

He lunged at me. I curled my hand into a fist and punched him in the stomach hard enough to knock the wind out of him. He doubled over and tried to breathe. I snatched the stake out of his hand and with a kick to the face—not exactly kung fu but sufficient to knock him off balance—he landed hard on his back on the snowy ground.

I clutched the stake and glared down at him. Every nerve ending in my body felt as if it was sparking and crackling with energy.

"Please don't kill me!" the hunter begged.

I knelt and pressed the stake against the creep's chest hard enough to make him flinch. "Then I suggest you make like Michael Jackson and beat it. And don't even think about coming near me again. Got it?"

He nodded. I stood up again, and he scrambled to his feet and ran out of the park.

The Red Devil had his arms crossed. "Hmm."

I turned to glare at him. "Hmm, what?"

"I'm surprised that, given your reputation, you didn't end his life."

"Maybe I'm feeling generous tonight."

"Or maybe it's true that your reputation is only rumors and speculation."

"Or that." I blinked. "How are my eyes?"

He studied me for a moment. "Back to normal."

"Thanks for the help, by the way," I said dryly. "I thought you were supposed to be some vampire-hero guy."

"Didn't look like you needed any help." He surveyed the park. "The woman who was here before, she cursed you to be a nightwalker, is that true?"

I nodded and felt my throat tighten. "I have two days to convince her to end the curse or apparently I'm stuck like this."

"And would that be so bad?"

I looked at him, at the thin line of his face and eyes visible through the scarf. His gaze seemed to burn right into me. I wondered, not for the first time, what he looked like under that get-up. "Yeah, it's bad. I kind of like going out in the day. It's a habit of mine."

"There are ways around such inconveniences. But you've gained so much by this transition. Your strength is equal to that of a centuries-old vampire. Your mind control, if practiced, could be extremely useful."

"Can nightwalkers turn into bats?" I asked.

"I don't believe so."

"In that case, I just want to be normal."

He laughed at that and I looked at him sharply.

"Normal?" he said. "Why would you want to be normal? You have the world at your fingertips. You've been given a true gift, Sarah, and you wish to give it away so easily?"

"A gift? Curses aren't gifts."

"It depends how you look at it."

"No, I'm looking at it from the only vantage point I have. I was just getting used to being a regular run-of-the-mill vampire, and I'd convinced myself I wasn't a monster, and now I am one. I don't want to be this way."

And that was it in a nutshell. Even if I had to get rid of the thrall, I didn't want to be this way. It felt wrong on every level.

"This has to do with Thierry de Bennicoeur and his view of nightwalkers?" he asked.

I clenched my jaw so hard that it hurt. "You know, Thierry thinks you're an impostor up to no good. I shouldn't even be talking to you because he'll be pissed."

"I saved your life."

That deflated me a little bit but not much. "You did. And thank you for that. But I'm not accustomed to trusting easily lately, and when I do make that mistake it usually gets me a stake through my chest. I am learning, though. I don't know anything about you. I don't know who you are under that stupid scarf. Maybe if you show me I might be a little friendlier."

His eyes narrowed. "Sorry, I can't do that. At least, not yet."

"Then I think this conversation is over."

He studied me. His black scarf was turning white from the blowing snow. "Let me ask you this, Sarah . . . before this curse, is it true that you had consumed the blood of two master vampires?"

"Maybe." I eyed him cautiously. "What difference does it make?"

"Perhaps none." His gaze was steady on me. "And there have only been the two? Thierry and Nicolai? No others?"

"You're a master vampire, aren't you? I've heard you've been around ever since the Crusades. History wasn't one of my better subjects, but I think that makes you even older than Thierry. Maybe I'll bite *you*. Three is my lucky number."

"An interesting suggestion." His eyes crinkled at the sides to show he was smiling, which, since I hadn't really been kidding, was a little odd. "When the witch contacts you again, will you allow her to break the curse?"

"In a heartbeat."

The amusement left his eyes. "That is a mistake. Know this, Sarah. That when the nightwalkers roamed the earth

they were misguided in their actions, but they weren't
stupid. They longed for the sun and for control of their
darker natures. Near the end, they had objects created
to help them achieve that goal. Some of those objects
remain to this day, but to the uneducated observer are
unremarkable and undetectable."

"What kind of objects?"

"Typically it was jewelry. Rings, bracelets, and necklaces that the nightwalker would wear to enable them to
appear as a daywalker. As long as the object touched their
skin they were, as you say, normal." He paused and I felt
his gaze heavy on me. "If my information serves, and I
believe that it does, you have already come in contact
with such an object in the very recent past. This would
confirm for me how you seem to be blessed with great
luck and coincidence."

I blinked at him. "Seriously? What was it?"

He shook his head. "What do you care? After all,
you will have the witch break your curse at her earliest
convenience."

"Yeah, but I'm all for having a Plan B."

"Sarah!" Thierry called out from across the street.

Oh, crap.

I clutched the Red Devil's long leather coat before he
could walk away. "You have to tell me what the object is."

I was close enough to him now to sense something I
didn't expect at all. In fact, it was the last thing I would
have expected. Past his cologne, which I recognized
as Acqua di Gio, I smelled something else. Something
unmistakable.

My eyes widened as I moved my searching nose up

his neck and immediate hunger curled in my stomach. "You're human!"

"I'm not."

"Yes, you are! The Red Devil isn't supposed to be human. He's a vampire."

"You're wrong." He pulled away from me and his eyes narrowed.

"Who the hell are you?" I reached for his scarf but he pushed my hand away roughly.

"Don't touch me," he growled. Then he turned and walked briskly out of the park.

"Sarah, are you all right?" Thierry's words were harsh and filled with concern as he reached my side. He watched the Red Devil disappear into the shadows.

"I'm fine."

But I wasn't. Not even close.

I frowned so hard it hurt. What the hell was going on?

Interlude

Where is your wife?"

Thierry looked up from the Red Devil's journal where he'd been keeping notes on the assignment he'd just completed. His friend Nicolai's wife, Elizabeth, regarded him from the doorway of the small inn they currently called home.

"Veronique has returned to Paris," Thierry said.

"And Nicolai is in New York. My goodness. All this time on our hands and however shall we occupy ourselves?" She smiled at him and ran her hand suggestively down her side.

Elizabeth was a beautiful woman. Blond hair, red lips, a peaches-and-cream complexion. As a human she'd been an actress whose talent and fame were rivaled only by that of the great Sarah Bernhardt. Men from miles around would come to see her perform and lavish gifts, money, or their undying devotion on her.

Nicolai was one who could give her all three . . . and he added immortality to the list.

His friend was completely smitten by the gorgeous actress who had agreed to marry him and then immediately be sired as a vampire. Nicolai was obsessed, devoted, and truly in love with Elizabeth and believed she felt the same for him.

Elizabeth was an excellent actress.

Her attire that night was, in a word, scanty, and showed bare skin that would bring a flush to a modest woman's cheeks. Elizabeth was not modest. She knew what she wanted and was shameless in her pursuit of it.

Currently, she wanted Thierry.

The thought made him very uncomfortable.

His marriage to Veronique continued to be tolerable. She tended to stay in Europe for long periods, occasionally showing up and expecting him to fall at her feet, and he knew that she was vaguely annoyed when he didn't.

She'd recently left with the promise not to return after a particularly unpleasant exchange in which she'd accused him of hiding from the world and not participating in life enough. But that had been his cover for several centuries. No one would suspect that a handsome but passionless aristocrat was the Red Devil, who had developed even more of a bigger-than-life reputation since Marcellus had been the man behind the mask.

Though, as much as he worked, as many vampires as he was able to save, nothing seemed to change. He had hoped helping the hunters slay the nightwalkers would be enough to appease their need for something to kill, but now that the nightwalkers were no more, the hunters had taken up their stakes against vampires who walked during the day. It was a wearisome battle that seemed to have no end in sight.

But life was not only about work. There were *distractions.*

Elizabeth strolled deeper into the room. She had a habit of touching everything, running her fingertips over the tops of furniture or woodwork . . . or men who were not her husband.

"You keep to yourself too much," she told him, her red lips turning up at the sides. "It's not healthy, this solitary life you lead."

"I'm perfectly fine as I am."

"Nicolai asked you to take care of me when he was away." She pouted. "I don't feel very well taken care of."

He remained still as she came to sit on the edge of his desk. "What is it that you want, Elizabeth?"

"Isn't it obvious?" She raised an eyebrow. "I want you."

He couldn't help but laugh out loud at that. "You want me? I'm quite sure Nicolai would not approve of that statement."

"Nicolai doesn't have to know." Her expression turned slightly sour. She stood up from the desk and began pacing the room as if she were a caged animal. "I can't live like this. I feel imprisoned in this inn. I need to be on the stage again, I crave it."

"Nicolai wishes for you to be safe as you adjust to the life of a vampire."

"Safe." She spat the word out as if it were a curse. "Safety is for cowards. I want to feel the wind on my face. Hear the applause of the audience in my ears." She approached him again. "I want to feel the hands of a lover on my body."

He sighed. Despite her beauty, she did not appeal to him. He already had a beautiful woman in his life whom he felt little for.

Only his secret identity as the Red Devil gave him any sense of peace, and even that was waning. Women were confusing and manipulative creatures. There were times when he longed to have someone in his life who would make him feel alive after such an already long life, but he had long since given up hope that the fortune-teller so many years ago had been correct in her prediction that true love would find him.

He stood up. "Elizabeth—"

"What's this?" She snatched up the notebook in front of him.

"Give that to me."

She smiled. "Ah, something to finally capture your attention. Very interesting."

Before he could reach for it, she ran out of the room. He followed. Her bedroom door slammed shut and locked behind her.

He knocked. "Elizabeth, let me in."

"I'm reading. It will only be a moment."

He stifled the feelings of panic that swelled in his chest. *Stupid*, he chastised himself. *Stupid mistake. I let down my guard.*

He kicked the door open.

"It cannot be." She looked up at him, her eyes wide. "You . . . *you* are the Red Devil?"

"No."

"But it says it right here."

"You are mistaken." He came at her and took the journal away from her. "It would be in your best interest to forget everything you have just read."

He turned his back on her and went back to his room, silently fuming that he had been so careless. The job that evening had not gone as well as hoped. Hunters in the dozens had shown up at their compound. The vampires they had imprisoned there were long gone, since Thierry had freed them. But one hunter had gotten a glimpse of him, albeit a fleeting one while he wore his mask, and he had worried that he'd been followed back to the inn despite his best attempts to cover his tracks.

The evening had been tense, but now at just after midnight he might begin to feel more at ease if not for Elizabeth's prying eyes.

She followed him. "I won't tell a soul, Thierry."

"There is nothing to tell." The thought that she knew his secret ate at his gut like acid. She was an insipid, vain, and impossible woman. He tolerated her since she was married to his good friend, but that was as far as it went.

"The Red Devil," she said as she came closer. "I have always wished to meet him."

"Go to your room, Elizabeth."

"Although, don't you ever feel that all of the time you spend leading this double life could be used in other pursuits?"

"Other pursuits?"

"The Red Devil saves only whom he chooses. His actions are ultimately pointless. That is what he says."

"What who says?"

"Nicolai. He believes the Red Devil, well, *you*, would be better off fading away. He believes your existence draws the hunters' hatred and pursuit of vampires more than if you didn't exist at all."

His jaw tensed. "Nicolai is entitled to his opinion."

"If it were me," she said, "I would either want the glory of everyone knowing it was me or not bother doing it at all."

"Then that is what separates us."

"Have you considered quitting?"

He didn't reply, since any reply would be an admission that he was what she believed. The truth was that he had considered quitting. As she said, his work was largely misunderstood. There were those who thought him a hero and those, such as Nicolai, who thought him a problem that made the hunters even more vicious.

"I am tired," he said instead. "I wish to sleep."

"You're lonely."

"I grow weary of this discussion, Elizabeth. Please return to your room."

"I know what you desire."

He would take her back to her room, push her inside, and lock the door. He might consider letting her out tomorrow morning. Possibly not.

"I do not desire you, Elizabeth."

Her smile was steady on her face. "Perhaps not. But you desire something else. I know it."

He looked down to see that she had a knife in her hand that she slowly drew over her forearm. The blood welled red against her white skin.

His body reacted to it.

He cursed inwardly. He had not consumed blood for a great many years. Veronique had explained rather explicitly that those of their age should be careful with blood intake. They could now exist without it entirely. Veronique had no problem with this, but for him it had become an issue.

Elizabeth was right. He did desire blood. It was a hot ache that began in his chest and spread through his entire body—a need that refused to be ignored.

"Here." Elizabeth raised her arm toward him.

He pushed her away roughly. "Leave."

Her expression darkened. "Drink from me or I will tell your secret to everyone I know."

Hell hath no fury like a woman scorned.

His eyes narrowed. Why did she wish to bait him like this? Was she that bored? Did her love for Nicolai not exist when he was more than a hundred paces from her side?

Nicolai would be heartbroken to know the truth about his beloved wife.

"Taste me," Elizabeth demanded, her voice going from seductive to shrill.

He felt his fangs sharpen and elongate. His hungers were controllable, normally. But his emotions were high, and that did not help the situation.

He grabbed her arm and brought it to his lips, raising his eyes to meet hers. Her eyes closed with pleasure as he drew his tongue along the self-inflicted wound.

"Yes," she hissed.

The blood stirred a darkness inside Thierry that only took seconds to overtake him. He'd overestimated his control, especially after so long. He wanted more. Needed more. The desire overwhelmed him.

He broke the connection with a growl.

"See?" Elizabeth gave him a slow, amused smile. "Was that so bad?"

"No." He grabbed her shoulders. The look she gave him made him believe that she expected him to kiss her and perhaps carry her off to his bed, but that wasn't what he wanted from her.

He pushed the light-colored hair away from the side of her neck and sank his fangs in.

She gasped in pain.

He drank until he felt her small hands on his chest. She was attempting to push him away. Finally his senses began to come back and the world widened to include more than just the taste of her blood.

She held a hand up to her neck, her eyes wide with shock. It hadn't been as exciting as she'd expected. He saw fear in her eyes now. He'd taken too much.

He swallowed. "I'm . . . I'm sorry. It's been so long. I misjudged my control."

She blinked at him. "I will tell Nicolai. I'll tell him everything. That you are the Red Devil. That you attacked me. He'll kill you for this."

She turned away, but he grabbed her arm. He had to stop her—to convince her to say nothing. His secret couldn't be revealed. "Please, Elizabeth. Listen to me—"

She wrenched away from him, then turned and ran out of the room and down the stairs of the inn. Thierry thundered after her. She opened the front doors and ran out onto the street—

—Where there were five hunters waiting. Thierry halted his steps and watched in horror as they grabbed her, pulling back her lips to see her fangs.

"Our information was half right about this place, but it's a female not a male. She is one of the monsters."

The others roared their appreciation before a stake was plunged into the beautiful actress's heart. She hadn't even made a sound of protest. She'd already been weakened by loss of blood and was too stunned by the sight of the hunters to scream.

Thierry's knees gave out and he collapsed, shaking, to the ground.

It was his fault. The death of his friend's wife was on his hands.

All his fault.

He felt certain as he stared out at her body, lying in the middle of the street as the hunters departed, that he would never recover from this.

The Red Devil died that day as well.

Chapter 13

In the park, after the Red Devil had disappeared, Thierry grabbed my hand and practically dragged me back to Haven.

"We must talk," he said. He didn't sound happy.

We entered the club and I glanced at George, Amy, and Barry, who all took a step back from us as we passed them on the way to Thierry's office. Even the patrons in the club glanced up in our direction with wariness in their gazes. Butch sat at a table holding a wet cloth up to his head.

I was a jumble of emotions, but the slamming of the office door helped me snap back to the present. I looked up. Thierry's gaze was filled with anger.

"Why would you go out there all alone? After everything that has happened to you? You could have been killed."

I crossed my arms. "George was with me."

"You'll excuse me if that does not fill me with confidence." His expression slowly began to soften a little around the edges. "Sarah, why must you continually tempt fate?"

I blinked back tears. "I had to meet Stacy. I had no other choice."

"There are always other choices."

"She called and I met her to apologize. She's thinking about breaking the curse, but it doesn't sound all that positive."

He was silent for a moment. "I'm very sorry."

"She confirmed that the curse was to make me into a nightwalker."

His expression was grim. "Yes, I have suspected that for some time now."

I felt so frustrated that I wanted to scream. "Are you going to kill me if I don't get cured from this?"

"What are you talking about?"

"Stacy told me that there used to be a bunch of night-walkers and you helped the hunters kill them all. Is that the truth?" It sounded so horrible as I said it I almost wanted to take it back. Why would I believe anything that witch told me?

"You aren't truly a nightwalker," he said simply and quietly.

"I have the symptoms."

"It doesn't matter. You are currently cursed. That is all. It doesn't change you from who you were originally."

"So are you trying to say that she was lying about the nightwalkers?"

"The nightwalkers were indiscriminate killers," Thierry said. "Focused on feeding and violence. They were an unfortunate by-product of vampirism—a rare mutation of the vampire virus that fortunately no longer exists. There weren't that many with this affliction. A few hundred at the most."

"The Red Devil told me that they had objects to make them able to go out during the day."

"The Red Devil told you that, did he?" There was a borderline mocking tone to Thierry's words I didn't particularly care for. "Then it must be the truth. He seems very trustworthy for you to be meeting him in parks without my knowledge."

"I didn't meet him there. He just showed up."

"He is an impostor." His expression darkened.

"You're right."

His eyebrows went up. "You're agreeing with me? This is a switch."

I crossed my arms. "He's human. I could tell when I got close enough."

"Human?" He seemed surprised. "I didn't expect that. But I do know that he's dangerous. Did he give you any indication what his plans include?"

"No."

"So he told you about this object a nightwalker can use."

"Maybe he was making it up." I absently touched my neck.

Thierry glanced at my throat, at the marks his fangs had left behind when we were literally necking earlier. "It's dangerous to be alone like this. For you."

"I'm feeling okay at the moment. The shots I did earlier must have helped with my . . . my hunger."

"I will be very careful and constantly vigilant of my own . . . hungers." His jaw was tight. "The last thing I want to do is hurt you, Sarah."

"I know that."

"And you have no reason to fear that I would eliminate

you because of these symptoms you now display. I don't look at you as a nightwalker. I am not proud of what I had to do in the past to get rid of the threat. Nightwalkers are mostly to blame for vampires' being considered monsters by hunters and humans alike. Of course there are vampires who are evil due to their destructive nature, but they have made the choice to be that way. The nightwalkers were all evil. I saw what they were capable of with my own eyes, Sarah. It was horrific."

"So you did what you did to save other people."

"Yes."

I hugged him and he tensed at my touch. "Don't worry," I whispered. "I won't kiss you. That seems to be what triggers it."

He leaned back and looked down into my eyes. "The thought of not being able to kiss you again is not a pleasant one."

I leaned back and grinned up at him. "I know. I *am* a fantastic kisser."

His lips twitched into a sad smile. "There was a time, Sarah, that I thought myself a very noble man who did things and made choices to help others. Now, after all this time has passed, I find that the only thing I care about is right here."

"The club?"

He shook his head. "*You.* I care about your safety and your happiness. Both, however, are currently compromised by this curse and the presence of the Red Devil impostor, and I will do everything in my power to help you."

I ran my hands down his warm, firm chest. "Keep talking like that and I'm going to kiss you. And that wouldn't be a good thing."

"No." He studied my lips. "It wouldn't be."

"I'll have to start writing you IOUs."

"An excellent suggestion."

I swallowed. "I should probably mention that Veronique called earlier. She got the annulment papers and she is freaking out over them."

He raised a dark eyebrow. "Veronique is *freaking out*? I don't believe Veronique has ever *freaked out* about anything before."

"She's not happy and she doesn't want to sign. She wants you to call her ASAP."

He nodded. "This is all my fault."

"You're having second thoughts about getting the annulment?" I asked, and felt a heavy weight press against my chest at the thought.

"No. However, I went about it the wrong way. Veronique has a tendency to act as if nothing affects her, but I would assume that having legal church documents delivered was very likely confusing for her."

I thought about our conversation. "She called me a silly, inconsequential girl."

"That sounds more like her." He smiled. "But she was wrong. You are in no way inconsequential."

I frowned. "What about the 'silly' part?"

His smile widened. "Do you truly want me to answer that?"

"Maybe not." I bit my bottom lip. "You know, if you'd rather I give this back to you, I can. It's not a problem."

I was referring to the ring on my right hand, which I now held up to show him what I was talking about.

He glanced down at it. "Do you want to give it back to me?"

"No," I said quickly.

"Then I want you to wear it until you choose not to." His smile faded. "I now realize that I should have let Veronique know my intentions."

"And what are your intentions?"

He took my hand in his and ran his thumb over the eternity band. Then he raised his silver-eyed gaze to mine. "To figure out a way to kiss you again. I've waited much too long for you to enter my life to allow this curse to come between us."

My toes curled at the tone of his voice, words that promised so much more than just kissing or even sex. It was a tone that promised a future together. My heart raced as he slid his hand through my hair, still damp from the snow outside, and then traced his fingers over my lips.

But then I felt the darkness begin to well inside me. My fangs began to ache and my vision narrowed down to the small pulse on his throat. Reluctantly, I moved away from his touch. "Better put the brakes on. We've just entered the danger zone."

He nodded and then released me completely to pace his office with his hands firmly clasped behind his back. "Now there is the matter of the Red Devil. I think it's a good idea if we draw him out of his hiding place and demand to know who he is and what his intentions are."

"Ever consider that he's just trying to help?"

"Help? I doubt that."

"Why? He did save my life once. He also tried to give me some good advice about the magic nightwalker object. He said that I'd come in contact with one recently. I'm racking my brain trying to remember any nondescript piece of jewelry I've seen lately—"

I blinked.

Wait a minute.

No, it couldn't be.

Three weeks ago I'd come in contact with an odd piece of jewelry. Yes indeedy, I had. It was a plain gold chain. Pretty ugly, actually.

In a nutshell, I'd been handed this piece of crap and told to hide it from the bad guys. The bad guys at the time were my bodyguards. The necklace ended up turning my stuck-in-werewolf-form pet dog back into a human when he came in contact with it. But who knows? Maybe that had only been a well-timed coincidence.

Ah, Barkley. I missed that biscuit-eating mutt.

I knew there was something weird about that necklace. But could it be possible that was what the Red Devil had been talking about?

And if so, how the hell did he even know I had it? *Nobody* knew. I hadn't even told Thierry.

"What is it?" Thierry asked.

"Maybe nothing, but there's one way to find out." I made a beeline to the door, but before opening it I glanced over my shoulder. "Am I allowed out, officer?"

He raised an eyebrow. "If you promise not to go running off in search of danger."

"Wouldn't dream of it."

He came to my side as I opened the door. "Stay close."

"But not too close."

"No, not too close." Our eyes met and held. "Much too tempting."

Damn, I had it bad for him. Sure he was a stick-in-the-mud about some stuff, he was sometimes cranky and easily annoyed, and he came with a ton of baggage, but he was also generous, caring, protective, and so incredibly sexy. Plus he wanted to be with me despite the fact that I was a mess and a half and had an unfortunate habit of running off headlong into danger.

I'd never been so in love with anyone in my life. It was a little scary.

No, actually it was a *lot* scary.

I'd figure a way out of this curse. I would. I wasn't going to let it get in the way of my being with Thierry. Not after everything we'd already been through. And if the witch wouldn't come to me, I was going to track her down and go to her.

But that was after I got my Plan B.

I'd given the necklace in question to Amy for her birthday. Doing this served two purposes. First, I knew she would hate it and hide it safely away in her jewelry cabinet where it would never see the light of day again. Second, I'd forgotten to buy her another present in time for her party.

I remember her reaction when she pulled it out of the gift bag, past the secondhand tissue paper.

Her eyes had widened at the glint of gold, and then narrowed with disappointment that it wasn't something good. "What the fu—?" She stopped, blinked, and looked at me. "Uh, I mean, what a fu-uu-abulous gift! Thank you, Sarah! I love it!"

And, just as I'd predicted, she hadn't worn it once. Perfect. It was safe and sound and locked away. I felt the oddest sense of certainty come over me. I didn't know how the Red Devil knew about it, and I didn't really care. If it did what he said it did, then I wanted that hunk of junk back. I would wear it proudly as I emerged into the daylight again. It had only been a day but I already felt starved for sunshine and was probably pastier looking than normal. I might even go get a spray tan to celebrate everything working out okay when this was all over.

"Amy!" I walked straight toward her. She eyed me warily.

"Um, yeah?"

I grabbed her arm and felt her flinch as I pulled her off to the side and out of earshot of everyone else. "I need to ask you a question."

"No, I don't want you to bite me."

I blinked. "I wasn't going to ask you that."

She crossed her arms protectively in front of her. "I mean, I know we're friends. *Best* friends. And I know you're probably looking at my neck and thinking about how delicious it must be. But that doesn't mean I want to experiment with you. I'm not into that, Sarah. I don't feel comfortable taking our friendship there."

"What in the hell are you talking about?"

She looked confused. "Barry told me that you're dangerous and I should stay away from you as much as possible, but I don't want to do that. I don't want to be afraid of you, but the things he's told me about nightwalkers . . ." She grimaced. "They're like sex-crazed mosquitoes who don't care who they seduce to get what they want."

Okay, that was an image.

"I'm not sex-crazed or a mosquito. And even if I was, trust me, you're not my type."

She appeared to relax a bit. "Really?"

"Really."

Then she frowned. "Why not? Is it the pink hair? Because I have an appointment booked to go blond again."

I cleared my throat. "Look, this is going to sound odd to you, but do you remember that birthday present I gave you? The gold chain?"

"Of course I remember." She appeared to stifle a shudder.

"I can't go into the major details right now, but I need it back for a little while. Maybe we can pop over to your house and grab it."

"You need it?" She looked confused. "But you gave it to me as a present."

I looked over my shoulder to see Butch still glowering at me. The sound system was playing Sinatra's "Lady Is a Tramp."

"I know, it sounds bizarre," I said. "Just humor me, please. I know you never wear it, so I can't imagine you would mind my borrowing it for a little bit. And I wouldn't ask if it wasn't excruciatingly, vitally important."

"Excruciatingly?" she repeated weakly.

I frowned. "What's the problem?"

"Is there any way another gold chain will do? I have a few you can borrow. Most are a little more wearable than that one." She paused and then added, "Not that I don't appreciate the thought, of course."

"I know you hated it. It's okay. And I promise to replace it with a much better belated birthday gift. But I need that one in particular."

"Oh, dear."

"Oh, dear, what?"

She began to wring her hands, and she met my eyes with what looked like . . . *guilt*? "I . . . I actually don't have it anymore."

"Excuse me?"

She twisted a finger through her short pink hair. "I'm so sorry. I know this is the absolute worst thing, but . . . but I knew I was never going to wear it. I put it in my jewelry box and every time I opened it up it was just staring up at me giving me the evil eye."

"A necklace doesn't have eyes."

"It felt like it did. I never in a million years thought that you would want it back, and if you had asked me in a couple of months or years why I never wore it I was going to tell you that I lost it."

"What did you do with the necklace, Amy?" I asked tightly.

"Well, one day I was at home vacuuming and the TV was on in the other room and I heard a commercial. It was this guy talking about . . ." She stopped and her bottom lip quivered.

"Talking about what?" I prompted her.

"Talking about selling your used and unwanted jewelry. For cash." She covered her face with her hands. "Oh, I am so ashamed."

"You sold the necklace?" I managed, not believing my own ears. "You sold it? I gave it to you as a gift!"

"I wasn't going to wear it." She touched her ear. "And I was able to buy these earrings with the money the guy gave me. It was only the day before yesterday."

I felt the blood drain from my face. On the one hand I was furious that she would sell a present I gave her, even though it was admittedly not really a present at all. On the other hand . . . those were some really cute earrings.

She hadn't known. Hell, I hadn't known that I might need that necklace again. Actually, I didn't even know right now that it was even the object in question that would help me.

All I had was my gut instinct. And my gut was telling me I needed that gold chain and I needed it as soon as possible.

I put a hand on her shoulder. "Where did you sell it?"

"It's a place called Sell Your Gold for Cash."

"Sounds classy."

"It's really not bad. A little cluttered."

"How much did you get for it?"

"Fifty bucks."

I nodded. My potential chance at a normal life had been pawned to some sleazy used-jewelry shop for fifty bucks. Great.

"Vampire or human owned?" I asked.

She thought about it. "I'm pretty sure the guy was human."

Thierry approached us and I told him what was going on. He shook his head. "I know the owner of this store—his wife is a regular customer here at Haven—but it's too late right now. They would be closed. It's nearly midnight."

"Well, as much as I'd love to wait until the stores open tomorrow morning, I'd prefer not to be fried by the sun when I stroll down the sidewalk."

"I will investigate the problem myself, then."

I shook my head. "No, I'm sorry. I don't mean to be all contrary here, but I need to go now. I need to get the necklace now. I can't wait."

Thierry studied me for a moment and then glanced at Amy. "You are sure this is the correct place?"

She nodded and fluttered her eyelashes. "Uh-huh."

He stood in silence for a while longer, his expression unreadable. "George will come with us. He has a talent we may require if I'm unable to contact the owner personally."

I raised my eyebrows. "I didn't know an affinity for tight leather pants would come in handy in a situation like this."

"George is very adept at picking locks."

This was news. "You learn something new every day. Do I want to know how he came to learn this?"

Thierry regarded me and a small amount of amusement slid behind his gaze. "We all have pasts and hidden talents, Sarah. I'm sure you do as well."

"I can tie a cherry stem in a knot with my tongue," Amy said, her gaze slowly moving over Thierry's body. "Does that count?"

I hit her in the shoulder. Hard. "Not in this case."

She rubbed her arm and pouted. "Ouchie."

After Thierry made a quick and mysterious phone call, and without telling anyone else where we were going, the four of us piled into Thierry's Audi, just returned from its extended stay in the Abottsville Motor Inn parking lot—he'd paid a couple of the employees to drive it over—and we left for a midnight pawnshop run to retrieve my Plan B.

Chapter 14

Sell Your Gold for Cash was a quick ten-minute drive from Haven, close to Front and Jarvis, and closed for the day, which, since it was after midnight when we arrived, was not unexpected.

George seemed excited at the prospect of a late-night break-and-enter, which I wasn't sure was a good thing.

"I'm excited," he stated, as he pulled out a pouch from his manbag that looked like a manicure set. He unzipped it to show that it contained several long metal rods of varying widths.

"What's up with that?" I asked him. "I had no idea you could do something like this."

"Well, it's not exactly the sort of thing one discusses with just anyone. But since I know you, I suppose I can come clean. In the fifties, I was a world-renowned cat burglar."

I was shocked. "You were?"

He blinked. "Well, okay, *assistant* to a world-renowned cat burglar. Dammit, I can't lie very well. I answered the phones and gathered together bail money when necessary. But he taught me a lot." Another blink. "Pierre now lives in Tahiti and collects cabana boys. But whatever. Bygones. I'm over it."

I felt like comforting him, but I was too stressed. I wanted to get the necklace and get the hell out of there. "Let's get started."

"That actually won't be necessary after all, George," Thierry said, and he leaned past me and pressed a buzzer on the side of the door.

"What are you doing?" I asked.

"I was able to reach the owner by telephone. He agreed to open the store for us."

After a minute, the lights flickered on inside the store and somebody approached the door.

George pouted. "Why am I even here?"

"I'm sorry, George," Thierry said. "Perhaps another time."

He tucked the lock-picking kit back into his manbag. "I am incredibly disappointed. Though the sensation is extremely familiar lately."

It was a man dressed in a brightly colored bathrobe, and he looked extremely sleepy. He had a puffy face, squinty eyes that he rubbed at the sudden brightness of the lighting, and a hairline so receded it was practically in the next room. He blinked a couple of times as he gazed through the door at us. Then he unlocked the door and swung it open.

I suddenly recognized him from his TV commercials. His name was Hans Christie and he had a great onscreen personality that made me want to gather up all my jewelry, such as it is, and bring it to him.

His expression at the moment was not a friendly one.

"Come in," he growled. I could hear his thick New York accent. "Let's make this quick. You woke me from a very pleasant dream. My wife will owe me for this."

"Your wife is a very good customer at my club," Thierry said. "If she had sired you, I would have been pleased to welcome you any time at my club, but unfortunately nonvampiric members of society aren't permitted in Haven. I'm sure you understand the security risks involved."

The man grunted. "The last thing I want to be is a bloodsucker. My wife's nightly excursions are her own business."

"You're human and your wife is a vampire?" Amy asked.

"That's right. Married for forty years now."

I thought of my cousin Missy and her husband. "I've always wondered how that works out. When one refuses to be turned. It must be difficult. Have you never considered it before? The chance to be immortal?"

Hans snorted. "Immortal? Life is difficult enough knowing I have seventy or eighty years to suffer through, let alone imagining hundreds of years. No, I never wanted an open-ended existence."

"But your relationship is solid?"

"We're going through a divorce right now."

I raised my eyebrows. "I'm sorry to hear that."

"Don't be. It was a mistake. Humans and vampires shouldn't become involved with each other. Besides, one in two regular marriages end in divorce. Do you know the percentage of human-vampire marriages that end in divorce?"

I shook my head.

"A hell of a lot more!" he said, and then cleared his throat. "I apologize. I don't mean to seem agitated, but this whole divorce is grating on my very last nerve."

"We appreciate you taking the time to open your shop so late," Thierry said. "Especially given your relationship issues with your wife."

I tried to see past him into the shop, wanting to scan the place as soon as I could, but the man was large and he blocked the entrance.

"Speaking of wives," Hans said, "how is Veronique? I only met her once in passing, but she has stuck in my memory as one of the most beautiful women I've ever seen."

"Veronique is fine," Thierry replied.

Hans shook his head. "If I was married to a stunning woman like that I might have considered becoming a vampire. My wife may look thirty, but it's an ugly thirty."

"I will pass along the compliment to Veronique."

He glanced at me. "So you're the problem, eh?"

"Excuse me?"

"The reason I had to open up my shop. You're the problem."

Yeah, that sounded about right. Veronique was the stunning beauty and I was the problem. Nothing new there. That was the least of my troubles right now.

Thierry touched my arm. "Sarah is looking for a gold chain that was sold here by accident. We wish to retrieve it."

"It was me," Amy admitted. "I was in the day before

yesterday with it." Her shoulders hunched. "I am so ashamed."

Hans eyed her. "I think I remember you. How could I forget that hair color? You said you wanted to get rid of it for any price."

Amy glanced at me and shrugged. "Again, so sorry."

"I'll pay you for it," I told Hans. "Can you please get it for me?"

He pulled a pair of round-rimmed glasses out of the pocket of his robe and put them on, pushing them into place on the bridge of his nose. I felt as if he was studying me at the end of a microscope. "I'll look."

I waited, feeling on edge and jittery, as he wandered over to the main counter, a glass cabinet filled with all sorts of jewelry. Around the rest of the store were other objects, not only jewelry. I thought he would look through the merchandise itself, but instead he consulted a list on a clipboard.

He looked at Amy. "You were in the day before yesterday, you say?"

"That's right."

His finger traced the line of the page. "Yes, I see. Here you are." He flipped forward a couple of pages, tilted his head to one side. "Hmm."

I glanced at Thierry and tried not to allow my current state of anxiety to show on my face.

"What do you mean, 'hmm'?" I asked. Had he found it?

"Just a moment." He took a key, opened the cabinet, and pulled out a few chains. "Come here, miss."

I did as he asked and I was looking at the necklaces

that he laid out on the counter on top of a black piece of velvet.

I frowned. "What about them?"

"Will any of these do?" he asked.

"Will any of these do?" I repeated. "No, they won't. I need the one that Amy brought in."

"According to my records, it was a simple gold chain. As are these. Any of these would make a fine replacement."

"We don't wish to find a replacement," Thierry said, and I felt his hand on my back. "We require the original."

"Well, I'm sorry, but that's not possible."

"If price is the object," Thierry continued, "we are willing to pay any price to get it."

Hans shook his head. "A generous offer, but not the point, I'm afraid. The chain you are looking for was sold earlier today. I didn't remember until I looked at the ledger."

"Sold?" I squeaked. "You're joking, right?"

"No, I'm afraid not."

I felt a tight sensation building in my chest. I think it was panic. Or possibly a massive heart attack. "But . . . but it was ugly. Who would even want it?"

"Yes, the same, I suppose, could be said about my wife, and yet someone wanted her." Hans took the chains and returned them to the cabinet before he locked it up again. "It was an odd situation. For a moment this after-noon I was quite sure that I was being robbed. The man came in and looked around. He approached the counter and pointed directly to the chain. I was almost ready to reach for the alarm when he produced a thousand dollars, asked me to give him the chain, and walked out without a receipt or a box."

I felt like throwing up. No. It couldn't have been sold. Who would buy something like that when there were a dozen other nicer chains in stock?

"I don't understand," I managed. "Why did you think you were being robbed?"

"The man wore a black scarf over his face that he didn't remove when he entered the store. I thought he was a criminal and was very relieved when he wasn't."

A scarf over his face? My heart took a nosedive straight down to my shoes.

The Red Devil. He'd been the one to tell me about the necklace in the first place, indirectly anyhow. He'd bought it before I could get to it.

"Thank you for your time," Thierry said, and, taking me by my arm, directed me out of the store and into the cold night air.

"A thousand dollars?" Amy said. "It was worth a whole grand? And I totally sold it for fifty bucks. I could have got the diamond earrings instead of these imitation ones." She blinked. "Not that that's the issue here at the moment."

"Perhaps it isn't even the object you were searching for," Thierry said as he regarded my stunned expression.

"It was," I said. My voice sounded flat. "I know it was. And now the Red Devil has it."

"Then everything is going to be okay," George said with a big grin. "The Red Devil helps other vampires. He's obviously planning to give you the chain. What a hero!"

Maybe. I frowned. Maybe that was it. He would give it to me because he was a good guy. But if that was the case, why did I still feel ill at the prospect that he'd beaten me to it? And why hadn't he said anything earlier about having it?

And if he was really human and not vampire, what the hell was he doing pretending to be the Red Devil in the first place?

The whole thing smelled seriously fishy. And it wasn't just the fact that we were around the corner from the Toronto Fish Market.

I slept on the leather sofa in Thierry's office that night. I hadn't realized how exhausted I was until we got back. I did a few more shots of B-Positive and then felt the need to be alone. Thierry promised he would be close, but not too close.

I lay down, my thoughts racing like Seabiscuit on amphetamines, but the moment I closed my eyes I was out like a proverbial light.

And I did dream. Whether they were prophetic dreams was another matter. I was accepting an award—an Oscar for Best Actress, no less—and thanking all the little vampires who helped get me to where I was. There was a standing ovation. Roses rained upon the stage and I felt fantastic and elated and all of those good things. But then the roses turned into sharp wooden stakes hurtling toward me and there were too many and I couldn't get away. All of a sudden, Thierry was on the stage with me trying to protect me with his body, but that meant he was riddled with the stakes instead.

Another dream that ended with Thierry dying horribly.

Another dream that ended with me sitting bolt upright and screaming my head off.

Then there were hands on my arms, pushing me back down onto the sofa, and a cool hand stroked the hair back from my forehead.

"It's fine, Sarah," Thierry's deep voice soothed. "You're fine."

I blinked and the room came slowly into focus. "Sorry."

Thierry knelt at the side of the sofa. "Don't apologize. You were having a bad dream."

I let out a long breath. "Is that all this is? Just a bad dream. Thank God. I seriously thought I'd been cursed to be a nightwalker."

His dark brows drew together. "I'm afraid that isn't a dream."

"I know that. I'm just kidding."

"I'm glad to see that you can find the humor in the situation."

"Who said anything about humor?" I looked at him. His black shirt was unbuttoned at the top and his jacket was off. "Did you stay here the whole time I was asleep?"

"I thought it best. I didn't want to risk you wandering off in search of your Red Devil."

"No, wouldn't want that." I sighed and looked up into his silver eyes. "God, Thierry, why do you put up with me? I'm such a pain in the ass."

He frowned. "I believe that you're right. I should abandon you to fend for yourself in this, your time of greatest need."

"Are you trying to be funny again?"

"Perhaps."

"You should really leave that up to the professionals." I managed a smile. "I know I can be a pain. I know I make stupid mistakes at least fifty times a day. I know I fly off the handle and get into trouble like nobody's business. I just want you to know that I appreciate your putting up with me."

"As I appreciate your willingness to adapt to . . . my difficulties."

I met his gaze. "Difficulties, huh? Is that how we're putting it now?"

"Do you have another way?"

I touched his face. "I love you, Thierry. I just wish I'd stop having dreams that ended with you—" I stopped talking.

"Ended with me what?"

I shook my head. "It's nothing. Just stupid dreams."

"You dream about me?"

"Constantly."

"I'm very pleased to hear that." He stroked my hair back and tucked it behind my ear.

I frowned. "They're not always good dreams."

"You dream of my death?"

My eyes snapped back to his. "Yeah. Sometimes."

"Since you met me when I was about to end my life, this isn't an unusual dream to have. Don't be concerned."

I blinked and felt tears begin to well. "You don't think about that anymore, do you? You haven't been scouting out any new bridges to throw yourself off? Because I seriously don't know what I'd do if I lost you."

He shook his head and gently pushed my few tears away with his thumb. "Thoughts of leaving this life have recently vanished completely from my mind. I now find myself newly inspired to wake up each morning. You have nothing to fear."

"Nothing to fear but fear itself."

He tilted his head to one side and a small smile appeared on his lips. "Oh, there is plenty to be afraid of, Sarah. I don't think you need me to make a list for you. But my suicide is no longer on that list."

"I'm very glad to hear it." I blinked and pressed my hand against the side of his face. "I really want to kiss you right now."

"That would be a mistake." He didn't move away from me.

"I know. But I still want to."

He traced his fingers over my lips and then took my hand in his. He brought it to his mouth to kiss it.

"That's a nice start," I breathed.

"Okay, break it up!" George shouted from behind Thierry. He clapped his hands. "Up and at 'em, Sarah. Chop chop."

Thierry didn't take his attention away from me. "I asked George to watch over you in case of emergency."

"You two are too close for comfort!" George continued. "I want to see some space. Back up, boss. Give our little nightwalker some air!"

"It's okay, George. Really. I'm feeling . . ." I blinked. How was I feeling?

A little cold and clammy, actually.

I pressed my hands against my face. Felt normal

enough. But there was something off. I couldn't pinpoint it exactly.

I sucked in a breath of air. That felt okay, too.

Then I gasped. "It's my heart."

"What about it?"

I grabbed his hand and pressed it against my chest.

"Hey, what did I say about getting too close?" George protested. "Am I going to have to separate the two of you naughty little monkeys?"

Thierry frowned deeply and looked into my eyes but said nothing.

"I don't have a heartbeat," I said. "What the hell is going on here?"

Thierry nodded slowly. "A lack of a pulse is another trait of the nightwalker."

"A lack of a pulse? But that means that . . . that night-walkers are . . . are . . ."

"Undead."

"And regular vampires are the opposite."

"Yes."

I jumped to my feet and walked out of the office, brushing past George, who was looking at me with very wide eyes. Dammit.

I froze in place as I felt my heart begin to beat.

Once.

And then nothing.

"Oh, my God," I said aloud, and the panic started to let loose again.

Nobody was in Haven at the moment except for the three of us. The chairs were all up on top of the tables. The lights were off. I stood there, in the middle of the ceramic-tiled floor that resembled a whirlpool of blues and mauves, and felt as if it was sucking me down into the pit of despair. And no, I didn't think I was over-exaggerating at all. This was bad. Really bad. I didn't have a heartbeat. *My heart was not beating.* There was nothing good about that. The metaphorical pessimistic glass of water wasn't even half empty anymore. It was bone dry.

"Okay," I said, and noticed that George and Thierry had followed me into the main area of the club. "Okay. I'm not going to freak out. There's still time left to fix this."

"What do you mean there's still time?" Thierry said. "Of course there's time."

I shook my head. "Stacy said that if the curse wasn't removed within three days from when she did it in the first place, it was sticking. Forever. But, it's morning now. We've got the better part of two days to take care of this, so I just need to think. I need to think about what to do next, especially since I can't go outside. It's not a cloudy day out there by any chance, is it? Of course it isn't. It's probably the brightest day of the year, with my luck."

George and Thierry exchanged a glance.

"I wish that you had told me about this timeline last night," Thierry said quietly.

"Why?" I looked at the clock above the bar. "It's 7:00 A.M. We've got all day to figure out where that skank is hiding out."

He shook his head. "I'm sorry, Sarah, but it isn't morning. You slept through the night and also through the daylight hours. *Nightwalkers,*" he said carefully, "often sleep through the day. They . . . thrive in darkness."

I swallowed hard. "You're kidding."

"I wish I was." His expression tightened. "But there is still time."

"Why didn't you wake me up?"

"I didn't want to disturb you. I didn't realize that time was an issue."

I felt as if I was in shock. The heart that let out one beat every other minute was also a bit distracting, to say the least. Like the gong that signified that my life was currently taking a long walk off a short pier into an ocean of crap.

I sniffed and ran my hand under my nose. "I think I'm actually room temperature right now." I blinked a couple of times and looked at Thierry. "You really still think everything's going to be all right?"

He nodded. "I have no doubt that it will be."

"You haven't figured out where Stacy lives yet, have you?"

"No. My sources have met with brick walls wherever they try. I believe she must be using some of her magic to help conceal her location. She obviously prefers to have the power solely in her hands."

"Did she call?" I asked hopefully.

"Not yet."

I began pacing to the bar and then back again. "She's a murderer, you know. She told me. She didn't kill the people herself. But the curses she put on people have led to their deaths. I think that's what she wants to do with me." I let out a shuddery breath. Weird that I still needed to breathe with a heart that didn't beat. Didn't all of that work together? I got a C in biology but some things are quite obviously not natural.

"I won't let that happen," Thierry said, and there was a strange fierce tone to his words. He exhaled deeply. "I do have a suggestion."

"What?"

"Your friend, the other witch from the reunion. We must call her and have her come here. Perhaps she can help us find Stacy. And when we find her, we will visit her personally."

Of course! I nodded quickly, ran to grab my purse, which currently had taken up residence behind the bar, and happily found the contact info Claire had given me. Without saying anything else I went to the phone and pecked in the numbers.

Claire answered on the sixth ring. My heart beat once in happiness.

I quickly explained the situation and gave her directions to Haven.

"Of course I'll come, Sarah," Claire said. "How exciting! I'll do a location spell. We'll find her. I'll be there in about two hours, okay?"

While I didn't agree with her assessment of the situation as "exciting," I did appreciate her willingness to come to assist with my problem.

I hung up the phone feeling nine parts hopeless and one part hopeful, but that one part was beginning to gain strength again, all things considered. Hope was a surprisingly durable emotion.

George approached me and patted me on the back. "I read your horoscope today. You do know that Scorpios are prone to lead exciting lives with loads of drama, right? Obviously everything is very normal. I believe your Mercury is also in retrograde. Or something like that. Not so sure what that means."

I sighed. "My Mercury has been in retrograde for so long I think it's still wearing bell bottoms."

He held out his arms. "Somebody needs a hug?"

I eyed him warily. "Since when have you become Mr. Touchy-Feely?"

"Ever since my last relationship ended. I'm all needy now. Humor me."

I glanced at Thierry, shook my head, and gave George a hug.

"I brought you a change of clothes," he told me. "I thought the new black jeans and smiley-face tank top would be a nice look. Put a positive fashion spin on this whole situation."

I clung to him. "Thank you."

George patted my back. "Feeling better?"

"Not really."

"Why not?"

I swallowed hard and dug my fingers into his shoulder blades. "In about five seconds I'm going to bite you. And I won't be able to control it. I suggest you step away."

He released me as if I had just sprouted sharp spikes.

I was breathing hard and the hunger welled within me like a living, breathing thing. I knew my eyes had gone from normal to black in no time flat because I saw the world differently. Like a predator looking for her next meal. And the predator saw two worthy candidates to munch on at the moment.

"I need blood and I need it right now," I managed, even though I could barely speak past the fangs.

And I got the blood. From a keg. As much as I needed, which was good, because as sickening as it was to admit it, I needed a lot.

Not a good or safe way to feel right after one has just woken up . . .

Undead and unfed.

Chapter 15

I thought Claire would have her fiancé with her when she arrived. Even though humans weren't allowed in Haven, I was sure that Thierry would make an exception this one time. But instead she brought a small dog, which looked more like a mangy mutt than any specific breed, on a harness leash.

He also wore a muzzle.

I nodded at the dog. "Is he friendly?"

She glanced at the dog. The dog glanced up at her. "*Too* friendly sometimes. Especially when checking out cute waitresses in Red Lobster."

"What's his name?"

"Reggie."

I frowned. "Isn't that your fiancé's name, too?"

Reggie growled at that.

Claire looked down at him sharply. "I swear, if you try to say anything right now you will be in even bigger trouble than you already are, mister. I'm mad at you."

The growl turned into a whimper that sounded vaguely like, "Ah ruvv yu, caaar."

She looked up at me. "Actually, this *is* my fiancé. When he's been bad I use a transformation spell to turn him into an animal as punishment. He's been a rat, a weasel, a ferret"—she frowned—"are ferrets and weasels the same thing? Anyhow, he's been a snake, a small, hairy pig, and now a dog."

I blinked and waited for her to tell me she was just kidding, but she looked at me with complete sincerity.

Ten weeks ago I didn't believe in any of this stuff: vampires, witches, demons, you name it. Now, Claire was saying that she had used her knowledge of witchcraft to turn the man she planned to marry into a dog as a penalty for looking at other women?

Not my business. I had my own issues to deal with at the moment.

I looked down at Reggie. He looked up at me and wagged his tail.

O-kay.

Thierry had closed the club. It would not be open to the general vampire public tonight. Which was a good thing, since we needed the space and privacy.

Tomorrow, Valentine's Day, would be the last night Haven opened for regular business with its current staff. After that, the new owners would move their people in. They'd probably even change the décor. Out with the old, and in with the new. I figured that the regular customers would keep on coming here despite the fact Thierry didn't own it anymore. Other than Haven, there was only one other vamp club in Toronto at the moment that I knew of. Four others had either shut down or been burned to the ground after the recent hunter blitz.

Butch stood guard near the door. I wasn't sure if it was

to keep other people out or to keep me in. He wasn't currently speaking to me after my tossing him around Thierry's office last night like a bodyguard-shaped Beanie Baby, despite a sincere apology to him earlier. In fact, he wasn't even making eye contact with me anymore, not even to give me the evil eye.

But not because he was pissed. I think he might have been a little bit afraid of me now.

Of *me*. That was so completely ridiculous.

Claire lit some candles. Actually, a whole lot of candles of varying colors and shapes. There was even one that looked like a cartoon whale.

"Did anyone else come in contact with Stacy at the time of the original curse?" she asked.

Thierry shook his head, as did George. Reggie shook his muzzle.

"Just lucky old me," I said.

"Then sit cross-legged in front of me. Nice and close." She did the same in the middle of the circle of candles. "And give me your hands."

Reggie let out a little growl that sounded like, "Raowrrr."

I glanced at George.

"Two women don't do it for me," he said. "But I'll try to use my imagination."

The only light in the club was from the candles. I sat down and Claire grasped my hands, pressing her thumbs into my palms.

"How does this work?" I asked.

She shifted position on the hard tiled floor until she got comfortable. "Since you came into contact with Stacy recently, you are the best conduit to find out her location now. Her mystical essence would have made an impression on you, whether you realize it or not. All I'm going to do is block out everything except that essence, and ask it where Stacy is right now. Simple."

Yeah, sounded simple enough. Maybe in the Twilight Zone.

"Whatever you have to do," I said, "I'm very willing to let you do it."

"Raowrrrrrrr."

"Reggie, hush." Claire closed her eyes. "Now, Sarah, concentrate on the last time you saw Stacy. How she looked. What she said. Close off any other thoughts. Empty your mind of troubles. Be like a river, flowing and free, with its energy coursing across the land."

Be like a river.

I could be like a river. Sure I could.

I focused on my memory of seeing Stacy in the park. Of her telling me that Thierry had been responsible for killing off nightwalkers in the past. That her other victims were now pushing up daisies. That she thought I was a horrible person in high school. Was I? Was I really that bad? I didn't remember. Maybe I was. Maybe thinking that I was nice and didn't deserve any of the bad stuff that seemed to come along with life, Scorpio with Mercury in retrograde or not, was wishful thinking. Maybe I did deserve all of this. Maybe it was karma for being a mean person.

"Focus," Claire said sharply. "I'm not getting a river. I'm getting a cesspool."

"Sorry."

I let out a long, steady breath and tried to center myself, pushing away all my stress and anxiety. It wasn't easy, but slowly and surely I relaxed and was able to concentrate better.

The park. It was cold there.

Stacy refused to help. She wore a red coat. Her face was pale in the moonlight. Her lips, red as her coat. Red like blood against my tongue. Hot melting sugar that slid down my throat to warm me.

So cold inside. Too cold.

No heartbeat meant that I was dead.

But I didn't feel dead. I felt alive. More alive than I'd ever felt before.

"I think I'm getting something," Claire said. "You're doing great, Sarah."

I opened my eyes, still breathing regularly, in through my nose and out through my mouth. My heart didn't beat but I was breathing. I held my breath to see if it made a difference. It didn't. I didn't even feel as if I ever had to take in another breath if I didn't want to. That should have been disturbing, but it wasn't. I forced myself to breathe again. It was a habit, after all. Any different and people might start looking at me funny.

I felt the fog slowly build inside me, so subtle I didn't notice it at first, but growing thicker with every fake breath I took.

In between us was a swirling cobweb of light. It didn't look like anything interesting to me, so I ignored it and looked beyond it to Claire. Her attention was on the light, her forehead furrowed with concentration. I could see the quick pulse at her throat.

I could taste it and sense it with every cell in my body.

I crawled toward her, focused only on that small patch

of warm pink skin at the side of her throat. What was it that brought this on? Relaxing, maybe? Letting the meaningless stress I was feeling slip far away. It helped make things better. Much better.

"Good, Sarah," Claire said. "Closer proximity is probably better to focus the energy." She focused on the light and then a big smile came over her face. "It shouldn't take long now to get a fix on her location."

I grabbed the front of Claire's sweater and pulled her closer, then tilted my head to the side. Her attention finally landed on me as her gaze met my own.

"Sarah," she began, "what are you doing?"

"Shh." I pressed my index finger against her mouth.

I could feel her heartbeat in my head, hear it thudding in my ears, as if it took over for my own silent one. So close now. The pulse was close. My mouth watered at the thought of sinking my fangs into her warm flesh. So alive. So vital. Blood from a keg wasn't sufficient for me. Too cold. I needed it fresh, from the living, breathing source.

"Uh . . . somebody?" Claire called out, but otherwise she was frozen in place. "A little assistance, please? I'm too weak from starting the location spell. Scary Sarah alert! Help!"

My fangs grazed her neck. I wanted to make this last. To enjoy every moment of it. It was a primal need. A driving desire to feed. And somehow, at this very moment, it felt so completely right to me. This is the way being a vampire should feel. This ache inside that could be relieved by only one thing: blood.

I heard footsteps pounding behind me, but I knew they couldn't stop me. I was too strong now. I could fend all of them off if they got in my way. They would be wise to stay far away from me until I was finished.

But before I could seal the deal, so to speak, I felt a strange sensation. Instead of grasping hands attempting to pull me away from Claire, I felt a sharp and painful jolt of electricity. I backed away from her with a snarl and looked up. Butch stood very tall and large next to me, and in his hand he held something that I foggily registered as a stun gun.

Thierry stood behind him with his arms crossed in front of him. "Again," he said tightly to Butch. "Do it quickly before it's too late."

My hands curled into fists and in one fluid motion I rose to my feet and lunged at him. Butch also froze in place; whatever he saw in my face was enough to stop him cold. Thierry grabbed the stun gun away from him and without hesitating, touched it to my chest where my stake wound was a fading memory, and the electricity coursed through my body, freezing me in my tracks.

My eyes widened as I met his gaze.

His expression was tense. "I'm sorry, Sarah."

I fell to the ground, feeling the cool ceramic tiles press against my face seconds before the world went completely and totally black.

When I woke, my eyes still felt too heavy to open, like little cinder blocks tipped with smeared, day-old mascara.

I didn't know where I was, but I could hear people talking.

"And what happens if that doesn't work? She's dangerous." That was Butch.

"Give her a break, she's been through a lot," George said.

"And what would you suggest I do?" Thierry's deep voice asked tightly.

"I would suggest that we take care of the problem before it becomes a larger one," Butch said.

"You are going to have to be more specific, I'm afraid," Thierry replied. "It has been a long couple of days, so I find myself unable to understand your exact meaning."

"If she's a nightwalker, for real, and we can't find this witch, then she needs to be eliminated. There's no other solution."

"Are you crazy?" George said. "This is just a stupid curse, not the way she normally is. No way. We can't hurt Sarah. I won't let you."

"Oh, yeah?" Butch continued. "You really think you could stop me?"

"Perhaps George alone could not," Thierry said. "But if you make one move toward Sarah that I find to be threatening, make no mistake, I will kill you myself."

"Look," Butch said. "You still don't understand what I'm trying to say here—"

"No," Thierry cut him off. "*You* are the one who doesn't understand. If you attempt to hurt her in any way, I promise to return the favor."

There was silence then.

"I can't be here," Butch finally said. "If you want to make a mistake and keep a potential disaster like that alive, all power to you. But I want nothing to do with it."

"Then you are relieved of your duties. Permanently. I will forward payment for services to date. You may leave now."

There was more silence, and then I heard the sound of heavy footsteps leave the room.

I managed to pry my eyes open then, and I looked up at George and Thierry. I was on the leather sofa again. Maybe I should invest in a nice comfy afghan, since it seemed to have become my new home away from home. Reggie, still in dog form, was curled up at the end by my feet sleeping and softly snoring.

"So, did I miss anything?" My words sounded as dry as my mouth felt.

"Claire, she's awake," Thierry said and I could hear the strain in his voice.

I felt something poke me and I looked down. Claire held a ruler and she prodded my shoulder with it. "Sarah, are you all there?"

"Oh, I'm all here, all right. Unfortunately." I looked at the ruler. "Didn't have any ten-foot poles to touch me with?"

"She is back to normal," Thierry said. "When the darkness descends she loses her capability for sarcasm."

I blinked at him. "Glad you noticed my subtle differences."

His jaw was tense. "I apologize for having to use extreme measures."

"That wasn't as extreme as you could have gotten. I heard what Butch said."

His throat worked as he swallowed, but his expression didn't change. "I'm sorry you had to hear that."

"No, I'm the one who's sorry." I looked at Claire. "Are you okay?"

She waved her hand dismissively. "Please. Not exactly the first time I've been attacked."

"By a vampire?"

"Vampire, demon, employer. What's the difference?" She put the ruler down and hovered her hands over me. "Just do me a favor and don't do it again?"

"I wish I could say that I had control over it."

"It's a matter of mind over matter. With enough practice, I'm sure you'll be fine. Just think like a river. You were thinking more like a waterfall. A big, scary one."

I frowned. "I can't think like water. It makes me need to use the washroom."

"Do you sense anything?" Thierry asked.

"Oh, definitely," Claire said. "I can feel the curse. It's super strong, too."

"Is there anything you can do to remove it?"

She shrugged. "I'm fairly powerful, but this Stacy chick is into the mega dark arts."

"So you're more like Glinda the Good Witch?" I asked. "Your magic is pure?"

She snorted at that. "Not really. I just can't afford the really cool spell books. Do you have any idea what they cost?"

"No idea."

"Some are a few thousand bucks. Those are the cheap ones. The really good ones are paid for with little bits of your soul. That's too expensive for me. Then again, you can always kill a more powerful witch and steal her library. That's an option, but then there's the risk of her vengeful spirit coming back to kick your ass."

"I can't believe anyone would want to live like this." I closed my eyes and thought about the nightwalkers who had roamed the earth many years ago. "And it seems to be getting worse by the minute. I can't live like this. I don't want to hurt anybody."

"You won't," Thierry said, his words firm.

I looked at Claire. "Did the location spell work? Do you know where to find Stacy?"

She shook her head. "There wasn't enough time. But we'll . . ." She swallowed hard. "We'll try it again."

"Are you well enough to move?" Thierry asked.

I nodded and struggled to sit up. Neither Claire nor George made a move to help me, but Thierry was there to grasp my hand in his and help me to my feet. He smiled at me when I didn't resist.

"What?" I asked.

"I'm surprised you would wish to touch me after what I had to do."

I raised an eyebrow. "You mean zapping me with the stun gun?"

"Yes."

"Wasn't a romantic moment I'll cherish always on this, the day before Valentine's Day, but it's not exactly like I gave you a choice."

"I'll make it up to you."

"Oh, yeah?" I raised an eyebrow. "How?"

"I'll think of something appropriate." He leaned over and kissed me briefly. I sighed against his lips.

"Hey!" George said. "Watch it!"

"It's fine," Thierry said, and looked at me. "It is, isn't it?"

I nodded. "At the moment, it seems to be."

The kiss helped me to clear my head and focus on what really mattered. Getting better so Thierry and I could be together. Getting better so my friends didn't have to be afraid of me anymore. More than anything, that was what was important to me. I didn't want to hurt anyone I loved. Hell, I didn't even want to hurt anyone I *didn't* love.

Well, maybe I'd make an exception for Stacy.

I seriously needed to be cured of this ASAP, but this wasn't exactly just a couple of germs to deal with.

What I wouldn't have given to only have a really bad head cold.

The phone rang and Thierry moved toward his desk to answer it. I wondered if it was Veronique again, but no, I could tell by his expression it was somebody else. Somebody worse.

He cupped his hand over the mouthpiece and looked over at me. "Are you feeling well enough to take a call?"

"From who?"

"Stacy," he said simply.

My eyes widened and I held my hand out for the phone. He brought it over to me, although his expression was tense and worried.

"Hello?" My voice was a whisper.

"Sarah," Stacy said, "I've been thinking."

"About what?"

"I know you tried to find me just now. I could feel the other witch at work—she's fairly powerful, actually. You're very determined to get rid of this curse, aren't you?"

"Yes, I am. Stacy, listen to me, you need to think rationally. I know you've been hurt in the past, but that's the past. You need to put it behind you and move on to the future."

"Oh, I know that now."

I was surprised. "You do?"

"Yes, it's . . . it's so crazy how life works out, Sarah. I've never felt like this before." She paused. "I'm in love."

"You're *in love*?" That was the last thing I'd expected her to say.

"I finally see the error of my ways and I want to atone for what I've done to you. The curse won't be permanent until tomorrow night. Come to my house right away and I'll take care of it. Then we can both move on with our wonderful new lives with the men we've fallen in love with."

Skeptical didn't even begin to cover what I was feeling at the moment. "And let me guess. You want me to come alone? Forget it. I'm not falling for that one again."

"No, no, bring whoever you want. Even bring Thierry if you like. I have nothing to hide anymore. After tonight I'm not going to do any more black magic. I'm going to be a healer. I want to help people instead of hurt them now. It's so crazy how finding the right man after all of these years has changed my attitude about everything. I feel more alive than I have in years."

I listened for the sound of my heartbeat and heard only silence. "Wish I could say the same."

"So are you coming or what?"

I hesitated and looked at Thierry, who studied me with a steady, concerned expression. There wasn't even a question of whether I was going to see Stacy. I could only hope that she was serious this time. If she was, if she'd really found a man who would love the crazy witch for who she was, then more power to her. It didn't exactly excuse the terrible things she'd done in the past, though. She was still responsible for, as far as I knew from what she'd told me, the deaths of six people.

Not exactly your average girl-next-door behavior.

"I'm coming," I said, trying to remain calm even

though it was a struggle. I would hate to get my hopes up only to have them dashed again, but hope was nudging me rather hard at the moment. Whoever had swept Stacy off her feet might soon have my eternal gratitude for appearing at the right time and right place.

Stacy told me her address and I jotted it down on a piece of paper.

"And listen, Sarah," she said, and then paused.

"What?" I prompted.

"I'm sorry. For everything. The past is over and the future is bright. For both of us."

I could hear that she was smiling.

After telling her that we'd be there in half an hour, I hung up.

"She's going to break the curse," I said quietly.

George let out a very long sigh of relief. "When do we leave?"

"Right now," Thierry said firmly. "The sooner this is over the better."

I honestly couldn't have agreed more.

Chapter 16

I filled a Thermos just in case something went wrong on the way over to Stacy's house. I don't think I need to go into detail about what was inside.

I held on to my optimism as best I could. That sliver of hope told me that even when things were darkest in my life, they always seemed to turn out okay in the end. The optimism had been growing by the minute since Stacy's phone call. Besides, I had very good backup: George, currently the keeper of the stun gun, a role he was taking very seriously; Thierry, the strong, silent type with the grim but determined expression; and Claire, our resident expert in crazy-ass witches.

Oh, and her little dog, too.

The four and a half of us made like *The Wizard of Oz* and went off to see the repentent wicked witch of the west end of the city.

I was surprised to see that Stacy lived in Rosedale, the ritziest neighborhood of Toronto and home to some of its rich and famous citizens. The area was surrounded by winding streets, parkland, and ravines that effectively concealed the fact that it was only a short drive to downtown. I seriously would have killed to live there. Luckily, though, at the moment, I was speaking figuratively.

I wondered if Stacy had killed to live there. Or used her magic somehow. Actually, I was willing to bet that she had.

Thierry parked down the street, and we got out and cautiously approached the beautiful home. The lights were off, which was unexpected, considering that she was expecting us, after all.

"I'm not feeling any warding spells," Claire said. "She's not trying to keep us out."

Thierry led the way to the front door. His determination was extremely reassuring. If Stacy reneged on her promise to break the curse, I had full faith in his ability to be . . . *convincing*.

However, I also had full faith in Stacy's ability to possibly turn him into a strong but silent toad. Or a moody, guilt-ridden armchair.

"Be careful," I warned him.

"I'll do my best," he said.

Stacy was a powerful witch. Check. She'd cursed me with a really crappy curse. Check. She also didn't seem to care if those who'd done her wrong ended up dead in a ditch somewhere. Also check.

But she wasn't completely evil, was she? I mean, she'd even apologized to me. If she was willing to reverse things before it was too late, that had to count for something. I wondered just who this mystery man who'd swept her off her feet was. Did he know she was a witch? Would she turn him into a furry creature if he did her wrong, like Claire had done to Reggie? More likely Stacy would do something much worse. I felt sorry for this guy, whoever he was.

I still felt extremely uneasy about this whole situation. I didn't want anything bad to happen. I didn't want to put Thierry's or anyone's life in peril for helping me. Was that what I was doing?

No, I assured myself. It's fine. This all will be fine.

If that was so, then why were the damn lights out?

Thierry rang the doorbell and we waited. My mouth felt dry and my heart let out a plaintive beat before going silent again. George whistled nervously under his breath. He'd brought his lock-picking kit with him again just in case of emergency.

After a couple of silent, beat-free minutes went by, Thierry knocked on the door. I literally forgot to breathe for two minutes. He glanced at me, his brow lowered into a frown, then he turned the handle of the door and pushed it open to find that it wasn't locked.

The interior of the house was dark. I swallowed hard.

Thierry met my gaze. "Stay behind me."

He slipped into the darkness inside and I followed. As soon as I passed over the threshold I frowned.

"Hold on," I said quietly. "How did I just do that? I thought I couldn't enter private homes without an invitation anymore. I figured that Haven and places like that were off the list because they were open to the general public, but this is an actual house."

Claire shrugged. "A witch's home must be different."

I frowned. "Maybe."

Where was Stacy? Had she given me the wrong address? I didn't like this. My skin had been crawling with bad vibes ever since being at the reunion and they'd just intensified.

"Hello?" I called out. "Anybody home?"

"I'm still not sensing anything," Claire said.

"What do you think you should be sensing?"

"A paranormal presence. Some sort of malevolent magic. It leaves an impression in a house like a stinky-cheese smell."

"Maybe she went to the convenience store for something," George suggested.

She shook her head. "I'd still sense her magic here."

"She's out," I said firmly. "That's all there is to it. She'll be back. This is the address she gave me, I'm sure of it."

"Then we shall wait for her to return," Thierry said, and there was an underlying darkness in his words. His patience had worn out with this situation. Maybe not with me, specifically—at least I hoped not—but with the curse itself and the witch who'd caused it.

Frankly, so had mine. I wanted this over with.

Reggie was sniffing the archway leading into the living room area. He turned to Claire and whined through his muzzle.

"What is it?"

"Ahh heeensh rumhing."

He turned and padded into the living room.

"I should have kept him on the leash," she said under her breath. "We'll check it out. You guys stay here and keep a lookout."

She walked after him.

"George," Thierry said. "Perhaps you should wait out front. Conceal yourself and keep an eye open for the witch's return."

"Sure thing, boss." He nodded and slipped back outside.

Thierry turned to me. "Are you feeling well?"

"Other than the fact that the answer to all of my problems is currently AWOL, I'm doing okay." I swallowed. "Listen, Thierry, about what Butch said earlier."

His expression didn't change. "What part do you refer to?"

I licked my dry lips. "About . . . about *eliminating* me. If Stacy doesn't come back or if she's changed her mind . . . if I don't fix this mess I've gotten myself into . . ."

"I wish you hadn't heard that."

"I don't blame him for suggesting it. This is all really bizarre. This whole situation."

He shook his head. "I won't let anything happen to you."

"You say that now, but . . ." My voice caught on the words. "What if I go all dark and dangerous again? I mean, I know what happened to the other . . . the other nightwalkers. That you knew they were evil and a threat and what you did was the right thing, but . . . if Stacy bails and this really is a debilitating curse that sends me permanently on a one-way trip to Monsterville—"

"It isn't."

"How can you be so sure?"

His determined expression didn't waver and he brought

a warm hand to my cool face. "Because you are not a monster, Sarah. There is nothing about you that is remotely evil, if that is what you're concerned about. Of this I am utterly convinced. Being evil is a choice one makes."

"So what happens if I am stuck like this?"

He turned so that he was completely facing me, and he reached down to take my hand in his. The one that wasn't currently clutching my emergency Thermos.

"I know there are parts of Alaska that are dark for weeks at a time," he said.

My bottom lip quivered. "Like that scary movie with Josh Hartnett and the bad vampires who ate everybody?"

His mouth moved into a small smile. "That was just a movie. But there are places that would suit one unable to bear sunlight. There are steps one can take to make such a life very tolerable."

"So you're suggesting I pack my bags and head to a place like that?"

"No," he said. "I'm suggesting that we will both head to a place like that."

I blinked up at him. "Both of us?"

"I, too, have a darkness inside me that I must deal with. I truly believe that we will be better off together than apart as we both learn how to control our inner demons. I know, now that I have the proper motivation, I can find that control, as will you." His grip on my hand increased. "We'll make this work. Whatever it takes."

My heart beat at that announcement. One little, barely audible thump.

A tear splashed down to my cheek. "That sounds like a very reasonable option."

His smile remained. "I thought so."

"But Alaska? You know I'm room temperature now. I'll be like an ice cube up there."

"I'll make sure we have many electric heaters available to us."

I sucked up the emotion I thought might overwhelm me. Butch suggested Thierry kill me because I was a nightwalker. Instead, if the curse wasn't broken, Thierry was going to take me to Alaska so we could be together in a place that didn't have sunshine all the time.

He was going to buy electric heaters to raise my body temperature.

It was the most romantic thing I'd ever heard.

"This is, of course, a worst-case scenario," he said. "But I have given it a great deal of thought over the last forty-eight hours."

I bit my bottom lip. "If you're not careful, I'm so totally going to kiss you."

He gave me a small smile. "You say that as if it's a threat."

"More like a promise."

He met my gaze. "Only a kiss?"

"That's just the appetizer."

He circled my waist with his hands and I felt the comparative warmth of his body against mine as he pulled me against him. I rested my head on his chest. "It will be fine, Sarah," he said softly. "Trust me."

"I do." I said it quicker than I would have expected. But I did trust him. More than anyone I could remember.

I felt safe with Thierry, even knowing that he had serious issues of his own to deal with. Now I knew for sure that he wanted to deal with his monsters while I dealt with mine. We were a pair, all right.

Claire cleared her throat and I looked over at her.

"Sorry to interrupt," she said. Her expression was grim. "But there's something you need to see."

She led us into the living room and through to a hallway beyond. Up a short flight of stairs and into an expansive, professionally decorated master bedroom with a king-sized canopy bed. Candles were lit and flickering throughout the room. Dozens of them. There was the scent of perfume in the air.

Stacy was lying on the silk sheets of her bed wearing black, lacy lingerie and high-heeled slippers. She was asleep with her long blond hair spread out on the black silk pillows like a macabre Sleeping Beauty.

I frowned. No, she wasn't asleep. I sucked in a breath that I didn't actually need anymore.

Her eyes were open and staring up at the ceiling, wide and glassy.

And very, very dead.

The silver hilt of a knife stuck out of her chest, and I touched my own chest, flashing back to my stake wound. But I'd recovered from my injury.

Stacy wouldn't.

I heard somebody sob and realized it was me. Thierry gathered me into his arms and held on to me tightly.

"We'll find another way," he said softly.

"Somebody killed her," I said out loud, and it didn't even sound like my voice, too shaky, too broken. "Who would kill her?"

Considering her recent black magic activity, I'd say that was actually a long list. But looking at the romantic setup of the room, from the candles to the lingerie, I'd have put money on the murderer's being her new boyfriend.

"I don't sense the murderer is still here." Claire had her eyes closed, her arms raised to her sides. "Whoever it was left only minutes before we arrived."

I pulled away from Thierry and looked down at Stacy's face, still as coldly beautiful as she had been last night in the park. I wanted to feel sorry for what had happened to her, because it was a hell of a way to go—killed by somebody you thought that you loved—but all I could feel was . . .

Nothing. There was a big, gaping hole inside me. A black hole that seemed to devour emotions. I wasn't upset or scared or depressed. At the moment, at the revelation that Stacy had died, all I felt was *nothing*.

I remembered something she'd told me last night along with the three-day time limit for curse reversal.

"It's over." I swallowed hard. "She told me that if she dies, then the curse is permanent."

"Don't say that!" Claire said, and she began rooting through the bookcase at the side of the bed. "I've never heard of a completely permanent curse. Look, all of her magic books are here. I'm totally taking these back to Niagara Falls tonight. I'll read through them. If there's anything I can do to help you out I'll be in touch as soon as I can, okay?"

I nodded stiffly, still too stunned to even make room for a little bit of positivity. "Okay. If you say so."

Thierry turned me away from the bed to look at him

instead of the dead witch. "Sarah, please be strong. This isn't the end."

"Just feels like it, right?"

He took my face between his hands and forced me to look at him. "Sarah, please. Don't lose hope. Hope is sometimes all we have."

"Since when have you become such an optimist?"

"Since about ten weeks ago."

I smiled weakly at him. "I'm tired. I know I've only been awake for a few hours today, but I think I want to go to sleep in my own bed tonight. I'll pull a Scarlett and think about everything tomorrow."

He nodded. "Perhaps that would be for the best. Let's leave this place. I'll contact the authorities when I return to Haven."

So we left, literally closing the door behind us on any hope of breaking my curse tonight. I went back to George's place, to my bed that I hadn't slept in for the week in which I'd stayed with Thierry at his townhome, stayed at the motel in my hometown, or slept on the sofa at Haven, and I pulled the covers over my head and tried to sleep.

Not too surprisingly, I dreamed. Vividly.

I was in Mexico with Thierry. A picture postcard of our trip to Puerto Vallarta shortly after we'd first met when I thought that I might have just achieved my little vampiric happily ever after with my handsome but angsty Prince Charming.

The sun was setting over the ocean, which sparkled like diamonds. The sand felt cool against my hands. I reclined on a lounge chair under the umbrella that had been up during the day. The sky was all shades of pinks, oranges, purples, and golds as the sun slowly slipped beneath the horizon. There was a slight wind that felt warm against my skin and I could smell a mixture of sea salt and that cocoa-butter aroma of suntan lotion.

I took a sip of the drink the waiter had just brought by—a Tequila Sunrise. My favorite and definitely appropriate to the location. The mixture of tequila, orange juice, and grenadine slid satisfyingly down my throat.

I wore the skimpy red bikini that I'd bought specifically for the trip. When I'd first put it on I felt strange and exposed wearing so little compared to the way we had to dress for winter in Toronto, but I'd quickly gotten used to it. A couple of beaches away the women went topless, so my small bit of red material was comparatively modest.

"You're so beautiful," Dream-Thierry said. He sat on the accompanying lounge chair. I turned my head and smiled at him. His shoes and socks were off and his black shirt was unbuttoned to the waist.

"You're not so bad yourself," I said.

He got up from his chair and knelt beside mine, resting his hand on my bare stomach.

"I'm glad you convinced me to come here," he said. He pulled off my dark sunglasses and set them down on the little table between the lounge chairs that also held our drinks. "I want to kiss you right now."

"Well, what's stopping you?"

His hand drifted down to my hip, over the tied strings at the side that held the bikini bottom in place, and then farther down to my thigh, my knee, my calf, and then back up again all the way to my face.

"When I'm with you, Sarah, you have a tendency to make me forget myself," he said, and his dark gaze returned to mine.

I frowned. "What does that mean?"

"It means that when I'm with you I feel like a normal man when I am anything but."

"You're normal," I said. "Very normal. Now are you going to kiss me, or what?"

A small smile played across his extremely kissable lips. "I'm not normal," he said as he moved his face up to mine and brushed his mouth against mine. "And neither are you. Not anymore."

"Are you talking about the nightwalker thing?"

He leaned back slightly. "That, yes. But much more than that makes you different now. My own mistakes have changed things that should have been left alone. *Les jeux sont faits.*"

"What does that mean?"

"It means that the games are set. The plays have been made. And now we must wait and hope that all is well, for I fear that there is no turning back."

"I remember the good old days when you didn't talk so much." I smiled and put my hand on the back of his head, twisting my fingers in his dark hair to bring him back down to me. His lips parted with the next kiss and I felt his tongue slide against mine, which made my entire body ache for more of him.

"What am I going to do with you, Sarah?" he mused.

"I can think of a great many things," I said. "None of which require a French translator. And we better get started right away or it'll be too late. There's not much time left."

"Indeed," he said.

He pulled me into his arms and lifted me off the lounge chair. I put my arms around his neck.

"Room. Now. Immediately."

"As you wish." He kissed me again.

Best dream ever. Yes. It was definitely number one, taking over from the George Clooney one back when he was on *ER* and I was a patient he had to "take care of."

But in my new bestest dream ever, Thierry didn't carry me immediately back to our hotel room to ravish me like something out of a romance novel. Instead he placed me back down on the lounge and I stared up at him.

"What's going on?" I asked.

"I forgot something very important," he said.

"What?"

"That little issue of you being a nightwalker."

I frowned. "I thought you said that didn't matter."

"I'm afraid you were wrong."

I gasped. There was suddenly a wooden stake sticking out of my chest. The same one that was there the other night when Heather's boyfriend tried to kill me. And I wasn't on the beach in Puerto Vallarta anymore wearing a red bikini, I was wearing regular clothes, jeans and my white camisole, and the only thing red was my blood.

"The weapon hasn't pierced your heart," Thierry said. There were people behind him. George was there. Amy and Barry. Butch. Claire and Reggie. And even Veronique looked over Thierry's shoulder.

"My poor, stupid, trusting dear girl," she said. "However did you come to be in this unfortunate situation?"

"Get it out of me," I gasped. Every breath I took hurt.

No one else approached me. It was as if they were afraid for some reason. But Thierry did. He pressed his palm against my chest and with one forceful pull, he removed the stake.

I looked down at my chest and watched as the wound healed itself before my very eyes. After a few seconds it was as if it had never been there in the first place.

I felt so relieved I began to cry. "That was a close one."

"It was," Thierry said. "You were almost lost to me forever."

I reached up to touch his tense, handsome face. "I love you so much, Thierry. Do you know that? Do you have any idea how much I love you?"

He kissed my hand and brought it back to my side. "I know, Sarah. That's why you must die."

Then he raised the sharp wooden stake above his head and plunged it directly into my heart.

I sat bolt upright in bed and stared at the large shard hanging across from me on the wall. It reflected a woman who had just had a very lousy night's sleep climaxed by a nightmare of epic proportions.

Poor thing.

I blinked at the reflection. My straight, dark brown shoulder-length hair was plastered across my face. I raked it back into place. My face beneath the hair was pale and damp with perspiration. My brand new *Ghouls Just Wanna Have Fun* T-shirt with the picture of designer-clad zombie chicks was twisted enough to almost cut off my circulation.

In other words: totally hot babe alert.

Riiight. It was a very good thing that I was all alone. What a terrible dream.

I heard a ringing sound. The doorbell. Maybe that's what had woken me up in the first place.

With my head in a just-woken-up-after-a-lousy-dream fog, I swung out of bed and grabbed my new—*free*—bathrobe, put it on, and walked to the front door. It was probably Thierry. Where was George? I blinked, feeling the side-effects of not getting a whole lot of nightmare-free sleep that night.

I twisted the lock and opened the door.

And that's when I remembered my little "aversion to sunlight" problem. How the hell could I have forgotten that little tidbit?

I screamed as the laser beams of death attacked my entire body, and I slammed the door shut. Even knowing I didn't have to breathe anymore, my chest heaved as I braced myself against the wall. Wisps of smoke moved in the air around me as my exposed skin recovered from leaving the fry-zone.

The doorbell rang again.

"Uh . . . delivery here for a Sarah Dearly?"

I approached the window, which I suddenly realized was blocked by heavy blinds and curtains. I braved a quick, very quick, peek outside, which very nearly melted my eyeball. A FedEx truck sat idling at the curb outside George's house.

Delivery. For me.

Staying behind the door, I opened it a crack. "Okay."

The delivery guy hesitated, and then I saw the edge of his tracking machine enter past the edge of the door. "Um . . . you're going to have to sign for it."

I grabbed the tracker, hastily scrawled my signature, and handed it back to him.

"Everything okay?" he asked tentatively.

"Just a really bad hangover," I explained. *Yeah. From the fiery depths of hell.*

"Been there," he said with a knowing chuckle. "Okay, here you go."

A small bubble envelope appeared then. I grabbed it.

"Have a great day!" he said.

"Yeah, you, too." I shut the door and stood there with my back against it for a good two minutes. Then I finally allowed myself to relax and walked over to the sofa, where I promptly collapsed.

The door opened again and a death sunbeam hit me dead on.

"Close the door!" I yelled, and then added a few choice expletives to hammer home my point.

"Sorry!" I heard George say from a sea of white-hot pain, and suddenly the room was blissfully dark again. I blinked and watched the swimming spots of color in front of my eyes begin to fade away.

"Where were you?" I asked.

"On an important assignment." He held up two coffees in familiar Starbucks cups. "Happy Valentine's Day. My new espresso machine broke so I had to go for reinforcements. You take yours black, right?"

"You brought me coffee?" I managed a smile at that. "You are the best."

I added a few packets of sweetener to the dark liquid that smelled good enough to bathe in. I loved my coffee. Even though my new vampire body had a hard time handling the cream I used to like, and the caffeine didn't actually do anything to help wake me up, I refused to give it up. Some habits die hard.

"Even after how mortifyingly awful last night went," I said, "this coffee helps a bit this morning. Thanks, George."

He picked up my discarded sweetener packets and stir stick. "It's not the morning. It's four o'clock."

I frowned. "It's four o'clock? In the afternoon?"

He nodded. "Thierry was here earlier. He stayed for a few hours but you didn't wake up. I watched to make sure he didn't try any funny business; after all, you do look fetching in that nightshirt. He decided to go to the club early. He says he'll see you there."

Valentine's Day was not off to a great start. My skin was still smoking a bit from the sun exposure.

"He's probably sick of me. I'm too much trouble."

"And your point?" He grinned and took a sip of his coffee. "Maybe you're worth a little extra effort."

I looked at him. "You are really super sweet this week."

His shoulders slumped. "I think I need to get out more. I've lost my edge. I'm going all soft and cushiony." He appeared to shake it off. "How are you feeling today? Okay?"

I shrugged. "Okay is a relative term. It still hasn't entirely sunk in that I'm going to have to avoid sunshine for the rest of my life." My throat tightened at the thought.

I told him about my dream. He looked concerned at first, and then laughed at the end of it. "As if Thierry would ever stake you."

"You don't think so?"

"Of course not."

I sighed. "It felt so real. Especially after I found out that Thierry's responsible for the fact that there are no nightwalkers around anymore. And it's not because he gave them five hundred dollars and a ticket to Hawaii."

"I hadn't heard that. Well, maybe he *will* stake you then."

My eyes widened.

He grinned. "I'm kidding. Maybe I haven't lost my edge after all." He nodded at the coffee table where I'd thrown the envelope. "What's that?"

"It came by courier a few minutes ago." I grabbed it and tore open the envelope and peered inside. There was a smaller envelope with a handwritten note.

Happy Valentine's Day, Sarah. From one who cares more for your well-being than you realize.

I loved Thierry like crazy, but he wasn't exactly a born poet, that was for sure.

He couldn't just say "I love you," or even end the note with "Love, Thierry," or how about "Marry me, Sarah, and spend eternity by my side."

Well, the last one was out of the question due to Veronique, but still, a girl could fantasize, couldn't she?

"Doesn't look like his handwriting," I said aloud, and then opened the little envelope expecting to see a gift certificate inside.

Instead, my mouth went dry and my heart let out a single, very surprised thump.

It was the gold chain.

I pulled it out slowly, my eyes widening at every gold link that emerged from the envelope. It was equivalent to an eighteen-inch necklace, a little thicker, and the gold had a brassy quality to it rather than a fine finish. Exactly like I remembered it.

It was cold to my touch and didn't feel like much of anything at all. I didn't feel any magical vibes from it, not that I ever had when it first came into my possession.

"Is that what I think it is?" George asked.

I licked my suddenly dry lips. "Would you help me?"

He nodded and took the necklace from me. I lifted my hair and he fastened the chain behind my neck. He leaned back to inspect it.

"All you're missing to complete the look is an extremely hairy male chest," he said.

I blinked and then realized our proximity. "Are you sure you feel okay about being this close to me?"

He raised an eyebrow. "I have the stun gun in a shoulder holster right now and I'm not afraid to use it. Don't take it personally."

I snorted lightly. "I don't blame you at all."

"How do you feel?"

"I'm not sure."

"Do you feel any different?"

I concentrated. "I'm not . . . sure."

He tilted his head to the side. "Does my neck look extremely delicious and appetizing to you right now?"

I looked at his neck. "Not particularly."

"I'm terribly insulted."

"Don't be."

He stood up from the sofa and walked over to the front door. "Well, how about another test?"

He swung the door open and the sunlight hit me square

in the face. I shrieked, held up my hands, and braced myself for sheer and complete agony.

But . . . there was nothing.

I slowly spread my fingers and looked through them at George and the very bright February day behind him.

"You're not on fire," he observed. "I'm thinking that's a good sign."

I touched the chain at my throat and rose from the sofa, moving over to where George stood. I stood in the doorway, closed my eyes, and felt the sun on my face.

"I can't believe this!" I said, and laughed out loud with relief and happiness. I tentatively took a step outside and then another, until I was standing in the middle of the snow-covered front lawn in my bare feet. Then I proceeded to do a happy little jig. "It works! The necklace works!"

"It wasn't from Thierry at all, was it?" he said, with a matching smile on his face. "It was the Red Devil. He sent the necklace to you. See? I told you he was all sorts of awesomeness."

I stopped dancing for a moment. He was right. The Red Devil had to have been the one to send this to me. And what did the note say? That he cared about my well-being?

I frowned then. "How did he know where I was staying? He had the delivery made here specifically. How did he know I was even here?"

"Who cares?" George replied.

Good point.

Human or not, the Red Devil was now my favorite masked man in the universe. He even beat out Zorro, and since I was a big Antonio Banderas fan, that was saying a lot.

"I love the Red Devil!" I said out loud.

"Me, too!" George agreed, and he joined me on the front lawn and we did a sun dance together as we celebrated my new chance at a normal life.

It was a very good way to start Valentine's Day.

Chapter 17

Feeling revitalized and happier than I'd felt in days, I took my time getting ready to go to Haven. I wanted to look extra good—after all, it was Valentine's Day. I told George to keep my new piece of jewelry a secret. I wanted to surprise Thierry with my fabulous news.

I put on some new lingerie I'd never worn before because it was too nice and I was saving it for a special occasion, and then got dressed in a bright-pink cashmere sweater and short black skirt. The sweater was high enough in the neckline to conceal the gold chain but tight enough to make up for the lack of cleavage. Black nylons and black stilettos finished things off nicely. I even used Velcro rollers to give my hair a little extra *oomph* and then spent a good half hour painstakingly applying my makeup, using my large shard to reflect how it was going.

Sometimes I wondered why vampires didn't have reflections. Really, it didn't make much sense, did it? I was solid, I felt solid. I wasn't see-through. But a regular mirror didn't show me or the clothes I wore.

Too weird.

But I was currently too happy to give a crap.

I finished applying my Viva Glam lipstick and smiled brightly at my well-made-up reflection. I'd ringed my eyes in black liner and had gone extra heavy on the mascara. My hazel eyes popped right off my face. Though, not literally, of course, because that wouldn't be good.

I'd taken it fairly light on makeup and fashion—all things considered—over the past couple of months. Strange that when you're scared for your life these things tend to take a backseat to other worries.

But a little polish sure did feel good.

Even George approved. When I finally emerged from my bedroom through a cloud of hairspray and Givenchy *eau de toilette,* he gave me an appraising look.

"Who's the Cosmo Girl?" he asked. "I don't think we've met."

"Very funny."

"Let's go. It's my last night to make tips."

I still wasn't sure what I was going to do to make money after tonight. However, with my newly optimistic outlook, I felt rather certain that everything would work out perfectly.

My plan for tonight was to show up at Haven, let Thierry get a load of my new and improved look and outlook, and then force him to take me out on the town for drinks to celebrate Valentine's Day and my new lease on life. Then we'd go back to his townhome and I'd show him a few other things, not the least of which was my brandnew lingerie, which I had a funny feeling he might like quite a lot.

So what if I was stuck as a nightwalker? As long as

I had my new necklace all was right with the world, because none of the symptoms even mattered anymore. I could forget about my problems and think only of my future. With Thierry.

Hell yeah. It was going to be a very good night.

The world seemed brighter. The stars were out. The moon shone large in the black sky above. The night air was cold and refreshing against my face. My feet hurt like a son of a bitch because of the four-inch stilettos, but it was a good pain. And one that, after a lifetime of wearing questionable footwear, I could deal with quite easily.

George and I entered Haven just before it opened. The bouncer, who I knew had a minor crush on me, eyed me warily as I passed him. That wasn't the usual look he gave me. Strange.

But then I remembered that everyone expected me to be all nightwalker-from-hell. They all treated me like a mental patient on the brink of having a final breakdown.

Not tonight. Nothing could go wrong tonight. I seriously wouldn't allow it.

Amy and Barry were inside, and they both looked worried, their expressions growing graver as I approached.

"Sarah," Amy said warily. "Good to see you."

I gave her a quick look up and down. "Somebody's a blond again."

To go with her back-to-normal blond hair she wore a bright red miniskirt and sparkly white shirt with a red sequined heart over her chest. Barry wore his usual minituxedo.

She touched her hair. "I had it done this afternoon. My scalp feels like it's on fire."

"I know the feeling."

Her bottom lip wobbled. "I feel so horrible about everything."

"Forget about it." I smiled at her. "What are you drinking?"

"Um . . . it's a chocolate martini."

"Can I have a sip?"

Her expression changed to one of confusion. Then she lifted the glass. "Of course."

I took a quick sip. "That is dee-lish."

"Are you feeling all right?"

"I'm feeling fantastic. And you?"

"I'm . . . I'm okay."

Barry eyed me. "You are acting erratically."

"Am I?" I lunged forward and grabbed the little freak and gave him a big hug. Then I kissed him hard on his right cheek, leaving behind a kiss-shaped imprint of my lipstick.

"George," Barry said. "I'm told that you have a stun gun at the ready?"

George laughed. "I do, but it won't be necessary. Sarah's just in a really good mood tonight. Go figure."

Barry pursed his lips as he began working on the kiss mark with a paper napkin. "I can't think of a single reason, given everything that has transpired, why she should be."

"You are a pessimist, little man." I pointed at him. "You need to take Amy out and have some fun tonight. It's Valentine's Day, for Pete's sake."

"That would be nice," Amy agreed.

Barry nodded. "Later. Definitely later." He still frowned. "You look . . . *well*, Sarah."

I raised my eyebrows and glanced at Amy. "I think your husband is flirting with me. Better keep an eye on him."

Barry gasped. "I would never!"

"I'm just joking." I shook my head and laughed. "Honestly, sense of humor. Seek one out. It'll change your life."

"Sarah?" Thierry said from behind me, and I turned around slowly.

"Happy Valentine's Day," I told him.

"And to you." His gaze slowly took me in. "Barry is quite right. You look very well indeed. I've been worried about you."

"I heard you were at George's earlier."

His expression shadowed. "I didn't want to leave, but I knew that George would keep a watchful eye on you. There were certain last-minute details I had to attend to here before the club transfers to the new owners."

"Come with me." I curled a finger at him and then turned and walked through the club to his office. Once inside, I sat on the edge of his desk and waited for him to follow me. He did and then closed the door behind him.

"You are acting strangely," he said. "I know that finding the witch dead was a traumatic experience, but you mustn't lose hope. I will do everything in my power to find a way to break this curse. I swear to you, Sarah. It is the most important—"

I slid off the edge of the desk, closed the distance between us, and kissed him. Very hard and very deeply. I smiled against his lips as his hands curled around my upper arms and he brought me closer to him.

"What are you doing?" he breathed against my mouth.

"Kissing you." I kissed him again to prove my point.

He pulled away with effort. "I realize that, but it's not safe for us to be this close. Not until we figure all of this out."

"I've already figured it out."

He raised a dark eyebrow. "Oh, have you? And what have you figured?"

"You really want to know?"

"Very much."

I gave him a wicked smile as I began to remove my sweater, a smile that grew wider when I saw how shocked he looked. However, he didn't try to stop me.

"This is not the time, Sarah," he said.

"Trust me, it is." I slipped the pink cashmere over my head so I sat on his desk clad only in my previously un-worn light pink push-up bra, which left very little to the imagination. I threw the sweater at him and he caught it.

"Sarah . . ."

"Notice anything different about me?"

His throat worked as he swallowed and his darkening gaze moved over my face, my neck, the pink lace of the bra, until it finally came to the "anything different" in question. His gaze snapped back to my own.

"How?" he asked simply.

I touched the chain. "It was delivered this afternoon. The Red Devil sent it to me personally."

His frown deepened. "He sent it to you? How did he know where to find you?"

"Exactly what I was wondering, but then I realized that it doesn't matter. He obviously found it at the pawnshop and bought it to give to me because he knew I needed it."

"And it works?"

"Come here."

After a moment, he approached me cautiously. I took his hand in mine and pressed it against my chest so he could feel the beating of my heart.

"Works like a charm." I slid my fingers over the metal.

He didn't move his hand, but leveled his gaze with my own. "That it does."

"Not the prettiest necklace I've ever owned, but definitely my new favorite. I can go outside in the sunshine. Also, you really don't realize how much a beating heart makes you feel normal until it stops."

"And your uncontrollable desire for blood?"

"Back to a humming white noise in the background of my life." I smiled at him. "And I can kiss you without going all Mistress of the Dark. As proven a minute ago."

He touched his mouth where my lipstick had made its second appearance of the evening. "This is all very good, Sarah."

"I thought you'd think so." My smile widened before beginning to waver a bit. "You're saying that, but you don't sound all that convinced."

He placed my sweater next to me on the desk and then clasped his hands together. "I do have concerns."

"Concerns," I repeated. "Like, for example?"

"Such as the fact that while it is a good thing that the chain works as a dampener to the curse, the curse still does exist. The chain is not a cure, only a treatment."

"That's true. But—"

"And also if you happen to lose the chain or it is stolen from you, then there are no other options. It is as if you are painting yourself into a corner by relying on unreliable magic of this sort, and we mustn't be lulled into a false sense of security and stop searching for a true solution."

The air began to go out of my happy balloon with an annoyingly squeaky sound.

"Yeah, I guess. But—"

"And then there is the very important matter of this Red Devil. Who is he? What is his motivation for assisting you in this matter? Where did he come from? What does he want?"

"That's a lot of questions."

"To which we have no answers." His expression softened a little, and he moved closer to me. "Sarah, I know you are overjoyed that you now have the necklace again and that it works. But we can't let our defenses down. Now more than ever we are vulnerable. Most hunters are out of town, but it doesn't mean we should trust anyone who waltzes into our lives so easily."

I frowned. "Are you saying that I'm too trusting? Even after everything that has happened to me?"

He nodded. "It is a wonderful trait to have, this trust in your fellow man. But as you've seen in the past, there are very few who are actually worthy of this trust. Others have their own agendas, their own desires to be met, and sometimes lies and deceit are tools of that trade."

I reached up to touch his face. "I know you've been hurt a lot in your life. Well, I don't really know that for sure, since you aren't exactly all that open with the amusing anecdotes, but I'm assuming a lot of bad stuff has happened to you well above and beyond what I already know. Why can't I accept the Red Devil's gift for what it is? A gift from somebody who cares if I live or die?"

His jaw tensed. "Because he is not the Red Devil."

"How do you know that?"

"You said it yourself, he is human, not vampire."

I shrugged. "Maybe I was wrong."

"I don't think that you were. He's an impostor attempting to worm his way into your good graces. And perhaps not today or tomorrow, or even a week from now, but one day he will expect a favor from you in return for giving you the gold chain."

"Then I'll do it."

He laughed at that but it was cold. "Just like that."

"Sure. He did me a favor. Why wouldn't I do one for him?"

He let out a long sigh. "He is *not* the Red Devil."

"How do you know that?" I asked again.

"Because . . ." His expression tightened. "Because I . . . I knew the *true* Red Devil. A very long time ago."

I stared at him. "Okay, I think we have a bit of a communication problem, because when I first asked you about this very subject you said that he was an urban legend. Now you were a close personal friend of his? Which is it?"

"His identity has been a closely guarded secret. I keep that secret as well."

"After all this time?"

"Yes. And the true Red Devil has not made an appearance for a hundred years."

"And why is that?" I asked.

"There are many reasons."

"Such as?"

He sighed. "Such as the fact that the world has changed. That one man cannot make a difference alone.

There is too much darkness in the world. The Red Devil grew weary of fighting against this darkness and not seeing an improvement."

"Was he killed?"

Thierry hesitated. "No. He is still very much alive."

I shook my head. "So he's been standing around for a hundred years watching all the bad things happening and he hasn't raised a finger to do anything about it?"

"Certain events transpired in his life that made that choice inevitable. Some of his choices only led to more pain and torture for those of his kind."

"Excuses," I said, and shook my head.

His eyebrows rose. "Pardon me?"

"This guy, whoever he is, sounds like he wasn't right for the job in the first place. I don't know much about the Red Devil, but I do know one thing. Other vampires looked up to him like a symbol of hope. As long as he existed they had something to believe in other than worrying about hunters being around the next corner."

"It is not like that at all."

"He sounds like a self-involved jerk to me. And the difference with the guy who's impersonating him? He's actually doing something. He's trying to make a difference. Just the mere glimpse of him around town has got everybody all excited. That has to count for something."

Thierry glowered at me. He was actually *glowering*.

I blinked at him. "What?"

"He is dangerous and he must be exposed."

"Well, I think you should e-mail your old buddy and tell him to get back on the job and maybe other people won't have to take over for him." I shook my head. "I mean, seriously. Especially with Gideon Chase dead and buried, this is the perfect time for vampires to rally themselves and start fighting back against the hunters in big numbers."

"Gideon's death will mean nothing to the hunters in the weeks to come. Another leader will be chosen and things will return to how they have always been."

"I disagree."

"This isn't surprising to me. Perhaps one day when years have passed and you have the luxury of looking back on history, you will see as I do. That people or their circumstances rarely change."

"That is such a defeatist point of view."

He gave me a smile. "I am pleased to see that your optimism has returned at its full strength."

I slid off from the edge of the desk and gave him a hug. "I don't want to fight with you. Not tonight."

"Neither do I. I only wish for you to be safe, Sarah. I worry that your optimism and trust lead you to danger."

I leaned back. "You have to stop worrying so much. It causes wrinkles."

His smile widened slightly. "Can we speak of other things?"

I nodded. "Sure."

"I didn't mention how beautiful you look this evening." His gaze moved down the length of me.

"Oh, yeah?" I smiled back at him.

"And I'm very pleased that you are feeling better about your circumstances."

"Way better. Any trips to Alaska are officially on hold."

"Is this new?" He ran a finger down the strap of my bra.

I nodded. "I bought it during my post-apartment-explosion shopping spree. Do you like it?"

"Very much." He raised a dark eyebrow. "And suddenly thoughts of your mysterious Red Devil benefactor seem rather inconsequential to me."

"I thought they might."

And as his lips met mine I found that I, too, forgot all about the Red . . . um . . . whatever his name was. I sank into the kiss, wrapping my arms around Thierry and holding on tight as he picked me up and carried me over to the sofa, where the kiss became deeper and more urgent. Urgent enough that I suddenly wondered if he'd happened to lock the door so nobody would walk in on us. My now regularly beating heart sped up as he ran his hands down my body.

How could somebody so my opposite in nearly every way make me want him so much? What was it about him that I fell in love with? He was like a strange recipe that had absolutely everything thrown into the mix. Things that didn't seem to go together at all or seem palatable. But mix it up, throw it into the oven, and an hour later out came the most delicious dish I'd ever tasted.

Yeah, that was Thierry.

Not to everyone's taste, but definitely on the menu for me. Breakfast, lunch, dinner, and a midnight snack.

I had once doubted his feelings for me, and even now I did at times. He was hard to read with that stony exterior of his. But I knew he loved me, even though he didn't exactly shout it from the rooftops. He proved it to me with his actions, his deeds, the unspoken things. And he murmured it to me when we made love.

He loved me. And I loved him. And nothing was going to come between us.

Did I want to bite anybody? Nope.

Was I feeling okay? Hell, yeah.

"I hope I'm not interrupting anything," a cool, female voice purred.

Thierry and I both turned toward the door to look. Veronique stood there, tapping her foot, with her arms crossed in front of her. She had an eyebrow raised.

Damn. Another couple of minutes and this would have been mortifying instead of just a really awkward and embarrassing situation as I made out with her husband on the sofa in his office.

And damned if she didn't look amused by the whole thing.

Reassessment.

Did I feel like biting anyone?

Yes please.

Chapter 18

Perhaps I should give you a little privacy?" Veronique asked, although she didn't make any move to leave the room. She wore a low-cut black dress with a high slit at the side. I was almost certain it was Gucci. Her raven-colored hair was long and sleek and fell effortlessly around her perfect face.

Thierry pushed up from the sofa and grabbed my sweater, which he handed to me with a definite look of apology in his still-dark gaze. I turned away and slid the sweater on as quickly as I could.

"Veronique," he said evenly. "I didn't expect you."

"No, I imagine not."

"You have come all the way from Paris to see me?" he asked.

"Yes, and I'm sure you know why."

"I would imagine it has something to do with the papers I sent you."

"That's right. An annulment?" She shook her head and smiled. "Really, Thierry. I expect much better from you after all these years."

"Oh? What do you mean?"

She smiled in my direction. "Sarah, so lovely to see you again, my dear."

"You, too," I said, and it sounded more like a squeak.

Dammit. Why did I feel so wrong? Their marriage was over. I had nothing to feel guilty about. I mean, it's not exactly like our relationship was a secret. Everybody knew Thierry and I were together. Veronique herself condoned the whole thing—encouraged it, even. She was fine with it!

Still, I was currently so embarrassed I wanted to crawl under the sofa.

She returned her attention to Thierry. "I thought we had an understanding. Our lives could be led separately. You can take part in your . . . dalliances . . ."

I frowned at that. *Dalliances?*

"But to take things to the next level by seeking an annulment of our marriage?" She shook her head. "Honestly. I don't feel that such a step is necessary."

"With all due respect, Veronique," Thierry said, "I feel differently."

She nodded. "I see. And was this your decision or something you were talked into?"

"I am rarely talked into anything."

"This is very true. But you are a man. Your head can be turned by that which is new and shiny. History suggests that all men will wander, but they eventually will return to where they belong. I am simply suggesting that you look at this situation from my point of view."

"And what point of view is that, Veronique?"

"How would you feel if some young man came

into my life and I decided to leave everything to be with him exclusively? If it were I who requested this annulment?"

Thierry stared at her for a moment and his lips curled to the side. "I would be fine with it."

She frowned. "Perhaps that was a bad example."

Thierry turned to me. "I think it would be best if you allow Veronique and me to discuss this matter alone."

That sounded like the best news I'd heard all day. Well, other than the fact that my nightwalker days were history. Leaving the room and letting Thierry and his wife hash out the annulment issue ran a very close second.

"No," Veronique said. "This concerns Sarah as well. After all, had you not met her, this wouldn't be an issue at all, would it?"

"No, you're right," Thierry said. "It wouldn't be an issue, because if I hadn't met Sarah I would be dead right now."

"Ah yes, she did interrupt your little plan to end your long life, didn't she?"

"That she did."

She seemed to be avoiding a laugh. "And this has given you such a new outlook on life that you wish to end our arrangement to, what? Marry her instead?"

He glanced at me and then back to her. "My plans are currently not up for discussion."

She sighed. "Such double talk. Truly, Thierry, had you not begun life as a mere peasant, I'm quite sure you would have become a lawyer."

His face showed a bit of strain. "Are you refusing to sign the papers?"

She waited so long to answer that I wondered for a moment if she'd even heard the question. "I haven't yet decided. I thought I would return to Toronto to find out your true feelings on the matter. I believe I understand all too well now."

"You should sign them," he said.

"Perhaps. Perhaps not." She took a deep breath and let it out slowly. Then she smiled again, a seemingly effortless expression. "I will be staying at the the Windsor Arms. If you need me, please don't hesitate to let me know. I may stay for a couple of weeks, now that I'm here. Good night."

She turned and left the office. Thierry made a move to follow her, but I grabbed his arm to find that it was tensely corded muscle.

"It's okay," I said. "Let her go."

"She is the second-most-frustrating woman I've ever known," he said.

I frowned. "Who's the first?"

He met my gaze and a small smile showed through his tense expression. "You are."

"Frustrating, huh?"

"Extremely." He took my face between his hands and kissed me lightly. "I must speak with her."

"No, let me," I said.

"You?"

"Believe it or not, she likes me. At least, she used to. If I can talk to her face-to-face and explain everything, maybe she'll listen."

"You are more than welcome to try."

"Wish me luck."

"Of course." He kissed me again, and then he pulled back and his expression was guarded. "If she doesn't choose to sign, will it make a great difference to you?"

I touched his face and looked up into his silvery eyes. "Absolutely. It will be so over between us."

He frowned.

"I'm kidding," I said. "My parents will not be happy that I'm with a married man, but I can deal with whatever life throws at me. It's been one of those weeks that has made me reassess what's important in my life."

He squeezed my hand and then brought it to his lips. "I as well."

Then he let go of me with a smile, and I left the office to, I hoped, talk to Veronique and get this whole unfortunate situation sorted out.

Fortunately, she hadn't left the club yet. She stood near the bar speaking to Barry. Amy weeded her way past the crowded tables to come to my side. The music was currently Nina Simone singing "Feeling Good." I hoped that was a good omen.

"That woman scares the crap out of me," she said, nodding in Veronique's direction.

"She's not that bad," I told her.

She raised her eyebrows. "I'm surprised you would say that given who she is. I wouldn't want to meet any of Barry's ex-wives."

I turned to her. "Barry has ex-wives? Why didn't I know this?"

She nodded. "He's been married five times before. The man is a love magnet but he's all mine now."

"Right. And he still doesn't know about your crush on Thierry?"

"I thought we weren't going to talk about that anymore."

"Sorry."

"I mean, it's not exactly my fault that the man is a total dreamboat."

"Dreamboat?" I repeated. "Do people still say that?"

She crossed her arms and studied me from my black stilettos to my slightly poofier than normal hair. "You seem a lot better than you were. Are you, like, cured or something now?"

I told her about my little windfall. She was very happy for me, and some of the guilt and fear finally left her expression. I pulled the edge of my sweater down so she could see the necklace in place.

She shook her head. "Wow, I'm so happy for you, but that is seriously *fugly*."

I patted it gently. "I love it."

"Hey, guess what I heard?"

I kept an eye on Veronique. Whatever she was telling Barry caused him to glare in my direction every few seconds. Great. I guess it was obvious who was his favorite contestant in this fanged version of the Dating Game.

"It's about Gideon Chase," Amy continued. "You know he was killed slaying a freaking demon in Las Vegas, right? Can you believe it? That's why the El Diablo Casino burned to the ground."

"Coming through!" George slid past us carrying a tray heavily laden with drinks.

"Actually, I didn't know all the details," I said.

"The casino burned to the ground from hellfire. *Hellfire!* How bizarre is that?"

"Hellfire. Huh." I was only half listening to her.

"That's what killed Gideon. Hellfire. Apparently it completely and totally incinerated his body. There was nothing left behind. It was a closed casket with only a picture and a pair of shoes inside."

Veronique pointed directly at me and Barry glowered. Damn. I wish my vampire hearing was better. I tried to pretend I wasn't paying attention, so I turned to Amy.

"So . . . this Gideon update. How did you hear this? Is it on the Vampire Hunters of America Web site?"

"No. Actually Quinn called ten minutes ago. He wanted to talk to you but I knew you were busy."

"Quinn? He called *here*? That's the second time this week."

She nodded. "He also called to say he's getting married and he thinks he's coming back to Toronto to do it since everyone else on the continent hates him or wants him dead. Those were his words. We're all invited to the wedding." She clapped her hands. "I love weddings!"

"Married?" That finally got my full attention. "Quinn's getting married? *Quinn?* To who?"

"That really nice girl who was your bodyguard. Janie." She touched her now-flaxen pixie cut. "She liked my pink hair."

Janie had been a liar, a double-crosser, and she'd tried to kill me by handing my ass over on a silver platter to her master vampire boss, Nicolai. Then she ended up saving me. And now she was engaged to Quinn?

Three weeks. Seriously. Three weeks and Quinn had gotten over me that quickly?

I laughed out loud and shook my head. "Well, more power to him. I guess."

"Yeah, so he called and told me about his engagement, and about the Gideon thing. He thought you should know."

Gideon. If there was ever a name I never wanted to hear again of a man I'd never even had the displeasure to actually meet in real life, that was the one.

Buh-bye, Gideon, I thought. *Can't say that I'll miss you.*

Veronique leaned over and air kissed Barry on both cheeks, then she swung her ermine stole over one shoulder and walked out of the club.

"Okay, thanks for the update," I said. "I've got to go convince Veronique that Thierry and I belong together."

"Sure. Good luck with that," she said, although she didn't sound all that convinced.

I quickly followed Veronique until she left the club entirely and was outside the red door in the alley.

"Veronique, wait," I called after her.

She turned and raised a perfectly penciled-in eyebrow. "Did you wish to speak with me, my dear?"

"Actually, yeah. Do you mind?"

"Why should I mind?" A smile grew on her full red lips. "Come." She held out a hand to me. "We shall have a drink together. There is a café down the street."

Well, that was friendlier than I'd expected.

The café was the same one I'd gone to with Heather and her boyfriend the night I'd been staked. I tensed as soon as I saw its sign, the French Connection, glimmering in the near distance. But I didn't say anything. I sucked it up and ordered a coffee when we went inside. Black. Veronique ordered a latte and a croissant with apricot preserves.

I never realized that she was one of the lucky vamps, even at her age, who could still stomach solid food. Apparently that trait was on a biological lottery system and Veronique had come out as a winner. Figures.

"Barry told me more about your unfortunate situation," she said. "How are you managing?"

"I'm much better now." I decided not to share my news about the gold chain with her.

"I remember when the nightwalkers roamed the earth. It was a different time."

"And they were all wiped out."

"That is correct."

"Because of the information that Thierry gave the hunters."

She studied me for a moment. "That is also true. In part. At the time I didn't agree with his decision. To me, even though the nightwalkers were fierce creatures who gave the rest of us a reputation as monsters, a reputation that has lasted to this very day, I didn't feel he was right in his actions. In fact, I accused him of being a traitor to his own kind. However, my opinion did change over time."

"Why is that?"

"One could not reason with a nightwalker. I, myself, was nearly a victim of one." She absently touched her throat as her expression shadowed. "It was a man who appeared very handsome and charming until we were alone. He restrained me with ropes and he very nearly tore out my throat despite my pleas for him to release me."

My stomach sank at that. "Oh, my God, that's horrible. How did you get away?"

"The Red Devil came to my rescue."

I must have looked surprised because she laughed lightly. "Yes," she said. "I have also heard that you have recently come in contact with him. That he has reappeared after so many years in hiding. It is a wonderful thing."

I didn't tell her Thierry's theory that he was a total and complete fraud. I gripped the hot mug of coffee in front of me. "So the Red Devil saved you."

She nodded gravely. "I would not be sitting across from you right now if he hadn't. I still remember the night vividly, as if it was not so long ago." She visibly shivered. "He was incredible. So tall, so handsome, so virile."

"So handsome?" I repeated. "You saw his face?"

She frowned slightly. "No, actually I didn't. He wore a mask. A red mask. But I have no doubt that underneath he was the most handsome man on earth." She pushed the croissant around the plate absently but didn't take a bite. "I will never forget that he saved my life. At the time, he suggested that we become lovers, as he was so taken with me, but I had to decline. Still, I sometimes wonder what it would have been like to have such a charming and wonderful man in my life."

I wondered what had happened to the mask. My Red

Devil just wore the scarf over his face. "He saved my life, too."

"Yes, I heard that as well."

"From Barry."

She nodded. "Barry tells me many interesting things about you, my dear."

My jaw tightened. "Yeah, I'm sure he does."

She studied me. "He tells me, for example, that you are very much in love with my husband."

That surprised me. Barry told her that? I wonder what the catch was.

"It's true," I said simply. "I love him. I'm sorry if that hurts you."

She smiled. "Why ever would it hurt me?"

"Well, you *are* married to him."

She waved her hand dismissively. "You are not the first woman to fall in love with my husband and I am sure you will not be the last. His cool exterior attracts as many as it repels. What he sees as a defense mechanism to keep others away from him, for their own safety as he likes to think, tends to sometimes act as a magnet to those lacking an instinct of self-preservation and common sense."

The smell of cinnamon drifted under my nose as the baker behind the counter removed a tray of freshly baked biscotti from the oven.

"Do you think I'm lacking an instinct of self-preservation because I'm in love with Thierry?" I asked dryly. "Or just common sense?"

"I'm not entirely sure."

"What else did Barry tell you?" I took a sip of my

bitter coffee. "Just for the record, he really doesn't like me, so whatever he's said about me should be taken with a big old grain of salt."

"I'm not so sure about that, my dear. He, too, puts forth a rather harsh exterior. When one has been alive for so long, dealing with the daily struggles of a vampire's existence, one must put up a certain façade, and barricades against those who may lead us to harm."

"If you say so."

I heard the bell over the door as a couple, bundled up in winter clothes, entered the café. They approached the counter to place their order.

Veronique slid her index finger around the rim of her latte. "Barry tells me that when you first came into Thierry's life he believed you to be a silly, insipid creature who was interested only in Thierry's power and money. He did not trust you and he did not understand why Thierry would willingly want to spend time with you. And when he found that you had raised Thierry's bloodlust to the surface, something that Thierry has fought to keep under control for a century, he was not pleased. He wanted you gone from his master's life."

"Yeah, this isn't news. He told me as much to my face." I remembered a small red face, clenched fists, and a great deal of foot stomping.

"But you refused to leave. You refused to leave even when my husband attempted to end things between you for good—he even went so far as to sell Haven so he could leave the country entirely. Why is that?"

When had I lost control of this conversation? Had I even been in control to begin with? This was so annoying. I felt like I was on trial.

I shrugged a shoulder. "I can be a bit stubborn at times. I'll admit it."

Her gaze was steady on me. "You remind me a great deal of someone."

I shifted in my seat. "Oh, yeah? Do I really want to know?"

Her lips curled. "You remind me of myself."

"Really?"

Her gaze moved down and then back up as if she was appraising my value on the open market. "Some will see a stubborn woman and believe she is an inconvenience. But I see something different. I see someone who knows what she wants. A woman of decisiveness. With a strength of spirit. There are many vampires I have met over the years, Sarah. Many female vampires. There has only been one master vampire who happens to be female because the rest have succumbed to weakness at the hands of a hunter."

I blinked. "You?"

She nodded. "It takes a great deal more than luck to have lived as long as I have. I had my doubts about you, Sarah. At first glance I had to agree with Barry's assessment. You amused me, and I thought you were an interesting diversion for Thierry, but that was all. And though it has only been a very short time, all things considered, I feel that I must re-evaluate my opinion of you. I don't believe you are interested in my husband only for self-serving reasons."

"I'm not," I said quickly.

"No, you're not." She tilted her beautiful face to the side. "You truly love him."

I nodded. My throat felt tight. "I'm sorry."

"Don't be sorry. One should never be sorry for falling in love." Her eyes got that faraway look. "Because of Marcellus, I know what true love feels like. It is all-encompassing. It is obsession. It can be utter pain and absolute bliss."

I nodded. "That about sums it up."

There was a slight crease between her eyebrows as she concentrated on me. "I have never felt that with Thierry. That deep love. He has never caused my heart to be elated at his presence. Nor has he ever caused my heart to break. After Marcellus's death, my heart cooled to all others. Perhaps that is one of the reasons I have lived for so long. My head has not been turned by emotion. I have been able to make decisions based on survival, not because of a need for romance."

I didn't exactly know what to say to that so I said nothing at all and took another sip of my coffee.

Her gaze was still focused on me. "It is a mystery, is it not?"

"What?"

"Love. The world around us finds it so easy to hate each other. There is hate bleeding from every part of the earth. But love can heal all. Why is it so difficult to accept that?"

"You got me."

She licked her lips and played absently with the rim of her untouched latte. "Barry told me something else. Something I found most interesting indeed."

"What's that?"

"He believes Thierry loves you in return."

I swallowed a gulp of coffee so quickly that it burned my throat. "He actually *said* that? *Barry?*"

She nodded. "That gives me great pause. For as long as I've known my husband, I have never known him to show deep emotion for anything. In fact, I thought he was impervious to such a thing. I found that to be as great a strength as it was a disappointment. That I did not love him didn't mean that I didn't wish for him to love me. It is a power a woman has—the love of a man. Her greatest power. For to have the love of a powerful man is to wield that power at your whim."

I shook my head. "I don't want to wield any power. Seriously. Not exactly a hobby of mine."

She took a breath in and let it out, and then a smile replaced her serious expression. She took a twenty-dollar bill out of her wallet and placed it on the table. "It has been a pleasant conversation, my dear. We must do this again while I'm in town. Now, I shall retire to my suite for the remainder of the evening."

"But you didn't even eat your croissant."

She smiled. "I don't eat, Sarah. But there is no reason why it shouldn't appear as if I can."

I stood up at the same time she did and was about to say something else when she leaned toward me to air kiss both of my cheeks.

"Bon soir, mon amie."

I followed her out onto the sidewalk where she was able to summon a taxi with an elegant wave of her hand.

"So what does this mean?" I asked, now smiling at how well our conversation had turned out. "Are you going to sign the annulment?"

She turned to face me. "Of course not."

My smile dropped away. "You're not? But I thought

you understood. I thought you believed that Thierry and I are in love and want to be together."

She patted my face as one might do with a slow child who didn't understand why she couldn't sit on the family dog. "I told you before, my dear, love has very little to do with a successful marriage. It is much more than that."

"But—"

"No, no. Listen to me. I understand your feelings. You and Thierry should be together as much as you like. You have my blessing to be as happy as is possible. But my marriage shall not end over such a small thing as a ten-week relationship. It simply cannot be."

I frowned. "Look, if this is about money, I'm sure Thierry can arrange some sort of alimony to keep you in the style you are accustomed to, or however that works."

She opened the back door of the taxi that now idled at the curb and looked over her shoulder. The amusement in her eyes was vast. "My dear, I am the one with all the money in our marriage. Thierry's finances have dwindled of late because of the fortune he has lost from losing so many nightclubs in town. His holdings in other cities have also burned to the ground. Due to the secret nature of owning vampire-related establishments, none of that property was properly insured. To my knowledge, all he has left of his personal fortune is what he will make from the sale of Haven. It is a good thing that it sold; otherwise it would have soon gone out of business anyhow."

I felt stunned by that. "I don't believe it."

She smiled. "If anyone would be getting money from our marriage ending, it would be him. But since that is not an option, all is well with the world. You see? This is the way it must be. Good night, my dear."

She got into the cab and closed the door. It drove away from the curb. I watched it fade into the distance until I couldn't see it anymore.

Well, that went really well.

Thierry was almost broke? When the hell did that happen? And why hadn't he said anything to me?

She was probably wrong. I mean, didn't he have a ton of cash in his pocket just the other night? Besides, how could a nearly seven-hundred-year-old vampire not have a huge nest egg just waiting for any potential financial difficulties?

Yeah, she was wrong. Had to be.

I felt deflated about the annulment, but I guess it didn't really matter. It would have been nice. I'd actually had a vision of myself wearing a long white gown and walking down an aisle to meet a tuxedo-clad Thierry with rose petals being thrown at my feet. I'd always wanted a fairy-tale wedding.

Unfortunately, I was more than a half a millennium too late to get to my Prince Charming before he was already snapped up by a woman who didn't believe that love was an important element in a successful marriage. Sure. Just my luck.

It didn't matter.

What mattered was that my trauma of the week had been fixed thanks to the gold chain. Maybe it wasn't the cure, but it was a reasonable fix as far as I was concerned. And Thierry and I were still together. Everything else would have been extra icing on a cake that was already extremely tasty just the way it was.

I breathed out and watched the cloud of frozen air drift up and dissipate into the night air. Then I turned and walked the block and a half back to Haven.

Yeah, everything was cool, I decided as I trudged along, mentally kicking myself for the fiftieth time that I hadn't worn more comfortable shoes. Then again, who would have thought I would be out for a stroll after having coffee with my boyfriend's wife? On Valentine's Day?

All alone.

In the dark.

At nearly ten o'clock at night.

With no bodyguard to speak of.

Again.

I stopped and turned around. Did I hear footsteps?

I picked up my pace.

The alley to the secret entrance of Haven was just ahead, and I relaxed slightly as I turned the corner before skidding to a stop.

"Sarah," the Red Devil said. He leaned against the cold brick wall. I recognized him immediately due to the scarf that completely obliterated his identity.

All I really knew about him was that he was tall. Really tall. And well built. Not too muscular and not too skinny. Athletic. That was all I could tell, since he was dressed from head to toe in warm winter clothing, including black leather gloves. Exactly the same as the last time I'd seen him.

Only this time he stood under a streetlamp. As he looked at me I could now see that he had green eyes—the only thing visible under that scarf.

"Hey," I said, and I was very glad that my voice sounded steady, considering he'd just scared the living undead out of me. "How's it going?"

"Well. Very well." He blinked slowly. "Did you receive my gift?"

I touched my neck. "I did. I can't even begin to tell you how grateful I am for this. It's made all the difference in the world to me."

"I thought it might."

"But I don't understand why you didn't tell me you had it the last time I saw you."

"I wanted to keep it a surprise. Were you surprised?"

I nodded. "Very."

He didn't say anything for a moment and simply continued to watch me.

"I should probably get back inside," I said.

"Inside where?" he asked.

I bit my lip. Haven was a secret vampire club. Emphasis on the *secret* part. Did he know he was twenty feet away from the unmarked entrance? Or was he simply here to speak to me? Maybe he was trying to trick me into revealing the location and then he'd . . . then he'd *what*?

I laughed a little at that.

"What is it?" he asked.

I shook my head. "It's nothing. I'm just really paranoid. It's been one of those weeks that have made me question absolutely everybody's motives."

He touched his chest with a gloved hand. "Including mine?"

"Most especially yours." I sighed. "Look, I don't know

who you are. I guess that's the point, right? The whole disguise thing. I get it. It's all superhero and you don't want to reveal anything, but you've got to admit that it's a little bit creepy. I mean, you could be anyone under that scarf, couldn't you?"

"Are you afraid of me?"

"Should I be?"

He shook his head. "I have no plans of hurting you, Sarah."

I frowned. "That's kind of a strange way of putting it. Just a 'no' would have been good enough."

"Why would I give you the chain if I was one of the bad guys?"

"That's a very good question." I forced a smile. "Obviously you're one of the good guys. Because without the chain I'd be in a great deal of trouble, wouldn't I?"

He nodded. "Especially now that the witch is dead and unable to remove the curse."

"Exactly." I stopped talking for a moment and frowned hard. "Uh . . . how exactly did you know that she was dead?"

"If she wasn't you wouldn't need the chain to be normal, would you?"

I crossed my arms. "But you knew that she was dead. Not gone. Not hiding. *Dead.*"

He exhaled slowly. "A lucky guess?"

My mouth felt very dry as I thought of the silver-hilted knife sticking out of Stacy's chest. "I think I should be going now."

"No, wait. Sarah, we must talk."

I cleared my throat. "Do you think it can wait for another night? I sort of have a date."

"With Thierry?"

I nodded. "And he does hate to be kept waiting."

"I'm sure that he does. But I'm afraid this can't wait either. I'd like you to come somewhere with me."

I shook my head. "I don't think that's a very good idea."

"You don't trust me."

"Why should I trust somebody who hides his face? Look, I don't mean to be ungrateful or anything. I appreciate that you gave me the gold chain. I do. But the odds of me coming along with you wherever it is you want to take me are seriously slim to none."

He didn't say anything for a moment, and then, "Would knowing who I am change your mind?"

I looked at him skeptically. "Not sure about that. Who are you? Brad Pitt? My friend thinks you might be Brad Pitt."

He shook his head. "Afraid not."

"Do I know you already?"

"Indirectly, I'm sure that you do."

"Are you one of Thierry's informants? Or another bodyguard?"

He shook his head again.

Great. He wanted to play games. "So show me. Show me who you are and maybe I will be a little friendlier. Although I'm not promising anything."

He reached up to his scarf but then his hands froze as if he'd had second thoughts. "Perhaps you're right. Tonight is not a good night for this."

I rolled my eyes. "What? Chickening out? That is so not something I'd expect from the Red Devil."

He laughed a little at that. "No, I don't expect that it is.

But . . . but I've been through a great deal recently that I doubt you'd understand."

I frowned. "What does that mean? A great deal of what?"

"I was involved in a horrible accident recently. My face . . . it's not what it used to be."

I raised my eyebrows at that. "Your face? Is that why you're wearing the scarf? Some sort of *Phantom of the Opera* role-playing thing?"

"That's one way to put it."

"Look, I saw the movie." In fact, I used to own the DVD until my apartment went up in smoke. "The phantom was a good guy who bad things happened to. I promise not to scream or freak out. As long as you don't start singing everything is going to be just fine."

His green eyes took on an edge of amusement that chased away the doubt that had been there. "There will be no singing at any point of this evening. That much I can promise you."

I was warming up to the guy again. Just a little. He was one of the good guys, he just had a little facial disfigurement going on. And the phantom thing was *so* Gerard Butler, and that was a very good thing indeed.

Besides, at the moment I was only screaming distance away from Haven's friendly neighborhood bouncer coming to my rescue. I allowed myself to relax a bit. Just a bit.

"All right, here it goes. At your insistence, remember," the Red Devil said out loud, and then slowly began to unwrap the black scarf from his face to reveal his true identity.

My now regularly beating heart picked up pace. I couldn't believe he was actually going to do it. He was going to show me who he was.

I pressed my lips together as he uncovered the damaged flesh. His face, on the entire right side, had been horribly burned. The damage trailed down his neck and, I assumed, continued along that side of his body.

"Oh, my God," I managed, feeling a huge swell of pity for the poor guy. "What happened? What caused that?"

"Hellfire," he said simply.

I frowned and my gaze moved to the good side of his face and my heart began to make an impression of the *Titanic* and sink like a stone into the cold, dark depths of the night.

"Oh *shit*," I said out loud as the untouched, handsome side of his face helped me click in to his actual identity—after all, I'd recently seen a picture of him from a computer printout.

Amy's words from earlier began to ring loudly in my ears.

"Hellfire. Apparently it completely and totally incinerated his body. There was nothing left behind. It was a closed casket with only a picture and a pair of shoes inside."

"Gideon," I said out loud, and my voice was barely audible. "You're supposed to be dead."

"I am, aren't I?" He studied me as a slow smile grew on his damaged face. "Now remember, you promised not to scream."

Every muscle in my body had tensed up. "A woman's prerogative is to change her mind."

"That is true."

I staggered back a step and held my hands up. "Don't come any closer."

He raised the only eyebrow he had left. "If you scream, I will start singing. All bets are off."

My throat felt so tight I wasn't sure I could scream at all. But I was willing to give it a try. I opened my mouth.

Before I could let out a single sound I felt a painful stinging sensation. I looked down at my chest and pulled out the small dart. I stared at it with wide eyes and then looked at Gideon, who now held a gun.

"This would have been much easier if you'd simply come with me when I asked, Sarah," he said. "Now I'm afraid we'll have to do it the hard way."

It was a garlic dart. Garlic worked as a tranquilizer for vampires and was one of the weapons in the arsenal of your average hunter—let alone the leader of all the hunters, who had, for weeks, wanted to come to Toronto and kill me himself.

I began to fall. Gideon moved forward to catch me before I hit the ground and then the world faded to black.

Chapter 19

My eyes snapped open. The room I was in was dim but not dark and I lay on a hard floor. I sat up quickly, immediately panicked, and my head swam from the movement. The last thing I remembered was being shot with a dart by Gideon Chase.

Gideon *freaking* Chase.

But I was still alive.

That was a good start, I guess.

"You're awake," Gideon said, and my head snapped to the side to see that he was sitting in a nearby chair.

"Wh . . . what the hell is going on?" I managed. "Where am I?" My mouth tasted like I'd been sucking on moldy cotton balls, although I certainly hoped I hadn't been. I looked down at my hands to see that they weren't restrained. I wasn't tied up. That was also good. At this point, I mentally latched on to any positive sign.

"We're in an abandoned factory close to your boyfriend's vampire club," he said. I must have looked at him with shock because he continued, "Yes, of course I know where Haven is. It always amazes me when people underestimate me. There are ways of knowing anything you want to know, Sarah. About anything or anyone."

He stood up. Damn, he was tall. I wouldn't be surprised if he was six-foot-five. As quickly as I could I also got to my feet and I looked erratically around at my surroundings. It was all dark and unfamiliar. A huge space. There was a single light shining above us that lit a ten-foot-by-ten-foot area.

I looked at him without saying another word. His face was so scarred, it looked like raw hamburger. That was from slaying a demon? And the entire casino burned down and everyone thought he was dead. He'd allowed his funeral to happen without letting anyone know he was okay. How many kinds of crazy was that?

He flinched a little at my stare and touched the damaged side of his face. "I had a witch attempt to heal me as best she could, but the damage has already been done. Burns, especially from hellfire, can't be fixed with only a simple healing spell."

I swallowed hard. "Does it hurt?"

"For as long as I have it, it will continue to cause me great and constant pain. An unfortunate side-effect of such an injury."

I shoved aside any feelings of empathy I had. This wasn't some poor guy who got a raw deal. This was the leader of all hunters. He was a mass murderer. A glorified serial killer.

"Are you going to kill me?" I hated asking it, because I actually didn't want to know the answer. But I had to know.

"Kill you?" His lips curled into a smile. "Why? Should I?"

"I'm going to have to answer that with an emphatic no."

"You are the Slayer of Slayers, right? I've heard many interesting things about you, Sarah. For weeks now. There are hunters in my ranks who are deathly afraid of you."

"I can be scary when I want to be."

"I did plan to kill you," he said. "I worked out many different scenarios. I believed that perhaps you would be an interesting prey for a change. Do you know how easy it is to kill a vampire?"

My hands trembled, so I squeezed them together. "I have no idea."

"It's easy. Trust me. Most will practically bare their chests to my stake to help make their deaths as quick and painless as possible. It has been extremely disappointing time and time again."

Despite the waves of panic I was feeling, I gave him a withering look. "Are you kidding me?"

He raised an eyebrow. "Excuse me?"

"What are you telling me this for? Because you expect me to feel sorry that vampires aren't more of a challenge for you? Do you know how sickening and completely disgusting it is that you take pleasure in murdering living breathing people who have lives and hopes and dreams?"

He cocked his head to the side. "How can I possibly take pleasure from something that is as easy as shooting fish in a barrel?"

"Then why the hell do you do it?"

"Because it is what I was born to do. I am the last in a very long line of hunters, Sarah. I went to Harvard and was first in my class. I could have become anything I wanted, but I chose to stay with the family business. Does that make me a bad person?"

"No, it makes you a sick, evil bastard."

He laughed. "A tongue as sharp as her reputation. And you feel no fear of me right now? I'm very impressed."

A line of perspiration slid down my spine. "No, you're wrong. I'm scared completely shitless. But if I'm going to die, I want you to know exactly what I think of you."

He sighed. "Sarah, how many times must I tell you? I don't plan to kill you."

"You don't?"

He shook his head slowly. "No."

"Then what do you want from me?"

He drew a sharp, silver-bladed knife out from the back of his pants. My eyes widened as the metal caught the light. He took a step closer to me and I took an immediate step backward. Then he smiled and leaned over to place it on the ground between us.

"Pick up the knife, Sarah," he said.

I stared at it, then at him, but I didn't make any moves.

His smile widened. "Your heart must be beating very quickly right now, isn't it?"

I frowned. My heart. It . . . it wasn't beating at all. I placed my palm on my chest, but felt nothing. My gaze snapped back up to his. He had his hand out, and dangling from his index finger was the gold chain.

"Took this back when you were snoozing," he said. "Hope you don't mind me borrowing it for a minute."

"Give that back to me."

"Here's the scenario, Sarah. And this should be interesting." He twirled the chain around his finger. "Pick up the knife. And then come over here and kill me. Then you can take the chain back. I even promise not to fight back at all."

I blinked. "What are you talking about?"

"You are the Slayer of Slayers. And look at me. I'm the biggest slayer of them all. I'm a very bad man who has done very bad things. You have every right to kill me, so go ahead and do it. Then you can have your chain back and return to your happy little life with your master-vampire boyfriend."

I bent over and snatched up the knife. My hands were sweating.

"Good," Gideon said. He slipped the gold chain into the pocket of his black pants, then sat down in the chair again and began to unbutton his shirt. "Let me make it easier for you."

He bared his chest. One side was smooth and perfectly chiseled muscle. The other resembled melted wax from being burned.

His throat worked as he swallowed. "Many women have gazed at me as you do now, only they did so with desire, not pity in their eyes."

My attention returned to his face. "Wow. Brag much?"

"It's not bragging if it's the truth."

"Just for the record, I already know about your rep as a ladies' man. Hooray for you. Second, the last thing I'm feeling at the moment is pity. More like disgust and hatred."

He stroked his chest. "Right here. Plunge the knife exactly here and you will get my heart."

I took a step closer to him. "Is this a trick or do you really want me to kill you?"

"It's not a trick. Kill me, Sarah, and then you can have your chain back."

I clutched the knife and drew closer until I was only a foot away from him.

Kill a man who had killed so many. Whose very existence helped fuel the hunter organization. Whose money went to pay for weapons and travel so hunters could come and get us where we lived.

Gideon Chase definitely deserved to die.

The Slayer of Slayers reputation was a false one. Mostly. But it had started because I had killed a hunter. The hunter had tried to put a stake in my chest. I'd managed to shoot him in self-defense before he got the chance. I had every right to do it, but I still felt bad about it. I wasn't a murderer. I'd done it to protect my life. It had been him or me.

This was different. Even though I knew Gideon was a horrible person who also deserved to die, probably even more than that other hunter had, this . . . this wasn't right. I couldn't do it. I couldn't kill somebody in cold blood.

This had to be a trick. It *had* to be. He sat there, his green eyes open and fixed on me, his bare chest moving in and out with his breathing. I expected him to reach up and grab me, to turn the tables and plunge the silver knife into my chest instead. But he didn't make any move as I touched the sharp tip of the blade to his skin.

I blinked and felt tears splash down to my cheeks.

Gideon raised an eyebrow. "Having difficulties?"

"Dammit," I said softly, and then louder, "*Dammit!*"

I threw the knife away and it clattered and clanged, the hollow sound echoing against the walls of the empty factory.

Gideon frowned up at me. "A lot of people would have welcomed the chance to kill me."

I sighed very shakily. "Yeah, well, I guess I don't belong to that club."

"Don't say that I didn't give you the opportunity."

"Screw you."

"Lovely." He smirked at me and then stood up from the chair.

I scanned my surroundings for an exit, but even with my improved vampire eyesight it was too dark. I couldn't even see the walls. I felt trapped and very afraid. "I have places I need to be. Since you said you weren't planning on killing me, I can assume I can leave now? With my necklace?"

"Not quite yet." He studied me, his gaze that was amused before changed to a colder one. "I want something from you, Sarah. There is something about you that makes you very special."

I crossed my arms tightly in front of me. "My sparkling personality?"

"Other than that."

I exhaled shakily. "The nightwalker thing? Yeah, I'm sure a nightwalker would make more interesting prey than a regular vamp. You kind of missed out on the original massacre, didn't you? Well, sorry to break it to you, but it's just a curse, even though it's a permanent one."

"Because the witch is dead."

"How do you know that, anyhow?" But I already knew the answer before he said it out loud.

"Because I killed her," he said evenly.

I sucked in a breath and tried to stay calm as I flashed back on Stacy lying in her bed with the knife sticking out of her lingerie-clad chest. "Why would you do that?"

His throat moved as he swallowed. "I had her use magic to try to heal me. She was able to relieve my pain for a short time but that was all. She failed me and she had to be punished."

I felt ill. My stomach churned. Gideon was the man Stacy thought she was in love with. The reason she planned to give up black magic to become a "healer."

He'd killed her and he'd also killed my chances to break the curse.

Gideon continued, ignoring the stricken expression on my face. "Your being a nightwalker, even only a cursed one, has nothing to do with what I want. It has a great deal more to do with your very special blood."

"My blood?" I repeated shakily.

"Two master vampires have allowed you to drink from them. It has changed something in your internal makeup. Master vampires do not share their blood, and if they do it is with only one fledgling. Multiple masters giving blood to a fledgling is a very rare event. In fact, it's an unwritten rule among their kind that they don't do this."

I shook my head. "It's only a rumor that it makes a difference."

"It's not a rumor. It is fact. However, I'm still not certain that two masters are enough." He frowned. "I have reason to believe that your blood can cure me. It can heal me."

That surprised me. I licked my dry lips. "Heal . . . heal your scars, you mean?"

"That's right. But also the hellfire I was exposed to continues to burn into me and cause its damage even as we stand here. It won't be long before it slowly consumes me completely, and when I die, hell itself will claim me, body and soul." His jaw clenched. "But I think that your blood has the potential to cure all of my ailments and make me stronger than I was before."

My temperature had plunged even more at hearing his full diagnosis. "You *think*."

"There have been others like you, many years ago, and their blood was a sacred gift thought to be sent from the gods as a cure for illness."

"So, what? You mix a little of my blood with some peach schnapps and call it a day?" My jaw was tight. "So what was with the whole song and dance? Why didn't you just do it a week ago when the stake was sticking out of my chest? There was plenty to go around then."

"I have to wait for the full moon two weeks from tonight." He sighed and it came out sounding very weary. "There are all these annoying rules with this sort of thing."

"So the full moon. Then what?"

"Then you will sire me as a vampire."

I blinked. "But you're the leader of the *vampire hunters*. Don't you see a bit of a problem with that?"

"I am dead to the hunters. I've been buried. I can begin a new life."

"You're crazy."

"Getting there."

"I'm not making you a vampire."

"I'm afraid that I'm not giving you a choice in the matter."

I took a deep breath. Okay, I'd had about enough of this. I walked over toward him and put my hand on his chest. My nightwalker juices had started to flow and the fog that had slowly rolled in was helping to chase away that petrified feeling and solidify it into something much different and a hell of a lot scarier. For *him*, that is.

With one push, he stumbled backward and landed in the chair.

He raised an eyebrow. "Interesting."

"Oh, I'm just getting started." I leaned forward so I was looking directly into his eyes, knowing without a doubt that mine had turned black, since I now saw the world a bit differently—more like a predator would. "I want you to let me out of here. Right now. Do you hear me?"

"I hear you." He didn't make any moves and his eyes didn't glaze over in that special mind-control way.

I frowned. "Let's try this again. *Let me out of here now.*"

"I believe I told you before, Sarah, that vampiric mind control only works on weak-minded humans. My mind, despite my obvious injuries, is very strong from years of training against potential dangers like this."

I hissed at him. Maybe I couldn't stab him in the heart with a knife, but his neck, on the good side, did look extremely appetizing. I settled down onto his lap and pressed my face against his throat. "What if I bite you right now?"

"I would strongly suggest against it."

He didn't flinch as my teeth grazed his flesh. The world began to narrow in and I felt the darkness gathering inside me. I could taste his pulse, and sinking my fangs into his neck seemed like the best idea I'd had in a very long time.

"Taking the chain away was a mistake," I whispered into his ear. "I'm a little different when I'm hungry these days. And I'm suddenly extremely hungry."

"I don't think Thierry would appreciate you sitting on my lap like this."

"I'm sure he'd understand." I traced my tongue along the side of his neck and tasted the salt of his skin and the smell of his cologne. Very tasty.

Then I felt his hand on my ass under my skirt and he squeezed. It made me jump and I got up quickly.

"What the hell was that?" I snapped.

He grinned. "What I normally do when a woman is crawling all over me." He flicked his head to the right. "Take a look at what's over there on the table. Perhaps we should move this meeting along a bit, although I did enjoy the lap dance."

I glared at him, drawing my upper lip back from my fangs. Then I moved toward the table to the side of the chair and looked down.

There were photos on top of it. Black-and-white surveillance photos.

"You see?" He stood beside me now. "I have been watching, Sarah. I know everything about you. And all I want from you is for you to sire me come the full moon. I want to be healed and I have no intention of going to hell—even if it means becoming a vampire to avoid that fate. In fact, I look at it as a great adventure."

I could barely hear him, since I was too focused on the photos. There was one of Thierry leaving through the back door of Haven and heading to his Audi. One of Amy and Barry laughing outside their house. George walking down the street holding a tray with two Starbucks coffees. The front of George's house with the blinds drawn and a FedEx truck out front.

There was a picture of the high school where I'd

attended the reunion. A shot of me and Thierry and Claire and Reggie outside after I'd bitten George. There was a picture of my parents' home with all the cars belonging to my relatives parked in front. Another photo showed my mom and dad putting birdseed out.

"I will kill them all," Gideon said softly. "I hate to do this with such a lack of finesse. It's not really my style. But I'm afraid if you leave me with no other choice, then what can I do? I'm a desperate man."

I turned and grabbed him by his throat and squeezed. His hands came up to claw at mine but I had a good hold on him. I pushed him back and he flew across the factory floor before hitting the ground hard, coughing and sputtering.

"You stay the hell away from these people!" I yelled.

He kept coughing. I could see the red, bruiselike imprint of my fingers on his throat. "You have quite the grip on you."

The need for blood had been replaced by anger. No fear, no panic, no anxiety, just a simple, hot line of fury that anyone would threaten the people I loved.

"Stay away from them or I will kill you myself," I said.

He struggled to get up from the floor. "I already gave you that option. That door has closed, Sarah. You made your choice."

"Maybe I've changed my mind." I took a step toward him.

"Harm me and all those who are pictured there are dead." He breathed out. "I haven't taken any chances. The other hunters may think I'm dead and buried, but my money still speaks volumes. And hired killers are a cheap commodity these days. Hired killers who, if they don't hear from me in the next hour, will go ahead with their assignments."

"So if I'd killed you when you gave me the chance all of these people would die anyhow?" I was shaking with anger. "You son of a bitch."

His now-blank expression didn't waver. "If you'd killed me I automatically would have gone to hell."

"It's what you deserve," I snapped. "So all you want from me is my blood when I make you a vampire. What if it doesn't work? What if you're wrong and it's only rumors?"

"Then so be it. It's better to try and fail than leave one's life up to nothing but fate."

My head hurt. This was too much to take in, especially when I was feeling foggy to begin with. But my anger was fading and being replaced again by uncertainty and a dark hunger.

I clenched my fists at my sides. "And if I do this you swear you won't hurt anyone I know."

He smiled. "Cross my heart and hope to die."

I had no choice. He wasn't giving me any damn choice.

"Then we'll meet again in two weeks," I said. "At the full moon."

"You'll do it?"

"It would be my pleasure to sink my teeth into your neck, Gideon. And I wouldn't say that about just anybody." I held my hand out. "Now, give me back the chain."

"Two weeks is a very long time." His gaze on me was steady. "A long time for you to go blabbing your pretty little head off to your darling boyfriend about my plans."

I dropped my outstretched hand. "And let me guess, if I say anything, you'll have everyone killed."

"Of course. But I want a show of faith from you. I want you to do something for me tonight."

"Sorry. Only one lap dance per customer per night. Those are the rules."

His smile grew. "That's not what I had in mind. It has more to do with Thierry."

My eyes narrowed. "What about him?"

"You're in love with him?"

"Is that a rhetorical question?"

"I have observed this relationship and have been very surprised that it has lasted, given the difficulties you've encountered."

"What's your point?"

"My point is that it is a good way for me to know how devoted you are to our little deal. This relationship that you value so highly, that you have already sacrificed so much for." He paused. "I want you to end things with him."

I blinked. "I'm sorry?"

"Break off your relationship and promise me you'll never see him again. Ever. It is the best way for me to see that you understand our agreement and will honor it. Besides, having Thierry too close, information could be whispered in intimate moments. Secrets could be told. And if he knows, then all bets are off. All those you love will die. So this is for your benefit as well as mine."

"Go to hell."

He touched his scarred face. "That's what I'm trying to avoid."

"I'm not breaking up with Thierry. Besides, he wouldn't believe it. He knows how much I love him."

"My research reveals that you were once an aspiring actress, Sarah. I suggest you use that talent to make it as real as possible. He will believe you. It's not as though it's been a long-term relationship. There are issues. He knows this. I'd be surprised if, given his history, he raises one finger to help salvage your love affair or tries to talk you out of your decision. The man has no passion for life, which is one of the reasons I've allowed him to live for as long as he has, hidden away in his secret clubs. I believe I'm actually doing you a favor."

"You're insane."

"This is how it is, Sarah. You will do this because I'm not giving you any other choice. You will end things with Thierry permanently tonight and you will not see him again. By doing so you are saving the lives of all those you love—including Thierry. I think it's a very even trade."

My throat felt tight. "You think this is fair?"

He studied me for a moment and then ran his hand along the ruined side of his face. "I'll tell you what. If Thierry actually puts up a fight, if he really loves you as much as you think he does, then maybe I'll reconsider. But if you don't even try to do as I ask or attempt to pass him the message that I have anything to do with this, then we have a very serious problem."

I opened my mouth to say something, to tell him off, but he stopped me with a wave of his hand.

"We're finished here. Do as I say. And make no mistake, I will know if you've reneged on our deal and will react accordingly." His smile twisted into something very unpleasant. "So make it good." He patted my cheek and then placed the gold chain in my hand.

I snarled and lunged at him, but felt the sharp pain as another garlic dart hit me at point-blank range. I yanked it out of my stomach and glared at him.

Fade to black.

Chapter 20

When I woke, Gideon was gone and I was all alone in the factory. He'd even taken the surveillance photos away. I would have liked to pretend that it had all been a horrible dream, but I knew it wasn't. My dreams lately ended much worse than this.

I shakily got to my feet and brushed myself off. I still felt unsteady but it wasn't from the lack of consciousness. It was because I wasn't wearing the chain that now lay on the concrete floor next to me. I took a moment to put it on and slipped it under my cashmere sweater so that it rested directly against my skin. Immediately I felt better as my heartbeat slowly started up again and the hunger faded away to nearly nothing.

I stood there for a few more minutes as I replayed my conversation with Gideon in my head. I suppose I could ignore his warnings and tell Thierry everything. He'd know what to do. He might be able to protect everyone.

Might.

And what did I have to go by? Gideon's word? I didn't know him. All I had was his reputation. The reputation of a cold-hearted killer who was now out of options and willing to do whatever it took to get what he wanted.

From where I was standing, it didn't look like a multiple-choice questionnaire. Gideon had been very clear about what he wanted from me. I suppose, if anything, I should be thankful that he hadn't killed anyone that I cared about yet to prove his point.

So yeah. I would do what I had to do to keep those I cared about safe. It wasn't even a question.

I was an actress. Forget all the ensuing years in which I'd done everything from being a personal assistant who fetched coffee to being a waitress and bartender who . . . well, fetched coffee.

Did I think that Gideon would hold true to his promise and kill everyone if I didn't do what he said?

Yes. I believed it. That belief had attached itself to me as a sick twisting feeling in the pit of my stomach. I had a strange feeling it was now a permanent fixture.

I finally left the factory and found that he hadn't been lying. I was close to Haven. So close that I was able to walk there in under ten minutes. Funny, my feet didn't even hurt anymore from wearing the high heels. I think I was numb.

Numbness would help.

It was just before midnight by the time I entered the club. I'd been gone for two hours. The club was now packed. Valentine's Day was a good night for business in a place that served blood and booze. This was the last night it would still be Haven. Tomorrow it might look the same, but it would be different—kind of like me.

"Sarah!" Amy called and approached me. "How did it go with Veronique?"

I blinked at her and then forced a smile. "It went okay."

"Glad to hear it. Listen, I wanted to wait until you came back to say bye. Me and Barry are headed out. He's taking me dancing."

"That sounds fun."

"Definitely. See you later!"

And then she was gone. I scanned the floor for George, but he was very busy waiting on all the tables for his last chance at getting tips here.

Ron the bartender waved at me and gave me a thumbs-up. He pointed to a shot glass in an unspoken question of whether I wanted a shot of my favorite blood type.

Be positive.

I shook my head.

And then I summoned my inner actress, the one who never had a chance to really shine because her little light had been snuffed out too early by feminine hygiene commercials, lousy auditions, and general bad luck, and together we went to Thierry's office.

The door was slightly ajar and I took a deep breath before I pushed it open.

Thierry's head was down as he studied some papers, but he looked up at me and smiled.

"Sarah, you've returned. I thought for a moment that Veronique had taken you back to Paris with her."

"Nope. Still here."

"Did everything go all right?"

I shrugged. "Depends what you think is all right."

"The papers?"

"She won't sign them."

His smile faded. "I see. Well, I will have a conversation

with her before she leaves town. Perhaps I can still persuade her—"

I waved my hand. "No, forget it, Thierry. It's not necessary."

He frowned. "Veronique is a very stubborn woman. But if she can understand that this is what I want as well—"

"No. Let's just drop it. Can we do that?"

"Of course." He leaned back in his seat. "Is everything well?"

I sighed and it sounded shaky. "Oh, yeah, everything's peachy. Just fabulous."

Inner actress. Summoning. Couldn't look directly at him. Had to make this quick. Quick like pulling off a Band-Aid and it might not hurt so much.

"It's not too late if you wish to go somewhere this evening," he said. "To celebrate Valentine's Day and your receiving the gold chain." He paused. "And I do want to apologize. I know I've been a bit overbearing when it comes to my opinion of this Red Devil impersonator. Perhaps you're right and he only has your best interest at heart. There's room in the world for heroes of all shapes and sizes."

"Overbearing," I said, and tried to laugh a little. "Yeah, you're definitely that."

His brow lowered. "Pardon me?"

"You're overbearing. Way. I normally don't mind so much but for some reason lately it's really been getting on my nerves."

"Is that so?"

"It is." I shook my head. "I think I should thank Veronique. She came at the exact right time to help a lot of things crystallize for me. I hate to admit it, but I think she might be right."

"Might be right about what?" His tone was even.

"The annulment being a stupid idea. I mean, seriously, Thierry, it's only been ten weeks. I've left milk in the fridge for longer than that. It's the blink of an eye for somebody your age."

"This is Veronique's opinion? That ten weeks is not long enough to constitute a worthy relationship?"

"Actually, I think it might be my opinion. Ten weeks. Almost all of it difficult."

"We have had our difficulties."

I laughed, and it sounded amazingly convincing. "Difficulties? Well, let's see about that. Yeah, there are difficulties. You being overbearing and unemotional. That's a couple of them. There's also you being judgmental, possessive, and jealous."

He stood up, his brow deeply furrowed. "And this little outburst was inspired by your chat with Veronique, was it?"

I put a hand on my hip. "Yeah. Your *wife,* Veronique. She made it very clear that's how she was staying, too. Seriously, what's in it for me?"

"What do you mean?"

"Exactly what I said. What's in it for me? I'm just supposed to stand by and be your mistress? For what? The next thousand years? Sorry, Thierry, but I need more commitment than that in a relationship. I thought I could ignore it, because there were a hell of a lot of other perks, but at the end of the day, there are way too many strikes against us."

"Such as?"

Dammit. "Veronique told me about your little financial difficulties."

His eyes widened a fraction. "Did she?"

"Yeah. I can't believe you didn't tell me. I thought you were rich."

"And this was a prerequisite for our relationship? The fact that I had money?"

"I didn't think it was, but now that I think about it . . ." I paused and tried not to cry. Oh, my God, I didn't want to say these things. None of it was the truth. I didn't care if Thierry only had two cents to rub together, it didn't change how I felt about him. "I guess it does. What am I supposed to do? Eat Kraft Dinners for the rest of my life?"

"You don't eat."

"Figuratively."

"I must say I'm disappointed to hear this from you." But he didn't sound all that disappointed. He sounded bland and emotionless. His expression was now completely unreadable.

"I'd be surprised," Gideon had said to me earlier, *"if Thierry raises one finger to help salvage your love affair or tries to talk you out of your decision. If Thierry actually puts up a fight, if he really loves you as much as you think he does, then maybe I'll reconsider."*

"I'm sorry to have disappointed you," I said.

"Barry did warn me that he suspected you were after my money, being one of very little personal means."

I shrugged. "A girl's got to do what a girl's got to do."

"Veronique had no right to tell you any of my personal affairs."

"She's funny like that."

"I'm sorry this evening has not gone as well as I'd planned."

"We've had worse evenings."

"Oh?"

Nail in the coffin alert. My heart ached so badly with every word I spoke to him, but I forced myself to hold it together. "Yeah, remember that crazy night you nearly tore out my throat and then left me for dead? *That* was memorable."

His expression went from bland to icy. "I do remember. It is one of my greatest regrets."

"I told somebody a while ago that I was involved with a married man who had a serious drinking problem. Sounds like a huge mistake, doesn't it?"

His gaze remained as cold as ice. "It does indeed."

I gave him a small shrug. "I think tonight is a really good night for us to . . . I don't know. Start fresh."

"I agree," he said slowly. "Perhaps we should spend a little time apart and meet tomorrow to discuss this further. I'm sure we can come to an understanding. I know that your words tonight are spoken out of frustration with Veronique and stress from dealing with the curse. I will choose not to take what you have said personally."

"That's not exactly what I meant." I felt like crying, but I held it inside. If I let one tear fall—if I let Thierry think for one moment that I didn't mean what I was saying—then I had no doubt that Gideon would find out and he would kill everyone I loved. Including Thierry. It was all up to me.

I willed my hands not to shake, and I pulled off the

eternity band and placed it on Thierry's desk. He eyed it before his gaze returned to me.

"I'm starting new," I said. "I haven't been happy for a very long time and I'm realizing that a lot of it has to do with being with you. We're not right together. We don't fit."

"They say that opposites attract."

"Maybe temporarily. But I'm not looking for a temporary relationship, Thierry. This isn't right. I can feel it. I'm trusting my gut on this one. It's over. I want to see other people. People who aren't so overbearing and moody. And when I leave, I would really appreciate it if you don't try to see me again. It'll just be awkward. Do you understand?"

He stared at me for a very long time. His eyes were gray and there was no warmth there.

"I see," he said finally, and there was no inflection to the words. Just a general statement. "And I do understand, Sarah. I feel no ill will toward you for this decision. I have expected it for some time."

"Well, that makes things much simpler."

"Indeed it does."

"Then I won't draw this out any longer." I took a deep breath. "I thought I loved you, but I was wrong. I'm sorry to have wasted your time and mine. Good-bye, Thierry."

"Good-bye, Sarah."

I blinked and turned around, and then all I could hear was the click-clack of my heels as they touched the ceramic-tiled floor and the accompanying thudding of my heart slamming against my chest.

I waited until I was outside in the cold February air before I started crying, great heaving sobs that made me clutch at the brick walls in the alley to stay on my feet. I'd never felt worse in my entire life. It felt as if all of my insides had been pulled out through my mouth and lay on the snow-covered ground next to me in a horrific steaming pile of pain.

And, no. Definitely not an exaggeration.

I loved him. Oh, my God, I loved him so much.

But it was obvious. He couldn't love me in return. What he'd told me before had been words. Just words. If he really loved me he wouldn't have stood there and listened to me without trying to defend himself. Without trying to fight for me. He didn't fight. He didn't care.

Gideon was right.

It was over. I'd never see him again. But at least he'd be safe. He'd be alive. That was all I could ask for. He'd never know how much this had hurt me. He'd never know how much I loved him.

But at least he'd be alive.

I tried to pull myself together and slowly, very slowly, I did.

Gideon would pay dearly for this. The devil would get his due. The ball was now in my court. *Les jeux sont faits.*

I sniffed. *And other sayings appropriate to the situation.*

I pushed my tears away. I'd go home to George's place and pull a Scarlett. Tomorrow was another day. My first day as a vampire without Thierry in my life.

Dammit. Here come the waterworks again.

Interlude

Thierry watched in silence as Sarah left his office.

She'd left him. His throat felt suddenly tight at the thought. He'd always feared that the day would come that she would see him for the man he truly was and that she would turn her back on him forever. However, he had never realized how much it would hurt.

He'd believed that she was different. That perhaps she wouldn't leave. That perhaps she was someone he could finally, at long last, open his heart to.

That perhaps the fortune-teller from so long ago had been right.

Sarah Dearly was so incredibly wrong for him. So different. So young and sweet.

It had surprised him to hear such cruel things from her beautiful lips, although he had to agree that a great deal of it was very true and needed to be said. Perhaps he should have tried to defend himself, but from what? He had hurt her. That was the truth. His fortune was drained, although not nearly as much as she seemed to think. His stubborn, estranged wife—who had her own life on a separate continent—refused to give him the freedom to truly commit to their new relationship.

All true. And all reasons for harsh words.

He leaned back in his leather chair behind the desk that would no longer be his as of tomorrow.

Sarah had always claimed to him that she once wanted to be an actress of stage and screen, but it had never worked out for her. He'd always wondered why.

But now he finally knew.

Sarah Dearly was a horrible actress.

Horrible.

Completely and absolutely dreadful in every way.

She had lied to him tonight. Completely and shamelessly.

Instead of making him angry, this realization made him happier than he had felt in centuries, if not ever.

She loved him. Of everything in his long difficult life, of this he had no doubt. His money meant nothing to her. If it had, she would have accepted his many attempts to give her spending money and then asked for more.

He loved her so deeply it made his heart ache.

She'd made every day a gift instead of a curse. Before he'd met her he'd believed that he had nothing left to live for. But now he knew that he was wrong. Now he lived for her and the promise of a future together.

It was all very clear.

It was also very clear that she was being coerced into her current actions. Forced to leave him. He frowned deeply at the thought.

It couldn't have been Veronique's doing. Of this, too, he was certain. Veronique might have many faults, but she wasn't an evil woman.

No, something else had happened. Something that had scared Sarah so badly that she had no choice but to lie to him. He had considered calling her on this during her tirade of hurtful words but had decided against it.

Something had happened. Someone else was involved with this, and he was willing to bet that it had to do with the false Red Devil.

He had threatened Sarah. It was obvious. She was afraid.

The thought made him furious. Whoever was responsible would be very sorry.

He picked up the eternity band from where she'd left it on his desk and slid it into his front jacket pocket.

Sarah had told him that she didn't love him. That it was over between them once and for all.

He'd once wished for this—for her to walk away from him and not look back. Only a short time ago he wouldn't have fought for her; fought for their relationship and for a future together. But that was before he realized how very much he loved her.

A small grin of determination turned up the side of Thierry's mouth.

He was different now.

Chapter 21

*H*ow did it go, Sarah?"

Gideon's low voice in the darkness of the alley outside Haven startled me. I raised my damp eyeballs in his direction, expecting to see him grinning or looking proud of himself for what he'd made me do.

Instead he simply looked at me. The black scarf was wrapped around his scarred face again so all I could see were his eyes, but that was enough for me to know that he wasn't smiling.

Neither was I. To say the least.

"How the hell do you think it went?" I managed.

He studied me for a moment longer. "You've done the right thing. I will assume he didn't question your decision to end your relationship?"

I swallowed past the large lump in my throat. "No, he didn't. Are you happy now?"

"This doesn't make me happy."

"Sure. I believe that." I started to move past him, but he stepped in front of me to block my path.

"Where are you going?" he asked.

"Home. To bed."

"Is it safe for you to be out all alone like this?"

"The leader of the vampire hunters is concerned that little old fanged me is going to get home safely? How sweet of you." I could practically taste the venom in the words. I took a deep breath and faced him again. "I agreed to sire you in two weeks. Does that mean I have to put up with you constantly being around between then and now? Because if I have a choice, I'd rather you stay as far away from me as possible and mind your own goddamned business about what I do."

He blinked. "I'm not leaving. I'll give you your space, of course, but don't think that I won't be near and well aware of whatever you do. There's too much at risk for me to give you too much freedom."

I wiped at my tears, which had turned from grief to frustration. "I did what you asked—I broke up with Thierry for good. On *Valentine's Day*. Now I just want to be alone tonight. Do you think you could do that for me, you scarred son of a bitch?"

His green eyes glittered. "Since you put it so politely, I suppose that's only fair. Good night, Sarah. I'll see you again soon."

He stepped to the side to let me pass.

I wanted to give him the finger, or possibly kill him where he stood, but I didn't have the energy. Instead, I slowly walked away, out of the alley and onto the sidewalk, all the way to George's, with my now-blistered, screaming-in-pain feet the only things to keep me company.

An hour later I was in bed with the lights off, and I tried to will myself to go to sleep. Maybe my life wouldn't seem quite so hopeless tomorrow, although I seriously doubted it.

Not too surprisingly, I couldn't get to sleep. I would take a few over-the-counter sleeping pills, but drugs, unless they were of the garlic-dart variety, didn't work on vampires.

Garlic sleeping pills for vampires, I thought absently. That quite possibly could be a million-dollar idea.

I lay awake, my attention on the dark ceiling above me, as I went over everything that had gone wrong in my life.

Never should have gone on that blind date, I decided. That's where the trouble had begun. If I hadn't, the obsessive creep wouldn't have bitten me so we could be "together forever." He wouldn't have turned me into a vampire. I wouldn't have been chased by vampire hunters.

And I never would have met Thierry.

If I hadn't met Thierry, he would have gone ahead and staked himself on the bridge that night, his remains falling into the river below to be washed away. He wouldn't have had to save me. He wouldn't have felt this solemn need to protect me ever since—which obviously was what I had confused for romantic feelings. He would never have even been a blip on my radar and my life wouldn't have been completely ruined.

I'd be the same Sarah I used to be—a fashion-loving, apartment-dwelling, party-going personal assistant with no direction in her life.

But I didn't *want* to be that Sarah anymore. Being a vampire had changed me, but not all of the changes were bad ones. At least, I didn't think so.

If I hadn't become a vampire I never would have met George or Quinn. Amy never would have met and married Barry.

And then, of course, there was Thierry.

I wanted these horrible feelings to turn into anger against him. That would be helpful. But I just felt empty and so very sad. I know he was difficult, overbearing, judgmental, and jealous, but he was also generous, wonderful, sweet, protective, and passionate.

I didn't want to love him, but I did.

I wanted to stop loving him, but I couldn't.

And if it meant I had to turn Gideon Chase into a vampire to save him and all of my friends, then that's exactly what I was going to do.

I let out a shaky sigh and closed my eyes.

Then they snapped right back open a moment before I sat bolt upright in bed.

What the hell had I done?

I got out of bed, straightening my bright pink *I'm a Rock Star* nightshirt (with the image of a cartoon star wearing sunglasses and playing an electric guitar—*chic* it wasn't) and left my tiny bedroom to scramble in the darkness for the phone. I pecked out the numbers instinctively.

"You've reached Haven." George's voice boomed in my ear. "How can I be of excellent service so you will strongly recommend to the new owners that I can keep my job here?"

"George," I whispered into the receiver. "I need to talk to Thierry. Please . . . can you get him for me right now?"

There was a pause. "Sarah? Is that you?"

"Yes." I was afraid to raise my voice to regular speaking volume.

"Do you have laryngitis?"

"No . . . just, please, George, get Thierry for me."

Bottom line: I *was not* Gideon Chase's bitch.

I don't care what he threatened to do, he wasn't infused with superpowers—he was only human. He couldn't possibly know what I might tell Thierry. I'd gone along with him out of fear and confusion, but now that I'd had some time to think things through, I was sure that I'd made the wrong decision. *Hugely* wrong.

Gideon didn't have to know what was going on, but Thierry did. He could help me. I wasn't exactly sure how, but at present I was at Gideon's mercy, and I didn't like that at all, since, from what I knew of the guy, he didn't have any honor or compassion to go along with his billions of dollars.

He was a murderer. He'd killed countless vampires over the years, and he'd even murdered Stacy last night. He was a very bad man. Not that this was a revelation.

I'd tell Thierry I had to talk to him. I'd explain what had happened and then wo'd . . . we'd . . . I didn't know what we'd do, but it would be better than waiting and worrying that Gideon would just kill everybody anyhow.

This was the best way. The only way.

And sure, it did bother me that Thierry had accepted our breakup without even standing up from his desk; with his expression only growing colder and more distant.

Then again, he might not believe me. After everything I'd said to him . . .

Oh, God, I thought. *He* has *to believe me.*

"Sorry," George said. "He's not here."

I licked my dry lips. "Where is he? This is urgent."

"Look, I'd get him to give you a call, but he's gone. Like *gone*, gone. I figured you already knew about this."

"What are you talking about?"

"I can't believe you broke up with him, Sarah. Wow. I didn't see that coming. He was in a foul mood when he came out of that office. *Foul.* I asked him where you were and he told me that you dumped him—although he didn't use those exact words, of course. He finished the paperwork and cleared out his office of all his personal belongings, which I believe amounted to a fountain pen and an extra black shirt. He said he was going to the airport."

My stomach turned over. "The airport?"

"I figure he's going back to Europe. Now that Haven's gone, and you're moving on, there's nothing to keep him here anymore. Are you okay, sweetie? Amy said you and Veronique had a talk earlier and I guess I can tell that it didn't exactly go well, did it?"

Thierry had left for the airport. He was gone. Shock quickly spread over me.

"It . . ." I tried to swallow. "It went fine. But it made me realize a lot of things about me and Thierry. And yeah, it's over."

"Sorry."

"Don't be." I was speaking at a normal level now and my throat ached with every word.

"Look, I want to help you through this, I do, but I have ten tables who need service glaring at me right now. I'll see you in the morning, okay?"

"Okay."

"Chin up. It might feel sucky now, but in the long run it's probably the best decision. You guys were really different. I guess opposites don't always attract after all, huh?"

"You're right." I sniffed. "See you later."

I hung up and put my hands over my face and sobbed until I was all out of tears and felt utterly exhausted. The proverbial bed had been made and now I had to lie in it. Thierry was gone and Gideon was still here waiting for our appointment with destiny.

I felt for a tissue, but the box next to the phone was empty so I reached to turn on the light. It didn't work. I stood up and walked over to the floor lamp next to the sofa, stubbing my already-blistered toe on the coffee table as I went.

I swore loudly.

Could the night seriously get any worse?

I felt at the wall for the light switch, but it didn't work either. I'd shut the lights off before I went to bed, so they *were* working. Was there a power failure? Had we blown a fuse?

I heard the floorboards creak and I froze in place. They creaked again.

Somebody, other than me, was in the house.

It wouldn't be George since he was still at the club. Then who? Was it Gideon? Had he followed me home and broken into the house? What was he going to do? Or, even worse, was it another hunter? I'd been bodyguard-free on my walk home, and somebody could have picked up my trail and slipped in through a window.

I didn't care who it was, my survival instincts kicked in and I knew I had to get out of there. I made a beeline to the front door, turned the lock, and put my hand on the knob.

Somebody grabbed me firmly from behind. Before I could scream, a hand came over my mouth and I clutched at him, clawing at his arms and imagining my death a thousand different ways. But if I was going to die, I was taking whoever it was with me. I waited to feel a sharp wooden stake at my throat, but there was nothing.

"Shh, Sarah. It's okay."

My eyes bugged. I released my death hold on his arms and he removed his hand from my mouth. I slowly turned around to face him.

"What is going on?" I managed in a hoarse whisper.

"Is that new?" Thierry asked, referring to my amazingly stylish Wal-Mart nightshirt. "I don't think I've ever seen that before."

It was dark in the house so I could barely see him, even taking my improved vampire vision into consideration.

"Shh." I peeked out the curtain to the outside. Gideon was nowhere to be seen, but I wouldn't expect him to survey the house from a visible location. "George said you went to the airport."

"Obviously that's not the case."

I could barely breathe. I wanted to tell him everything in a rush of words but I held back, too stunned to think rationally. "I figured you'd never want to see me again."

He cocked his head to the side. "Those actually were *your* words, not mine."

"You shouldn't be here."

He moved closer and studied me. "You've been crying."

I shook my head. "Allergies."

"I came here because there are a few things that must

be said between us before I will accept once and for all that our relationship is over. That's why I'm here."

I glanced out the window again.

"What are you looking for?" he asked. "Or, should I say, *who* are you looking for?"

I blinked. "You shouldn't be here."

"Why not?"

"I told you that this was over, Thierry. I . . ." I swallowed hard. "I still mean it."

"I don't think you do."

I sucked in a quick gasp of air at that response. "Then you're wrong."

His gaze grew serious. "Who is responsible for this, Sarah? Who is coercing you to say these things to me?"

This was bad. Very, very bad. I'd already had second thoughts about telling him everything. It was too risky. Was I willing to put the lives of my friends and family in jeopardy just so I could tell Thierry I hadn't meant all the cruel things I'd said to him?

I shook my head. "It's me. All me. And I don't know why you're here. You obviously accepted it when I told you the first time and didn't care one way or the other. It's better that way. You and I are through and it's never—"

Placing a hand on either side of my face, he leaned over and kissed me. I gasped against his lips before wrapping my arms around his waist and opening my mouth to his. After a moment he broke it off and stared down at me.

"We're through?" he said softly. "Are you so sure about that?"

I cleared my throat. "I can't help it if you're a good kisser."

"Who forced you to end things with me?" he asked again. "Was it the Red Devil? Who is he? What does he want from you? Please tell me. You don't have to be afraid."

I tried to pull away from him but he held on to me tightly. "Why do you think that? Maybe this is the way I feel. I mean, your money—"

"A lie. You don't care about my money."

"I totally do. I love rich guys. The richer the better. Money makes the world go around. And, to say the least, you're way too old for me. My parents think you're eight years older than me, which sounds a lot better than 650 years older."

"You knew that from nearly the moment we met. I've tried to push you away for your own good because of our many differences, but you wouldn't let me. How is it any different today?"

How was this different? The fact that Thierry didn't want to take my breakup at face value was unbelievable, especially since he'd reacted so coldly only a couple of hours ago.

"Look, Thierry, this isn't right—"

"You love me," he said. "I know this more certainly than anything else in my life."

I glared up at him. "Somebody needs an ego check."

"And I love you." He swallowed. "I love you, Sarah. I know if I tell you that in my many years I've never felt like this for anyone else, you probably won't believe me, but it's true. I had my fortune told two hundred years ago, and it said that my true love would one day arrive and that I would fight for her. I always thought it was a lie until I met you. I love you. Only you. That's how I know that you were lying to me earlier. And that's how I know you're afraid. But I'm here now and nobody is going to hurt you."

It was obvious. I was dreaming. I guess I'd been more tired than I'd thought. I'd come home, turned off the lights, and fallen completely unconscious enough to have a very vivid dream starring the man who was now out of my life forever. The real Thierry would never say these things to me, would he?

But then Thierry kissed me again and it felt very real.

A tear slipped down my cheek and that felt pretty real, too.

"How did you know?" I whispered against his lips. "How did you know I was lying?"

"I just knew." His lips curled to the side. "Now are you going to tell me who has you afraid, or do you want to continue to keep this terrible secret from me?"

I bit my bottom lip and let out a long, shuddery breath. "It's Gideon Chase."

I'd never seen shock on Thierry's face before. It didn't really suit him. "But . . . Gideon is dead."

I shook my head. "Empty casket. He's horribly burned, but he's not dead."

And then, as quietly as I could, I told Thierry everything and with every word I spoke I felt the horrible weight that pressed against my chest lift little by little. I told him about Gideon's plan for me to sire him, and of his threats if I didn't. I told him that Gideon was the one who'd killed Stacy. And finally how Gideon had forced me to break up with him.

His expression grew more grave and serious with everything I said, and there was a fierce look of determination on his face by the end when he met my gaze.

"And yes," I said. "The Red Devil obviously isn't the real one. Hindsight is twenty-twenty and all that."

"I will refrain from saying I told you so."

"I'd appreciate it." I let out a long sigh of relief. "I'm so glad you know. Now we can fix this together."

He didn't say anything to that.

"Thierry?" I prompted. "How are we going to fix this?"

"That is a very good question," he said. "Gideon Chase is a formidable hunter, and one who has never shown any mercy. Now he's desperate to be cured even if it means becoming the very thing he's hunted his entire life. There is no easy answer to this."

"But we'll figure something out, right?"

He stroked the hair off my forehead and tucked it behind my left ear. "Yes, we will. But until then we need for him to believe that I know nothing. It's safer if we play along with his little games."

"So what do we do?"

"I'll be leaving on the next plane to France, and you can sort all of this out here by yourself. Please let me know how it all turns out."

I gaped at him. "Please tell me this is another attempt at that humor thing you've been trying lately."

He frowned. "I'm not very good at it, am I?"

I shook my head. "I love you even without the knock-knock jokes. Seriously."

His expression softened. "This is good to know."

"Gideon is convinced I was successful at breaking up with you."

"Then he must continue to think that. As far as anyone will know, we're no longer together."

"Everyone? Even George?"

His dark eyebrows rose. "*Especially* George. If George knows, the world knows."

"Good point." I twisted my hand into the silky material of Thierry's black shirt. "So we'll stay away from each other until this is over."

He nodded slowly. "That would be best."

"Then you probably should be leaving now."

"I should." He kissed me again deeply and it nearly took my breath away. "I'm very glad you have the gold chain. Much safer that way, isn't it?"

"This doesn't feel very safe to me," I breathed against his mouth.

He picked me up in his arms. "George is working until 6:00 A.M. at the club. That, I believe, gives us four hours until he returns."

I wrapped my arms around his neck. "For a master vampire, you're very good at math. But . . . but we need to figure out what we're going to do about Gideon. And how can we make everybody believe that we're not together? Obviously I'm a really bad liar if you figured it out."

"We'll find a way. But not tonight. Or, at least, not in the next four hours."

"But—"

"Do you love me?" he asked very seriously.

"Yes." My eyes filled with tears again. "I love you so much."

"Then that's all that matters. You haven't known me that long, Sarah. You don't know how I can be when there's something I want and someone's standing in my way. And I want you." He frowned then. "However, there is one thing that troubles me more than anything else at this very moment. More even than Gideon Chase."

"What?"

He met my gaze and smiled. "That nightshirt definitely has to go."

My heart swelled. I hugged him tightly against me and felt right then that everything was going to be okay as long as we were together.

And, quite honestly, my nightshirt was seriously ugly.

"I can definitely deal with that," I said just before I kissed him again . . . and again.

About the Author

To me, writing is a way to get stories I want to read. I remember seeing a movie once whose ending, in a word, *sucked*. I left the theater thinking about how I would have done it differently and rewriting it in my head as I walked to my car. When I'm writing I can get whatever ending I want. It's a power thing. I'm greedy that way. Don't judge me.

Being a writer is a dream come true and, when I'm not wrestling with my stubborn characters (Sarah Dearly, I'm looking at you!), I'm having the time of my life immersed in my worlds of vampires, demons, and other strange, hilarious, and angsty creatures. I hope you enjoy coming along for the ride!

Please visit me at my Web site at www.michellerowen .com and feel free to send me an e-mail at michelle@ michellerowen.com. I love hearing from readers!

Dear Reader,

I hope you enjoyed *Stakes & Stilettos!* You might be wondering what's up next for Sarah Dearly and her friends since this is obviously not the end of her story.

Tall, Dark & Fangsome (September 2009) is the fifth and final book in my Immortality Bites series. Sarah tries to keep her ongoing relationship with master vampire Thierry a secret while she does whatever she can to save herself and the people she loves from Gideon Chase, the leader of the vampire hunters, who plans to use her special blood to become a supervamp. And there's still that nasty little nightwalker curse to complicate matters further for her. Things continue to be difficult for my little fledgling vampire and her search for her fanged happily ever after in this funny, exciting and, I hope, satisfying conclusion to her story.

Head on over to my Web site at www.michellerowen.com for a sneak peek at chapter 1!

Happy Reading!

Michelle Rowen

THE DISH

Where authors give you the inside scoop!

♥ ♥ ♥ ♥ ♥ ♥ ♥ ♥ ♥ ♥ ♥ ♥ ♥ ♥ ♥

From the desk of Michelle Rowen

Dear Reader,

When I began writing my Immortality Bites series, I thought it would be fun to play with vampire myths. As a long time fan of vampire fiction, I wanted to see vamps more as heroes than villains. To do that, I had to humanize them a lot. Gone went death-by-sunlight—my vamps can go out during the day. Gone went the compulsion to sink their fangs into any unsuspecting neck—my vamps get their blood from sterilized sources and well-paid donors. Gone went the idea that vamps are undead—my vamps breathe and have regular heartbeats. I kept a few things, though: immortality, extra strength, no reflection, and the fact that my vampires were pursued by hunters who really wanted to slay them.

Now with the fourth book in the series, STAKES & STILETTOS, I asked myself, at this point, what's the absolute worst thing that could happen to my heroine, Sarah Dearly? And it was very simple, really. Now that she's somewhat accustomed to being a regular, everyday vampire who doesn't have to worry about any of those nastier vampire myths, I should give all of them to her in full force.

So I cursed her—or rather, she's cursed by a vengeful ex-classmate who's gotten into dark magic big-time since high school—to become a "nightwalker." These are the nasty vamps who gave other vampires a bad reputation; the vamps who are the reason vampire hunters and their sharp wooden stakes exist.

Sarah now has a big problem. She can't control her thirst for blood. She can't go out during the day. She can't enter a house without permission. Her heart has stopped beating and she's officially room temperature. Her immortal life has gone from pretty good to absolutely horrific as she searches frantically, along with her master vampire boyfriend Thierry, to find a way to break the curse before it's permanent.

Life for Sarah, forgive the pun, *sucks*.

In the most entertaining way possible, of course.

Happy reading!

Michelle Rowen

www.michellerowen.com

♥

From the desk of Larissa Ione

Dear Reader,

Ah, my boy Wraith. Of all the demon brothers, he's the most, well . . . *screwed up*. Which, of course, is what makes him so fun.

As an avid reader and obsessed moviegoer, I've always found that my favorite characters are often not the heroes, but either the shadowy bad boy or the charismatic and/or messed-up buddy who hangs out with the heroe.

In the TV series Angel I adored Angel, but there was always something darkly yummy about Spike. In the TV series Firefly, Malcolm was my favorite (after all, he is a bad boy), but the selfish, immoral, and wildly funny Jayne held a strange appeal for me, as well. And the movie Sahara? My favorite character wasn't Matthew McConaughey's Dirk Pitt, it was his goofy yet oddly competent sidekick, Al.

In my mind, Wraith was always a blend of those types of characters. Someone you either love or hate, maybe both at the same time. Because when these characters reveal their soft side, you still know that deep down, there's a scary male in there, just waiting to emerge and kick someone's butt. And when their dark side breaks the surface, watch out, because only a very special woman is going to be able to peel back those layers and find the tenderness inside.

In PASSION UNLEASHED, the third book in the Demonica series, Wraith finds that special woman, but having her means killing her, and suddenly, the wild, irreverent bad boy must make a choice that, no matter what he chooses, means someone will die.

I hope you enjoy Wraith's story. And when you finish, please feel free to stop by my Web site at www LarissaIone.com to learn more about my work and to download the free Demonica demon compendium, which is full of definitions for all the demon species mentioned in the Demonica books, as well as some extras, including a short story that tells the tale of how Shade and Eidolon met Wraith.

Hope to see you soon!

Larissa Ione

♥

From the desk of Lori Wilde

Dear Reader,

With ALL OF ME, I'm closing a chapter and leaving behind four very special friends who've been part of my writing life for the last two years. From people-pleasing Delaney in THERE GOES THE BRIDE to avant-garde Tish in ONCE SMITTEN, TWICE SHY to starry-eyed Rachael from ADDICTED TO LOVE and now cynical Jillian in ALL OF ME, I'm going to miss them.

Jillian's story is the final installment in the Wedding Veil Wishes series and while I'm sad to know the books are over, I'm thrilled that Jillian finally gets her happy ending. But the road to happiness is a bumpy one, because Jillian doesn't believe in love. I saved Jillian for last because I knew her story would be the most emotional.

You see, the man who is her destiny, widower Tuck Manning, has lost his faith in love. After losing his wife to cancer, he's raw and hurting and unable to believe that lightning can indeed strike twice. Getting these two together was at turns painful, funny, sad, and heartwarming.

And I don't want to forget Mutt, the Heinze 57 stray, who through his endearing doggie antics melts resistant Jillian's heart and shows grieving Tuck that it's never too late for a second chance at love.

But that's not all. There's also the close-knit mountain town of Salvation, Colorado, and all the quirky characters who reside there. From Tuck's sister, Evie, a renowned pastry chef who moved to Salvation to be near her brother, to Evie's mystic Native American husband, Ridley Red Deer, to the crusty old matchmaking southern gentleman lawyer Sutter Godfrey, the town captivates Jillian and gives her a place to finally call home.

So I bid adieu to the Wedding Veil Wishes series and for me it's on to the next book. If you enjoyed the series I'd love to hear from you. Please visit me at www.loriwilde.com and let me know your thoughts.

Much love,

Lori Wilde